CRESCENDO OF DESIRE . . .

She was not fighting him.

Oh, God, he thought. *Just this once!*

His kisses fell on her silken cheeks, then roamed desperately to her ears, to the soft spot beneath, to her throat, her shoulder. . . . What skin she had! So perfumed, so velvety!

He kissed her passionately, holding her to himself with one big hand pressed on her slim hips. He felt her move against him, and desire rose in him so hotly that he was afraid of his own passions. Yet he could not let her go. . . .

Dell books by Janette Radcliffe

STORMY SURRENDER
HIDDEN FIRES
LOVERS AND LIARS
THE HEART AWAKENS
AMERICAN BARONESS
THE COURT OF THE FLOWERING PEACH
VIENNA DREAMS

VIENNA DREAMS

Janette Radcliffe

A DELL BOOK

Published by
Dell Publishing Co., Inc.
1 Dag Hammarskjold Plaza
New York, New York 10017

Dell ® TM 681510, Dell Publishing Co., Inc.

ISBN: 0-440-19530-6

Printed in the United States of America

First printing—September 1982

Chapter 1

Diana Ballantyne was trying hard to control her rising anger.

"But, Herr Professor Schenkendorf, you knew from my note that I was a female. Why did you agree to see me, only to refuse my request to become a student?"

Several men in the large conservatory room turned to gaze curiously at Diana as her voice became more agitated.

The heavyset professor chuckled, his red face beaming cunningly under a fringe of gray hair. "If you had been old and plain, I might have taken you as a pupil. But a young beautiful lady—nein, nein! You will marry and have children, and my work would all be in vain. Education does no pretty girl any good!"

Diana flinched as he let his eyes wander over her trim young figure, clad in a changeable silk gown of white, blue, and rose. Suddenly she was uncomfortably aware of his friends laughing in the background, nudging each other, amused by the scene before them.

"Herr Professor," she persisted in her fluent German. "I am a serious student of the piano. I have come to Vienna to study music. I assure you I am not of a frivolous nature—"

He interrupted, his expression changed to a portentous frown. "Then you should be! A pretty young lady like you should go home to her papa, and find herself a husband! It is children you require, not a music score! *Kinder, Kirche,* and *Küche*—that is a woman's lot, and rightly so!"

Nursery, Church, and Kitchen! A woman's place! Diana burned with rage at the old masculine refrain. In June of 1893, in Vienna, the city of music and dreams, she had hoped to find a more advanced attitude than this! But no, the men here were even more set in their attitudes than her own father back in England. At least Homer Ballantyne had allowed her a year to devote to music before she settled down.

Diana noticed one man among the group behind the professor who was not chuckling. He was a tall handsome man, his hair golden, his vivid blue eyes staring from a face tanned from time spent outdoors. But his cold look was as disapproving as that of the others. She turned her back on them all, turning so abruptly that the wildflowers of blue and rose adorning her straw hat seemed to tremble with her outrage.

"May I ask you, Herr Professor, if in your kindness you would be so good as to recommend some other professor of music to teach me?"

He bellowed at her, in spite of her elaborate and courteous speech. "Recommend you? Recommend you, dear Fraulein? Nein, nein, never! I tell you, I do not approve of women who fancy careers! They are bold and brazen! They forget their place! They forget their destiny as women!" He looked about proudly, as though expecting applause.

her blond head firmly. "No, I thank you." She turned away.

He persisted in a soft musical voice. "But, Fraulein, permit me! You are alone, yes? Allow me to take you in my carriage, and drive you wherever you wish to go! You will be as safe as in the bosom of your mother! Look at me, am I not an honorable man?"

Unwillingly, her blue eyes met his laughing black ones, and she found not safety there, but a devilish glint. Without thinking, she smiled. That was all the encouragement he needed to stride nearer to her, holding out his white-gloved hand.

"Fraulein! Come with me, my carriage is just around the corner. Pray tell me your lovely name—it must be as beautiful as your exquisite face." He smiled alluringly down at her. "I am Captain Gardell Mueller, at your service—"

"Captain Mueller!" The voice behind Diana snapped with such harsh command that both man and girl started in shock. "You will leave the woman alone! She comes from the Conservatory; you must know she is not a woman of the streets!"

Diana flushed deeply as she turned to face the man. Even before she saw him, she somehow knew the voice belonged to the man with the vivid blue eyes who had frowned at her before.

He was even taller and more rugged-looking close up than from a distance. His eyes were bluer, his golden hair shone in the sunshine, his black silk top hat was politely held in one black-gloved hand. There was a dueling scar on his left cheek, very like the one shining red on the cheek of the handsome captain before her.

"Thank you, sir," she said quickly in her anger. "I am not so foolish as to go with—"

"The Fraulein may go where she chooses," said the

captain, and held out his hand again to her, coaxingly. "Come, Fraulein, I will take you to my carriage. I promise you you shall go where you choose—"

"Go," said the blond man uncompromisingly. "Captain Mueller, if you do not wish trouble with me, you will depart at once! The woman is a music student, not one of your playmates!"

"Can she not be both?" He smiled, but his face had turned red, and the black eyes seemed uneasy.

"Nein!" The man raised his right hand and pointed down the street with his top hat. "Go!"

For a breathless moment Diana thought the handsome blazing-eyed captain would challenge him. But then he lifted his cap to her, turned, and stalked off. "My regrets." His words floated back to her.

Quickly the blond-haired man turned on her. "And as for you, Fraulein," he snapped, "you should not flirt with such riffraff unless you mean to spice your *musical* career with love affairs!"

She gasped at his heavy sarcasm, her eyes flashing back at him. "How dare you say such a thing!" she cried in English, too flustered to speak German.

"If you did not encourage such men, they would not linger," he admonished, his mouth straight. "Such loose behavior is not tolerated in Vienna, I warn you, Fraulein. If you wish to remain here, you will not behave as you undoubtedly are permitted to do in England!"

She gasped at him again. What presumption! Her father was so strict and anxious about her that she rarely went out alone in England! And while she did not have her own maid in Vienna, her cousin accompanied her to any formal occasion.

As she rallied her wits to answer spiritedly, she noticed him transfer his black hat to his left hand, and then snap the fingers of his right hand for a fiacre. His left arm scarcely moved.

In an instant, it seemed, one paused beside him, and the driver jumped down to hold open the door to the little double-seated carriage, so popular in Vienna.

"Herr Baron wishes—?"

"Nein. The Fraulein requires transportation to her home. You will take her there, and see her to the door!"

Money rapidly changed hands, and a strong arm lifted her inside the carriage. Then, lifting his hat to her, the man turned his back and strode down the wide street.

Fuming, Diana settled back in the carriage. The driver had given her a look of such thinly veiled contempt, as though she had begged for a ride with the stern-faced man!

Her mind whirled on the short drive to her cousin's boardinghouse. Herr Baron—was he a baron, or had the driver been indulging in the Austrian talent for promoting men rapidly with flowery speech? She closed her eyes, even though she usually enjoyed looking at the lovely wide streets, the tall plane trees, the flowered gardens. How scornful he had been, how he had dismissed the military man! What harm did it do to talk to a man? After all, she would not have gone anywhere with him without a proper introduction from some mutual friend!

When the carriage stopped, the driver jumped down and solemnly escorted her to the door of the boardinghouse. His look was a little more kindly when he saw where she lived. Her cousin's boardinghouse was a respectable place for a young woman to stay.

The maid opened the door, neat in her black-and-white uniform. "Good afternoon, Fraulein." She bowed.

"Good afternoon, Gretchen," answered Diana, and without pausing she hurried up the curving stairs to the first floor.

Unlocking the front door of her suite, she entered the cold, darkened room. The maids had closed the curtains again.

Immediately she reopened the dark draperies, letting in the bright sunlight. She was accustomed to sunlight in her English home, at both the house in London and the country estate. She had always ordered the draperies opened there first thing in the morning, to allow the warmth of the sun to enter. Even on a rainy day she enjoyed seeing the open skies, the glorious trees and green grass, and the flower gardens she herself supervised.

She had to admit that she missed England. She had had more freedom there than here in Austria because of the difference in the attitudes toward women. Oh, her father was strict, but she had been his hostess since the age of sixteen, when her mother had become ill and died of some fever the doctors could not cure. She had taken over his household completely, and her word had been law among the servants.

Her two older brothers had entered the family trade. Ballantyne's had traded with China for almost one hundred years, and the company warehouses were always full of the richest imported goods. Diana had been gowned in China silks and jade from the time she was small.

Her father would take her for treats to the warehouse to choose teas, ivory, porcelain, from the best China had to trade, and all her own silk lengths to be made into dresses and cloaks.

As a child she had sat with her mother in the drawing room, demurely attentive to the guests. In this setting she had learned what her mother could teach of society, of manners, of morals, of spiritual matters.

Her father had seen that she received a formal education far beyond that normally accorded girls of her time. One fine governess had taught her music and German, while another had instructed her in French and Italian, arithmetic, reading, and history. She had learned and absorbed like a sponge, her mother used to say, with a faint smile of pride.

Moreover, from her brothers she had learned to be a good sport, to play the new game of tennis in a gown that reached only to her ankles, to be good-natured when losing and polite when winning.

However, despite the advantages of her upbringing, it seemed that what Diana wanted most she could not have—because she was a female. She had loved music since the time her mother had put her tiny hands on the keys. She had heard it in her mind when she could not sleep; she hummed when she could not play. When she was silent through conversations at dinner, as the men discussed business in the formal London town house, she would hear the music she would later put down on huge music sheets. She had lived music, dreamed music, loved music since childhood.

She played the harp and the flute, but her first love was the piano. And she composed for the piano, mostly in secret, because the men teachers she had tried to work with had scorned her compositions without listening to them. She had come to deprecate that talent, though she knew that she had a fine gift. Only no man would recognize it! Someday she would have the right teacher, she vowed, and he would encourage her!

She pulled the hatpins from the yellow straw hat, and set it down carefully on one of the mahogany tables.

She laid her jacket on the sofa, and went over to the large piano in her suite. Sitting before the keyboard, in her anger she began to play.

Her long and skillful fingers moved to the bright march. She hit the keys crisply, her foot on the pedal to magnify the sound, and she raced through that march ferociously, as though she would send every man through it in double time! Her hands, unusually strong for a woman, moved with swift accomplishment through the long runs and trills.

"There," she muttered at the end, then began to play another piece, more calmly, but still with firm strength. Thinking again of the rude professor, and the man with blue eyes, she scowled, and unconsciously began to bang the keys.

When she had finished, her hands dropped to her lap. It was then she heard the gentle knock at the door. Rising, she went to open it.

The older woman at the door was smiling with gentle understanding. Her black silk frock rustled as she moved through the door into the room.

"Cousin Helena, I am making too much noise!"

"Nein, nein, dear Cousin Diana. However, I think you have had another disappointment, ja?"

The woman's plump face showed motherly understanding toward her young cousin. Diana moved forward and pressed her face for a moment against the cool cheek of her older cousin. The woman was childless; it was the grief of her life, as much as the early death of her beloved husband, Andreas. The two had married when the English girl was twenty, her Austrian beloved forty. He had brought her to his land, and together they had run a fine tourist hotel in the Alps. He had died some eighteen years ago, and she had returned to Vienna and turned their large residence there into a boardinghouse for musical girls of good families.

The fine four-story home had become refuge to many homesick girls of England and America. Frau Helena Lewisohn was known for her strictness and goodness and piety. Fathers did not hesitate to trust her with their girls. She was highly respected all over Austria.

"Oh, Cousin Helena, he turned me down, too, and he did not even listen to me play!"

"Oh, my little girl!" breathed Helena fervently, her arms closing protectively around her young cousin. Her plump body shook with emotion. "And you play so very well, my darling!"

"Thank you." Diana moved back, sighed, and tried to smile. "Ah, well, there are other teachers in Vienna, and I shall see them all!"

"Of course, that is the spirit! Do not despair! Someone will recognize your fine talent! You say he did not hear you play?"

"Ja, he regarded me with contempt as just a woman." Diana had slipped into German. She and her cousin both spoke English and German fluently, and moved easily from one to the other language. "I asked why he had allowed me to come to him, and he said it was because if I had turned out to be old and plain he might have taken me as a pupil!"

"He did not—he did not attempt—" Frau Helena's plump face grew stern. "You did not go to his room alone!"

"Come, sit down and let us chat," said Diana, and moved her jacket from the sofa. Both women sat down and continued talking easily. They had not met until April of this year, yet Diana felt she had known the woman always. She was so comfortable, so understanding and gentle, for all her firm discipline and strict morals.

"Yes, yes. Let us. So, he brought you on a vain journey. That is bad of him. Did he insult you, my dear Diana?"

"Yes, he asked me to come to a café, after refusing to teach me!"

The woman frowned, and Diana knew they were now filed away in her memory, the facts about that professor. She would allow none of her girls to go to him again.

"Well, well, you shall not despair. Tell me, Diana, your father did not approve of this year abroad?"

"No, not really. He wished me to marry Addison Montague. Mr. Montague is of a trading family, like ours. They, too, deal in spices. The firms would merge, probably."

"And this Mr. Montague, you do not care for him? You have no soft emotion for him?"

Diana grimaced. "His hands are always damp," she said.

"Ah—so." She understood at once. "So—you will have your year, to make the music and live a little. You have had so many years of much work, my little Diana," she said sentimentally.

"Cousin Helena, I did not mind the work. I love my father and my brothers. It was a pleasure to make the house comfortable for them, entertain their friends. I do not mind housework, I even like to cook. Meal planning was a pleasure, and I enjoy arranging flowers, and keeping up the decorations, and all that. But, cousin—I feel I have a talent—it has not been used enough—I hear music in my mind—can I ignore that music? Because I am a female, must I forget the melodies that race through my mind? Because I am a woman, must I neglect the piano for weeks, while we have guests for the hunt? I had to give myself a chance to see if I have a true talent."

Her blue eyes blazed with her fervor. Helena eyed her tenderly, but with apprehension. "I wish I could encourage you, dear child, to hope for this career. But you are young and lovely, and your father is wealthy," she said simply. "What chance do you have to live a single life, and pursue a career as a pianist? My dear, I fear the most you can hope for is a year of freedom."

"Then a year I shall have!" announced Diana fiercely. "I shall take that year, and if I can find a teacher I shall work hard to improve my ability. And I shall try to find an honest opinion of my talent, to see whether it is worth the fight to go on!"

"Brava, brava!" applauded Cousin Helena, clapping her hands lightly. "You shall have all the help I can give. Let me search my mind, to think of some other professor who might teach you. Meantime, come down to tea. We shall have a pleasant interval in my small parlor, just the little group of us. I wish you to become acquainted with the new American girl."

"The red-haired girl who moved in across the hall?" asked Diana, rising as her cousin did. "Now, she looks strong of will!"

"Indeed. Her father and mother brought her last week and left her with regret. Americans, you know, and newly rich in railroads and steel. They deny her nothing. She plays the violin with strength, but not enough feeling. Still, she has talent. I think she's running away from a marriage they plan for her."

"Really?" Diana's interest in the pretty American was growing: "We may have much in common!"

"Come down, and see!"

Diana followed her plump cousin down the stairs,

feeling a renewed warmth toward her. She had strength of will, that lady, to conceal her grief, turn her home into a boardinghouse, and keep her head held high during the years of loneliness.

Cousin Helena managed her house with a mixture of dignity, reticence, and warmth that encouraged "her girls" to look to her for guidance. She loved music, and any musician had her respect and admiration.

They approached the small parlor behind the large drawing room. Two maids in black and white stood by with two tea trays, and several of the boarders were talking among themselves.

The red-haired American was talking in lively fashion and broken German to the little flirtatious Rosalie Stamitz, an aspiring operetta singer. Rosalie had a pretty figure and was diminutive as a china doll, with long curly brown hair, and huge brown eyes. The redhead was dressed in a white shirtwaist of the type popular among American women, and a long green skirt of twill. A broad belt encircled her slender waist, and her green eyes flashed in the lively discussion.

In another corner the quiet stately Frau Johanne Weiss sat silently, alone, a cup of coffee in her hand. She stared down at the full cup as though not seeing it. A huge blond German woman with large blue eyes, she resembled a figure out of a Wagner opera. It was said she studied opera, but one rarely heard her voice. Though she wore a gold ring on her left hand, a maid had whispered to Diana that she was *divorced*. Diana had never met a divorced woman, and eyed her with secret wonder.

Little Frau Hemmel completed the group. A longtime friend of Frau Lewisohn, she had moved in after the death of her husband, and the two women frequently went to the opera and concerts together. Though tiny and timid, she had a sweet sense of humor, and maintained a certain gallantry despite the rheumatism which bent her figure.

Frau Helena Lewisohn had rooms available for more boarders, but she did not take in just anybody. In spite of the critical shortage of rooms in Vienna, she was very particular and took only girls of good birth and fine talent. The house tended to be fuller in winter, she had explained to Diana, when more girls came for the winter season and took lessons.

Gretchen and Maria wheeled the tea trays around the parlor with silent efficiency. Helena had chosen them and trained them, and made sure they appreciated music also! They had to, for the rooms were often filled with music when all the guests were practicing. The drawing room contained a large piano and harp, and the small parlor an upright piano and music stands for informal gatherings.

Diana relaxed on a sofa, and listened to the lively talk. The American girl was arguing with Rosalie, an Austrian, about modern music.

"It is the waltz, the operetta, which is the popular music," argued Rosalie, with a little lilting laugh. "You will see when you are longer in Vienna, Fraulein. Our beloved Johann Strauss will convince you."

"That is music for the masses," declared the American girl, who had been introduced as Alicia Huntingdon. "The real music of today and tomorrow is the music of masters like Richard Strauss—quite different! And of Anton Bruckner, and Gustav Mahler!"

Rosalie looked very shocked, though dimples peeped into her pretty pink cheeks. "Nein, nein, nein! You do not understand of what I speak! Wait till you waltz all night to the music of our orchestras!"

"I think you speak of two different matters," said

Diana, unable to resist joining in. "There are two kinds of music, really. That of the classic masters, and that of the popular ones. I like both, I confess! But they are quite different."

A lively argument followed, a good-natured one, in which only Frau Weiss did not join. Frau Helena Lewisohn finally looked to her, thoughtfully, and spoke. "Frau Weiss, you are worried about your audition tomorrow?"

Mournful large blue eyes lifted to Cousin Helena's. "There can be no audition, Frau Lewisohn. My accompanist is ill. His wife refused to let me in. I went all about, trying to find someone to accompany me. None would risk it on such short notice!"

All gasped, genuinely upset and anxious for her.

"Oh, my dear," said Frau Lewisohn. "Oh, what can we do? That audition—it is so important—"

"Ja. I have heard Herr Baron is casting for the first opera he has written. If only I could sing for him—but how can I? I must have an accompanist."

"I'll play for you!" said Diana impulsively.

"It is most kind of you to offer, Fraulein Ballantyne." The unhappy look in Frau Weiss's blue eyes did not diminish. "However, it would take many hours of practice—I could not impose—I do not know what I shall do!"

"I can sight-read," urged Diana, now won to the cause of the unhappy woman. She was so large, so strong, it was a pity to see how sad she was. She should laugh and be happy, like a goddess with humor, thought Diana. "Do let me try, it can do no harm!"

"Nein, nein, no harm." Cousin Helena beamed. "Cousin Diana is talented, you will see! And she also has a disappointment, another professor has refused to teach her only because she is a pretty female. Let her do this, perhaps someone will hear her and believe in her!"

"I appreciate your courtesy," Frau Weiss said with a sigh. "However, the audition is in his home. And he was a formidable pianist at one time. He is most particular. It might even do you harm."

Diana believed strongly in her talent, and her mind was made up. "If I believed that, I would not be here in Vienna," she said. "Come now, do let us practice after tea, and you shall judge whether I shall come with you or not."

Frau Weiss hesitated. "I should send a message to the Herr Baron if I am not coming tomorrow—"

"Let it wait until the morning," urged Frau Lewisohn. "If you cannot go, I myself will send our man with a message."

"Then I accept your kind offer," said Frau Weiss to Diana, relaxing slightly. She lifted the coffee cup to her lips and sipped gratefully. "Thank you very much."

Diana smiled, and nodded to her, and went over to speak to her. But before they had exchanged words, the red-haired American spoke.

"So you also have had trouble getting a professor to teach you! So did I! When we came to Vienna, Papa and I went about, finding the very best teachers, only to be turned down. Finally Papa found one Herr Professor Wendler, who had a good reputation for the violin. And when he began to refuse, Papa put a bundle of notes on the table before him, and said, 'How much to teach my daughter for one year?' And the man swallowed and agreed."

Rosalie Stamitz laughed, but the others shook their heads sorrowfully. Little elderly Frau Hemmel said soulfully, "Ah, what fools mortals be! Their principles

are drowned in a sea of money! And does he teach you
well, Fraulein Huntingdon?"

"Please, all of you call me Alicia. I dislike formality," said the cheerful American girl, tossing her red
head. The golden-red waves rippled down her back,
against the white lace-trimmed shirtwaist. "Does he
teach me well? Ah, yes! He does not mean to, but in
our two hours together I force him to do what I wish! I
ask questions, I try out passages, I work him hard!"
She laughed naughtily, her well-shaped nose wrinkling.

Diana was busily wondering if she could try the
same ploy, but her father was not so indulgent, and he
was chary with his money. Still—if that was what it
took. . . . But no, she had just enough money to live
on from month to month. She had enough set by to
pay a decent amount to a professor, but not an extravagant amount.

"I have a lady teacher," announced Rosalie, "but
she is very straitlaced. What I need is a man patron,
one who will see that I get a position in the operetta he
is producing. That is the only way to get somewhere in
my field."

Frau Lewisohn looked grave. "You must be careful,
my dear! Such men make promises, only to make fools
of young girls like you, fresh from the country."

Rosalie smiled mysteriously and smoothed her
flounced embroidered skirts. She looked as though she
was ready for an operetta today, with a peasant costume from the Austrian Alps, and red stitching on her
fluffy blouse. She had made it herself, she had told Diana proudly. She always looked the part of a waltz
princess, she said.

"Ah, but the men in the country are like the men in
the city," she observed, laughing. "Flattery goes to
their heads just as quickly. One needs to know how to

handle a man, and that knowledge must be acquired early, if one wants to achieve her ambitions!"

Diana eyed her wonderingly. Was that how it went? Or was the pretty little girl headed for a bad downfall?

"Do not be too cocky, my dear Fraulein," murmured little old Frau Hemmel. "Pride goeth before a fall."

"I know I am talented, and I shall proceed with caution mingled with daring," said Rosalie sweetly, and ate another cake smothered with whipped cream.

After tea Diana took Johanne Weiss to her suite of rooms on the next floor. The piano there was excellent. Johanne spread out her music on the stand, and they began to work. Diana was pleasantly surprised at the voice that swelled out into the large room. Johanne had a fine soprano voice, full-bodied and rich, that hit high notes with seeming ease, and rang with deep emotion in the lower tones.

Johanne had a good presence also, standing well, moving easily about the room as the music moved her, holding her arms up, her chin high as she sang. Diana could imagine her performing in an opera, building to passionate crescendos and reaching her audience with both her voice and her magnificent figure. She stood about five feet nine, taller than Diana's five feet six, and with a good form.

Johanne seemed equally surprised and pleased with Diana's accompaniment. Diana let her lead and followed her with quiet chords that never overwhelmed the lyrics. They paused to discuss the music after the first three arias.

"You play so well. Have you played these before?"

"One of them, not the other two."

"Then you do sight-read well. I am most fortunate!

You will accompany me tomorrow? The Herr Baron is formidable!"

Herr Baron—surely not the same Herr Baron! No, that could not be, thought Diana.

"Of course I will. I have no other engagements, and no teacher," she said, with a rueful grimace.

"You are good and kind; good fortune will come to you," said Johanne Weiss seriously.

"Thank you. Do you want to try something else, one of the song cycles?"

"We had heard that the Herr Baron is casting for an opera, one he has written. My accompanist, who is also my teacher, suggested I sing only arias. However, he may ask for something else. What do you suggest?"

Now that Johanne had stopped singing, she looked more helpless, and seemed to be looking to someone for advice. Diana had the feeling that men often bullied her and pushed her about.

"I think you should be ready with other music, if he is interested. What about some lighter songs for contrast, some of the waltzes of Johann Strauss, so he can see how you can sing other numbers?"

"Ja, ja, that is a good idea, Fraulein!"

"Please call me Diana, if you will."

Johanne smiled for the first time, and her serious face lit with a shy charm. "And pray to call me Johanne, if you will."

After two hours of practice they were friends. Johanne followed directions well, and had a natural singing ability enhanced by years of practice. She told Diana she was twenty-five and had been singing for three years. She had left her husband then, she admitted quietly. He had given her some money to live on at first, but now she earned some by singing in cafés every weekend.

Their session finished, they put away the music and went down to dinner together at eight o'clock. Frau Lewisohn set a good table, and the ladies sat about enjoying the wholesome Austrian food and conversation.

They retired at ten o'clock. Diana played softly for another hour, then went to bed.

Chapter 2

~~~~~~

Diana rose early on Tuesday, played for half an hour, then washed and dressed in a gown of rose silk. Johanne would wear gray twill with a blouse of white silk, she had said. The maid Gretchen brought a breakfast tray to Diana at eight, and she ate while thinking of the day ahead. She must do well for Johanne's sake, she resolved, and help the girl keep her confidence. She had a magnificent voice, but she was shy and easily intimidated by criticism.

When Diana came downstairs at nine thirty, Johanne was waiting in the lower hall. Frau Lewisohn had sent the odd-jobs man for a fiacre, and he returned with it shortly. The girls got in, and with Cousin Helena's good wishes as farewell, they set out.

Johanne gave the directions, then settled back with her thick packet of music clutched in her arms.

The girls were silent as the fiacre clip-clopped with its single horse over the pavements into the elegant Ringstrasse. Before long the driver pulled the horse up in front of a large classically-designed gray mansion in a quietly fashionable district. Tall pillars framed the huge windows of the four-story building. Diana's eyes widened as she took in the huge mansion. It was about the same size as her family's country home, twice the size of the London town house.

The gardens inside the iron fences were blossoming in roses, twined luxuriously about the fences, and huge beds of other blooms, reds, yellows, and some blue flowers she did not know.

"What are the blue ones?" she muttered to Johanne.

"Alpenblumen," said the girl absently.

Alp flowers. So pretty and deeply blue, like the sky.

They did not even have to touch the large bronze door knocker. A butler swung open the door silently, and bowed to them.

"Frau Weiss and accompanist," murmured Johanne diffidently.

"You are expected, Frau Weiss. Pray come with me," he said solemnly, and bowed them inside into the huge hallway. The parquet floor shone, and in the distance rose a dazzling dark red staircase leading to the upper floor, a runner of red Persian carpet covering the center of the stairs.

Diana caught a glimpse of someone on the stairway—a woman, half-turned toward them. She was so beautiful that Diana blinked as at a vision.

The woman was tall against the railing, her black curly hair crowned by a dashing red hat with a slanting brim. Her mouth was scarlet, twisted in a slight smile of mystery and seduction. She carried a riding crop, and now Diana realized she was gowned in a black riding habit of sleek fit. A dash of gray mud marred the gown near the knees.

Otherwise, she was perfection, a Viennese charmer in the dusk of the stairwell. As Diana stared, she

climbed another few stairs, turned the corner, and was
gone.

Who was the woman? The butler eyed Diana from
the corner of his eye, and motioned to them.

"Ladies—if you will come—"

She had a strong feeling he was upset that she had
seen the woman. Who was she? Someone—come to entertain the master? No, she looked like royalty, that
imperious lift of her chin, that grace of figure. She was
no street woman.

Above their heads glittered a chandelier of Austrian
crystal. They were led into the front room on the left,
and this huge room shone with another, even larger,
crystal chandelier.

Diana's eyes took in the formidable drawing room:
the grand piano, the harpsichord, the golden curved
harp, and a dozen sofas and chairs in red silk brocade,
all set against walls of the same rich red silk in cut velvet.

Then before them came a man in a blue silk suit,
with vivid blue eyes. The man who had rescued and insulted her yesterday!

"Baron Lukas von Korda," murmured the butler. "I
have the honor to present Frau Weiss and accompanist."

The baron bowed slightly; Frau Weiss curtseyed and
so did Diana, deeply. She straightened, and he said,
"And which one is Frau Weiss?"

"I am she," said Johanne, and curtseyed again. "I
have to announce, Herr Baron, that my accompanist
was ill, and could not come. Fraulein Ballantyne kindly
offered to accompany me. We live at the same boardinghouse," she added, in a confused mutter, and as a
sort of apology.

"Ah, so," he said gravely, and bowed them into the

room. The butler retreated, closing the huge carved door after himself, and they were alone with the famous musician, Baron von Korda.

In her slightly more than two months in Vienna, Diana had heard of the Baron von Korda. He had been a formidable concert pianist of handsome appearance, and adored by all Austria. Then he had suffered an illness or accident—some said he'd fought a duel—and his left arm had stiffened. He had not played during the last two years.

Rumor had it that he was composing. He conducted sometimes now—an orchestra or an opera. He took no pupils, some said, and Diana had not even tried to find him. He was a true baron—Lukas von und zu Korda; he and his family still owned their castle in the countryside west of Vienna. He had a town house too, and a place in the Alps, and other property as well.

He was conducting Johanne to the huge grand piano, a fine rosewood piece, its top raised. The music rack stood ready for the sheet music, and the bench was positioned at proper distance from the keyboard.

"You may wish to remove your hats and jackets, ladies," he was saying courteously. "Make yourselves comfortable enough to forget everything but the music."

Diana removed her hat, taking out the several hatpins, and setting the hat on the nearby sofa. She also removed her rose wool fur-bordered jacket, and set that down also. Johanne took off her wide blue hat and light gray wool jacket.

The baron waited until they were ready, and then turned again to Johanne.

"Now, Frau Weiss. I wish you to sing what you will—arias, to begin with. I shall walk about the room, in order to listen to your voice from several angles. Do not allow this to disturb you. You will stand where you will, read from the music, make what gestures you will. Is this understood?"

"Yes, Herr Baron."

"And you may address me as 'Maestro,' as they do in Italy," he said, with a slight charming smile at her.

"Thank you, Herr—I mean, Maestro."

Diana had seated herself at the piano, and adjusted the bench to her liking. She found the pedals with her long narrow walking boots, and tested them. She tried a few notes with chords. The instrument had a crisp mellow tone.

He nodded to her, then walked away to the window. Drawing back the dark red draperies and the white lawn curtains, he gazed outside at the June sky and the gardens.

Johanne drew a deep breath. Diana began the first aria, Rosina's from *The Barber of Seville,* by Rossini. The "letter aria" began *"Una voce poco fà,"* and they were off in the light brilliant music.

At the end he did not turn. Diana began again, a more somber aria from Verdi's *Aida, "Ritorna vincitor."* Johanne's expressive voice turned dark in tone and grew ominous with the words.

During the singing of this one Baron von Korda turned from the window and began to walk softly through the room. His steps made no sound on the thick Persian carpets, but both girls were well aware how he prowled the room. He walked as far as the opened double doors into the next salon, moved farther into that room, and beyond to the far library, then returned, moving like a quiet panther.

Diana thought he was testing the tones from a distance. Johanne seemed to be nervous. Her voice closed up twice, and she put her hand to her throat. Then, recovering, she continued, and Diana matched her moods with softer music, or louder and firmer, following her lead closely.

Still no word when they finished. As planned, Johanne and Diana began another piece, in still another mood, from *Carmen*. The throbbing rhythmic *"Habanera"* filled the rooms with gaiety and defiance.

At the end the baron nodded briskly and asked "Something from a song cycle, if you will. You know something?"

"Ja, Maestro," said Johanne, and exchanged a relieved look with Diana, which the man caught with a flash of his vivid eyes. She sang two songs, then paused, as he made a gesture.

"One other song if you will, Frau Weiss," he said. "Do you know some lullaby?"

Nervously, Johanne clutched her hands to her breast. She gulped and said, "There is the lullaby of Brahms."

"Ja, sing that."

Diana did not have the music for that. Johanne sent her a desperate look, then came to the piano and whispered, "Shall I sing alone?"

"I can play it," said Diana. "I suggest, loud and firm to begin with, then *piano,* then *pianissimo,* as though the baby falls asleep."

Johanne nodded, relieved, certain that Diana could play it. Diana remembered the music from having heard it. She had never played it before, but could play the melody, and improvise the chords in the left hand. Baron von Korda had overheard her. He said nothing, but watched them both earnestly as they began.

Johanne's voice began firm and soothing, clear and supple. Then gently she eased into softer tones, moving her arms in a cradling motion. The baron watched

her intently now, leaning against the back of a brocaded chair. With the final verse her voice softened to
a lovely *pianissimo,* and Diana stopped playing after
one phrase and allowed the voice to continue alone.

The last line was sung so softly that one could
barely hear it. Like drops of rain falling into a clear
pool, each note fell softly, eloquently into the elegant
room.

There was a short silence after she'd finished. The
baron nodded, shortly, then strode about the room, his
hand to his chin. His left arm was at his side, not quite
stiff, but suggesting some injury.

"Pray, be seated, ladies," he then said abruptly, coming to a halt. He held a chair for Johanne. Diana left
the piano and he held another of the straight-backed
brocaded chairs for her.

Her limbs trembled, anxious for Johanne, now that
the audition had concluded. She was glad to sit down
in the chair.

The baron drew up a chair for himself, and faced
them both. "Frau Weiss, you are married?" he asked.

Johanne started. "Ja—that is, I was—Maestro. I
am—divorced," and her voice went down into her
boots.

He nodded, his face expressionless. "Children?"

"Nein, Maestro."

"You are then free to carry on a career, Frau
Weiss?"

"Ja, Maestro." Her large hands were twisting and
twisting in her gray lap.

"Your full name?"

"Frau Johanne Weiss, Maestro."

"And your schooling?"

She named two teachers, then spoke of the singing
she did in the café. From his face Diana could not see

whether he was moved or very interested. Yes, surely, he would not ask all that if he were not. He would not be so cruel, she felt that. He might be wealthy, perhaps very critical, but he had listened the way a man does who loves music. He had been deeply moved by the lullaby. His face had changed; his eyes had closed briefly.

The baron opened his coat, as though warm, and a bright gold waistcoat appeared, rich and elegant against the somber blue of the silk suit. He wore little jewelry, only a signet ring on his right hand and a blue sapphire in his flowing blue tie.

"Ah. And you both live—where?"

"In the boardinghouse of Frau Helena Lewisohn."

"Ah, yes."

"She is the cousin of Fraulein Ballantyne," added Johanne anxiously, as though to assure respectability to them both.

The vivid blue gaze turned on Diana, as though he would see clear through her and search out all her secrets.

"Your cousin, Fraulein?" he barked.

Knowing the Austrian passion for family lineage and total accuracy as to relationships, she answered precisely, "Frau Lewisohn is the first cousin to my father, Homer Ballantyne. She was raised in her home in England and married Herr Andreas Lewisohn some years ago. Together they owned and ran a fine inn in the Austrian Alps. When he died, she returned to Vienna and turned their house here into a boardinghouse. My father entrusted me to her, knowing her excellent reputation."

So there, Herr Baron, she added mentally, and thought he read her mind. A flicker of amusement passed briefly over his fine features, then disappeared.

"And your father now lives in Vienna also?" he asked pointedly.

"No, sir!" she said in English, irritated. "My father lives in London or in our country home in Kent. He is head of the firm of Ballantyne and Sons, Merchants and Traders. Our firm is in the China trade, sir, and sends some three or four ships each year to Canton for the silks, porcelains, chinaware, and teas."

"Ah—so." He rose and went over to a small side table of polished ebony. From it he took a rose vase and handed it to her. "What is this, Fraulein?"

"Famille rose, sir, from the Ming period. A fine example, I believe," she said handing it back to him with gingerly care.

"Even so." He returned the vase to its place and sat down again. "Now, Fraulein, your mother?"

"Dead, these six years, sir. When I was sixteen. I have since run my father's household."

"Your brothers?"

"Two—both Lewis and Andrew are now in the firm. Each received on his majority a trip on the continent. I asked for a like year in Vienna, on my majority, and father agreed."

"Willingly?" There was a slight smile on the firm lips, the blue eyes sparkled.

She gave him a full look from her speaking blue eyes. "He agreed, sir! And I am to have a year, to April of next year, to play music, and learn all I can. And I mean to do so."

"Good," he said, unexpectedly. "And what does your father do for a hostess this year?"

She sighed. This was a sore point. "I had hoped my brother Lewis would marry," she said frankly. "However, he has not, yet. So I trained a fine woman as housekeeper, and hope all goes well."

Her father wanted her to marry Addison Montague, join their two firms. Diana would remain in their home, with the addition of a husband, and soon children, they hoped. And he would have his hostess, and future grandchildren, to help carry on the business.

However, Diana had not the slightest intention of confiding all this to Herr Baron Maestro von Korda!

He waited, politely, to see if she would continue. When it was clear she would not, he said, "I wish you to return on Thursday. I would like for my friend Herr Conductor Otto Kliegl to hear you, Frau Weiss. Are you able to come at the same time, at ten o'clock in the morning?"

"Oh, ja, ja, Maestro!" Johanne gasped.

"Good. One moment." He went to the door, spoke to the butler briefly, and returned. He lifted Johanne's jacket, holding it for her as she slipped it on. As Johanne nervously jammed on her straw hat and stuck the hatpins into the hat and through her golden chignon piled on top of her head, Baron von Korda picked up Diana's rose wool and fur jacket and held it for her.

"I wish both of you to return, on Thursday," he added, unexpectedly, staring right at Diana. "Fraulein, I wish you to accompany Frau Weiss as you did today. You understand? I do not wish the other accompanist to come. Illness or no, he does not come. Understood?"

"I shall be happy to come, Maestro," said Diana simply. "And thank you for your kind attention today."

She saw Johanne was almost too overcome with excitement to thank him properly. The other girl finally stammered, "Ja, I thank you so much, Herr Baron—Maestro—I am so grateful—"

He escorted them from the room, across and down

the hall, away from the front door. The side door was
opened by a footman, and the baron led them outdoors
onto a graveled driveway where a fine golden and
ebony carriage waited. The driver jumped down, but
the baron waved him off.

He lifted Johanne into the carriage, bowed, and
lifted Diana inside after her, bowing again.

"The boardinghouse of the Frau Lewisohn," he said
briefly. "Until Thursday, dear ladies!"

"Thank you again, Maestro," said a gasping
Johanne.

"My coachman will call for you on Thursday," he
said, and smiled in a kindly fashion at both of them,
his stern face softening marvelously. "Until then!" He
bowed, and watched while the driver whipped up the
horses and drove them out the carriageway into the
wide street.

The girls could not speak much, as the coachman
would be sure to hear. But Diana and Johanne clasped
hands exultantly, and beamed at one another. Surely,
surely, this was hopeful! He would not have them
come back in vain!

The coachman drove them at a sedate pace through
the Vienna streets to the Lewisohn house. How grand,
to be driven in such a fine carriage, to have people
stare at them, peering into the carriage to see who went
there! Passersby, noticing the heraldic pattern on the
carriage door, must surely believe it was the family of
Herr Baron von Korda!

The fine houses went past, the beautiful tall trees, the
flower gardens in full June bloom. The seats were
plush, and the magnificent pair of black stallions pulled
the carriage so smoothly, the coachman had no need of
his long curling whip. But he cracked it anyway and
sang as he drove, as the Viennese did.

The odd-jobs man ran out to open the carriage door, his beaming grin happy and curious. Gretchen opened the front door, curtseying again and again as the girls came in.

"You have good news!" she sang to them as they entered. "From your happy pink faces your news is good!" She smiled as though she herself had made it happen, and ushered them into Frau Lewisohn's parlor, where the lady waited.

Cousin Helena opened her arms to them both. "It is good news, I feel it, it is good news!"

"Not yet, not yet," said Diana hastily. "We are to come back on Thursday. But he listened to Johanne, and he liked her voice very much, I could tell. How well she sang!"

"You are just in time for luncheon. We shall have wine today, white wine from the valley, and you shall tell me all that happened," Cousin Helena chanted. She could not have been happier if she had arranged it all herself, or if she had been the one who had auditioned.

Frau Johanne Weiss sat in a daze much of the luncheon, and was unaware of what she ate. Much of the telling fell to Diana, and she told it with her own embellishments: how the baron had listened, how he was moved by the lullaby, how grand the house was, how the walls were of velvet brocade, how he had Ming vases on the tables, how fine the piano was.

"And he wants Johanne to come back on Thursday, for his friend to listen! Herr Conductor Otto Kliegl!"

"Ah, yes, one has heard of him." Both Helena and Frau Hemmel nodded. "I have heard they are good friends from days in the Conservatory, and later in the military, where both were captains of cavalry. Both ride well. They are often in the parks, riding of a morning. Baron von Korda has sponsored Herr Kliegl in his career as conductor in an opera house, and he has done well."

After luncheon Diana and Johanne rested, then practiced again for much of the afternoon. On Wednesday Johanne did not return to her teacher-accompanist. Instead she practiced alone or with Diana much of the day, working on everything they could think of that might further impress Herr Baron von Korda. They would be well prepared!

In the midst of all their practice Diana could not help thinking several times of the mysterious lady on the stairway. She wondered if she would ever know who she was.

Oh, well, a Viennese nobleman probably enjoyed his affairs, as other men of the world did. Yet he had scolded her for even speaking to that Captain Mueller. He must have double standards, like all men. For he had brought that beautiful woman into his house, and sent her upstairs to wait, until he was free to entertain her!

Her lips curled scornfully as she thought of that woman and the Baron von Korda. Yet—she felt odd also. For he was a very attractive man. And the way he had gazed at her had stirred her briefly.

Chapter 3

Lukas von Korda was amused at himself. He had been eager for today to arrive—and not just for the second audition of a singer who seemed to fit perfectly into his opera plans.

His first opera *Juditha* was a project he had worked on four years, since the idea first came. If it succeeded, he would be well on his way to a new career.

Now that he could no longer play the piano as he wished, he must find something else in the music world that would fulfill his passion for music. He stood at the window waiting for his carriage to arrive with the two ladies. His mouth curled up with bitter resignation as he felt his left arm with his right hand. He had been so bitter at first, so hardened that he could not even think about music. Life had seemed dead for him without his beloved piano.

He had forced himself to start again, writing out compositions, playing with his right hand, conducting, going about in music circles. But his lost piano music—how he hated that loss—and for what? A woman of no virtue, a cause of no value—a duel with only terrible results on both sides.

Even as Frau Weiss was singing so beautifully, he had found himself staring with envy at the strong capable hands of the girl at the piano. A slim English chit of a girl—to be able to reach octaves easily, to produce sounds he no longer could produce.

Then as he had listened and observed, he had finally been struck by the realization that here was a fine pianist! She played with emotion and some control—not enough. She had been badly taught, she had some bad pedaling and poor phrasing, but it could be corrected in time.

"Hum." He was frowning and still musing when his carriage drew up. He heard the butler going to the door, opening it. Another carriage pulled up behind his. The conductor had arrived on time as usual.

At the drawing room doors he greeted them all. They entered, flushed with the crisp June air, all with sparkling eagerness that raised his spirits. He was smiling as they came to him.

He welcomed them all warmly, and ushered them in. The ladies shed their jackets and hats with shy charm, and he introduced his conductor friend to them.

"Herr Conductor Otto Kliegl—Frau Johanne Weiss, whom you will hear sing today. Fraulein Diana Ballantyne from England. She speaks German well."

Diana Ballantyne gave him a questioning look from her deep blue eyes, but gave a deep graceful curtsey at the introductions. How graceful she was, how lovely her figure. Her clothes spoke of wealth: blue silk today, shot with a gold thread, and a matching jacket trimmed with mink. Little golden earrings that spoke of both wealth and good taste, a ring set with a blue sapphire on her right hand.

He felt a slight irritation at her. What was she doing here, alone in Vienna? She should be under the protection and close observation of her parents, someone who cared that she not roam Vienna alone! She should be engaged to be married, loved devotedly, shielded. Did no one in England realize the dangers of a lovely girl alone here? And an obviously wealthy girl? Before long she would probably be married, a mother, mistress of some fine home, her music career forgotten. Women had no time and energy for careers, their uses were elsewhere. His mother was a good example of that, a talented musician, but giving up all for the sake of her husband and children, the castle and estate, her duties.

The ladies were settled, Diana at the piano bench, Johanne standing beside her. He nodded, and they began one of the same arias as they had performed two days earlier. He looked to his friend Otto and saw his face begin to beam with surprise and pleasure at the full rich sound of the soprano voice.

All went well. Johanne Weiss was nervous at first, but Diana composed herself well, and managed to calm her soprano. The baron noted this sharply. Diana had self-esteem, presence, nerve. Her hands were firm on the keys, her eyes sparkled with delight in the music, and she did not keep looking worriedly at the conductor, as many who auditioned for him did.

He watched Diana as much as he did Johanne, yet Johanne was much more important to him, really. He frowned and began to pace from drawing room to study, and beyond. Still the full rich tones followed him easily, the voice carried well.

When he returned, Otto was nodding and sighing with pleasure. Their gazes met, full of meaning. Otto nodded and smiled happily at his friend and mentor.

They were agreed. After many trials, this was the right woman.

"We agree," said Lukas softly, seating himself on the sofa beside his friend.

"Yes, yes, she has the full big tones, the generous size, the quality of a Judith," said Otto, with satisfaction. "Now, with the baritone and the tenor, we need only the bass."

"Yes, our Holofernes. Someone large and formidable in size as well as with a huge voice and dominating presence."

The aria ended, Lukas rose and set chairs for the ladies.

"I would like to tell you my project, Frau Weiss, and Fraulein." He nodded to Diana. "Pray, listen, if you will, and I will outline it."

They composed themselves, and listened with keen attention, eyes shining.

Lukas moved about the room as he talked, his excitement growing as he told the story of Judith from the Old Testament of the Catholic Bible. Johanne Weiss seemed to know the story, judging by the way she nodded abruptly from time to time as he made the points. However, it seemed new to Diana, who frowned in puzzled attention. She must be a Protestant, Lukas thought. He felt a little disappointment, yet it was to be expected that a well-off English girl of good family must be a Protestant, for the Episcopal faith was the main faith of England, just as Roman Catholicism was that of Austria.

He set that aside for later contemplation, rather irritated that it should bother him.

He finished, "So Judith manages to cut off the head of the enemy of her people, and returns in triumph to her town. The enemies flee in dismay, the people are saved, and sing a song of triumph. The widow Judith, a virtuous woman, has saved her beloved people, the people of God."

"Holofernes will be a bass, the villain," said Otto, his hands drumming on his knees as he thought of the music. "The tent will be rich in silks, and there will be a chance for a ballet of women to amuse him. The music there is light and exquisite, Lukas, some of the best you have written!"

"I thank you," said Lukas drily. His favorites were the dramatic arias in which Judith prays and resolves to sacrifice herself and risk her virtue for her people, and the one in which the high priest Joakim blesses Judith and sends her on her mission. However, his friend and protégé Otto Kliegl was popular in Vienna for conducting light waltzes and operettas, and Lukas had chosen him deliberately for this popularity. He wanted very much for *Juditha* to be popular and accepted.

Lukas was a practical man for all his wealth and musical genius. He understood his audience, and he wanted his music to gain acceptance. It was all very well for some to compose music that was heard only by the musical elite. But he wanted more. He longed for acceptance, praise, and to have his music played in the nightclubs and cafés. "I want the moon," he had confided to his mother, sheepishly. "I want to compose well, but also to have my music loved."

"You shall have both, my son," she had said to him calmly. "You have talent, yes, and more, you have an understanding of people. You will give them the beautiful music for which their souls hunger."

He wondered at times if she missed the music career and the limelight she had had before her marriage. She never said. Certainly she loved her children, and her grandchildren, with a gentle devotion that won the praise of all her wide circle of friends.

Pushing aside such thoughts now, he listened as Otto Kliegl spoke to Johanne Weiss.

"I understand your accompanist has been very ill. Friends tell me he moved to the country for the summer to recover. I should like to arrange for you to be changed from his teaching to that of a friend of mine, if you will, Frau Weiss."

"As you will, it is most kind of you, thank you, sir." She was stammering and blushing, not at all as poised in conversation as she was musically. She must learn more control, thought Lukas.

"Not at all. It will be a good time for us to undertake your training," said Otto Kliegl kindly. "You will be learning the Judith arias. Copies are being made and some will be delivered to you shortly. The opera will have its premiere in September and then we shall see! Eh, Lukas?"

Lukas came forward to join again in the conversation. "Yes, yes, we shall see if it is booed and closed on the opening night, or if it is cheered and goes well!" he said, with a shrug and a smile at the nervous Johanne. "However, whatever happens, I must say, Frau Weiss, that you have a magnificent voice, and shall go far in your career. This work in the cafés on the weekends—you will give it up? I should say you will have a salary beginning today." And he named a sum that made her eyes widen.

"Who will pay for the teacher?" asked Diana quickly, before Johanne could agree. "Her expenses have been heavy, and she should not give up her job unless they are covered also."

Johanne looked shocked. Noticing this, Lukas covered his laughter with an effort. This English girl did not lack business sense! She may have inherited her father's business ability.

"You are quite right," he said, before Otto could interpose. "Her expenses for teaching and accompaniment will be covered also. I want her free to practice on the *Juditha* music. The sum will be for her own expenses. We will take care of the remainder."

It would come out of his own accounts, but shy Frau Weiss did not need to know that. He nodded to Otto, and the man nodded in return, looking wise. Lukas was known among his friends for his kindness and generosity to poor music students. Even in the two years following his duel and the terrible results, he had not forgotten the young ones dependent on him.

Otto Kliegl and Johanne Weiss began to speak together of rehearsals and practice, of arrangements for a music room, and other details.

Lukas turned to Diana Ballantyne. "And you, Fraulein, what are your plans? You have a professor now, yes?" He thought she had not, but wished to make it quite clear.

"Not yet, Maestro," she said naturally, her pretty face frowning slightly. "I shall try again next week. You may perhaps have someone to recommend?"

She looked at him with open faith and hope. Gazing into her lovely deep blue eyes, he felt a twinge in his heart. She was so young, so talented, so doomed to her own fate as a female, who would be married and have children, and almost forget music! Yet there was a determination in that rounded chin, a firmness in the sculpted pink lips, that made him wonder.

"I have someone in mind, Fraulein. Tell me again, how much time have you been allowed by your excellent father?"

"He gives me one year, which will be up next April, Maestro."

One year of freedom, he thought. One year in which she would work and hope and try, and fail. And then she must return to England and her destiny. One could pity her, fighting blindly against her fate. She was too wealthy and too lovely to go unmarried. He wondered if her husband had been chosen for her. What an indulgent father, to allow her freedom for one year! Yet, it could be a good year for her, a happy year, in lovely Vienna, in beautiful Austria, with music for her eager ears and hands, with laughter and waltzes and joy. Perhaps he could help. And then she would have a year to remember always.

"I have been considering a matter, Fraulein," he said, realizing he was committing himself to long hours of work. Yet he could not resist! He was a temporary victim of those blue eyes—and those lovely hands that played so well.

"Yes, Maestro?" Hope lit fires in her eyes. They sparkled.

"I have been considering offering to teach you myself," he said deliberately. "I do not have much time for pupils right now, but I could take on one—yourself. You realize I cannot play with my left hand, but I can see and comprehend what teaching you require. Will you commit yourself to my teaching?"

"Oh, sir!" She jumped up in her eagerness. The two men rose automatically. She laughed aloud, she clasped her hands together. "Oh, sir, do you mean it, really?"

She smiled, and they had to smile with her, indulgently. "I mean it," said Lukas von Korda. "You will come twice a week, on Monday and on Thursday mornings, from ten to twelve. That will suit you, Fraulein?"

"Oh, yes, yes, yes! I cannot thank you enough—I will work very hard—I promise you, I will work hard!"

He was amused at her joyous reaction, and put out his good right hand, and gently pressed her clasped hands. "Then we will work hard together, Fraulein," he said. "Come, let us choose some music, while Kliegl and Frau Weiss speak of the opera."

He had a stack of sheet music on a side table. They went over to it, and he chose several selections for her. She pressed them to herself, such joy and happiness in her lovely face that he could not repress another smile.

"It means much to you, Miss Ballantyne?" he asked in English.

"Oh, sir, I have been turned down by eight teachers!" she burst out. "All because I am a female. I was so angry and thought I might have to go home. Now I can remain in Vienna, and really learn."

"Good, good," he said, nodding. Yet he thought, and all this work in vain. Too bad. A woman can get nowhere in the world of the concert stage, and this beautiful creature will have her year in vain. He knew she must go home later—but somehow that thought was distasteful. "And you will come on Monday. Do not attempt to memorize these musical numbers, Fraulein. I wish you to think about the music, to think about emotion and control, of reaching the composer's meaning. Will you do this?"

"I will try, sir," she said simply. "I have never had as skilled a teacher as you."

He was flattered and wondered if she meant to flatter him. He said coldly, "You do not know how good a teacher I am, Fraulein. And I do not know your ability as a pupil. We shall see, hum?"

She gave a firm nod. "Yes, sir, we shall see!"

She returned on the following Monday, playing the

numbers ostensibly from the music, but he knew she had memorized them, without trying. It both irritated and surprised him. She must have a fantastic memory.

She played rather well that day, but her pedaling was abominable. He corrected her mercilessly, over and over.

"No, no, you must use it softly, carefully. One does not step on the pedal as if it were a stirrup! You ride, Fraulein? You do not ride the pedals the same way!"

She took it patiently, calmly, listening with all her attention and trying to follow his directions, no matter how irritated he became. He fumed to himself. What miserable teachers she must have had!

Then, too, he was critical of her lack of feeling for the music. She tried to please him, and he could tell she had some training and natural ability in her playing, but the emotions were often wrong. He strode about the room, writhing that he could not sit down and show her just how to do it. He silently cursed his stiff left arm. "No, no, Fraulein! Gently, now, gently, yet with firmness. The composer writes of his homeland; he is moved, he has the soldiers marching, but inside he is weeping, for the rape of his homeland!"

When she went home he wondered if he had been too rough on her. Would she return after his hard criticisms? He had had no female piano students before this, and he did not mean to be too harsh. It was simply that the piano meant so much to him—it was his first, his most beloved instrument.

She returned on Thursday, cool in blue silk, her face bland. Was she so cold, so English, that his fury meant nothing? He eyed her with suspicion as she began to play the same selections he had so criticized.

She was better today; she had worked hard. He relaxed. But the pedaling—so very bad.

"Nein, nein!"

He went over to the piano bench and pushed her. She stood up, sliding hastily out the other end as he sat down. "Listen, watch, my feet on the pedals are not like a cavalry charge, Fraulein!"

He began to play with one hand. His left arm he bent enough, painfully, to lay his left hand on his thigh. He remembered the days when he had made the piano sound like a small whimpering child or a massive thunderstorm, like a whispering breeze or a storm at sea. All those days were past. The applause, the worship of an audience were gone for him as a pianist.

As he played, he was surprised to see her bending down to see his shoes on the pedals. When she sat down on the rug and frankly stared at his feet, he could no longer keep silent. The well-polished shoes halted; he turned to her. "Fraulein, what are you doing, for the love of God?"

She met his question with an innocent gaze of her sapphire-blue eyes that momentarily gave him pause. On the rug, curled up in her silk dress, she looked so young. Her hair falling in curls about her flushed cheeks, dimples in the pink flesh, she could have been a child. He had a quick vision of her as a girl of about six, sitting on the floor, demurely playing with her dolls.

But it was a musician that answered him. "Sir, I am observing how you pedal. Nobody ever taught me to use the left pedal; I only used the right. What effects you are getting! No wonder I did not do well!"

He glared, uncertain at first whether to be stunned or amused, but amusement quickly won out, and he had to bite back a laugh. Such emotions she made him feel, one after the other, and sometimes all at once.

"It is not dignified, Fraulein!" he said sternly.

"Nein, Maestro, but I want to learn!" she said earnestly. "Pray, do it again!"

Helpless for once, the Herr Baron von Korda obediently played the Chopin again, with care for his pedaling, for she continued to peer and stare at his feet like one fascinated. He had never felt so conscious of his audience, nor so inwardly amused, so moved by another's desire to learn. He played the étude with as much skill and feeling as he could evoke.

When he was finished, Diana sat still on the rug, her head bent, and he frowned down at her. Could she say nothing? Had his one-handed playing displeased her?

He stood. "Get up, Fraulein, and play it again, this time with feeling, and not thumping!"

"Yes, Maestro," she said calmly, and stood, shaking out her skirts. She seated herself with composure and began to play. He could see she was now concentrating on the pedaling, neglecting the emotion, and he turned and stopped her.

"Tell me, Fraulein, are the English islands always covered with rain and mist?"

She stared up at him. "It—it rains often, Maestro."

"That accounts for it, then! There is water in the veins of the English! They have no blood in them, they cannot feel and think with their hearts! How can you play such an étude with such indifferent calm, when poor Chopin felt such boiling emotions? How can you treat it with such chill precision? Have you no heart?"

He waited, intent on her reaction. If she smiled and bobbed her blond curls, he would strangle her! He felt too keenly about music to allow such reactions.

When she responded by banging her hands on the piano with a single loud crash, he jumped in his shoes.

"How can you say such a nasty thing!" she cried, in English, too furious to speak German. Her cheeks were pink, her eyes flashing, stormy. "We have blood in our veins! Can you forget Waterloo? Can you forget Nelson at Trafalgar? Can you forget the Crimea and our Florence Nightingale?"

"It is like you to mention the wars," he taunted, to see her reaction. "I have heard the English can conduct a good clever war. But what about the arts? What about painting? What about music? We have Haydn and Mozart, and so on. You have Gilbert and Sullivan!"

"We may not have great musicians yet!" she cried. "But one day we will have great composers also, you will see! One day, we, too, will look back to great music and art. Just now we are too busy making our country great, and fighting the wars that Austria is too weak to undertake!"

He gasped, choking back an angry reply. He was painfully aware of the weakness of Austria. It was said the country lived in the past; that the empire was dying under the aged revered Franz Josef. Prince Rudolph of Hapsburg had died under mysterious circumstances in 1889 at Mayerling, and with him had gone hopes for the throne. Some whispered that these years were the twilight of the empire—and perhaps they were. Was there decadence in the air, in the feverish search for pleasure, in the gay waltzes with which the Viennese filled their evenings in a mad rush for pleasure?

His brother Theo was given to discussions about this very question; sober thoughtful discussions as befitted a university student of philosophy. Was he right? Was this English girl right too?

Lukas paced away from her. After a pause her soft clipped English voice pierced the silence. "I beg your pardon, Herr Baron. I had no right to insult you and your country."

He bent his head and returned to the piano. "You are forgiven, Fraulein. I provoked you. We shall speak again of this one day—when you are not in such a temper!" The sight of her flushed cheeks and the anger in her eyes pleased him. Yes, there was emotion in her after all!

Teasingly he bent, and without thought he pressed his lips to her soft pink mouth. He found it warm, sweet, fresh. But no sooner had his lips met hers when she gasped. Lukas drew back in alarm. What had he done? Insulted her? Frightened her? He saw the look of shock and confusion on her face.

"Forgive me again, Fraulein. I am too impulsive." His tone became formal once again. "It pleases me that you show emotion. It bodes well for your playing. Now, try again the Chopin étude, and we will plan the pedal work for you. The first lines, if you will."

Diana hesitated, as though unsure what to do. Deliberately he sat down beside her on the piano bench, close enough to feel her slim body tremble beside his thighs.

He put his right hand on the keys an octave above her right hand. "Now, if you will—play with me."

Her hand shook as she tried to play the notes. He turned to her.

"Do I disturb you?" he asked softly.

She blinked her silver-gilt lashes without answering. He bent to her, and cupped her chin with his right hand. How soft was her face, like silk—no, softer than silk.

He bent again, his gaze on that trembling mouth. This time he touched it tentatively with his lips, then more deeply. When he lifted his head a moment later, her body stiffened against him. He brushed his hand gently against her slim bare throat.

"Have you had a lover?" he asked.

"Sir—Maestro!"

"Have you?"

"Oh, no!"

"It might be better if you had. It would release the emotions inside you," he said evenly, and turned back to the music. "Begin again, Fraulein," he instructed, as though he had not just treated her so intimately.

She began again after a pause. For the remainder of the morning she seemed embarrassed in his presence, yet he was pleased. He had learned something about her. He had seen she was capable of powerful emotion. She was cool from training, not nature. He wanted her to play well; he was fiercely determined that this year should not be wasted. Even though she went home to England at the end of the time, she should be as well trained as he could arrange it. He would present her in concert, and prove to the world that he was a fine teacher of music!

That evening the baron was to preside over a dinner party attended by some of his relatives. He arrived early at the restaurant, and looked in at the room he had engaged. The flowers had arrived, and a maid was skillfully arranging them.

He checked to see that the dinner places were set as he wished: his mother at the foot of the table, he at the head, the aunts and uncles seated in order of their rank in Austrian society, and the young cousins scattered here and there, tactfully. Having attended to this, he returned to the office of the manager, and checked the menu. These were details a wife would have handled, he thought, a little amused at himself. Perhaps his mother was right. He was thirty-two, and should think seriously of taking a wife! Yet, who would look at him without a shudder—with his stiff left arm? And he had not danced for two years. What kind of social companion would he be?

Returning to the formal room, he met Captain Gardell Mueller. Surprised, he halted. The captain bowed deeply, mockery reflected in the black eyes, and in the set of the dark curly head.

"Herr Baron von Korda!"

"Captain Mueller." Lukas bent his head slightly, clicked his heels together. "You are dining here?"

"Ja, Herr Baron, my sister entertains in the next room. May you have a good evening!"

With more bows they parted. Lukas strode on, burning with rage. When the manager appeared with the special menus he had requested, he said abruptly, "I understand the Countess von Hulsen entertains in the next room. You know my request?"

"Ja, ja, Herr Baron, I am so sorry! She had reserved a room for last Saturday night. I had made all the arrangements, and then she changed it to tonight! There was nothing I could do!" There was a sly look in the small eyes.

"You could have notified me," he said stiffly. He hated the gossip that had spread through Vienna about himself and the Count von Hulsen, since the duel. Would nobody allow him to forget?

"I beg your apology so humbly, my high Herr Baron," began the manager, offering a string of elaborate flatteries mingled with lavish apologies. Lukas dismissed him curtly, hiding his anger.

Soon his own guests began to arrive. He stood at the threshhold of the doorway to greet them. Mingled among them were the von Hulsen guests, military men, gambling men, some titled women of loose reputation. Along, too, came the husky middle-aged Count Heinrich von Hulsen. His pale blond-gray hair was the color of weak tea, his pale blue eyes glittered. The count was lavishly clothed in a black silk suit trimmed with silver gilt.

On his arm was his wife, the Countess Elza Mueller von Hulsen, stunning in black velvet trimmed in silver against which shone jeweled necklaces and bracelets and, on her hands, brilliant rings of diamonds and colored gems.

At sight of the baron she broke into gay smiles. "Lukas! Dear man, what are you doing here?" she cried. "Do come and join us."

He bowed, making his apologies formally, aware of the hostile gaze the count directed toward him.

A guest paused, engaging the attention of the count.

Elza moved closer to Lukas and took his arm. "Dearest Lukas," she whispered, "it was so kind of you to give me refuge the other day."

"It was my pleasure to aid you," he said uneasily. Why did he still feel the lure of her sensual nature? The fragrance she wore still awakened his desire. Their affair had been brief but intense, and Elza, he knew, still felt attracted to him.

"You are so sweet. I was quite shaken by the fall."

"Your horse is too strong for you. I hope you will not ride that brute again."

Her mouth curled in a slow smile, and gazing at it he remembered long hot afternoons lost in her arms. That sultry mouth, those black eyes half-closed with passion, her white arms, her taut breasts, wide thighs— "I can ride him, I can ride—anything," she murmured, her gaze on his lips.

Abruptly he remembered the soft pink mouth of the girl he had kissed that day. The contrast was startling. Diana had a mouth like a pure pink rose. Elza's was more like a scarlet camelia.

"I wish you would meet me again," she muttered urgently. "Please—Lukas—you said you had forgiven me."

Lukas stiffened. "Never again," he murmured, smiling politely to someone who, passing them, was staring with open curiosity.

Elza patted his shirtfront, as though commenting on his decorations. Her long slim hands had known his lithe body, had given him pleasures almost as intense as those he had taken from her. Was he a fool to try to forget her? Why not take her as they both wished? Make her his mistress again? What could her husband do that he had not already done to him?

He could kill, true. Perhaps.

It was painful for Lukas to think back on his confrontation with the count.

During their duel the count had struck Lukas in the left arm. The resulting injury had crippled the limb and ruined Lukas's career as a promising young pianist. Lukas in turn had felt his sword slip from its intended mark in the count's side, wounding instead the private parts the count held dear. After the duel all Vienna whispered that the injury had left the count impotent.

Life since the injury to Lukas's left arm was not so sweet as it had been. But perhaps in Elza's arms he could forget the abandonment of his career on the concert stage. Perhaps if he tasted her lips again, he could forget that he could no longer hold a woman strongly with both good arms, forcing her to him, holding her helpless as she laughed and protested, and yielded.

It might be worth the risk.

But no. She was—what she was. He knew now the malice and cruelty that hid behind her sweet smile and bright eyes. She had wanted him, and yet he knew she'd been proud that her husband had dueled for her. And her husband knew of her unfaithfulness, and was brutal to her, sometimes leaving bruises on her body.

Lukas eyed the beautiful young countess dispassionately, but inside he felt hatred and resentment toward her. How sweetly she had pleaded with him! How she had wept over her vile treatment at the hands of her brutal husband! How she had begged him to find release for her! Lukas had been too sorry for her, too often in her tantalizing company, and the gossip had reached the count. The duel had been the inevitable result.

And now—how she smiled, how she waved her fan, how she eyed his left arm with cruel curiosity!

He bowed and left them, to greet more of his guests. Later, as the noise in the adjacent room rose above the level of their polite conversation, his mother whispered, "Who in heaven's name has the next room? I cannot hear myself speak!"

"The von Hulsens, Mother," he said, biting off the words. "The restaurant manager made a mistake. He shall not make another at my expense! We shall dine no more at this place!"

"Of course not, dear Lukas," said his mother. Her color had paled, but she retained her magnificent composure. She was an attractive woman. Tonight her blonde-gray hair was piled in beautiful masses, her blue gown a lovely contrast to her pink cheeks. Although widowed, she refused to wear black any longer. It was not her color, she said. Lukas wondered if she missed their stern father, but suspected she had felt relief at his passing.

His father, Karl von Korda, had been a stern hard man, devoted to the estates. He had refused to allow his lovely wife, Constantia, to continue her musical career. She was only to play for amusement, he had insisted.

Since his death, Constantia had begun to play again. Lukas felt a curious pang. Would his wife, if she were talented, resent him, and welcome his death? How sad that would be—for both of them! Yet that was the way life was—wasn't it? The man was the ruler of the family, and of his kingdom. Lukas had inherited the castle, the town house, the chalet in the Alps, the title, the duties of his rank, the responsibility for his family, servants, and tenants.

The man had a duty to them all, and to himself, to conduct his life honorably. According to the dictates of society, all must play his or her part. A woman was expected to honor her husband, to bear his children, to make him comfortable, and be a credit to him. She had no time for playing the piano—or other diversions. And no time for a career. Yet Lukas knew that despite the dictates of society, his mother was happier since his stern father had died!

A series of crashes in the next room signified that a toast had been drunk and the glasses smashed against the wall. Laughter broke out immediately afterward. Theo frowned, and looked away uneasily. His mother compressed her lips. And Lukas cursed the restaurant manager who had had the nerve to place them there, to remind him of the past.

He wished they would not continually remind him, these Viennese who adored a scandal, watching with such intense interest all that went on under their noses.

He wished he himself knew what he wanted. He had lost the one career that meant most to him. He had no desire to marry. It was up to Theo now to carry on the family name one day.

Lukas felt uneasy at the very thought of marriage.

Many of the women he knew were unhappy in their marriages; some of them were driven to seek excitement in the arms of one lover after another.

Perhaps he *would* yield to the wishes of Elza von Hulsen again. It would harm nobody, he thought cynically. And she was a voluptuous stunning woman. Everyone seemed to think their affair had continued anyway. Why not enjoy the sweets along with the reputation?

Chapter 4

Diana gazed from her window wistfully. It was a bright sunny Sunday afternoon in June. The trees were green, the flowers in colorful bloom. Must she stay in another afternoon and practice?

She had worked hard these weeks, inspired by the brilliant teaching of her Maestro. She respected Lukas von Korda; he was so fine, so smart, so talented. She enjoyed working with him. In fact, in these past weeks she had felt almost ecstatic with happiness.

But—she had taken off no days at all! Upstairs, Rosalie Stamitz was singing a gay waltz. The music made Diana want to dance, to run in the lovely sunshine, or ride a spirited horse. But such thoughts were impossible. Here in Vienna she had come to work.

There was a tap at the door. Perhaps Cousin Helena had come to chat for a time, she thought eagerly. "Come in!" she called.

The bright red head of Alicia Huntingdon poked through the opening, her scarlet mouth laughing, her green eyes bright. "It is such a pretty day," she cried. "Do you want to go out with me?"

"Out! I'd love to!" Diana sighed. "Shall we go for a walk?"

"Yes—in the Prater!" Alicia answered, beaming. "I've heard so much about it. Do let us see if Frau Lewisohn will come with us. I'd love to walk about, and drink that heavenly chocolate in one of the smart cafés!"

Alicia was dressed in a deep green gown with black braid, and Diana wore a blue silk. They each put on short jackets that matched their dresses, jammed hats on their heads, and went downstairs to urge Frau Lewisohn to accompany them.

Alas, Cousin Helena had engaged herself with friends for tea. But she would send her best maid with them—Pauline, a dependable older woman.

A fiacre was sent for, and the three women started out happily. Pauline sat facing the other two, demurely, but with a smile across her broad face. "The Prater will be fine today, Frauleins! Many come to see the puppets, and to stroll and stare at each other! And there will be gentlemen on horseback, and musicians to play for pennies. . . ."

So it was. The driver deposited his passengers in the gardens and promised to return for them in three hours. Joyfully the three women began to stroll about, eagerly taking in all the sights.

It looked as though all Vienna had come to stroll in the Prater that day. Crowds gathered about every puppet show, the children clustered in front so they could see. Pauline pointed out the amusements, the rides, the little platforms of musicians, the cafés for beer, chocolate, and the famous Viennese pastries. There were advertisements for some naughty evening amusements, too, and the girls shyly averted their eyes from the gaudy posters featuring female entertainers.

The afternoon was made for carefree amusements. Diana felt in the mood for fun, and so did Alicia. They had both been working very hard. They wandered about, trying to choose which café they would eventually return to to sample the sweets and chocolate.

"My violin instructor has finally received the word that I am serious about my music," confided Alicia, with a sharp nod of the green plumed hat on her bright red hair. "He fooled about for a time with simple pieces, until I drove him wild with my demands for more difficult things. Now we are really getting to work. I hope to arrange a concert somewhere, but he shakes his gray head, and says, 'Who will come? Who will come?' until I long to pull out his hairs one by one!"

Diana laughed merrily with her, and the sound drew the attention of two smart-looking men in scarlet uniforms. They began to follow the beautifully dressed ladies at a short distance, poking each other and nodding with pleasure. The girls did not notice them for a time, but sharp-eyed Pauline did, rather dubiously.

Diana told Alicia about her lessons. "I am so pleased with my Maestro," she said. "He is so very talented. What a pity it is that he had to cut his career short. He must have played magnificently at one time."

"We are being followed," Pauline interrupted sharply. "My Frauleins, shall we depart? I can get a fiacre for us."

Alicia was more alert than Diana, catching her meaning at once. "Who is following us?" she snapped. "Some mustached old gents?"

"No, no, young and smart military men. They look very handsome. Ah, one is now trying to catch my eye!"

"Ah, ha," said Alicia, relaxing. "So they are attracted to you, Pauline. We must watch out for you!" She managed this in her somewhat broken German, and the older woman giggled involuntarily.

"Nein, nein, you tease poor Pauline! The gentlemen stare at the so-lovely English ladies!"

"I'm not English, I'm American," asserted Alicia, a little crossly. "There is a difference!"

"Yes, you became independent more than one hundred years ago," said Diana, seriously.

"Not I, I wasn't born," said Alicia, with a laugh. "But I'm independent enough! My father says, too much so!"

"So does my father." Diana sighed. She had not broached the subject of their mutual troubles with unwanted suitors, but one day she would. "However, I have my year of freedom to study music, and I mean to make the most of it."

Under Pauline's suspicious eye the two uniformed men had managed to approach. As the girls paused to talk, the men caught up with them, snapped their hands in salute, and studied the girls' lovely faces with cautious hope. Diana turned to scowl and rebuke them, stopping when she recognized the face of one.

"Why—it is—" She hesitated, not remembering the name of the merry officer who had accosted her before.

He beamed, then bowed and swept off his hat with his gloved hand. "It is the beautiful English musical lady!" he exclaimed in accented English. "What luck I have today! You are more lovely than before, if it is possible! Vienna agrees with you. She has added sparkle to the most lovely eyes in all Europe!"

"And the other lady has hair as beautiful as my own," exclaimed his companion, sweeping off his cap to show a head of bright carrot. He was eying Alicia's mane of bright red with humorous admiration.

Diana and Alicia had to laugh. The initial awkwardness overcome, the officers each took possession of one girl's arm, and swept them along through the Prater.

They immediately introduced themselves. "Captain Gardell Mueller, at your service!" offered the dark-haired one. "Captain Ernst Schmidt," said the red-haired one, smiling at Alicia fondly. He had something of an Italian accent; which he explained to them. "My mama is Italian. She calls me Ernesto, and you may do so also. Italians make great lovers, you know!"

His words were delivered in a comic vein, not to insult, but to make them laugh. Which they did again and again that lovely afternoon.

As they walked about the sky seemed to become more blue, the gaudy lights of the Prater amusements more beautiful, the puppets funnier, the breeze more refreshing. Gallantly, the officers included Pauline in their strolls, sometimes on Captain Mueller's arm, and sometimes on that of Captain Schmidt, each protecting her from the pushing crowds as they stood to watch the puppets, or observe the swans in the lake, or read the political posters calling for Hungarian independence.

Later in the afternoon the women and their escorts stopped for refreshments. Captain Mueller chose the café, then proceeded to seat Pauline between the girls, with an officer on either side to protect them from the shoving patrons of the busy café.

He ordered hot chocolate all around, and a large plate of pastries. "You must try them all," he said generously. The girls pretended to groan at the temptation but were obviously delighted at the sight of the extravagant pastries—chocolate, raspberry, strawberry ones; custards, coffee-creams, and Napoleons—all topped with clouds of fresh whipped cream.

Alicia asked the men about the political posters they had observed. "Why are the Hungarians demanding independence? I thought this was the Austrian-Hungarian Empire," she asked curiously.

"Yes, it is, and our beloved Emperor Franz Josef is the dear father of all," said Captain Schmidt.

Captain Mueller added, "But Austria is made up of many nationalities of peoples, of Italians, like my brother officer here—"

"I am Austrian!" broke in Schmidt indignantly, licking the last traces of a chocolate pastry from his fingers. "Of course, I am Italian also, in my ability to laugh and love and sing," he bragged comically.

Schmidt drew a deep breath, dramatically placed his hand on his muscular chest, and opened his mouth wide. Mueller pointed his finger at him in imitation of a gun, and ordered, "You will not sing here, not today! Idiot!"

The girls giggled at their antics, and Mueller, pleased, went on with his story.

"As you see, we are all part something. I am Austrian, but also Hungarian. Schmidt is Austrian, but also Italian. There are Slavs, Bulgars, Germans, Bohemians, Dalmatians, Croatians—people of many nations have come together under our beloved emperor, God bless him!"

The young officer's face was suddenly reverent and devoted. Diana gazed at him with surprise. He was obviously capable of deep loyalty and devotion, a trait she respected him for.

As they enjoyed the rich pastries and hot chocolate, the two officers proceeded to tell the girls more about their backgrounds, and their country. Their conversation showed intelligence as well as humor.

Eventually Mueller changed the subject. "But tell us

about yourselves, beautiful ladies! You cannot be serious about your music—can you?" he added, with mock sadness. "I have not seen you in the Prater before, and we come almost every Sunday when we are not on duty."

"But of course we are serious," said Alicia decisively. "I have come to study the violin, and am working hard. Diana is studying the piano, and she practices all day and some of the night!"

"Well, I'm sorry I am bothering you," said Diana, with teasing hauteur.

"You don't bother me, you play like an angel!" said Alicia.

"I should like very much to hear you," said Mueller. "Above all things, I adore music!"

Above his head Diana suddenly saw a sight that stunned her. The face of her Maestro, scowling, his blue eyes blazing at her. Suddenly she was speechless. Fortunately Alicia did not know him, and went on merrily. Diana, however, was too distracted to hear what she said. Lukas von Korda was staring at them all, with obvious disapproval.

But surely he could see the maid was with them! What was the matter with him? They were not acting in a loose depraved manner, as his stern reaction seemed to imply! She remained quiet, letting the others speak. Von Korda turned on his heel and left the building, his small party trailing behind him. He appeared to be in the company of an older gray-haired woman and several small children. Children with him? She wished she had looked more closely.

Suddenly curious about the time, she glanced at the golden watch pinned to her lapel, a gift her father had given her on her eighteenth birthday. It showed four thirty.

"Oh—the fiacre driver will be waiting for us!" she exclaimed hurriedly to Alicia.

"So he will—we must go!" The arts of flirtation were not lost on Alicia. She knew that their early departure would leave the young men eager to see them again. She stood, and Diana and Pauline followed her lead.

As expected, the young captains were ill-disposed to allow them to leave. They walked them to the entrance of the Prater, kissed their hands, begged to see them again.

"I don't know—we will see," said Diana evasively, as Captain Mueller handed her gallantly into the little carriage.

"But we must see you next Sunday—here again. May I call upon you on Wednesday evening—what about going to a concert? an opera?"

"No, no, no," laughed the girls as the carriage pulled away. Even Pauline's cheeks were flushed at the men's gallantry and humor. It had been a delightful afternoon.

Monday morning Diana went to her lesson in a happy frame of mind, having almost forgotten her Herr Professor's scowling face in the café. She sat down to play at once, as was her habit. However, his upraised hand stopped her before her fingers touched the keyboard.

His frown quickly recalled their encounter the previous afternoon. "One minute, Fraulein Ballantyne! I must speak to you seriously, as your guide and mentor in Vienna!"

"Sir?" she asked, startled, her blue eyes widening.

"I do not know if you are as innocent as you seem! I have warned you about the uniformed menaces of Austria. They have little regard for a young lady's reputation. And the two young specimens with whom you were yesterday—"

"Sir, I can explain that. My friend Alicia and I went with a maid to the Prater, as my cousin was unable to accompany us—we met the captains. . . ."

Under his scornful look her tone died. She swallowed uneasily.

"Those two are particularly depraved men, dear young lady! Even among their own kind they have bad reputations. They drink heavily. They gamble away all their earnings. But worst of all they are unscrupulous in attacking the young ladies who are stupid enough to trust them! No mother in Vienna would think of allowing her precious daughter to go out alone—"

"We were not alone! Pauline was with us—she is a very respectable—"

"Silence! I would like it if you did not continually interrupt me! Is this how you treat your father?" He thundered so loudly at her that she was stilled, and sat with hands folded meekly in her rose silk lap.

"So!" He began to pace the room, his right hand holding the left arm, as though not conscious of the gesture. Beneath his frown his blond face resembled a mountain of snow under clouds. His blue eyes flashed lightning. "I do not know how to express myself to you in polite language, my dear young innocent girl! How can I speak so you will understand, yet not offend your childish ears? These captains—these military popinjays—these seducers of young women—these ruthless abductors of ladies—"

He turned, saw her shocked face, and modified his tone sharply.

"They are not fit company for young women, Fraulein!" he said more quietly. "Ask your Cousin Helena. She knows the world! We Austrians know that young English girls are too independent, have been given too much freedom. And the American girls are worse! The European men misunderstand this freedom. They consider you girls to be ready prey and willing. Be careful, I warn you. You are not in your protected English village now."

When he had finally stopped, she drew a deep breath. "You are kind to be concerned, Herr Baron," she said with angry formality. How he insulted her and berated her and treated her like a child! "I will keep your words in mind, as I roam Vienna like a brash Englishwoman of little virtue!"

His fine mouth tightened. "If you were brash, and of little virtue, I should not have been so angry," he said, in soft menacing tones. "However, it is up to you. You are on your own here in Vienna. Only common sense can guide you. If you lack that, what more can I say?" He gave a vast shrug and turned his back on her to stare out the window. "Begin!" he barked.

She began, and had the feeling he did not hear her at first. Finally he turned about and approached the piano, with a suggestion about the sonata she was playing.

"You will note the music is marked *pianissimo*. I suggest that you make it *piano;* you have a delicacy of touch already. Then increase to *forte* in the next theme."

She did as he suggested, and could hear the improvement. Forgetting their angry words, she concentrated on the rest of the lesson. She absorbed his teaching eagerly, and in the afternoon went over and over what he had said as she practiced in her rooms.

She went downstairs about four o'clock, pleasantly tired, to take tea with her cousin and the other ladies of the boardinghouse. Alicia was there before her, questioning Cousin Helena about the military men of Vienna. Diana found it easy to confide in her cousin about Herr Baron von Korda and his words.

"My instructor, Herr Baron von Korda, was very angry this morning, cousin," she said, looking into her teacup. "He berated us for sitting with Captains Mueller and Schmidt, and said some nasty words about them. Are they so notorious?"

"Ah," said Cousin Helena, eyebrows upraised. The others listened intently as she revealed the gossip. "There has been much talk these three years. You see, Captain Gardell Mueller is the fond brother of the Countess Elza Mueller von Hulsen. Of course, he took the countess's side when she was insulted by her husband for her association with von Korda! Yes, yes, all Vienna seethed with the story, especially when they dueled."

"Von Korda—dueled Captain Mueller?" Diana gasped.

"No, no, with von Hulsen! You see, the countess was seen alone several times with the handsome baron, accompanied only by her maid. Her husband quarreled with von Korda, and struck him. A duel was arranged—and one heard several versions of it. When it ended, von Hulsen was in a hospital at one end of Vienna, von Korda in a hospital at the other end! Von Hulsen emerged, evidently none the worse for wear. But von Korda, ah, his poor left arm! And such a fine pianist! He retired to his castle to the west, and did not return to Vienna until last year. And he has never played again in public."

Diana scarcely heard the babble of voices, so shocked and disappointed was she in her Maestro. He had dueled, over a married woman and his attentions to her! And he had dared to berate her for having chocolate with two young men in the presence of two other women! What a hypocrite! Somehow the story did not make sense.

She frowned, thinking it over. Von Korda's attentions to Captain Mueller's sister, the countess, had led to a duel with the count von Hulsen. The captain and his sister were clearly the injured parties. Why, then, had Captain Mueller allowed the baron to intimidate him that first day he had approached Diana on the street? Why had he accepted the authority of the baron, by turning and walking away from her at his command? Von Korda had acted as though with righteous wrath, and Captain Mueller had acted guilty!

"Is it the titles?" asked Diana suddenly, amidst the babble of voices. "Would the von Hulsens bow down to von Korda because he is a baron? Or much richer?"

Cousin Helena looked bewildered and shook her graying head. "No, no, no, that is not it. They have almost equal wealth; in fact, the count has the higher title. No. I don't know much of the matter. I respect the Herr Baron von Korda for his fine reputation both as a musician, and as a gentleman, or I would not have allowed him to take you as a pupil. The Captain Mueller I do not know well, but I hear little about him."

By the end of this conversation Diana was all the more confused. She certainly did not understand Austrian society and the military! As for the men, they all had dueling scars on their faces. Maybe they enjoyed dueling, even though she found the idea distasteful.

Pauline interrupted them, entering the room with two huge bouquets of flowers in her arms, and trying not to be too obvious in her delight. One massive bouquet of pink roses she laid in Diana's lap, and the other, a mass of red roses, in Alicia's. Gasps of admiration could be heard all around.

"Who sent them?" demanded little Frau Hemmel in great excitement. "Some gentlemen, it is sure!" She clasped her tiny wrinkled hands in delight.

Alicia had found a white envelope among the flowers and opened it. She began to laugh. "It says," she said, reading the card aloud without reticence, "To the beautiful lady with the hair like mine, I adore you! Will you come to the summer opera with me on Wednesday evening? I await your word, adored one. Captain Ernst Schmidt, your Ernesto." She began to giggle again.

They turned expectantly to Diana, who was holding another small envelope. Her cheeks were the color of the pink roses. She read the card silently, then sighed, and gave in.

"It says, 'To the pink English rose: Will you come to the opera with us on Wednesday evening? Captain Schmidt is taking your friend, Miss Huntingdon, and we will all go together. I await the evening with much anticipation. Captain Gardell Mueller!"

"Well, they certainly take our response for granted," remarked Alicia, trying to look stern, without succeeding.

"You shall not go out with them in the evening," announced Helena Lewisohn firmly, though it was clear she was sensitive to their feelings. "Their attentions and flowers are all very well, but your fathers would not approve! No, it would cause too much gossip. When you wish to go out at night, I will accompany you, and not permit much box visiting, either! I will not have you talked about!"

Diana was not sorry at the dictates of her cousin, and sent a firm letter of refusal, as did Alicia. But the men continued to send flowers and notes. They haunted the Prater on weekends and took the girls for chocolate in the cafés whenever they met up with each other. They were amusing company, and Diana felt relaxed with them, especially when Cousin Helena accompanied them and kept a firm watch over the goings-on.

Perhaps von Korda had made those nasty remarks because of the enmity between him and Mueller's family. Diana continued to find Captain Mueller and his friend amusing and charming, and their attentions remained respectful.

It was certainly exciting for her and Alicia to have handsome young men vying to escort them, being so devoted and sending such magnificent flowers. Diana could not take their attentions seriously; the shadow of Addison Montague and her father's plans for her future continued to haunt her imagination. Besides, she could not visualize her father allowing her to marry a reckless gambler of a guardsman! However, it made her happy to have such diversions during the week.

She was working hard, practicing the piano and secretly writing musical compositions that she hoped one day she might dare to show her Maestro.

She and Alicia became good friends; they were much alike, serious about their music, but longing for fun and good times during this period of independence from their families. As Alicia once said, wisely, "This may be the only time we are allowed off the leash, Diana. So far I have protested being married against my will. But one day Papa will get me married off to some husband or other, and I expect he will want to keep me in line, just as Papa has tried to. So—eat, drink and be merry—someday we will be married!"

Diana laughed at her cynical friend, but inwardly

she knew she spoke the truth. Once back in England, married, with children, these days of June sunshine, amusing young men, and flowers would seem like a distant dream. She wanted to enjoy it while she could.

Meantime, she had much to occupy herself. She played much of the day and still found time to work with Johanne on her music. Rosalie Stamitz came down twice from her room to sing over some of the songs she was preparing for an audition. Diana liked Rosalie and hoped she would be chosen for the part in the operetta that she wanted.

Rosalie had much self-confidence for one so young. Diana wondered to herself where that confidence came from. She said herself she was a farm girl. Yet she had poise and assurance far beyond her years.

The girls in Frau Lewisohn's boardinghouse were certainly an interesting and varied lot, thought Diana.

Chapter 5

Rosalie Stamitz eyed her competition from under the thick fringe of her dark brown lashes. All inexperienced except the girl near the door, she thought. They were all about her age—twenty-two—but she would warrant she had the most experience of any girl there.

As she waited her turn to audition, she thought about the contrast between her present situation and her earlier life.

She had been born on a farm in the Alps near Innsbruck. Her parents had reared a large family; Rosalie was the middle child among eight girls and five boys. All had helped on the farm as soon as they could toddle about—bringing in the cows, milking, haying, making butter and cream, taking the dairy products to the town below.

Her father owned much land and worked hard. Rosalie's childhood was uneventful until, at age thirteen, a tragedy befell her that changed the course of her young life. A cruel ambitious farmhand waylaid young Rosalie when she was walking alone one afternoon, and raped her. Then he had had the gall to go to her father and demand her hand in marriage!

Once her enraged father had cooled down, he had actually considered the match. It would suit him to have one daughter married, and to a good worker. But Rosalie had other plans.

Mature for her age, always thinking of herself, she connived to put off the ardent young man. She had discovered in herself a way to escape this rough life and go to the city. She could sing, better than any in her family of singers and musicians! Her silvery voice rang with merriment and she could yodel better than anyone around. She told her father she wanted to wait on marriage until she was older, and at thirteen, she had a point. As his wife told him, "Young Rosalie has much to learn about housework first!"

So Rosalie was put to work at cooking and sewing, instead of the outdoor chores. She discovered a talent for sewing, and for a time she made her own and her sisters' dresses. During this period she also made sure other young farmer lads noticed her. She flirted with them openly, and her suitor finally gave up, sulkily, settling instead for her older sister. The two of them now had a piece of the farm and seven children, and her sister already looked twice Rosalie's age.

At sixteen Rosalie had taken a job in the local café without her father's permission. As a waitress she had worked long hours, serving huge steins of beer with steady small hands, but also managing to perform songs often during the evenings.

With her wages she purchased material and made herself dresses patterned on the traditional costumes of the Alps. She knew they flattered her: the short pretty aproned dresses of white with blue and rose embroidery, adorned with lace on the sleeves and about her beautiful throat. Rosalie knew she had talent and looks, and learned early how to make the best of both.

Early on she had made herself a vow: she would make a life for herself! She would be no man's chattel!

Rosalie's thoughts returned to the present. She watched another girl leave the room, eyes downcast, cheeks flushed. She had heard about Herr Franz Vogler—he was middle-aged, married, a father. He was known to like young operetta singers, and had promoted the careers of several girls who had gone on to become famous.

What price would he ask of her? Rosalie felt sure she knew. It would be the same price as that of all the men who had helped her on her way from farm to town, to city, to Vienna.

Years ago she had learned about the certain times of the month she was free to engage in sex, and not get "caught" by a pregnancy. Thereafter she had flirted, slept with the men who could help her, and, moved freely from one to the next. First there had been her accompanist at the café, and then a traveling salesman who had taken her to Innsbruck and installed her at his cousin's boardinghouse and café. There her singing found a new audience, and her stage manner improved.

In Innsbruck she became rather well known. She had sung for the tourists, specializing in the songs she knew they liked. In addition she had memorized the songs of every new operetta in Vienna and the countryside, and sang them often, making sure she was on stage whenever visitors came in from the great city of Vienna.

Her fondest dream was that one day she would be the toast of Vienna. Then she would earn so much money, she need never fear being the pawn of any man!

Another girl was called to audition, and then the experienced-looking girl followed. Rosalie was next. When it was her turn, she drew a deep breath, stood up and shook out her flounced skirts, and moved prettily into the audition room.

The heavyset man who awaited her was not much taller than her own dainty five feet. Dressed in her Alps costume of white with pink roses and an apron of lace, Rosalie made a lovely picture, and knew it. The conductor's eyes lit up, surveying her slowly from her waves of shining brown hair to her tiny black slippers. Rosalie gave him a well-rehearsed shy smile.

She curtseyed deeply, fluffing her wide white skirts so he had a good view of her excellent ankles. "Herr Professor Conductor Vogler," she sighed in a mock-shy voice.

His eyes widened in appreciation, he stroked his thick black mustache. "Ah, you are—let me see . . ."

"Fraulein Rosalie Stamitz, from near Innsbruck," she said softly. "At your service, Herr Professor Conductor Vogler!"

"It is Herr Conductor Vogler," he said, reluctantly giving up one of the titles she had just awarded him.

"One has heard so much of you, sir!" She opened her big brown eyes in awe. "What an honor you have done me, to allow me to audition for you! The greatest conductor in Vienna, no, in all Austria! Even on the farm, we had heard of you!"

He preened, his chest swelled out like that of a pouter pigeon. So he did like flattery, but she must use it carefully.

"Farm girl, my child. Ah, yes, the pink cheeks, the fresh complexion!" He dared to fondle her cheek, and she only averted her eyes modestly.

"And what training have you had, child?" he asked

more practically, turning to the piano, and arranging some sheets of music.

"I worked as waitress in cafés, Herr Conductor Vogler," she answered briskly, as if to show she could learn quickly. "I enjoyed my work, but I liked to sing so much that music would burst out from me many times. People liked my music. I learned from whoever would teach me."

This roster had included an actor, a young man with many skills. In exchange for some artfully bestowed favors, Rosalie had persuaded him to teach her some stage tricks: how to enter and leave the stage, how to bow, how to use her body gracefully. He had been willing to teach, and she had been eager to learn. They had parted with regret.

"Well, let me hear you sing," he said with a sigh, and a glance at his turnip watch. Evidently he did not expect much. With a flourish he seated himself at the piano. "What will you sing, Miss—er—"

"Rosalie!" she urged demurely, not showing her disappointment that he did not recall her name. "Pray, call me Rosalie—I feel you are like—an elder brother!" He was her father's age, she guessed, but would not like to think so.

He glanced at her sharply but met her smile with his own. "Ah—and you will sing what, Rosalie?"

" 'The Pretty Girl from My Own Hills.' " She named a song from his own recent operetta production. "I like that one so much!" She knew it was his own favorite; he requested it to be sung in the cafés he visited.

He nodded, then began the introduction. She swung around so her skirts whirled, like the girl in the operetta, and softly began to sing.

The conductor watched her while he played. He needed a girl with good presence, as well as a good voice. Rosalie embellished the music with dramatic gestures that matched the lyrics. As the score required, she began to sing faster and faster. Her flutelike voice trilled into the higher notes, pure and clear and lovely.

She knew her voice was good, but it must be better than good. She must be radiant, starry, attention-getting. That was what Herr Vogler wanted—another star.

After she sang the last pure high C, she stopped and bowed.

Herr Vogler stared at her thoughtfully. At first he said nothing. She held her pose, smiling, looking, she hoped, much calmer than she actually felt.

"We will now try one of the songs of Strauss," he said, and turned back to the keyboard. He named one brusquely, and at once began the introduction.

He was really testing her! Determined to impress him, she began the song, quickly recalling the words. She had sung many songs during those years, and had memorized them all carefully, every word, every note, every trill and nuance.

She gave herself to the music. Her tone was alternately plaintive, arrogant, pleading, and, at the poignant ending, half-weeping.

When she was finished Herr Vogler gave no hint of praise. "Another one, Rosalie," he instructed, and he began again.

She sang for an hour. Finally Herr Vogler's secretary crept in, a lanky young man with hair falling into his eyes. He knew to dismiss the other girls, even without being told. He prepared tea, and the master drank, and the younger man took his place at the piano.

Herr Conductor Vogler watched and listened more as he drank his tea. Rosalie flirted with him as with an audience. She twirled as she sang, using her arms and hands and her eyes. But most of all she gave of her voice, making the room ring with her melodies. Her effortless tones rippled up to the highest notes, then trilled down to the low tones, gently as a lovely murmuring brook.

She knew the songs, she knew how to sing, and he approved.

"Fraulein," he said, dismissing the young man. "Come over here and have your tea. Now, tell me, are you willing to work hard?"

"I always have worked hard," she said simply, and sat down opposite him gracefully. "I always shall work hard, Maestro, because I love music, and I love to sing. And I know what I want; to sing for Vienna, for those who love music."

"And be well paid for it, Rosalie," he said gently.

"I hope so, Herr Conductor Vogler." Their eyes met, and he knew she would pay any price to fulfill her ambitions.

"Um. I am preparing a new operetta for the autumn, Rosalie. There are two places in it for fresh talented young girls. There may be a place for you. But you have some things to learn."

"Ja, Herr Conductor?"

"I would like to teach you myself, when I have time. You do not have another instructor at present?"

She had never been able to afford formal instruction, but she did not explain this.

"Nein, Herr Conductor."

"Good. I will teach you. You will come back on Tuesday afternoon to my apartment. My rooms are near the Opera House. This is the address." He gave her a slip of paper. "We will begin to practice the songs from the new operetta, so I may see how well you learn. For now, you are not to tell people you are in this operetta. Let them think you will appear in a revival of one of the others. I do not yet wish people to know what we are doing, you see?"

She saw, all right. He wanted to know what price she would pay for success. She beamed her flashing smile, her brown eyes dancing.

"I shall be so happy to sing for you, and to learn from you, Herr Conductor!"

He got up and began to pace the room. She watched him anxiously. Though short and rather pudgy, he was an attractive man. She liked the sensuous curve of his large mouth, the pride in his walk, his dramatic style at the piano. He cared about music as she did.

He was married, she knew, but she cared nothing about that. A married man could be safer than a single man—he would not want a permanent commitment. Besides, he had warmth, knowledge that she wanted to absorb, power that could assure her career. And he liked her.

"Rosalie!" He paused, returning to her with determination as though he had made a decision. His eyes fell on her, on the soft lace about her rounded breasts. "I have a suggestion."

Would he be crude, and suggest an affair at once? She must be coy and put him off for a time. Experience told her men like him did not like an easy victory.

"Ja, Mein Herr?"

"I wish to appear in a fashionable café on Thursday morning, with a pretty singer on my arm. It is time to start generating some gossip in the journals about my new operetta. You can help me. We will make a show of whispering excitedly, letting our talk of music and operettas be overheard—"

She quickly grasped his meaning. "To talk about your new operetta! Yes, yes, yes. And they will wonder and gossip all the summer. You are very smart!"

He basked in her admiration, nodding happily. "Yes, and there will be mentions in the newspapers, talk in the cafés, speculation over the dinner tables of Vienna. By the time I announce my new operetta in September, the people will be wild with impatience to see it."

"Of course!"

"So you will come at eleven, and meet me at the Café Schubert, eh? With a very pretty dress, like this one." He flicked his finger at the laces on her sleeve. "And a pretty bonnet with blue ribbons, eh? You shall greet me with a smile and open arms, and I will be deliberately coy about introducing you to my friends!"

Her heart leaped at the idea. "Oh, I shall do as you say, sir! I shall be there on the moment—"

"Good, good, and next Tuesday afternoon, at my apartments. We shall begin to practice together."

She went home, almost dancing with pleasure. She told Frau Lewisohn about her new instructor, and how hard she planned to work. But she also had to tell her she would require a fiacre to meet him the following Thursday—alone.

It was a sensitive request, and naturally it was met with whispered gossip among the others at the boardinghouse. Rosalie had anticipated this, and continued to go about her work as usual. The next afternoon, as she was laundering one of her fragile lace dresses—a task she never trusted to anyone else—Diana Ballantyne came into the laundry room.

Rosalie greeted her cheerfully. "Good afternoon, Diana. And how does your music go?"

"Well, thank you, Rosalie. And yours?"

"Well, I think. I have my new instructor, and we begin work soon."

She knew Diana had come with a purpose. She and Alicia always had their laundry done by maids, and had no reason to frequent the laundry room.

Diana waited until Pauline had finished with the iron and left the room with an armful of fragrant linens. Then she said, "Cousin Helena is most distressed about your meeting Herr Vogler alone in a café. Shall I come with you?"

Rosalie knew that would not do. She shook her dark brown curls. "Nein, Fraulein Diana! Nein, you must not be seen there. It is rather risqué. Your Maestro would be furious if he found out. For me——" She shrugged.

"We are all concerned for you, Rosalie. You are our age, and new to the ways of the world," said Diana firmly.

Rosalie concealed a sad smile. The English girl was as innocent as a bird in its nest, compared to her.

"For an operetta singer, Diana, it is necessary to be seen, to be wondered at, to appear in beautiful gowns and let men wonder if they might see her in some stage production. A pianist's career—that is different. Your teacher will arrange some formal occasion for you to be heard. For me—my instructor is not a fool, and he will present me as such singers are presented. He will welcome gazette gossip. You see?"

Diana looked troubled, swinging her long legs where she sat on a heavy laundry basket—like a child herself, Rosalie thought.

"Is that really necessary, Rosalie? Or has Herr Vogler persuaded you that it is, for his own purposes?" Her blue eyes met Rosalie's brown ones in a knowing gaze. "Men can take advantage of a girl's wish for a career."

Diana did not need to say that to Rosalie. How well she knew it, and had so far managed to turn their wishes to her plans! Rosalie continued to press carefully the fragile lace and silk of her newest apron. She had embroidered the delicate roses on it herself, in ruby red and pink silk thread, as well as the trailing vines and leaves in several shades of green.

She considered how to put Diana off without insulting her, or scorning her own reputation with men.

"I think I must make appearances in public, Diana. It is necessary for my career. I have noticed other operetta singers—how careful they are to appear in public on the arm of some notable or other. Most are unmarried, and it is often whispered they are someone's mistresses, but usually I think they are not," she said wisely. "I think they wish to cause talk, so people will pay to see them on stage. It takes all kinds to make an audience, and only some are music lovers."

"I think you are cynical," said Diana, shaking her golden head. Rosalie thought her hair a strange marvelous color, golden in some lights and more silverlike at other times. And her lovely silver-gilt eyelashes! Rosalie thought that on an operetta stage Diana would draw all eyes from every other girl. Thank God she was studying the piano!

Rosalie smiled. "I call it practical. I think I am very practical," she told Diana seriously. "People think because I look small and fragile that my head is full of sawdust. But it is not. I have made up my mind to earn a living as a singer, and I will do what I must to earn money. One day I will be famous."

"I wish you good fortune," said Diana. "It is a difficult life, as we all know. The ladder of success is steep, and sometimes teeters dangerously. If I can help hold the ladder, let me know."

Rosalie looked up from her ironing in surprise. She was used to having to fight her own way with cunning and guile, and every bit of her iron will. She saw Diana was sincere, and looked at her with some respect and a vague appreciation.

"I thank you very much, Diana," she said, but with no intention of taking her up on her offer. She would make her own way, whatever the price.

Diana waited until Rosalie had finished, then cheerfully helped her gather up the fragile silks and lace and take them to her room upstairs.

Then together they went down to tea, and chatted with the other ladies. One topic they avoided in Rosalie's presence was her intended excursion to the café.

At eleven promptly on Thursday she met the conductor in the café entrance. Dressed in her best costume, with a beautiful summer straw bonnet trimmed in blue, she held out her gloved hand for him to kiss. Their merry eyes met. He winked at her covertly, then took her on his arm and paraded half about the room before attracting the attention of the headwaiter, who bowed low and beckoned to them.

The men and ladies stared at her as Herr Vogler led her to his table in the corner. How everybody whispered and murmured to each other as they drank chocolate and ate pastries!

"See how they watch us," exulted Herr Vogler. "I have dropped such words as *songs* and *waltzes* in their ears. Now they will begin to wonder."

The headwaiter hovered near. Rosalie murmured,

"All new, Herr Vogler? A different waltz?"—making sure the headwaiter overheard.

Moments later he bent to whisper to a notorious gossip writer for a gazette, who paid him some clinking coins. Herr Vogler pinched Rosalie's finger in ecstasy.

Having played their little game a while longer, Herr Vogler took her to luncheon in still another restaurant where he made sure they were again seen by a journalist and their musical gossip overheard by another waiter. They lingered a long time at the table, until almost everyone had departed.

Vogler held up the large menu, and behind it he leaned and kissed Rosalie quickly but warmly on the lips. "My *Liebling,* you are adorable, and so quick! We will work well together. You will come on Tuesday morning, and we will begin!" His dark eyes made promises and hers sparkled in answer.

When they rose to leave, he offered to send her home in a fiacre, but she shook her head. "Thank you, I must shop for some laces. Again I thank you, and I shall come on time, I promise you!"

"I look forward to our next meeting, Rosalie!"

She danced down the cobblestoned street, turned onto another block, and proceeded more soberly to the dark corner building where the artists lived. Her stomach was comfortably full of rich foods, and he had paid for it all. She had a feeling that fate was on her side now, that she was progressing rapidly toward her goal.

And Herr Vogler was so attractive in his plump way! She liked small men her own size. They did not intimidate her as the farmhand had done. She pushed the thought from her with distaste; that part of her life was gone, and she would never think of it again. No more meadows with cow paddies in them, no more barns smelling of pigs. No more hot airless rooms over beer- and onion-smelling restaurants. She would live one day in an apartment of her own, with silken and velvet coverlets and draperies, with perfume in the air, and powder on her face and arms.

She raced up the first three flights of stairs, then took the other three flights more slowly. It was good for the figure to climb stairs, but her corsets made it difficult to breathe freely.

The door at the top attic room was open, and from it floated the sound of someone humming tunelessly. The one thing wrong with Peter Hering was that he could not sing.

Peter was at the easel. "You are very late, my most darling," he rebuked her amiably, turning his face to accept her quick greeting kiss on his brown cheek. "Go sit at the table, and be quiet, my own. I like your hat. I shall put it in the painting."

She frowned, and took it off. "I want my hair to show," she said defiantly.

"As you will, love. Um, that dress is fine. Yes. Fluff out the skirts, and turn sideways." He came over to help pose her.

She had posed twice for him, and he had paid generously. He liked her in the Alps costumes, and the paintings had sold at once to tourists. He sat her in a chair at the table, but painted her sitting on a rock with mountains behind her. Such is art, and imagination, Peter had explained.

Now he arranged her to his liking and returned to the empty canvas. He sketched her head quickly, while she talked without moving her form.

"Guess why I am late!"

"You overslept."

"Stupid! I never oversleep. My life is too important to spend it sleeping. I went to the Schubert Café with Herr Vogler. We are going to do an entirely new operetta. He will conduct and I will star."

"It is certain?" He stuck one brush between his teeth, and took up another without pausing in his painting.

"No," she admitted. "But I am on my way. He is going to be my instructor! I like him. He is plump and older and sure of himself, and he will carry me with him."

"You will like that, love. And your voice is magnificent. He will show it well. What price, darling?"

She frowned at his daring. She did not answer. She would keep all that to herself. She smiled dreamily into the distance.

"Keep that smile, love. That's good. Maiden dreaming of her rustic cowherdsman. Ruffle up your hair, that's a love. Breeze blowing through it, you know."

She ruffled up the curls obediently. Peter was a bright though poor young artist. Nights he painted brilliant paintings that he stored leaning against the wall. Days he painted girls like her, and scenes of mountains and cows and Alps flowers of blue and gold. The tourists bought them, and the money covered his food and rent, and the occasional party he gave for his friends.

As she posed, her mind wandered. She pictured herself on stage, singing, hitting the high notes, dancing gaily in the steps she did so well. All Vienna would cheer her! All Vienna would love her! And she would go afterwards to some smart café, on the arms of several handsome men, and smile at them all.

And afterwards she would go home in a carriage, rich with gilt and velvet, to her own apartment, and dismiss them all! Alone with only her maid to undress her, she would lie back on her soft couch, and gaze out at the night sky of Vienna, and glory in her fame!

"The next step up, uh, darling? Being in an operetta, and someday the star of one. And this Herr Vogler, what will he demand for payment, Rosalie?" Peter had three brushes in his mouth. He must have painted three colors and was beginning on a fourth.

"Hush your dirty mouth," she scolded him, and laughed. He understood her, though she would not admit it.

They were both young and determined, and knew where they were going. That was why they worked together so well. Someday she might sleep with him. He was handsome, after all, and he fancied her, too. But he was poor, and she knew nothing would come of that.

Next Tuesday she would go to Vogler. It was an off week for her; she could not risk sex with him. Too soon anyway. But she would let him kiss her hand, and her cheek. Better to go slowly.

Besides, she liked to go slowly with a man, to let him anticipate the final erotic meeting with her! It made the meeting the more thrilling.

Yes, she would let him kiss her hand, perhaps her lips once more. She liked his big firm mouth, and he knew how to kiss a girl.

She wriggled on the chair as she thought of being in close embrace with him. It would be exciting, and good. And she would make sure to make him wait, and be very excited, so he would give her much pleasure as well.

She would pay him well, and he would be pleased, and she would get the starring role in his operetta this autumn. Madame Fifi, his French girl in the current operetta, was wearying him with her fresh demands for more salary and privileges. Yes, by autumn, he would be ready for a new affair, and she meant to be the mistress he could not forget.

And all Vienna would toast her in champagne!

Chapter 6

Alicia Huntingdon laid down her violin carefully on the top of the practice piano and smiled at the nervous young composer.

"It went very well, I thought," she said kindly.

He smiled, shook his wildly curly head, and rubbed his cheeks with both hands. "Do you think so, Fraulein?" he asked, half-mournfully, half-excitedly.

Such a gentle guileless young man, talented beyond his own imagining. His little orchestra compositions were of such a purity and cleanness of line; she loved playing them. But they were not flashy, not waltzes, not bold and arrogant. They were simply beautiful and clear and with a counterpoint for the various instruments that made them difficult and exciting to perform.

Her violin instructor was conducting today. Herr Wendler came over to them. His gray hair stood up around his bearded face like the hairs on a ruffled porcupine, but actually he looked more like a bunny rabbit, she thought, suppressing a grin.

"Well, well, it went nicely," he said, nodding and nodding. "We shall meet again tomorrow afternoon, and practice once more before the performance on Friday evening. Well done, Herr Osterley."

"You liked the composition?" asked Moritz Osterley eagerly, his brown eyes shining with hope under his tousled brown hair.

"It is very good writing, Herr Osterley," said the instructor honestly. "The people of Vienna prefer waltzes and marches, you know that. Still—I think they will listen, and some may appreciate it. One hopes!"

He went away. Moritz's open young face showed his disappointment. Alicia felt sorry for him, and impulsively she asked him, "Do you have anything written for piano and violin?"

"Dozens," he said, with some humor, grinning at her. "Do you want one?" He picked up some sheet music, mimed throwing some at her.

She laughed aloud. He had courage, this shy young man. "Yes, I want several," she said. "Herr Wendler has arranged for me to play at some countess's house for tea, and I need an accompanist and something fresh to play. It is next Sunday. Could you come with me?"

"Oh, yes, yes, yes," he said happily, his eyes alight. "Let me see—what do I have? But we should play some waltzes also, nein?"

They laughed again. She liked him.

He gave her one sonata for piano and violin, and they arranged to meet at the same place two hours early the following afternoon. When she came, he had with him a dozen sonatas, two of which he had written for her just the previous evening!

She was amazed, and still more surprised to find they were beautifully written, with a sweet melody in each. They were short, just right for the tea.

"I can write anything to order. The melodies in my

head—they will not be silent," he explained simply and modestly.

Alicia realized he was one of these geniuses who are born with music in their heads. Like Mozart he heard melodies complete and full, and had only to write them down. He was very talented, but poor and dependent on the favors of such conductors as Herr Wendler.

She herself had improved much this summer. Herr Wendler was a gifted musician, and had finally resolved to work her hard, and be very strict. It had benefited them both. She was pleased with her progress, and had paid him more. She now dreamed of stunning everyone with her prowess, giving concerts in Vienna, then in Munich and Paris, and finally New York. She would show her father, and still his doubts forever!

He had come up the hard way, wheeling and dealing in railroads and steel, making such a fortune that it dazed his whole family. She had three brothers, who were all older and married, and vice-presidents in their father's firm. Her mother was quiet, shy, ambitious for them, but scarcely able to cope with their sudden changes of fortune.

Alicia had been born in a two-room cabin in Pennsylvania where her father was rail boss. Her next home had been in a five-room house in Pittsburgh. Then the family had moved to a fifteen-room home in New York, and finally to a mansion on Fifth Avenue.

By that time she was in a boarding school for wealthy girls, making friends among the daughters of other newly rich families, and a few among the established rich. She had always felt on the defensive, having to dress smartly and appear self-confident, concealing her unease in these situations.

The attempt to marry her off to a German baron

had been the last straw. She had stubbornly refused to marry him. She wanted a career, she had told her parents. She would play the violin. She would go off to Vienna to study. Her fond adoring father had consented and told the baron no.

The baron had been furious and upset. Her mother had been apprehensive until she met Frau Lewisohn, in whose care she felt comfortable leaving her precious only daughter. Alicia had, with both relief and fear, seen her parents depart Vienna. What was she doing, she asked herself, living alone in Europe?

However, she had settled down, and now she enjoyed her new freedom. Pauline went everywhere with her, listened to the music, enjoyed it, was discreet at all times. She had no worries at all—except—

Marriage. Would she have to marry someone like the baron, or could she go home, and find some nice ordinary American?

"There," said Moritz Osterley. "You learned very quickly, Fraulein! You play my music the way I hear it in my head."

She was pleased. His shy compliment meant more to her than all the baron's flowery ones. Baron Stanislav von Neumeister! She had been glad to leave him and his lavish compliments behind her in Germany. She knew he had never meant them. He had laughed at her behind her back with his relatives, she knew it. When she came into a room, the laughter had stilled and he had come and kissed her hand, and laughed no more.

The little orchestra concert went well. Diana attended with her Cousin Helena, and both praised the performance lavishly. Of course, the waltzes and marches were more applauded than Moritz's pure compositions, but that was to be expected.

She and Herr Osterley agreed to meet at the entrance to the home of the Countess Marsh on Sunday, and both arrived promptly. They were shown to a huge elegant ballroom, where tables were set for tea for at least fifty guests. Amid the clatter of cups and saucers, teaspoons and gossip, Alicia felt dismay.

"It is the usual," Moritz whispered simply as he sat down at a piano half-hidden by a huge potted palm. Alicia wordlessly moved the flowerpot, to have room for her music stand. She sat down also, and tuned her violin.

She had chosen to wear a tea gown of beige lace, a simple color that would not make her noticeable among the elegant guests. But the ladies were staring, and so were the few gentlemen present. Her darn red hair, she thought, made her show up anywhere.

They began to play. The nearest ladies listened for a few moments, then one turned to another and hissed, "And did you hear about the Countess von Hulsen? She cut that man cold! And one knows they were rather intimate for a time, though she denied she even liked him!"

The gossip was a delight to them. They put their graying heads together and their guttural hissing went whispering through the room. The guests talked all through the music. Alicia was furious. Moritz was mournful.

They did not even seem to hear his most beautiful new compositions. The hostess did pause and listen, and waved her hand in time dreamily. She did seem to care genuinely for music, and a few of her guests strained to listen from time to time. But the talking and the dishes defeated most of them.

Alicia and Moritz paused to take tea, which the countess sent to them. In that intermission several young officers entered the room, magnificent in their scarlet-and-gold uniforms. Alicia saw Captain Mueller and Captain Schmidt among them, but they did not notice her for a time.

Partly hidden by the palms she resumed playing. As before, voices rose to be heard over the music, and she and Moritz were drowned out. They played more softly, in disgust, and were glad when they were finished. Several noticed they had stopped, and clapped their fragile gloved hands, smiling in their direction. The countess merely nodded and smiled.

Alicia stood and placed her violin in its case. "Well, your music is beautiful," she said encouragingly to Moritz. "And one day we will play where we can be heard."

"Well, I did not expect much else today," said Moritz simply, apologetically. "These occasions are—like this."

"I am sorry I asked—"

"I need the money," he whispered, his eyes gleaming with unexpected mirth. "Do not apologize; she pays well!"

Alicia giggled a little and patted his arm. More and more she felt like his elder sister, though he was a few years older than she. Suddenly she noticed an older lady in black beckoning to her, and leaving her violin with Pauline, she made her way to her at a nearby table covered with tea dishes and leftover pastries.

She bent courteously to hear from the lady. If only one woman heard their music and liked it, it would be worthwhile, she thought.

"Pretty dress!" proclaimed the small lady, in the tones of the almost-deaf. "Where did you purchase it?"

Alicia bit back angry words. "In New—York—City!" she shouted into the proffered ear-trumpet.

"Oh! I never go there! Too many Indians!" shouted the lady. "Dangerous!"

Alicia was convulsed with laughter, and straightened to meet the merry eyes of Captain Schmidt. He greeted her, kissed her hand, yielded the hand to Captain Mueller beside him.

"What a pleasure to see you again, beautiful Fraulein!" said Captain Schmidt.

"And did you hear our music?" demanded Alicia, her head tossing. The men eyed her glorious red hair with appreciation.

"Yes, over the crash of teacups," murmured Captain Mueller, with sparkling black eyes.

She beckoned to Moritz Osterley. The tall military men eyed the small mussed composer with the look of lean greyhounds finding a frisky French poodle at their feet. He tossed back his hair and bowed to them. Shiny boots clicked sharply, handsome backs bent slightly, they shook hands.

"Herr Composer Moritz Osterley," she titled him cheerfully. "Captain Gardell Mueller, Captain Ernst Schmidt. Gentlemen, my friend here is a fine composer, and he plays the piano divinely!"

"We are having a party tonight!" said Captain Schmidt. "Will you come, Fraulein Huntingdon? You can both play for us, and we promise to listen carefully to every beautiful note!"

By the twinkle in his eyes she knew he was teasing, and Pauline's scandalized gasp told her it was forbidden. She glanced at the black-clad maid, to meet a decided shake of her graying head.

"I regret I cannot come, but Moritz can," she said quickly. "He will play well for you!"

Trapped, the two captains nodded. "Well, well, he shall come with us now!" they said. Mueller told him,

"We go right on to dinner, and will not stop until morning! Are you game?"

"I should be most happy to come," said Moritz. "But perhaps you have already arranged some entertainment? This is late notice for you."

They patted his shoulder, as if comforting a pet to be treated kindly. "Nein, nein, you will come! We can promise you good food, all the beer you can drink, and ladies very pretty—not as beautiful as Fraulein, but pretty!"

So it was that kind of party. Alicia knew they had not meant for her to come, but it was rather an insult they had invited her. She kept a smile on her features and listened to the gay chatter about her.

The countess came over, thanked them prettily, and paid them discreetly with envelopes for both. Alicia tucked hers into her beaded handbag, Moritz stuffed his in a pocket.

He turned to her. "Thank you very much for the engagement, Fraulein. You are most kind."

"We will play again, Herr Osterley," she said quickly. "I admire your talent enormously. And we shall be heard!"

The captains overheard, and smiled approvingly at her defiant words. "Yes, yes, you will be heard," said Captain Schmidt. "We hope to see you again soon, Fraulein!"

They bowed again over her hand, cast longing eyes over her flattering cream lace dress, and made their farewells. Then they departed, leading Moritz Osterley between them.

The countess kindly sent Alicia and the maid home in her own carriage.

In the carriage Alicia sulked. Pauline eyed her with understanding.

"Some ladies and a few gentlemen did listen to your music, Fraulein Huntingdon," she said gently. "And how well you played! The music was most beautiful."

Alicia brightened and thanked her. At least one person had enjoyed the concert! And Pauline had good taste! Alicia ran upstairs to tell Diana about her day.

On Tuesday she met Moritz Osterley once more in the conservatory. While the others gathered and chattered, she went over to him at the piano, where he was playing dreamily. He jumped up, kissed her hand, beamed on her fondly.

"Good afternoon, Herr Osterley!"

"I hoped you would call me Moritz again." He sighed. "Only my dear mama still calls me that."

"Of course, dear Moritz." She drew out a small card. "I have been asked by a friend of the countess to play for her tea next Sunday. Are you willing to come again?"

"I am game to go wherever my beautiful friend wishes!" he said gallantly. "What shall we play? You wish more?"

"More," she said firmly, in her still-halting German. "And do let us play your Sonata no. 3, and the five little sonatinas. I love them so."

Moritz brightened still more. "Thank you, thank you a thousand times, dear friend!"

"And how was your party with my military friends?"

He chuckled, his round face mischievous. "Oh, dear Fraulein! I had a marvelous time. I played all the night, and until noon of the following day! I had my dinner, my breakfast, and my luncheon with them! And they paid me so much I paid my rent for a month, and bought many more music sheets!"

"Good, good!" She could imagine such an all-night

party, though he did not describe it further. "Did they listen to your music at all?" she asked with some sarcasm.

He gave her a sweet smile. "Some did," he said. "Captain Mueller likes music. Sometimes he sat at the piano with me, on the bench, and kept time. He will recommend me, he told me. He was most kind!"

"I am glad of that. Oh, here we go," she said as the conductor took his place. Hastily she tuned her violin and sat down in her appointed chair. She resolved to keep Moritz under her wing and promote his talent. It was a good deed she could easily do. And he was so deserving.

After the regular rehearsal she asked her instructor to practice with her and Moritz, and he did so, contributing some good suggestions for the performance. Soon afterward he found another engagement for them, and Alicia and Moritz began to go about quite a bit together—always, of course, with Pauline as chaperon.

Alicia liked her role as champion of Moritz. She pushed him gently into the limelight, encouraged him to demand more money for his compositions and performances, and asked outright for higher fees for their engagements at teas.

She got them, too. She didn't need the money, but he did. He thought she was marvelous, and praised her, and once as they sat enjoying pastries asked half-guiltily if she would manage his career.

"But I am already!" she had laughed.

"I mean, with a contract. You are so—so business-like, Fraulein! You are not insulted?"

"No, no, not at all. I take after my father, I believe!"

"He is a smart businessman?"

Alicia thought of her board-chairman father, his

shock of gray hair and piercing green eyes, the brusque voice that only knew how to command. She nodded. "Very smart."

"But you will not manage me?"

She hated to disappoint him. "I will be here in Vienna only until next spring."

She was turning him down kindly. He sighed. "Well, I shall much enjoy the autumn and winter!" He had paid for their chocolate and cakes out of the little sum in the pocket of his worn brown coat.

One afternoon after an engagement she felt high with pleasure when she returned to the boardinghouse in the hired fiacre with Pauline. "It went so well, Fraulein," said Pauline, knowing her need to be reassured.

"Yes." Alicia sighed with pleasure, smiling at her companion. "And the next time will be next Sunday at the Baroness Puff Puff," she added.

Pauline giggled at her version of the difficult German name. They were in high spirits when the fiacre left them at the door.

"You have letters, Fraulein!" announced Gretchen, and helped her remove the stiff boots wet from the rainstorm.

She hoped her mother had written, with nice homey news of the family, of the birth perhaps of her little new niece or nephew. Her sister Jenny was about due.

In her rooms the letters lay on a rosewood table near the piano. She removed her wet coat, hung it up on the peg, and sank down to read.

The first letters were from home. Jenny had given birth to a son, and her father was ecstatic. Another boy to carry on the family business! Her mother described the goings-on in satisfactory fashion. She had stayed with Jenny for a week after the birth.

Her brother had also written—a nice manly letter about his joy in fatherhood, and about the business, punctuated with some veiled worries about his "reckless" little sister.

The third and last envelope was addressed in a firm masculine handwriting, in German script. She glanced at it without recognition and finally opened it. Perhaps it was a request for a performance.

Her shocked gaze took in the first lines. "My dear Alicia," it read, in bold writing.

"Really!" she gasped, and skimmed down to the bottom, on to the next page, to find the signature.

"Oh, really! How dare he!"

It was from Baron Stanislav von Neumeister—from his shabby castle, she thought scathingly. She had refused him very firmly, and now he dared to write to her. And where had he obtained her address? Her father must have given it to him!

In growing anger and amazement she read through the missive. It was in German, with a few English words. He had been idly studying English when they had met. Probably to impress her, that was all.

"My dear Alicia," read the letter.

"I have thought much of your recent visit to my home. Some memories are very precious to me. Such as our riding on my fine horses, and how quickly you learned how to ride!"

Her cheeks burned. She put one hand to a cheek as she set down the letter. She had been out with him one day, and they had ridden recklessly, leaving the others far behind.

She had pulled up, laughing, and looked down to her foot in the stirrup.

"Is something wrong?" he had asked. He had swung down and come to adjust the stirrup for her. Then as she had bent over to look at her foot, he had looked up at the same moment.

She had found herself gazing deeply into dark blue wide eyes framed with dark blond lashes, set in a deeply bronzed tanned face that was strong and bold and hard. She had gasped to find herself so close.

He had straightened, and managed to brush her lips with his. "Sir!" she cried, when he released her shoulder from the strong grip of his hand. Blindly she had reached out and struck him lightly with her riding crop.

"I could not help it. Will you marry me?"

She frowned down at the strong handwriting. She had ridden off, leaving him to follow after. And she had told her father she would not marry him, and her father had told the baron. They had departed the next day.

She had told no one her real reason for going. Not the kiss, but the conversation she had overheard.

She had gone down early for dinner that evening, guiltily wanting to see him alone. She had heard voices from the study, had crept to the half-opened door, and heard her father and the baron—talking about the castle roof that needed repair!

"It will cost a great deal—about half a million dollars to repair the roof of the castle," the baron was saying. "You see, it is very old, and rambles on, over nine wings, with the small chapel and bell-tower in addition. And then there are the lands—some are overgrazed, some were much neglected in the time of my father and grandfather."

"I was thinking about giving my daughter a dowry of about five million dollars," said her father smoothly. "She is my only daughter, and will not be taken into the company, of course. But I wish her to have what the others have in value."

"That sounds—very generous," the baron had said in his deep musical voice. "There is much to do here to make my home comfortable for her. But you may be sure I shall do it, and make Alicia most happy."

"That is what I want for her," her father was saying, when Alicia had turned and fled again up the stairs.

She had met her mother in the upstairs hall. "A broken strap at my waist," she had lied breathlessly, and she went to her room to catch her breath and make her angry plans to depart. How had they dared! To sell and buy her—her father and that man! She knew it was done; some of her friends had been sold for French titles and English, as well as for German. But for her dear loving father to do this to her!

Her mouth set grimly. She would not be so treated! She picked up the letter and read it through.

My dear Alicia,

I have thought much of your recent visit to my home. Some memories are very precious to me. Such as our riding on my fine horses, and how quickly you learned how to ride!

In the evening, when you played for us, how much I and my family enjoyed it. My mother asks for you often, and cannot understand why you departed from us. You did not explain how I had offended you.

I had thought at the time of our ride that you were not offended!

I remember well the flash of your beautiful green eyes, the look of the candlelight on your magnificent red-gold hair. How lovely you are, how bright your mind, how wonderful your musical talent. You haunt my lonely castle, a very beautiful ghost.

With your father's permission, I am coming to Vienna to see you again. I hope to arrive soon. Will you make me welcome? I hope so. My heart has seemed empty, as well as my castle.

Your devoted,
Stanislav.

Stanislav von Neumeister, Baron, Von and Zu Neumeister.

She flung the letter to the floor. "What impudence! What crass impudence! Coming to see me without my invitation!" she fumed aloud. "I have already turned him down. Is that not enough for him? Does my money so draw him? Can't he find another heiress to his taste? I haunt him? Well, good!"

She jumped up and roamed the room restlessly. Her cheeks were hot with anger. Her face in the mirror looked very pink and flushed.

There was no music coming from Diana's room. On impulse she picked up the letter and crossed the hall to tap at the door. Diana opened it with a smile of welcome.

"Come in, how did it go today?"

"Well, but then I come home to this!" She showed the bold handwritten letter.

"What is this?" Diana drew her in, seated her, and gazed at her curiously. "You are really angry. Did someone write an insulting note?"

"Yes, in a way. I suppose *he* does not think it insulting!" She calmed down enough to explain. "You recall, I told you about the German baron who wants to marry me—and get lots of money from Papa! Well, I

turned him down. Now he writes and says he is coming
to Vienna to see me!"

Diana pushed another cushion behind her back.
In an ice-blue satin gown with a cream lace bertha at
her slim throat and a long strand of pearls to her waist,
she looked cool and sure of herself. Her hair was up
high in a smooth roll, secured with pearl hairpins. More
pearls dangled from her ears.

"I suppose you did not like him at all?" she asked.

Alicia frowned. "Well—I did rather like him at first.
Until I saw it was just the money that attracted him!
So pushy, so greedy—he cannot bear to let the money
go!"

"What does he look like?" asked Diana.

"Oh, bronzed, and hard—he takes care of the estate
mostly by himself, riding about. He is a hard worker,
I'll say that for him. His father gambled away much of
the money, and he is trying to save the estate for the
family.

"He's very tall, very husky, with dark blond hair and
dark blue eyes. He has a scar on his face from dueling.
They all seem to love dueling," she said drearily. "That
and horses."

"He doesn't sound so bad. Unless he is a bully?"

"Well—he did try to bully me."

"I guess all men do." Diana gave her a sweet smile.
"It is like my situation. Only, Addison Montague does
not even pretend to want to follow me about. He is
quite content to let father push me! He knows father
wants him in the firm."

"I wonder what it would be like to be loved for myself alone." Alicia sighed. "Would it not be romantic?"
She pictured Moritz Osterley at her feet, quoting po-
etry, and it felt rather nice to think about it. Yet—he

was rather weak and easily pushed about. That was
why she liked being with him. She liked to order him
about and set his life straight for him.

"My father is almost as wealthy as your own," said
Diana drily. "I suppose we will never know what it is
to be loved for ourselves alone."

"Come now! You sound as cynical as I am!" Alicia
laughed. Sharing her troubles made her feel better. She
lifted the letter, ripped it in two, and in two again.
"There, I shall throw it in the wastebasket, and forget
him! He isn't worth a second thought."

"You don't suppose he would come to Vienna anyway?"

"Hardly! He is too fond of his estates."

Alicia returned to her room, and then went down to
dinner with Diana, where the talk was about music and
Vienna, and cafés, and the coming autumn season. August was half-over, and already people were talking
about the upcoming operas and operettas. Rosalie was
always dashing about, talking eagerly and mysteriously
about a part she hoped to get.

The torn letter still lay on her table. When she returned to her room after dinner, Alicia was about to
pitch it into the wastebasket when she caught the
words, in the bold black writing, "the flash of your
beautiful green eyes . . ."

She picked up the torn paper, fitting one page together again. How he flattered her!

She frowned, then fitted the other page together and
pasted each on another page to get the letter back together again. She would keep the letter, to remind herself that there were such brazen greedy men in the
world!

Yet—yet his flattering words were rather sweet! She

remembered the way he would sit in the drawing room listening to her as she played the violin and his sister played the piano. How he had stared at her, as though his deep blue eyes would swallow her up!

Chapter 7

"You must keep to the exact rhythm," said Lukas von Korda, beating the time carefully. "Recall, you will be with five other players. I wish you'd had more experience with a chamber group before you were to play in public!"

He was worried and nervous for her, she thought. She, however, felt gay and confident and very optimistic. If she did well, and earned the pay for the afternoon concert in the park, she would get other jobs.

If she could begin to earn money from her piano playing, then one day her father would have to be convinced that Diana was serious about her career. She did not *need* money. Her father was wealthy, and she had her mother's income from *her* father's èstates. Nevertheless, her father would push her into matrimony, probably with dull Addison Montague, if she could not prove to him that she was serious about music.

Money would be the key. If she could show him her accounts at the end of the year, and show she might even earn her entire living from playing—! Well, then, she would have won her point. This was the first performance for her as a paid musician.

They continued going over the music, and finally the baron had her play the Beethoven piano quartet twice. That would be her big piece this afternoon.

At twelve thirty he finally stopped and laid down the baton. He had agreed to conduct today, because his pupil would be the piano soloist. They anticipated a good performance. He had rehearsed the players for more than a week, and the paid attendance was flattering. All wanted to see Baron von Korda conduct in public once more. He rarely did so in the summer park concerts.

"Well, well, we must stop. Mother is waiting for us, and lunch will be ready."

Diana stood up and brushed out her skirts. She had chosen to wear a dress of white voile embroidered with lovely small blue cornflowers. The sleeves were wide, so she should be comfortable playing in the summer sunshine.

She saw the baron gaze thoughtfully at her gown.

"Is it all right?" she asked.

"Yes, yes, you look like a flower yourself," he said unexpectedly, then frowned, and led the way from the large piano room. She picked up her blue cloth handbag and followed him to the hallway and up the winding circular staircase.

She had never been above the ground floor of his huge town house before, and she was curious to see the upstairs. The lower rooms were large and formal, with stiffly arranged huge pieces of furniture of mahogany and velvet and gilt. The staircase was wide, covered with thick, dark red carpeting, and lit by a crystal chandelier that hung halfway between floors.

At the top of the stairs, was a wide long hallway

leading to the front of the house. He paused and opened a door. Diana looked into a fresh blue-and-rose bedroom, and the open door of a bath.

"My mother's room—she invites you to refresh yourself here. A maid will be waiting to show you to the dining room," he said curtly, and went on.

Diana walked in, glimpsed the lovely dainty accessories, and went on to the bathroom. As she washed her hands, she noted all the little feminine touches, the silver brushes and combs, the powder boxes of crystal and gold, the blue towels and rose rug before the bathtub. In the air hung a faint lilac fragrance that was dainty and pleasing. His mother's rooms were lovely!

When she had finished freshening up, the maid was waiting for her, smart in her black-and-white uniform with a starched small cap on her dark hair. She smiled, leading the way to the front hall, where she indicated that Diana should enter the door to the left. At the right, through an opened door, she caught a glimpse of a massive drawing room, which was situated above the drawing room where she took her lessons. The furniture was dark and heavy, the decor dark rose, brown, and gold. Another piano was there, just as large as the one downstairs. She guessed these were Lukas's rooms.

She entered the room at the left to find a lovely drawing room evidently used also as a family dining room. The round table in the center was set for four, with white lace place mats, and a charming floral centerpiece of gay summer flowers of blue and red and white.

Lukas rose upon her entrance, and greeted her formally as though they had not worked to exhaustion for three hours. "Good afternoon, Fraulein Ballantyne. Permit me, Mother, to introduce to you—my pupil, Diana Ballantyne. My mother, Frau Karl von Korda, by name Constantia."

She wondered at his use of their familiar names. She went over to bow and shake the hand of the woman on the rose sofa. Frau von Korda smiled at her kindly, her round plump face shining with good humor. She was rosy-cheeked, her gold hair turning gray, her blue eyes as bright and vivid as her son's.

Instead of releasing Diana's hand, she held it firmly, and turned it over in her hands. "Ah, large and fine, and strong, eh, my son?" she said. "She is a musician, I can see this, and I have been listening happily to the music you play, my dear child!"

Diana relaxed, comfortable with the lady's charm. "Thank you. I see that you also have large hands, more than an octave?"

"Yes, yes," and she held them out. "I have begun to play once more, now that my children are grown!"

"I should like to hear you."

"And I should like to play for you, but not today. It is the big day, eh? I am going with you, and will enjoy the concert."

The maid came in, and set three bowls of fresh fruit compote at the places. Frau von Korda rose and approached the table, gesturing to Diana to take the place near her.

Lukas von Korda was frowning. "Theo is not here yet?"

"No, he is often late coming from university," said his mother placidly. "We will not wait for him. He will rush in late, and not even know what he eats!" She smiled gaily at Diana, her lovely face crinkled in laughter.

"I told him we had a guest!" Lukas seated Diana after his mother, then sat down at the place to her left.

The round table made the luncheon seem pleasantly informal. Diana felt she was being honored by dining with them en famille.

Lukas's mother turned to Diana. "He will not remember," she said. "His mind is so absorbed with his studies in philosophy, he will be surprised to see you! I hope you will not mind!"

"Of course not. My father was the same when he had a business problem," said Diana calmly. "I had to have his valet lay out his dress clothes when we had a dinner party, and force him into them, or he would not have appeared!"

She laughed with her hostess and found Lukas staring at her thoughtfully.

"And what does he do, now you are in Vienna?" asked Frau von Korda, picking up her spoon.

Diana tasted the fruit mixture, delicious with strawberries and raspberries, peaches and liqueur. "I hired an excellent housekeeper, who has good humor and common sense," she said. "And of course there is father's valet, who has been with him many years. My two brothers are also in the firm, and have been of much help to him. If only they would marry, my problems would be over! His daughters-in-law would be his hostesses."

"Hum. That sounds most interesting—may I call you Diana? I feel I have known you for a time, my son has spoken so often of you."

This was an unexpected familiarity. Diana felt almost overwhelmed. Lukas did not change expression, but simply went on eating as though he'd expected this exchange. Did he speak of her to his mother as Diana?

"Please do, I should like that."

"Good. Then, Diana, pray tell me about your family

and your homelife. The English girls seem to have such freedom. Do they really?"

"I expect we do have more freedom than the German or Austrian girls, but less than the American," said Diana, thinking of how boldly Alicia went about. She was not brazen, but seemed accustomed to making her own decisions and going where she pleased.

"And your mother—she has died, my dear?"

"Yes, and I have been hostess for my father for some years. He wished me to remain—but finally consented to this one year for me to study music. I do hope to convince him that I can make a living at it, and not—" She stopped abruptly.

The kindly curious blue eyes urged her. "Pray, do tell me. Do you have a young man eagerly waiting for you in England?"

Diana hesitated, then told her. "There is a young man, yes, my father wishes me to marry him—but I—"

Lukas had stiffened and set down his spoon. He was looking at her, as was his mother.

She managed to go on, shyly. "I do not wish to marry—yet. And I would like to be able to make a career of music. I love to play the piano, and also—I have been composing."

There—it was out. She dared to look at von Korda, who was gazing at her with no expression on his hard brown face.

"How splendid!" said his mother. "And the young man—he approves, no?"

"No," said Diana. "He does not even like music." The maid silently took her dish and removed the others. She returned with a tray of plates and served them breaded veal cutlets, beans, and a fresh green salad.

"That is a pity. Ah—what does he do?"

"He is in his father's firm, Montague and Company.

It is a long line of British traders, similar to my father's company, Ballantyne's. We trade in the Far East, they in the Near East. Father is considering a merger, most seriously. It will probably go through."

"Trade in what?" Constantia von Korda was as full of curiosity and frankness as a child. "Silks, spices?"

"Yes, and tea, jade, porcelain, mostly from China and the Indies. Montague's has specialized in silks and Persian carpets, but the company has fared poorly lately because the father has been ill. A merger would be of benefit to them."

"And you think to make a career of music?" von Korda asked unexpectedly, for the first time taking part in the conversation. "You know it is very difficult for a woman!"

"I know," said Diana, her expression firm. "But I mean to make a darn good try of it! I love music, and I think I can do well at it. I shall not be easily defeated. And if men can make a living at it, I think I can also."

There was a little silence. Then Frau von Korda spoke. "I, too, wished one day to make a career of my music. I played the piano and the violin, and I composed some. My grandparents encouraged me, but my father shook his head. I was married at twenty to Karl von Korda. He was very kind to me," she added absently, frowning at her plate.

"And the music career?" asked Diana boldly.

Constantia glanced at her son. "I had Lukas at once," she said gently. "What a pleasure he was. Then my daughter Margarethe, and then my young son Theophilus. I was busy with the tenants on the estate as well as with my duties at the castle. I still live there, but my son-in-law manages all very well."

"And there was little time for playing the piano," said Lukas gravely. "She played only for her amusement and ours. Never in public again, eh, Mama? Except for family groups."

"Yes, and not seriously again—until my dearest Karl died," said Constantia. "Then I had time on my hands. . . ." Oddly, she spread out her large hands and gazed at them. "And so I played once more," she said, with a quiet satisfaction.

Diana was easily reading between the lines. Constantia's father and husband had not approved of a career for her, not even playing in public and continuing her lessons. She had been put in her place as chatelaine of the castle, wife and mother, housekeeper, nurse, all the traditional roles of a woman in Austria. But they had not approved of her career in music, so it had been halted, thoroughly, for all the years her husband had been alive.

Into the little silence burst a young man. He was as tall as his older brother, but lanky, mussed, his brown suit rumpled, his golden hair on end.

"Theo!" roared Lukas. "You are very late." He stood, frowning, the napkin in his good right hand.

"I'm sorry—Mother, there was the best professor today! He was magnificent! How he explained the universe to us—oh, I do beg pardon!" He stared open-mouthed at Diana. "You have a guest." He came around to kiss his mother's hand. "Mother, I am so sorry. I forgot!"

Diana had to smile as he bent and kissed her hand also, and her eyes met the guileless blue eyes of the student. "How do you do, Theo?" she said merrily.

He blushed, he stammered, he finally sat down and let the maid serve him. "How pretty you are!" he said, still staring at Diana. "Are you the one who plays the piano?"

"Yes, I am," she was saying, when her Maestro broke in.

"You call him Theo at once, and I am still Herr Baron!" he complained, surprisingly.

"I am sorry. Should I call your brother Herr University Student von Korda?" she teased.

Even Lukas von Korda laughed, his hard face relaxing into laughter lines which simply made him more attractive. His mother patted Diana's hand between gurgles of laughter.

"You understand our silly titles, dear girl!" she said. Theo watched them both, with surprise in his blue eyes. "Are they not strange? I am sometimes called Frau Baroness High Excellency of the Castle von Korda, and on and on! It is too outrageous, really!"

"I wonder what I would be called?" mused Diana, a dimple in each cheek. "Perhaps Fraulein English Student of Piano Foreigner Ballantyne!"

They all laughed again, and then the subject was changed. Theo told eagerly of his marvelous class that morning, the lecturer who had opened their eyes to the wonders of the universe. "And all in three hours," his older brother teased him. Theo took it well, and teased his brother in return. Diana enjoyed the ease in their manner toward each other.

It was evident to Diana that Lukas von Korda was very tender and considerate of his mother. She wondered if it was because she was a good mother, or whether perhaps he felt regret that her career had been taken from her? They spoke of Constantia's lessons, how she played the piano each day for three hours. Lukas was going to arrange an appearance for her. Her daughter Margarethe wanted to come to Vienna for that.

Diana was shown a portrait of Margarethe and her

four children. In the background stood a tall dark-haired man, with a strong face and square chin. Margarethe was a blond version of her mother, tall and a little plump, with a wistful sweet face. The children were in stairsteps. Karl, dark like his father, was nine. Roderick, seven, was more blond and musical; he already played the piano. Julie, at five, looked fiercely independent, sitting on the floor before her mother and glaring at the painter. Little Kristel sat on her mother's lap. At two, she was adorable with fat blond curls on either side of her plump cheeks, and wide blue eyes that gazed in wonder.

"What a lovely family," said Diana, studying them all, seeing the family resemblances.

"Margarethe is expecting again, this September. I hope all goes well," said her mother, worrying visibly. "She had a difficult time with Kristel. Ah, well, the nurse is good—"

"Heinrich manages the estates very well. We consult from time to time," said Lukas. "He is a very smart man. The marriage was good for the family."

Did he have a rather defiant tone? Constantia glanced again at the portrait, her gaze lingered on her daughter with the wistful face. "Yes, he manages very well," she agreed. "Karl approved him very much. It was he who arranged the marriage. Karl had hired him as his manager for two years."

"Of a good family," said von Korda, sighing. "He is tough on the men, makes them work hard. All goes well."

Diana was silent, fearing to say the wrong thing. It was evident none of them were fond of Heinrich, yet felt they must in all fairness say he worked very hard for the von Korda estates. And what about Margarethe?

Diana thought Lukas was probably like his father,

concerned with the good of his family, believing women were suited for making good marriages that would benefit the family. He probably would not approve of her career ambitions! She wondered again why he had agreed to teach her. Obviously he did not need the money. Why, then?

At the time he had offered to teach her, she had been so joyful she had not stopped to question his motives. Now she had begun to wonder. He was strict, he worked her hard, he praised only in moderation. He was the best instructor she could have had, she thought, for he had no patience with any weakness, and insisted on perfection as near as she could manage.

"And so you compose, my dear Diana?" asked his mother, so unexpectedly that Diana blinked.

She blurted it out, this secret she had kept from her Maestro. "Oh, yes, Baroness. I have composed much for the piano and harp, and recently for the piano and the violin. I do hope to play my compositions in public one day!"

Lukas was staring at her keenly. "I should like to hear what you do one day, Diana," he said, so naturally, she could scarcely realize he had never said that name to her before. "You have them written down?"

"Some of them, Maestro," she said.

"Bring them next time," he ordered. "I wish to see what you do."

"You should also show Diana your compositions for the piano, my dear Lukas," said his mother. "Perhaps she will play them for you!"

He frowned, and his right hand clutched his left arm. "Perhaps," he said. "I have not touched them for a time."

Oh, how Diana longed to see them! She would like

to play his music for him. He must have missed so
much not being able to play with both hands. And she
knew his opera contained magnificent music. How did
he compose for the piano, his favorite instrument by
his own admission?

By then it was time to depart for the park. The carriage was made ready. Diana and Frau von Korda sat
facing the horses, Theo and Lukas with their backs to
them. They clip-clopped through the Vienna streets,
past the beautiful stately buildings, the green plane
trees, the little parks with gorgeous crimson autumn
flowers. It was almost the end of August. Soon September would be upon them, bringing the debut of von
Korda's first opera, and more concerts, and more performances in public by Diana.

Did she truly have a chance to make this a career?
She must, though she was a woman. She vowed to do
so well this winter that her father had to be convinced!
He must allow her to continue with her beloved music,
not to be drowned in an unhappy marriage for the sake
of the Ballantyne Company. She would fight for the
right to determine her own future! She wanted to play,
to be applauded and recognized for her talent, no matter that she wore skirts instead of a dark frock coat!

There was a breeze in the park, welcome on such a
warm day, but a nuisance to the musicians, whose
music fluttered on the stands. Diana pressed her music
sheets back as she settled herself on the piano bench.
She found the baroness beside her, Theo following with
a chair for his mother.

"I will turn the music for you, dear girl, and hold it
when the wind blows," she announced simply, and sat
down beside Diana.

"Thank you so very much!" Diana did not want to

be distracted from her playing, and she was grateful to the thoughtful woman.

Lukas von Korda was on the platform now also, talking with the first violinist. The flutist was playing a few tentative notes. Diana struck a note for the violinist and violist to tune up.

A fine crowd had already gathered in the enclosure, and others gathered outside, some students and children unable to pay the price of admission. There must be almost five hundred paying guests, however, Diana thought, glancing over the group. She saw Alicia, easy to distinguish with her red hair, and guessed that others from the boardinghouse were with her. Two scarlet uniforms hovered behind Alicia, and she knew who they would be! She only hoped von Korda did not notice them. Fortunately his back would be to the audience most of the time.

Von Korda drew out his gold turnip watch, and glanced at it. In response Diana glanced at her little lapel watch on her dress. It was one minute until four o'clock.

Promptly on the hour von Korda lifted the slender wand of his baton. The orchestra began to play the merry overture which would open the concert and draw the murmurs of the audience into silent attention.

The piece was well received, and at the end there was much applause. Afterward a few minutes were granted to let latecomers be seated. Von Korda waited with unusual patience, splendid in his blue silk suit, his golden hair blowing from the usual smooth waves. His blue eyes shone and he looked natural in these surroundings. His mother gazed at him fondly as she waited at Diana's side. Theo, at his mother's side, held the rest of the music carefully in order. They could not risk putting too much music on the rack at once, for the breeze had come up more strongly.

Again von Korda lifted his baton. Diana began to play, with strong firm touch, the Haydn quintet. The others joined in, and the lovely melodies rang through the park. The crowd had become silent, listening. Diana felt their attention all through her.

Oh, this was why she had been born, she thought joyously, as she played and the others played with her, and the crowd listened appreciatively. She caught a glimpse of faces rapt with the music. Von Korda, with blue eyes sparkling, guided them through the intricate melody. With a gesture of his baton to Diana, she began the next movement softly, then built slowly, deliberately to the *forte* section.

How they applauded at the end! The clapping rang through the trees. They all stood and bowed. Von Korda bowed himself and gestured to his musicians. Some of them stared admiringly at Diana, and she beamed back at them.

They played another short piece, then paused for a brief intermission. After that came the difficult Beethoven quartet and Diana gave all her attention to the music. She knew most of it by heart, but she would not risk losing her place, so she followed the sheet music. The baroness was quick to turn the pages and keep the sheets from fluttering to the ground. One page got away; Theo rescued it swiftly, but Diana did not need it. She knew the music and continued on smoothly, oblivious to von Korda's look of anxious concern.

When they ended, the applause was loud and appreciative. Some men whistled and cheered, and she even thought she heard Mueller's voice! But she did not look toward him, and hoped von Korda did not either.

The enmity between them could spoil the afternoon for Lukas in his rare public appearance.

Von Korda had cleverly chosen as the last number an arrangement of his own based on waltz melodies from the well-known composers. This was much appreciated by the paying crowd and by those on the fringes outside the seats.

They laughed and danced on the lawn, and some whistled along and sang as the small group played the merry songs. Diana was amused at their antics, and was amused also at von Korda who seemed to dance on the podium, unconsciously taking one waltz step and another as he conducted. Yes, there was certainly music in his blood and waltzes in his feet! His smart shining boots stepped lightly as he turned from one side to the other, cueing in the flute, bringing in the piano, motioning to the violin.

At the end, the performers rose and bowed to much loud applause and Diana smiled and smiled with pleasure. They had pleased the crowd, and done well also. Von Korda was happy. She could tell by the curve of his back as he bowed, and the way he tossed his head to get the long golden locks out of his eyes.

"Oh! well, well done," said the baroness as she stood back near Diana. "Well, well done! Bravo!"

Theo yelled with the crowd, "Bravo, bravo, bravo!" And he was clapping with all his might, holding the sheet music under his arm.

The applause continued until they played a brief encore. Then von Korda motioned to Diana to come forward for more applause. The crowd gave her a hearty hand and cheered her.

Finally it was over, and the crowd drifted away. The park manager came to von Korda. Words were exchanged, accompanied by smiling and nodding on both sides.

Would he agree to another performance? There were a few more afternoons to play. She watched anxiously, relaxing as the two men shook hands and made notations on pieces of paper.

Then von Korda came to where Diana and his mother and brother waited. "They were all pleased. We are engaged for another concert," he announced to her and to his players. "We will rehearse next Tuesday at the convervatory. I will have the music ready—" And he named several quartets and a quintet for them. "And also some mazurkas I will arrange."

He gave them each an envelope of money. Diana put hers carefully into her blue cloth handbag, the first money she had ever earned as a professional pianist. She was radiant with joy. Von Korda watched her skeptically.

"Fraulein, do not allow this to go to your pretty head!" he said. "There is a long way to go."

She tossed the head he'd mentioned. "They did not frown and go away because I am a female!" she dared to defy him. "I think a woman can play the piano in public as well as a man can! And I shall go on and on!"

The baroness listened in silence, her eyebrows slightly frowning in thought. Theo did not say a word either, clutching the music sheets. Alicia was wending her way to them with Frau Lewisohn and Pauline.

"I wish you well," said von Korda more gently. "However, do not set your hopes too high. As you say, you are a female. You will play in public, yes, but what happens when your ambitions go higher, when you aim for the critical audience of the concert hall, not the park? I shall help all I can, you know that. But I would warn you, the critics will rip you to shreds if they think you aim too high."

There was no time for more. The ladies had come up to congratulate them. Alicia's exuberance made them all laugh with her. "I think that was the best concert in the world!" she cried. "I want to play in your next one!"

"Why not?" said von Korda gallantly. "What do you play?"

All were laughing as she said spiritedly, "The violin! And I am not too bad. Ask Diana!"

"I must hear you, then," he said more seriously. "Will you come to the conservatory with her next week? We shall all practice together. Who is your teacher?"

She told him, and they chatted together as easily as though they had known each other for years. Diana felt a strange little pang as she watched her friend with her Maestro. How easily Alicia got along with people! She made friends so quickly, and all responded to the charm she possessed in such abundance. Would Diana have dared go up to a famous conductor and demand to join in the next concert? She shuddered at the very idea, yet she was not without courage. It was just—she did not think she would have managed it in that way. She would have arranged an introduction, gone through proper channels, and so on.

Alicia did what she chose, and usually got what she wanted. It was odd to think she and Diana shared a similar predicament with regard to marriage, though. In some ways they were both trapped.

If only there were some way out—Diana was determined that her career must succeed! The more freedom she had, the more she wanted. She could never go back meekly to London and marry Addison Montague now! It was out of the question. Her father must see that. She fingered the blue cloth bag, the notes in the envelope. She could earn her living as a pianist!

Chapter 8

Johanne Weiss stood on the large rehearsal stage and watched the conductor carefully. It was September, and outdoors the cool winds had begun to blow, but in here it was warm and stifling.

She was glad she had taken Diana's advice and worn a summer voile of bright blue, rather than her dark gray wool. She would have been so uncomfortable, and she was nervous enough.

This was one of many rehearsals they would have. She had memorized her part as Judith for the opera, but now she must learn to sing along with the other soloists, learn their mannerisms, where she stood on stage, how she moved. Thank goodness Herr Baron von Korda was here today. He was strict but fair, and knew what he was about. Herr Conductor Otto Kliegl was in charge during practices, but all knew it was the Herr Baron who had the final say, as it was his opera.

It was a beautiful and powerful opera. Johanne loved the part of Judith, a good-hearted widow without children, who had courage and compassion for her people and the drive to do what must be done. Most of all she had religious faith in her God that carried her through the difficult times.

"Frau Weiss—" Maestro von Korda motioned to her. She stepped forward quickly. "Move through this part with the bass, and let me see where you should stand next."

She moved for him. He changed the positions so she was facing the audience, with Holofernes half-turned from them. The bass did not like it. He was the villain, trying to persuade Holofernes to have nothing to do with the foreign woman. Nor did the bass Holofernes like turning from the audience. But von Korda was firm, the solo was Judith's and Frau Weiss must face the audience. He had his way.

Thank God for him, thought Johanne fervently. She would never have the courage of some opera divas to insist on their rights and positions. Would she ever? She knew she had a good voice. She had trained all her life, and she wanted so much to do well. She would work hard—but that was not enough. One needed presence, and she had to work at that.

Most of all in the opera world one needed a backer, a mentor, or sometimes a powerful manager. She had none of these. But von Korda was backing her in this opera. She was his choice—they all knew that, and dared not treat her badly.

"Good, good," said von Korda. "Frau Weiss, you may step down for a time while we move the ballet through the scene."

Thankfully she left the stage by the side stairs, and went down to sit in the audience. She had noticed the small children waiting there so quietly, and involuntarily glanced toward them as she moved to the seats.

She had seen them come in earlier with their father, a cellist in the orchestra. He had carried his large instrument case, a harassed look on his face, as he held the smallest child by the hand and the two others trailed him obediently.

Von Korda had stared in surprise, frowning. Herr Lindau had come up to him, setting down his instrument.

"I beg pardon, Herr Baron, but it is an emergency. The woman who stays with them had a death in the immediate family, and had to go to the funeral today. She will be back tomorrow, she promises, but I could not get anyone else to stay with them."

"Must they remain here? Well, well, they must be quiet," said the baron with a kind but concerned look at the children.

"I promise they will be quiet. They are good children," said the man, quietly. With relief he smiled when the baron nodded, and turned again to the conductor.

He had settled the three children in the seats, and there they had remained through the long hot afternoon. They rarely moved, they rarely made a sound, listening intently to the music. For a time the littlest one had gone to sleep, leaning sideways in the plush seat, her head on the shoulder of her older sister. Now they were all awake, and stared at Johanne with similar round brown eyes, peeping through lovely long fringes of lashes.

In the three years of her bitter marriage Johanne had had no children. Her husband had jeered and mocked at her in public. All had laughed at her: his smart friends, his clever friends, and his beautiful young mistress.

The more Hermann Weiss had mocked her, the colder and more frightened she had felt. Was he right, was she frigid? Was she barren? He must be right. And when he had said he would get a divorce from the Roman Catholic Church for reasons of barrenness, she had numbly agreed. She could do no more than free him to have children with another woman.

But he had not. He had married another woman, kept his mistress, lived freely, but he had no children. She had wondered about that in her two years of freedom, but perhaps he was not ready yet to have children by his new wife. Or could his new wife be barren also?

It had hurt her even to sing a lullaby, and there was one in the opera *Juditha*. She forced herself to sing it, but at home when she practiced, the tears rolled down her cheeks. She longed for children. Her long arms were empty, her breast felt full and choked with tears.

On impulse she went over to the children and sat down beside the older girl, about five. "How are you?" she asked softly.

They stared. "We are well, Frau," said the boy, about seven. He was sober, anxious of face, thin, with neat clothes but a gray shirt that should have been white. She had noted Herr Lindau's shirt. Someone did not take good care of him, for his too, was gray, and the frills were not ironed well. He must have a sloppy housekeeper; it was known he was a widower.

All the opera company gossiped. One heard more than one wanted to know about everybody. It was like a small town, with all knowing everyone else's business. They must all know about her also, she thought sensitively.

"Good, good," she said, in a soft voice.

The smallest girl between the others was staring at her intently, her head turned sideways to look more closely. She had beautiful brown eyes and a sweet little round face, and as Johanne looked at her she gave the woman a sudden sweet smile. Johanne smiled back at her. What a beautiful little child.

Then with a suddenness that surprised them all the littlest child, about three, launched herself across her older sister and into the lap of Johanne. Johanne gasped, her arms folding about the child automatically, to catch her. She cuddled down as her sister and brother stared in horror.

"Oh, father will be angry," whispered the boy.

"Maria, you come right back here!" ordered the girl, pointing at the chair beside her with a great show of authority.

Safely in Johanne's arms, the girl shook her curly head of thick brown waves. It was mussed. Johanne longed to brush it gently, caress her soft cheek, hug her. She sat stiffly, but her arms could not help curving about the small warm tired body.

"Maria!" hissed the other girl. She gave Johanne an unhappy look. "Usually she is good."

"She is all right," said Johanne quietly. "Let her be, until I have to go back and sing again. Shush now."

They quieted obediently, and leaned back in their chairs while the orchestra played and the ballet group pranced and danced for the great Holofernes. This would be a popular part of the opera, especially for the men in the audience. Many came only on sufferance to hear the singers, but were rewarded by a show of pretty legs in the dancing. This dancing was unusually good for an opera, however, thought Johanne. The lead ballet dancer was a strong man who moved his troupe briskly through their paces, and the ballerina was his wife, and a fine dancer also. There was much applause at the end of the piece, and von Korda shook the male dancer's hand and complimented him gravely. She thought von

Korda had chosen him carefully, for he would not put up with sloppy work.

During the break in the rehearsal Herr Lindau came over to Johanne and his children. He looked anxious yet pleased, a smile on his thin face. He was wiping his brow with a huge linen handkerchief, gray like his shirt.

"Frau Weiss, I am sorry. My children disturb you?" he asked, rather hopefully.

"No, I enjoy them," she said.

"Thank you. I am Herr Arnold Lindau, at your service."

"Frau Johanne Weiss," she said, though he knew her name, and they shook hands formally.

He sat down in the next row, half-turned to them, looking over his children fondly. "You have been good, my angels?" he asked.

"We tried to be good, Papa," said the boy. "But Maria was naughty! She sat on the lady's lap!"

Maria, sucking her thumb, removed it long enough to give him an adorable smile, and put her thumb back into her mouth. He shook his head. "May I introduce the children to you, in your goodness, Frau Weiss? This is my eldest, my son Hugo, aged seven. My daughter Cornelia, aged five, and such a help in the kitchen, you would not believe!"

Hugo and Cornelia preened and shook Johanne's hand gravely. "And this little mischievous one is my Maria, aged three. Her mother Anna, God rest her, left me when the little one was one year of age. What a good mother she would have been." He sighed. The children listened gravely. Evidently they had heard this before.

"And do you have children, Frau Weiss?" asked Hugo.

"Nein," she said abruptly, and Herr Lindau shook his head at his son. So he had heard the gossip about her.

The orchestra was tuning up. He turned his head alertly and said, "I must return. Thank you for your goodness, Frau Weiss."

"It is nothing," she said.

Just then one of the older men in the orchestra, a fat bassoon player whom she had met several times in the company of her husband, came by along the aisle. "Ah, Frau Weiss! You have some children now, eh?" And he laughed to his companion, the flutist.

She flinched as though she had been struck, without attempting to answer. But gently she set Maria back in her place and stood up to shake out her skirts.

"I must go back," she said, and left them to go up on the stage. She stood in her place, her face bleak. Her husband had made such dreadful remarks in public about her frigidity, and this brought it all back to her.

He had mocked her singing also, and as she stood there she felt the old paralyzing fear and shame rising in her. She put her hand to her throat. She must not think about this, she must not. But her throat felt dry, so she tried to clear it.

Under the baton of Herr Conductor Otto Kliegl the orchestra began to play. She watched under her lashes the radiant face of Arnold Lindau. He was a tired and overworked man. But when he played, all that fell away from him, and he was a cellist, a musician, playing glorious music! He had a sweet full tone, she noted, as the cello rose over the other instruments following a cue from the baton.

Kliegl motioned to Johanne to begin to sing. But her throat felt pinched, and the notes would not come out full and mournful, in her solo. She reached for low notes, only to have them die out. She put her hand to her throat again as Kliegl stopped the orchestra.

"Frau Weiss, what is the trouble?" he asked impatiently.

"I am sorry, Herr Conductor. I will do better," she assured him in a faltering voice, and they began again.

In the solo she was supposed to go on into a trilling high aria. But she could not reach the notes she had reached so easily early in the day. It was the old story; she had become self-conscious, ashamed, inhibited, and it had altered her singing. She stopped abruptly, tears in her eyes.

Von Korda stepped forward, pulled out a gold watch, and glanced at it. "It is five thirty. Already we have gone on too long today. Forgive me, all of you," he said smoothly.

Johanne could have died of shame. He had been aware of her trouble and he had graciously taken the blame for the long rehearsal. Silently she picked up her handbag and waited for Diana to come up. The other girl had come to the rehearsal from her own practice with von Korda, at his invitation, and had been seated at the side of the stage near the piano.

Diana took her arm and squeezed it in silent sympathy. Johanne took out her handkerchief and wiped her face, furtively drying her eyes also.

"It is really warm in here," said Diana.

"Yes."

Von Korda was speaking to others, talking of the next rehearsal. She listened for the time and nodded. Then he came over to her and Diana.

"I will take you home," he said kindly, then paused as Herr Lindau, the cellist, came up to the small group.

He had a red face and he was frankly wiping his

brow, but he beamed at Johanne with an honest open expression. "Frau Weiss, my children have been so good, I am going to take them out to dinner now," he said. "Out of the kindness of your heart, would you come with us? They are asking for you."

She could not look at the children trailing behind him, nor could she look into his open face. She shook her head quickly, and muttered, "I cannot come to dinner."

His face fell. "Then perhaps tomorrow? The children—"

"Nein, nein, I cannot come!"

"Forgive me," he said, and moved away, speaking to the children. "No, the pretty lady cannot come, no, she cannot. Do not fuss, Maria! Come with me, we shall go to dinner now. You have been good children, be silent now!"

She felt miserable, as though she could have died with shame. She felt everyone was staring at her, condemning her for her failure this afternoon. She could have wept, but instead she moved stiffly with Diana, following von Korda out of the hall.

Ah, God, would it follow her forever? Probably. She could not trust men, she could not trust her emotions. She could not be honest and open; she was a failure as a woman. All knew she had failed as a wife, for she had not had children.

Would she fail as a singer as well? Would von Korda want to dismiss her? She had never appeared in a major opera before, much less in the lead. He had taken a chance with her. Was he sorry now?

In the carriage she waited miserably for him to say the words that would release her to emptiness. She had failed.

Courteously he sat with his back to the horses. What

a true gentleman he was. She hated having failed him. Her hands clutched together in her lap, she kept swallowing, imagining that she could almost taste her shame.

Diana said, "The ballet went so well. It should be popular, the music is so very gay and pretty."

"Yes, the gentlemen in the audience should feel they have their money's worth," said von Korda drily. He was opening his music case and taking out some sheets. "Here are the two compositions for piano I have written. You will see they are not complete."

Diana took them, pleasure showing in her face. "Oh, I shall enjoy trying them. Are you sure you want me to mark the pages, if I have an idea for the counterpoint?"

"Yes, I am sure. My left hand does very poorly," he said quietly.

"And you will tell me honestly what you think of my piano compositions and the sonata for piano and violin?"

"Quite honestly," he assured her.

Even in her misery Johanne was surprised at this exchange. So Diana was composing, and von Korda was permitting this? It was amazing for a woman to compose. Perhaps they were light airs—but no, she had said a sonata for piano and violin. That was no frivolous bit of music.

"You will want time to compose and practice. But I wish you to come with me to the opera rehearsal on Thursday as today, following luncheon with my mother," von Korda was saying. "Note particularly the orchestra accompaniment to the death scene. Do you think it too heavy, too ominous? After all, it is a victory for Judith."

"I did think it was too ominous," admitted Diana.

"What if you lightened the bass cello part? And the music later could turn from heavy to lighter as she and the maid move across the stage carrying the head of Holofernes. Yes, it is a stark scene, but after all they have succeeded, and later the high priest sings the song of victory. It seems a bit abrupt to lead into that."

She dared to criticize von Korda! Johanne sat in a daze as they talked it over as near-equals. Diana deferred to his judgment, but he kept asking her what she thought.

"Well, well, here we are." He glanced out the carriage as it pulled up. Jumping down to help them out, he smiled at Johanne kindly. "Get some rest tonight, eh? And some honey and lemon for your throat. We cannot damage it, eh? Good evening, Diana. Rest well."

"Thank you, Maestro. May you rest well, and not stay up all night altering the opera!" She said the words teasingly, and he smiled, his hard brown face charming.

He bowed over their hands and waited until the black-clad maid opened the door for them before reentering the carriage. The large carriage drove off with the two black horses high-stepping on the cobblestones.

It was past six o'clock. "It went well, Frau Weiss?" Gretchen asked as anxiously as though she had a stake in the opera's finances.

"Nein," said Johanne abruptly. "I did poorly. I am so ashamed!"

The words burst from her, and quickly she put her hands to her face.

Diana said to Gretchen, "Please, bring up a tray of tea for two to my rooms, if you will?"

She urged Johanne gently up the stairs to the first floor and into her rooms. "There," she said, pulling off her hat. "The rooms are cooler here, thank goodness. I'll just open the windows again." And she did so.

Johanne went into the small bathroom, admiring the blue-and-rose appointments of the brushes and jars. She washed her face and brushed her thick blond hair back into its usual prim arrangement. She was feeling a little better when she returned. Gretchen was just entering with a large tray of tea and pastries.

She had also brought a glass of honey and lemon with, she said, smiling kindly at Johanne, Frau Lewisohn's compliments.

"This will help your throat, said the good Frau," Gretchen told her, and handed her the glass. While Johanne sipped, Diana excused herself to the bathroom, then returned a few moments later with her beautiful silvery-gold hair shining and sleek in its coronet.

"There, now." She sat down to pour the tea. "What is wrong, Johanne? You sang so well early in the afternoon."

Johanne's face twisted. Confronted with genuine sympathy and interest she was vulnerable. She had had no one in whom to confide.

"It was the children," she said, then put her hands again to her face. "I was sitting with them—that man said—" and she began to cry.

"Oh, Johanne, my dear!" Diana jumped up, and came to sit beside her on the couch. Her slim arm went about Johanne, and tall Johanne put her head on the round shoulder and wept aloud. Diana patted her, and offered soothing words, and patted her again. "Oh, it is too bad, too bad, my poor dear girl, don't take on so, it cannot be so bad—poor dear girl, it will be all right—it will be all right. . . ."

"They all stared, they all sneered," wept Johanne. "I

am so ashamed—everyone—my husband mocked—
terrible—I did so badly—let down von Korda—what
will he think?"

"He was concerned about you," soothed Diana. "He
will understand. He admires you so much. He thinks
your voice is magnificent; he has told me again and
again."

"I am not a woman," wept Johanne, and put her fist
to her mouth. "I had not meant to say it—but my husband divorced me—barren—no children—everyone
knows—how can I sing the part—I am a coward—
poor fool . . ."

Diana soothed her, and finally made her stop crying.
Then she brought a cloth and washed her face with the
cool water. "There, now, tell me about it," she said.
"What about your husband? Who was he? What did he
do?"

Under her friend's prodding Johanne straightened
and clutched the cloth in both fists. "He is an owner of
three inns that do much business. He is important and
wealthy. He married me—I was twenty—but we had
no children—he wanted me to sing in the inns. I did
that, but I became so tired—and he mocked me about
being unable to have children. I could not sing then,
and he was angry and struck me. It was his right—as
my husband—but after he struck me before his
friends—and they laughed—I could sing no more for a
month. He divorced me, and pays for my lodging, but I
must one day earn my own living."

Diana listened in silence, her mouth tight, her face
strained. When Johanne finally stopped, she said,
"What a brute of a man! What a beast!"

Johanne stopped crying with a hiccup. What had Diana said? She surveyed her friend with round eyes. "A

beast? But he had the right—I am barren. He divorced me with the consent of the Church."

"But what if he was the one who could not have children?" asked Diana fiercely. "It does happen!"

Johanne was silent in sheer surprise. "Could that be?" she finally murmured. "But no—he is of a large family—"

Diana shook her head. "But what happened this afternoon?"

"I sat with Herr Lindau's children. What angels they are, such pretty ones. Maria sat on my lap of her own accord! How she felt in my arms—but that fat bassoon player—you know him—he made a remark—and then I could not sing afterward. My throat closed up, I felt sick at my stomach, and so nervous. Oh, what will the Maestro think of me!"

Diana patted her hands. "He thinks you are marvelous," she said firmly. "Now, sit up and drink your tea, and calm down. What a beast you were married to! He disgusts me! You are lucky to be done with him!" she exclaimed fiercely.

This was a different point of view. Johanne drank tea, ate two cakes, and felt much better.

"I saw you with the children, little Maria on your lap," Diana said presently. "How gentle and feminine you looked. You are a very womanly person, Johanne."

"I? No, Hermann said—"

"Herr Hermann was a fool!"

Johanne drew a deep breath. It was quite an adjustment, to think of wealthy Herr Weiss—a formidable man, a man she had wronged terribly by not bearing a child to him—as a brute and a fool! It was oddly comforting, though.

"Herr Lindau liked you at once. He was obviously

drawn to you. How tall he is. He must be six feet three or four!" said Diana. "He admires you, I could see that. And he did not mean to insult you by asking you to go out with him to dinner!"

"Oh, he did not insult me!" exclaimed Johanne, in horror at the very thought. "I am sure he would have taken us to a small family restaurant, not to a smart café to be seen in public! No, no, he is not that sort!"

"I am sure he is not," said Diana, nodding. "No, no, he seems a nice man, and with all those children. A widower, I believe?"

"Yes, his wife died when Maria was one. How he manages, I don't know. His shirt looked gray and mussed, and the children wore neat clothes, good things, but not laundered well."

"He needs a good wife," said Diana demurely, and caught Johanne's big blue eyes and laughed. "But not you, of course, Johanne! You are going to be a rich and famous opera star, too high for a mere cellist to reach to! Though he plays well, and has a good sweet tone to his instrument."

"Good heavens, no! He is a fine man—not too low for me—a fine cellist—what did you say?" stammered Johanne. "You go too fast! I only met him today!" She was blushing, and all at once felt very hot.

"Well, I saw the look of admiration in his eyes," said Diana, rising and glancing at her watch. "It is almost time for dinner. I should not have eaten two pastries! What the cook will say to us, I don't know!"

"Oh, I must go." Johanne rose also, and picked up her handbag. "I thank you so very much—Diana," she said shyly. "You are most good and kind."

Diana hugged her and kissed her cheek impulsively. Johanne returned her hug gratefully, feeling some of the loneliness melt inside her. Here was a friend, a kind good sensible friend, who had wiped her tears and made her feel better. "Take courage, Johanne, you are a fine woman as well as a brilliant singer. Forget that stupid brute you were unfortunate enough to marry, and live again! He is not worth one more tear!"

In her room Johanne hastily washed again and brushed her hair into a shining coil at her neck. She felt so good now! She felt on top of the world. She could sing, and tomorrow she would sing gloriously, and turn up her long nose to the stupid fat bassoonist. Just because he had eight children did not mean he was a kind good man! And that was more important than cruel Hermann Weiss and his harsh words or all the jeers in the world.

Herr Lindau was kind and decent, one could see that at once. His children were good and obedient and clung to him. Their devotion to him was further proof of his gentle kindness. Yes, she liked him, and if he did ask her again, she just might go out to dinner with him and his children!

Nothing serious, mind, she was not ready for another relationship, and she did not quite trust men yet. But one could see there were men of kindness in the world, like Maestro von Korda and his consideration, and Herr Lindau.

Chapter 9

~~~~~~

Diana felt so happy, she wanted to sing all the day. Even better, she wanted to play and write out the music she was hearing in her head. She worked from morning to night, so intent as the hours flew past that she could scarcely stop to eat or go out for a walk with Alicia.

How well things were going! Von Korda had arranged for three concerts this month and four next month, in spite of his opera rehearsals. She knew he needed neither the money nor the engagements, and before this he'd been reluctant to perform in public since his injury to the left arm.

He must be doing this for her! She felt a warm excitement in her because of his great kindness, his faith in her. What a good teacher he was: so strict, yet so fair; so interested in her performances, in her growth as a pianist, and yes, her compositions!

She was still his only student, so he spent much time working with her and encouraging her. He had even taken her compositions, gone over them with her, and shown her how to improve them. And he had not only allowed her to complete the bass parts for several of his inventions, but he had even praised her work on them!

After a break for tea with the lively boardinghouse group she happily started in again. It was becoming impossible for her to stay away from the piano. She set out one of von Korda's sheets of music, admired the solid black notes he had written, and began to play the right-hand part again. She had been thinking this one over in her mind. She would like to make the bass part a rolling thunder of chords—solemn, and firm, yet exultant—

A tap at the door interrupted her concentration. Answering it, she found Gretchen smiling in apology, proffering a long thick letter on a tray. "The post was late, Fraulein!" she murmured, as though it had been her fault.

"Thank you, Gretchen." Diana accepted the letter and closed the door. From her father—oh, dear. She turned the letter over in her hand. He had written about once a month, in answer to her faithful letters about her progress. Had he received the one telling him how well she had done in the public concerts? He might not approve that she was beginning to earn money by her playing.

After slitting open the envelope, she sat down and took out the thick sheets written in her father's familiar script. She could picture her father at his wide desk, dipping his pen in the black inkwell that was replenished with ink every day.

The letter began, "My dearest obedient daughter," and Diana felt a chill of fear ripple down her spine.

It went on:

I bring greetings from your brothers, your fiancé, and his father. I regret to tell you that Mr. Montague has taken a turn for the worse, and is now housebound most of the time. We are proceeding with the merger plans, which await only your approval and your presence.

I am sure you have been in Austria long enough to get this piano-playing nonsense out of your system. It is not a profession for a female, as you know. Addison Montague is a patient fiancé, but patience is not unlimited. Besides, his house is in an uproar. Because of his father's illness he is distracted, and some days he cannot concentrate on his work.

We have decided that you must come home now, Diana, my dearest daughter, and take your place once more in our household. I miss you, and your brothers miss you, too. I had hoped that Lewis might marry, but that engagement is off. The young lady was reluctant, the foolish girl. However, both my sons are working hard, and I am happy with them.

It is you who concerns us. I think of you, alone in a strange country, and think what mischief you might get into. I am not happy that you are so far from us.

I think you should come home now, and be married. It has been long enough. The housekeeper does as well as she can, but she is not nearly as good as our faithful hardworking Diana, who always saw so well to our comforts!

I have told Mr. Montague that after you are married, he shall move in with us all. You can manage the households for all of us, my dear, which should give your talents a wide scope! He is most relieved. The housekeeper was dismayed when I suggested that Mr. Montague move in at once, and in fact she threatened to leave. However, when I told her you would be coming home shortly, she agreed to reconsider, and she awaits your return as eagerly as we do.

I know I promised you a year. However, I shall make it up to you. I have some fine lengths of Chinese silks laid aside for you, some fine blues and rose, and a length of purple that will amaze you. Also your brother Andrew purchased a fine hunter, and said there was a splendid mare for you, if we can pay the rather high price for it. Come home at once, and many delights will await you, I assure you.

My dearest Diana, I want you married and settled. If your brothers do not marry for a time, I shall not have the grandsons I long for. I know I am getting older, though I do not feel it. Come, marry the suitor who awaits you, and make your old father very happy. I await your return impatiently, and send the fond regards of us all. If you need more money for the return journey, draw on my name at the bank. Your loving father,

Homer Ballantyne.

It was a blow so crushing that she could only sit and bow her head. She was too dazed even to weep or speak.

Her precious year taken from her.

Come home at once, marry, and take care of two more men!

She would never play again! She could picture her life, filled with the managing of three or more households, including the Montague town house. To have to

care for an invalid, her husband, and three men of the
Ballantyne clan! All telling her what to do, ordering
her about. And she would sleep with a man she detested—have his children—and stagger up again each day
to see that everything went smoothly for them all!

And in return her father offered some silks and a
mare she would have little time to ride!

It was so outrageous that it stunned her. So selfish,
yet so like her father and brothers. She knew that once
they had made up their minds, there was nothing for
her but to comply. Her hopes for a career would end.
She had no money but her allowance and the small
amounts of pay from the concerts—not enough to live
on if her father cut her off.

And her precious lessons—and the frequent contact
with a brilliant musician, a good teacher, a fine man,
Lukas von Korda. Yes, she would miss—miss *him*,
most of all, she admitted, and put her face in her
hands.

How could she endure it, never to see him again?

She went over and over the letter, but could see no
way out. The message was clear. She must go home
without delay. They needed and wanted her now, at
once.

Her year shortened by half. And now, with winter
coming, the opera season starting. Why, she would
miss the opening of von Korda's first opera! With luck
she might see a brief notice of it in some London
gazette. But she would not be here to witness the triumph that was sure to be his.

She could not bring herself to go to dinner. Alone,
she wept in secret, standing at the windows as the rain
poured down, like her tears. Her insides raged with
stormy defiance. But what could she do? Without
money a woman had no choices. Eventually she had

hoped to earn money with her playing, but it was too soon for that now—she needed more concert experience, exposure to influential critics, and more instruction from von Korda. A year would scarcely have been enough time—and now even that was to be denied.

When she went to bed, she could not sleep much. She tossed and turned, trying to think of some way out—but all her thoughts led back to the issue of money. She had to have money to live on. And her father had all the family's money tied up, even the sum left her by her mother. He had invested it at once into his business, and she had seen none of the income.

In the morning the sleepless night showed in her drawn face and reddened eyes. The rain still poured down, a gray sullen disagreeable rain that matched her mood; a late September rain that foretold a cold winter to come.

She put on a dark blue serge dress, pressed a dark blue matching hat on her silver-gold coronet of hair, yanked on gray gloves, and picked up her blue handbag. She put her father's letter in the handbag, in case she needed evidence to break her lesson contract with von Korda.

His carriage was waiting. The coachman handed her up with a beaming smile which she could scarcely meet. Her mood did not go unnoticed; he had been picking her up with the carriage each day since June, and she had never before failed to give him a bright good-morning.

Halfway there she realized she had forgotten her case of music, including von Korda's compositions. Oh, she must go back—but there was no time, and he would be upset if she were late. Miserably she arrived at his home. The carriage drove up into the side carriageway, and a footman appeared to help her out, shielding her from the rain with a huge black umbrella.

Von Korda stood at the entrance to the huge drawing room, waiting for her with a pleasant smile. But as he stared at her, the smile disappeared. "My dear girl, what has happened to you?" he exclaimed.

The hem of the dark blue dress was splashed with rain, her boots were wet, but she knew he did not mean that. At the warmth of his concern, she wanted to burst into tears. She drew a deep breath and preceded him into the waiting room, all the time fighting back the tears in her eyes.

He took off her jacket and turned to the hovering butler. "Bring a tray of coffee, at once," he said curtly. The butler disappeared. "Sit down, dear child," he said to Diana.

She sat down on the couch, took out her handkerchief, wiped her eyes, took a deep breath. "My father—sent me a letter. . . ." she began.

"And—" He was pacing the room before her, turning again and again to study her, as though helpless. "So—what did he say, your father?"

"He said—I must come home—at once—marry—" She gulped, felt tears overwhelming her words, pressed her handkerchief tightly to her mouth. "My year," she wailed. "My precious—year—gone!" Her voice broke, and she closed her eyes tightly, willing back the flood of tears. She must not cry before him; he would be so embarrassed and cross! Her father hated it when she cried, those few times.

"You have the letter?" His voice was strange. She opened her bag, and he took the letter from her brusquely. She had meant to read him only a few lines from it, but he took it over from her, and went to a chair near the lamp to read it through.

The butler and footman solemnly rolled in a huge

silver tea tray. Von Korda glanced at them, nodded for them to serve, and turned his eyes back to the long handwritten sheets. Diana thought she ought to get the letter back from him, but by now she was too exhausted to care.

The butler poured out the steaming coffee. When he handed her the cup and saucer, they rattled noticeably in her shaking hand. The footman set a small table before her, and she gratefully set down the hot cup. She was all a-coming apart, as her Irish nurse used to say in bad times. She clasped her hands together tightly and tried to control herself. She must be dignified, not disgrace herself before her Maestro.

The butler and footman departed, closing the door after them. The sheets of the letter crackled. Von Korda had turned back to the beginning and was starting over again. She heard him mutter: "Outrageous—silks—a mare! Great God in heaven," and a couple words she did not know, but that she suspected to be impolite.

Finally he set down the letter and walked over to the tray. He poured out a cup for himself, saying, brusquely, "Drink up while it is hot. Come, come, we must do something," and began to stride about the room, the cup forgotten in his hand. She watched him anxiously. Was he angry with her? Was he thinking of the concerts they'd promised to do in October?

She drank her coffee and set down the cup, while still he paced and muttered to himself, going to the window, drawing the draperies aside, staring out at the pouring gray rains. He stood there for a time, sipping the coffee with his back to her. Her eyes took in his smart blue silk suit, his golden hair shining in its slight wave, the way the bright lights from the chandelier blazed on him.

How handsome he was, how fine. And how she would miss him! Her gaze lingered on him. She would miss sitting in this room, at the piano, playing for him, hearing his words of criticism and praise. Would she ever play again?

Her precious year—snatched from her! And she would never see him again. She noticed, absently, that he held the coffee cup and saucer in his stiff left hand, but lifted it with his right hand to drink. When he had finished he turned back to her, set down the cup decisively and drew a deep breath.

"Well, well, this is a shock, I can see it. It is a shock to me also," he said heavily. He drew up a chair, shoved away the tea tray that sat between them, crossed his ankles, and eyed her gravely. "Now, Diana, what do you think about this?"

"I am—very upset," she said. "I can—scarcely believe. I mean—he had promised me that year! I had counted on it. Father usually keeps his word. But you can see—he is distressed, Mr. Montague is ill—he wants the merger. . . ."

"And you will be the sacrifice," he said.

She met his look, was about to protest politely, then nodded. "I do not mind housework, Maestro," she said. "But—I will never have time to play again! I know it! And I had so hoped—I mean, I wanted a career of playing, you have said I play well. . . ."

"You have a fine talent, Diana, even more than I had thought when I first took you as a pupil," he said, and the words were very sweet to her. "I thought then, She has a good talent; let us see how she can improve, what we can do with this. Let her have her year, I thought, she will go home content."

"Not content, Maestro," she said, in a low tone. "I wanted to prove myself, to prove I can have a musical career, just as a man can have. I wanted to earn money at my music, then build up a career, perhaps teach a few pupils, ladies. Stay on in Vienna, work hard, compose, perhaps be able to perform my own compositions one day. And now—that is all—all—" She could not go on. She fought back her emotions, she wanted so not to disgrace herself before him.

"Tell me of your life at home. We have spoken little of this. You are the youngest—go on."

While he watched her closely, she told him more freely than ever before of her life. How she had been housekeeper from a very young age, had been her mother's right hand, then had taken over at sixteen. How she had snatched time from her duties to play and compose. How she loved to play and how she had always heard music in her head. Her face shone as she said, "When I hear the music at night, I get up and go to write it down quickly before I lose it. And in the morning I go to the piano and play it again, and sometimes it is beautiful, the way I heard it in my head! Oh, Maestro, I love music so much. Must I give it up—for this?" Her hand indicated the letter lying on the couch beside her.

"You do not love the young man. I think you do not even like him," he said bluntly.

She shook her head. "He is disagreeable, moody," she said frankly. "He seems ill at times, with his very tempers. His father is like that, and to take care of him also, an invalid—as well as bear children, take care of them all—the houses—we have the London town house, the country estates—all take so much time."

"And there would be no time for your precious music," he said gently. He stood up and paced about. "Well, well, something must be done, something can be done," he announced, and returned to sit down again.

"Oh, what, Maestro? What can be done?"

"You have no money of your own. That is the problem?"

"Maestro, I have money from my grandfather's estate, through my mother. But father put it all into Ballantyne's, and uses it. He is allowed to do so by law."

Von Korda frowned. "Yes, yes, that is the law here, too. Women do not manage their own money. It simply is not done."

"If only they did, I would be free!" she said passionately, her blue eyes shining. "Do you think I could get money from Papa, since I have an investment in his firm?"

"I doubt it," he said drily, dashing her sudden hope. "My mother had such an income, but she never saw a penny of it until her husband, my father, died," he added abruptly, then stood and paced again, as though angry he had divulged this.

What then, she thought silently. What could she do? She had to obey her father until she married—and then she must obey her husband! And then must she obey them both? Would she be the rope they tugged between them, until she broke? Her father was very strong-willed, and Addison Montague had a will of his own. With a shudder she remembered the petulant droop of his lip, his sullen anger when he was thwarted.

Von Korda came and stood beside her, gazing down at her. Her hands were clasped together in unconscious pleading.

"There is a solution," he said abruptly. "It is this. I have faith in your musical talent. If you do also, you will let me take charge of it and assist you. Forget about my fees as a teacher. That is no consequence to me. I will pay your living expenses at the boardinghouse, and give you an allowance to live on, if your father will not. And you will have some small income from the concerts. What about it?"

"Oh—Maestro!" She could not believe it. "Can I?" she thought. "I must!" With shining incredulous eyes she studied his hard face. "What will people—"

"No one but your father need know. Write to him. I will write too, and tell him. If he does not have faith in your talent, I do! Were it not for the social conventions, I would even have you stay here! We must see each other almost every day, anyway. However, my mother is not here now, and it would not do. But I will provide for you sufficiently to take care of all your expenses. What do you say?"

"Oh, yes, yes, yes! And one day I will repay you!"

He hesitated, then nodded. "Of course! But I will not worry about that, and you must not. Now, come, let us write to your father at once!"

Still dazed, she hesitated. He bent over her, took her hands in his, and drew her to her feet. She gazed up at him, doubtfully, wanting to believe, yet—could it be true? Would he be willing to help her in such a marvelous way? For what motive? Did he truly believe in her talent?

He drew her to himself, and abruptly she felt the warmth of his body against hers. She gasped, her eyes huge. He studied her face, a half-smile on his lips, a look in his eyes she had never before seen. A look of slumberous passion, desire—

His touch was gentle, yet firm. Shocked, she felt his arm slide about her waist but she did not think to pull away. Why? That was a question she would ponder later, during long sleepless nights. She wanted to remain, near to him, held to his body, feeling every hard muscle, the heat of his thighs on hers—

His mouth was moving in silent need. He bent his head, and she felt his lips brush her forehead in a soft caress. His lips went to her cheek, gently brushing her silken skin. Then the large generous mouth moved lower, meeting her lips.

At once she could barely breathe. Her lungs seemed to be full, her throat closed, all her being stalled in a pulsating moment of time. His mouth was on hers—heat, softness, passion, drive—pressing on her lips, twisting a little to force a response from her mouth.

He moved her with him, and together they sank onto the couch, his legs half on hers. She could not think, could not struggle, though any other man she would have fought desperately.

This was her Maestro, her teacher, her mentor—and she felt she would let him do anything he liked with her. Her mind was dazed, her hands closed around his upper arms, feeling the hard muscles under the silk suit. How strong he was, how different his hard body from her soft one. He was man, she was woman. He was masculine power, she was feminine yielding. As he slid on her body, she wanted to die in his arms.

His mouth was moving on her mouth, whispering against it.

"My God, my God, you are so soft, so sweet. What am I doing? I must stop. Honey, I could take you now—but I must stop—this is madness."

He lifted himself up, his face burning warm from hers. He gazed down into her bewildered eyes, as though to look through her to her very soul.

"Diana," he said huskily. "Diana!"

What did he want of her? She could give him every-thing—yet—no! She shifted one hand up in involun-tary protest.

"I know," he said with a groan. "I must stop. This is wrong—I did not mean to do this."

"I was wrong to—to ask you—" she replied, gasping. Did he think because she would accept his financial aid—

She flinched from the thought, and from him. Surely he would not think to make her his mistress! She remembered again the voluptuous woman glimpsed on his stairway that first day, that glamorous creature moving up the stairs silently as though she belonged.

Lukas rose from the couch abruptly, striding away from her to the window. Both fists were clenched at his sides and he was breathing hard. Diana gazed after him in breathless bewilderment. She put both hands to her breast, feeling the crushed fabric and the pain of her bruised body where he had held her with his hands so cruelly tight. Yet his mouth on hers had been welcome.

Was she mad? She was not a loose woman. Why had she welcomed his embrace?

He turned about, looking at her from across the room. "This changes nothing," he said harshly. "Forgive me for this moment. I was moved with emotion at your plight. I did not mean to—insult you. Forget this if you can. It is over."

She stared at him blankly. Forget this? How could she? She would never forget.

Stunned and bewildered, she gazed up at him. He bent over her, placed his large hands one on each cheek, bent down closer, and put his mouth gently on hers. She felt the kiss deepen, grow more warm, then abruptly he stood erect again and released her.

"Come to my study, let us write," he said, and started from the room impatiently. Hastily she rose and followed him through several intervening rooms, to the huge back room.

She had never seen it before, except from a distance. Today she scarcely noticed it either. It was a large book-lined study, furnished with a huge mahogany desk on which papers, folders, and books were neatly laid. On a stand stood a magnificent bust of Beethoven. Quartos of music were filed neatly on the large bottom book shelves.

He held a chair for her opposite to him, and took out several sheets of crested stationery, a pot of black ink and some pens.

"We shall both write. I shall send the letters together today, at once," he said. "No sense in waiting. He shall know at once that you are not coming home to take care of the invalid, the husband, the father and two brothers, the hunter, and the mare!"

Diana laughed a little nervously, and he smiled at her kindly across the desk.

He pushed paper and pen toward her. "Now, let us say for six months, I shall be your mentor," he said. "All expenses paid, no worry about Papa. I shall give you a check today to put into the bank—you have an account?"

"Yes, sir."

"Good." He opened his checkbook, scrawled some lines, and handed her the check. She accepted it shyly, then noted the huge amount and opened her mouth to protest. He frowned at her. "Go ahead, write your letter! I want to get it off in the post. The butler shall take it at once."

She nodded and composed herself to write. Her hands were still shaking from all that had happened.

> Dear Papa,
> I have your letter of recent date, and hasten to answer. You did promise me a year, Papa, just as

my brothers had. I spoke with my teacher, and he has made a suggestion.

He said, that since he has much faith in my musical ability, and I am beginning to earn money, that I must have my six months more. He will sponsor me, he will waive the fees, and also pay my living expenses, if you will not.

As to the invalid Mr. Montague—

She hesitated over the page. The Baron von Korda was writing steadily, filling a page with his firm black handwriting.

She went on.

As to the invalid Mr. Montague, I strongly suggest that you do not take on his care. I would protest as the housekeeper does. I have much to do as it is. And I do intend to continue my music. Also, I have told you, I do not wish to marry Mr. Montague. I feel we are not suited to each other. If you wish to merge the company, that is your concern, dear Father. But please do not include my marriage in those plans. When I marry, I wish to admire and respect my husband and to feel that he does admire and respect me in return.

I am sorry to seem disobedient to your wishes, dear Father. However, I do feel that for once your good reason and common sense have not held sway, and you have let the business problems submerge them.

She frowned over these lines, then let them stand.

"In conclusion, dear Father, may I say that I am your always loving daughter, Diana.

Von Korda was waiting for her to finish. He had sanded his letter and laid it aside to dry. He sanded hers for her, and pulled it to him to read it. She longed to read his also, but he had set it on the far side of the desk.

She waited until he had finished reading. "Does it sound all right, Maestro?"

"Yes, yes, firm but loving." He folded them both and rang for the butler as he addressed a large business-sized envelope.

The butler came in.

"Take these to the post office at once and mail them by an express mailing to England, to the address here written. Here is the money for it." Sums exchanged hands.

When the butler had departed, Diana said, "I thank you so very much, Maestro. I cannot express my true feelings, I am so very grateful—"

"You may express them by continuing to work hard, as you do, dear child," he said. "Now we are going to have lunch upstairs as soon as dear brother Theo arrives from university. Then we shall talk, and you shall play for me when you are calm. After that we shall go to rehearsals, and you shall listen and comment on how it goes. All right?"

Her nerves melted under his smile, and she beamed back at him. "Oh, yes, thank you!"

He had told her to forget that time in his arms, and she would try to obey him. But oh, how sweet had it been, to be held and kissed, almost brutally, as though he would join her to himself. As his coachman drove them to the boardinghouse, he spoke lightly. It was as though nothing unusual had passed between them.

She wondered later if he remembered the kisses he had given her, and thought not. The last one had been like the soothing kiss one gives to an injured child. She did not know if he thought of her as a woman or as a child.

To her, it was a revelation of the feeling she had for him. He was so kind, so good, so intelligent, and such a fine musician! She admired and respected him so very much! And his mouth had been warm and gentle on hers, yet showing his strength and emotions. She lay awake sometimes at night, touching her lips gently, remembering how his lips had felt on hers.

In due time, her father wrote back. He was furiously angry, that was evident in his tone. But he sent her another check, and said he would not have another man pay the living expenses of his daughter.

> If von Korda chooses not to charge for your stupid musical lessons, that is one matter! I regard them as idle and frivolous anyway. But he shall not pay for your food and lodging and your clothes. That is not at all proper. I wonder at you for considering it seriously! It makes me wonder if Vienna and your freedom have not turned your head. You do not sound like my sensible daughter.
>
> However, you will have your year. I shall come for you in April, and brook no opposition at that time. Do not get into trouble; I warn you, I will not endure it. I am writing to your Cousin Helena to keep a stern eye on you.

Because of his letter to Cousin Helena, Diana had to explain something of the matter to her, along with what von Korda had suggested. Frau Lewisohn listened in silence, shaking her head in surprise and wonder.

"So he offered to pay for it all? And he no longer

charges for lessons? Well, well, well. I am surprised. But it shall go no further than myself, dear child. Of course you are a good discreet girl. However, I shall write to your father and reassure him of your care for the proprieties. I do fear that you may have to marry that Mr. Montague, though. It does sound that your father is set on it."

"But if I can make a living at music, I shall not have to return and do so, dear cousin!"

"Dear child," sighed her cousin, and patted her cheek and kissed her tenderly. "I hope all will work out as you hope! But life has a way of surprising us! Still, you have a will and a talent, may God watch over you!"

If her cousin had any idea of how Lukas von Korda had kissed her, Diana thought later, perhaps she would not be so willing to allow her to stay. But those moments would not be revealed to anybody in the world. Even she found it difficult to believe the embrace had ever occurred.

Chapter 10

~~~~~~

Gretchen came up to Alicia's room, just as she was arranging her hat on her red curls. Did the green silk look fresh enough? she wondered. She really needed a new dress; she had been wearing the same ones again and again. At home she would be outfitted at this time of year with all new gowns for the New York season.

But she was in Vienna—enjoying more independence and freedom than she'd ever known. That in itself was enough. She did not really need anything new—

"Fraulein, you have a visitor! He is in the drawing room downstairs!"

Alicia said, "Oh, it must be Mr. Osterley—is the Baron von Korda here?" She and Diana were going together today to the dress rehearsal of von Korda's opera. Johanne was very nervous, and von Korda thought they would help soothe her by their presence.

"Nein, not yet, Fraulein!" Gretchen trotted away, and Alicia picked up her handbag and prepared to descend the stairs.

Diana's door was still closed. She was always very

prompt so it must be early. Alicia shook her watch on the gold chain. Yes, it was fifteen minutes before the hour.

She went into the drawing room, quite unsuspectingly. There before her she was met by an immense gentleman clad in blue silk suit, white ruffled shirt, blue and gold waistcoat—huge, and formidable.

"Baron!" she gasped.

He reached out and clasped her hands in delight. "My dear fiancée!" he half-mocked, and kissed her hands, one after the other. She drew them back sharply until he finally let them go.

"How dare you come!" she gasped. "I told you—"

"You told me nothing, my dear Alicia! You did not write to me!" he reproached. "I finally came, in anxiety, but I see you are quite well!" His blue eyes roved over her boldly, from her red curls to the toes of her green slippers and back up again, lingering on the roundness of her breasts. "*Quite*—well!"

His tone infuriated her, but his presence even more so, now that she realized he was actually here in Vienna.

She drew herself up. "Well, you can turn about and go back home," she said coldly. "I am working here in Vienna, practicing very hard, and I have no time for—for foolishness!"

"And you are going out now?" he asked mildly.

"To an opera rehearsal!" she snapped.

"Permit me to go with you. We have much to talk about. I have a letter from your father. You know, he permits me to continue to see you. In fact, he encourages our marriage. I will show you some of his letter—"

"I am—not—going to—marry you!" she said, with slow burning emphasis. "I told you that!"

"But your father consents!"

"Then marry him!"

She blushed at his frown, aware she had been very rude. But she would not apologize. She stood her ground, unwilling even to invite him to sit down. And where was Frau Lewisohn? Why did she permit Alicia to see this man alone? Had he dared say they were engaged?

"I do not want you to stay here in Vienna," she blurted out at his steady stare. How blue his eyes were, dark blue and large, staring at her directly, as though he would eat her up with them. How did she look? If only she had worn her pale silvery green, that was so stunning. But no—she did not wish to attract him! She wanted him to go away!

"I wish to visit with you. We have not had time to become acquainted," he said seriously. "At the castle I felt we had no time to talk. I spent so much time explaining to your father about matters—"

"The repairs to the roof!" she blurted out. His eyes narrowed, his look turned thoughtful.

"Did I speak to you about that? I must have. Yes, we discussed the roof repairs, and other matters; my tenants, my duties to my people," he said with a quiet dignity she had to admire. "He understood what I said. I wish to explain to you."

She stared at the carpet, sullenly. She did not want to talk to him, to become better acquainted. And she felt betrayed. Her father should not be writing to him and encouraging him! She had made it very clear to her father that she would not marry the baron, and favor him with a huge dowry to help him with all the expenses of his impoverished estate. She did not feel like sacrificing herself to help Stanislav—

She squared her shoulders. "I have been working

hard on my violin," she said firmly. "I am interested in a career as a musician. I love it here in Vienna, and I don't mean to leave very soon! My friends are here—"

"Of course, of course," he said, with unusual patience. "I understand perfectly. But I would share this with you, meet your friends. I want us to become better acquainted."

"I don't want to!" she cried, childish again. "I don't want to get to know you better!" She felt instinctively that he would at once try to dominate her.

"Are you afraid to do that?" he asked, his voice lowered seductively. He took a long step toward her. She backed up, but a sofa barred her way. She eyed him warily. "Are you afraid you might come to like me—very much? You have been spoiled. I think you are afraid of feeling too much emotion."

At the glint in his blue eyes she took warning. But there was no place to move.

He caught her firmly by her arms and pulled her to him. The hard warmth of his body in the silk suit made her gasp. "Don't you—dare!"

"But I must dare—and my fiancée has not greeted me properly," he laughed, bending his head. His hard warm mouth covered hers. He kissed her long and harshly, until her teeth bit into her lips. His sudden fierceness alarmed her and though she tried, she could not pull herself from his rough grip.

Fire swept through her slim tall body. He was taller than she, more bulky, more powerful. She was helpless in his strong arms. As she tried to turn her head, he kissed her cheeks and her chin, then was back at her mouth, holding her still against his shoulder as he took a leisurely taste of the sweetness of her lips. She had opened her mouth to cry out, but he pressed his opened lips to hers, and she was overcome by the wet warmth of their touch.

Time slid away, and she was conscious of nothing but the warm pressure of his body against her slim form. His arms were hard, the muscles strong. She remembered how she had seen him one day, sleeves rolled up above the elbows, his arms taut as he helped lift a fallen tree trunk from the carriage it had crushed in a storm.

He was not afraid of hard work, and his body showed it—tough, sinewy, pressed now to hers so that she was only too aware of every movement of his muscular limbs. His arms held her to him, so she could not move away. One arm circled her waist, pressing her cunningly to his body. The other arm was at her shoulders, and his fingers played with her thick red hair. He would muss her up!

Fretfully she tried to move away, but, smiling at her with a broad white-toothed grin, he pulled her back again, masterfully, and bent his head to hers once more. "Don't," she began to say sharply. "I don't want—"

His lips touched her open mouth again, and this time he slid his tongue inside. Shock made her gasp, and her eyes went wide. How dare he! It was too intimate a touch. She felt as though he had invaded her body.

He wrestled her back to himself smoothly when she tried to yank away once more. Alicia was strong. She exercised and walked and rode, and skated on the ice. But she was no match for him.

Fury sent the blood rising in her cheeks. He was a bully and a beast. She did not want to be kissed by him! She writhed in his hard arms, and he laughed softly under his breath, and let her struggle, as though he enjoyed the twisting of her body against his.

And she was all too aware of his muscular strength, the barrel chest beneath her cheek, as he held her tightly to him, the curve of the arm behind her waist, and a strange thrilling sensation in her thighs. He had pulled her so tight that she half lay against him.

He was aroused, and she could feel the rising excitement in him as her thighs were pressed to his. She felt panicky, though she was in a public parlor and anybody might discover them at any moment. Would he—rape her? Would he try anything—oh, God! He was moving against her, as though the feel of her body pleased him immensely.

With one hand he cradled her neck, and he held her head still while he took his leisurely taste of her lips once more. He moved his large mouth on hers, and thrust his tongue between her lips, as he moved her nearer to the couch. She struggled more violently, tried to slide away from him, but he would not allow it. The couch was very close now; she could feel the soft fabric brush her knees.

Stanislav pushed her back, so that she lost her balance. Instinctively she kicked at his leg with her pointed shoe.

"Ouch! You vixen!" he cried out, in German, and let her go, hopping back from her, eyes glaring.

She moved out of his reach, toward the door. She was flushed, hot, furiously angry. Yet—she had felt—but no! She hated him.

"You are a brute and a bully—and you are disrespectful and arrogant! You can go back to Germany and live in your leaky castle. I hate you!"

She stormed at him as he hopped about clasping his shin with his hand and staring at her.

"And you are a spoiled child!" he said, with some restraint. "I will enjoy taming you!"

"Oh! That you will never do!" Her tone was angry. "I will marry an American. They are kind and good and know how to treat a girl nicely! I—I despise you! I hate you!" She turned and rushed from the room, and rushed right into the Baron von Korda.

"What is going on?" he asked sharply. He looked from her flushed indignant face to that of the stranger. "Sir, have you been bothering her?"

He had overheard the last few words, as he and Moritz Osterley were entering the boardinghouse together.

"Yes, he has! I hate him!" cried Alicia fiercely. She caught hold of Moritz's arm. "Come on, Moritz, take me out of here! Let's go!"

The young composer gazed helplessly from one to the other. "I have not been introduced," he began. "Herr Baron—what shall I—"

Von Korda was drily amused at the American girl. She tugged and pulled at the amiable young man until she got him to the door, though he tried to click his heels and mind his manners. Moritz did not have a chance.

"Let us go! We can get a carriage up the street. I won't stay here a minute—"

She hauled him with her out the door and into the street, letting the door slam shut behind them. Von Korda moved on into the drawing room and clicked his heels.

"Baron von Korda, at your service," he said curtly. The stalwart young man before him was a few years younger than himself, and about his own height, but more stocky, with darker gold hair, deeper blue eyes, and a scar on his cheek.

The German clicked his heels, bowing. "Baron von

Neumeister, at your service," he said. "I have the honor to be the fiancé of Fraulein Huntingdon."

"Indeed?" von Korda concealed his shock, and looked him over more carefully.

"Yes, though she will not acknowledge it. Her father consents," the man blurted out. "And who was that puppy?"

"A composer, fine talent, rather immature person. Moritz Osterley. I will introduce you later," said von Korda drily. "We are about to attend the dress rehearsal of my opera. It opens tomorrow night. Will you accompany us today? I think we should talk."

The gloom on the handsome face lightened. They shook hands as friends. "You are most kind! I shall be happy to come. I say, you must be the composer von Korda!"

These words were sweet to Lukas. He had once thought of himself as the pianist von Korda, and now that was over forever. Now to hear himself called the composer von Korda—that was good! Yes, he must think of himself now as composer-conductor.

"Yes, I am he. And you are from Germany." He had identified the accent.

"Yes, my castle there is at Neumeister. You may have been nearby. . . ."

Their conversation was interrupted by the three ladies who entered the room. Frau Lewisohn sailed in first, smartly dressed in black silk taffeta, with pearls about her throat. After her came tall Frau Johanne Weiss, pale in blue, her face rather white from nerves. Following them was lovely Diana, her calm face pink and white, her sparkling blue eyes nearly matching her lovely blue dress. How pretty she was—how truly lovely, he thought, as he stepped forward to greet each of them in turn, courteously.

He introduced them to the Baron Stanislav von Neumeister. Diana has heard of him, he thought after noting a slight flicker in her expression. Yes, she would be in the confidence of the impetuous Alicia. In his thoughts he imagined that the life in the boardinghouse radiated about her. She hovered over Johanne more like a sister than a casual friend. He knew she calmed her, and gave her confidence. She soothed Alicia from her tempers, and was like a daughter to the uncertain Frau Lewisohn.

"Well, well, where is Fraulein Huntingdon?" asked Frau Lewisohn. "I had thought she was here."

Her look seemed to accuse von Neumeister, who shrugged and looked embarrassed.

"She went on with Mr. Osterley," said von Korda, quickly. "I believe she was anxious to depart."

"But we are early—the naughty girl, to go on without a chaperon." Frau Lewisohn sighed. "Well, well, she is not bad, she is only too quick, and her life in America—well, well, she is a good girl, only too quick!"

The party composed itself. Once settled into the huge barouche, they were off. Lukas had had no time to be nervous about the rehearsal, he realized with amusement. He was too caught up in the little merry drama of the American girl and her unwanted German suitor. He must learn more about this. He was fond of the bright-haired girl and admired her fine musicianship.

He wanted to know more about von Neumeister, too, and resolved to become better acquainted. Appearances could be misleading, but so far he did like the man, and thought him open and frank.

The rehearsal went very well. The small audience was moved to tears by the lullaby, as Judith sang of her sadness at not having had any children with her beloved husband. Now she had nothing left of their love but his earthly possessions, and what good were they?

The audience was enthralled by the strong story, and listened intently, though many had heard the music and songs over and over. Von Korda found himself glancing toward Diana's face as the scenes progressed. Her eloquent expressions told him everything. At times she smiled, at other moments she went grave, then she was radiant with deep feeling. At the end she was smiling through tears. How she felt music! She was very talented; she played so well, and composed beautifully, more like a man than a woman, he admitted to himself. Her strong hands played runs and chords with ease, and oh, how she could make the music sing! He especially enjoyed hearing her play his music. At her touch it sounded the way he wanted it to sound, and could no longer perform it himself.

As the scenes went on Johanne grew more confident. Her voice gained in color and depth, and her high notes rang clear and pure. What a fine voice she had; she only needed more sureness, von Korda thought. Today she did well; would to God she did as well tomorrow night!

He could count on Diana to reassure her, he thought gratefully. The two girls had become close.

The scene where Judith sliced off the head of Holofernes evoked a slight scream from a woman in the audience. Von Korda wondered if it would have that effect on the opening night. It was a powerful and memorable moment. When the scene ended, the hall rang with the applause of the small group.

The last act was played, climaxing in the glorious triumphant choral finale. When it was over von Korda leaned back and wiped his face with his handkerchief.

It had gone so well—would it go this way tomorrow night? One never knew. An opera could fail after one performance, and then never be heard again. He must have faith.

After the performance he motioned to Theo. He had already introduced his brother to Baron von Neumeister. "Ask the baron to join us for dinner," he murmured quickly. Theo nodded and von Korda went backstage for final directions to his players.

Lukas found Diana there in Johanne's dressing room. He motioned her to join him in the drafty hall.

"She did well. Reassure her for me. I am sending you home in my carriage," he said quickly, into her ear. Diana nodded.

"I will. She did beautifully." She sounded as satisfied as he felt. "It all went well. It is such a magnificent opera!"

"Thank you. Pray for me tomorrow night!" he grimaced.

"I shall. Do not worry, it will go well. They are well rehearsed, and so well suited to their parts."

Diana's calm soothed him, and Lukas felt his stiff shoulders relax. She was so lovely in her silvery-blue gown, with the dark blue cape hung over her shoulders and her silvery-gold hair like spun silk. "Thank you. Is she ready to go?"

"I'll see."

She returned with Johanne, and they hurried out to the carriage. Lukas saw them on their way, then returned to discuss a few last details with the conductor. By the time his carriage had returned, he was more than ready to leave.

Theo and he took von Neumeister home with them. Lukas was mulling over a plan in his head.

In the small family dining room the three men sat

around the round table and talked. Baron von Neumeister was quick of speech and showed a happy disposition, yet a serious attitude about his duties.

"There is so much to do. So much was neglected." He sighed. "I cannot remain long in Vienna. Yet I had to see Alicia, talk to her. I had thought to find a meek wife!" He laughed at himself. "Her red hair matches her fiery disposition! Yet she can be sweet, as I saw when she was with her parents. I call her spoiled, yet she was gentle and thoughtful toward them. My mother adored her. And when she played for us, how the violin sang!"

"A very talented woman," said von Korda, choosing with care some grapes from a bowl of fruit. "She has improved in her playing, in just a few months under the guidance of a good instructor. And she is eager to work. I have attended two of her concerts, and been impressed at how well she performs in public. She and my pupil, Diana Ballantyne, are going to perform some piano-violin sonatas."

"This Miss Ballantyne—she is talented also?"

"Very," he said. "Even more so than Miss Huntingdon. She plays very well, memorizes quickly, but even more—she has a sureness of touch, a sensitivity to the music—and she composes."

"Composes! A woman? That is rare indeed. But how well does she compose? A few cute little tunes?" The baron was frowning.

"She has a great talent for composing. I have watched her. She takes a melody and arranges for it so quickly, so brilliantly, that I could close my eyes and think a man was doing it!"

"Indeed! Unusual. It makes me uneasy to see a woman with such talents. It seems so unnatural. A woman's place is in the home, with her husband and children." The baron nodded decisively. He was eating some grapes absently, toying with them. He had much on his mind, it seemed.

"I agree," said Lukas, nevertheless thinking uneasily of his mother. "A woman is happiest when she has her children, and all goes well in the home. When she makes her husband comfortable, and soothes him. When her children do well morally, for her example. Yet—yet these two ladies have such talents. . . ."

"Well, well, they can have their music as a hobby when they marry," said Baron von Neumeister. "I am sure I would not stop my wife from playing."

Again Lukas thought of his mother, playing late in the evenings, her shoulders stooped from weariness, yet unable to stay away from the piano. And how his father would call her with irritation, to come and do something for him. Sometimes Lukas thought his father had disturbed her deliberately, jealous of her talents, wanting her full attention.

And now his mother could play again. He would return from an outing in Vienna, late, to hear music coming from the rooms downstairs, and he would find her, seated at the piano, playing almost as brilliantly as she had years ago. She was working hard on her music, yet she never performed in public.

Why, then, did she play? It must be to satisfy something inside herself, some drive, some deep emotion.

She was a good mother and had been a loyal and devoted wife. But now she suddenly seemed like a free bird, escaped from its cage, flying high toward the sun. Her face was radiant when she played, her blue eyes sparkled with joy.

Involuntarily his thoughts turned to Diana Ballantyne. He burned inside when he thought of the letter her father had written to her. He took her so for granted! How contemptuously he regarded her great musical talent. In return for long hours of work, he would offer her silks! He did not understand his daughter at all.

Yet Diana could not stay forever in Vienna. Her dreams of a career were destined to fail. Lukas had originally thought only to give her a year to remember, yet—yet—how sad when she would have to go home again, to a life such as his mother had had. A husband who was hard on her, children to drain her energies, a house that demanded all her energies, people pulling her in all directions—

A husband who did not appreciate her! Lukas flinched to think of Diana married to some brute of a fellow. Or a man indifferent to her charm, her beauty, her musical talent, her bright mind. An unfeeling brute, who wanted only to order her about—and control her money!

Diana was right. Money was the root of it all, for if a woman had money, she could do as she pleased, and no man could stop her. Diana was a lovely girl becoming a beautiful woman. If she had money, she could also have her career. If the critics scoffed, as they were sure to do, she could shrug and play for herself.

But she needed money. She wanted to play for a living, and she must be able to teach and give concerts. After this year, after April, he knew she could not. Her dreams were in vain, and he felt uneasy that he might be unjustly encouraging her by his actions. She was acting as though she had all her life to do this—but he knew better. One day she must return to her fate—and the man her father chose for her. He did not like the idea; in truth, it made him ill to think of it! But what could he do?

"It is interesting to me," his brother Theo was saying, in his slow thoughtful drawl, "how you are speaking of women, their place in the home and all that. Yet, Lukas, you have composed an opera about a different kind of woman."

Lukas looked at his brother in puzzlement. "What do you mean, Theo? Judith was a good faithful wife, who mourned her husband all her life."

"Yet—she did not remarry and have children," said Theo thoughtfully. "The Bible says, she went out, did this very brave courageous thing, and you know the song—how she sings that a woman did this courageous act, when the men could not! Remember that?"

Lukas nodded.

Stanislav said, "Well, no man could have gone out and seduced Holofernes, after all!" And he chuckled.

"Yes, well, it did take courage, and she volunteered, like a soldier in the army," pondered Theo, as though figuring it out in his brilliant head. "Then she went and did that, that horrible thing, you know—cut off his head with two strokes of the sword. That would take strength and courage, you know, lifting that heavy sword, daring to cut off the head, right in the enemy camp. And figuring out the whole thing, setting it up. Clever thing, that!"

"Well, women can be devious," observed Stanislav, nodding.

"Clever," insisted Theo. "Strength of mind and body. That would take physical strength—to cut off his head. But also mental strength, lots of thought, to figure out the whole plot. I have read several translations that differ in small points, but all agree in the main story of what she thought and did. Judith was a very strong woman. She figured out how to save them all, and they didn't lose a man!"

They all sat there, thinking about it.

And then Theo went on, drawing little lines on his place mat with his finger, "And then after the victory, and the celebrations, and all that, they gave Judith some of the loot from the camp. She gave it all to the altar at Jerusalem, not keeping any of it. She was wealthy, you know, had money of her own. She went home, and lived to a very old age, and she was respected more and more. But she did not remarry, though the Bible says she was very beautiful. Many men sought her, but she refused them all. She took care of her estate and that of her dead husband, and at her dying she freed her maid and gave all she had to relatives. Then she died an honorable death. She did not marry or have children—she just lived alone and did what she wanted, and everybody honored her. Not a usual good woman, was she?"

"She was mourning her dead husband, as a good woman should," said Baron von Neumeister.

Lukas was thinking, "But if she had had a close male relative, she might have had to marry him, so he could have control of all those riches!"

"Or he would have married her off to someone, so some man would have had control of it," said Theo placidly, nodding. "Instead, nobody had control of her, so she took care of it all and managed very well. How about that? Was she an unnatural woman? According to our lights she did all the wrong things! So—are we wrong?"

All three men were silent, while the maid brought in hot coffee and poured for them. Then she retired softly, leaving them to their coffee and brandy.

"But women today are inclined to be too headstrong and independent," said Stanislav wearily. "And when I marry, I would want a woman who would listen to me and not argue. She doesn't have to be meek, but I want to be the head of the family! I must be—I cannot divide my authority!"

"And I also," said Lukas. But he kept thinking of Diana, her face so radiant as she played and lost herself in the music. What if she did marry someone who did not appreciate her, who condemned her to a life so busy she had no time for music? Would that not be a waste of such a rich talent?

And she added so much to his life, had made him feel eager again. She had given to him as much as he had given her. He taught her, yes, but she made him listen, made him appreciate music even more. Her gentle compassionate nature had eased matters at the opera for him, too. He had worried about Johanne, but Diana had soothed her, had helped her become more confident, so that she sang well.

They communicated well about music. He was eager to hear her opinions and she was respectful, but told him what she thought. She had arranged several of his compositions beautifully, and he loved it when she played his music, as he no longer could. But for her talents his music would be lying incomplete and unplayed. In her company he felt more eager for life, and he did not mind his injury so much. Surprisingly enough she did not even seem to notice his crippled arm.

And when he had kissed her, she had not flinched. Her mouth had been soft and yielding under his. He longed to kiss her again—but knew he really must not. After all, she trusted him; she was his student.

He roused himself. "Well, it grows late. I have a suggestion for you, Stanislav." They had taken to using familiar names as they had become more friendly during the evening. "Why don't you check out of your hotel tomorrow and come and live with Theo and me? We come and go freely, and you may also."

"Well, well, it is very kind of you! I am rather poor, you know," said Stanislav sadly. "I should like to stay for a time and court my Alicia! I think she will take much courting, and I need time."

"Good, I think so also," said Lukas. "We shall take you back to the hotel tonight, so you can pack. Tomorrow my coachman and footmen will assist you in removing to us. We shall enjoy your company. The opening night of my opera is tomorrow night—you shall be my guest. And I would like you to come to rehearsals with us when you can, and see more of your reluctant fiancée! And, too, we shall become better acquainted."

"It is very kind of you. I am most grateful." Stanislav accepted the invitation gracefully and seemed genuinely pleased. Theo had taken to him also; he would be good company for them both. "I think my Alicia is somewhat fearful of me, and needs more chances for conversation with me. We shall get along better together when she comes to know me. I shall not give up easily, I assure you."

Chapter 11

In late November a cold snap had come, freezing a pond in the Prater. Captain Gardell Mueller and Captain Ernst Schmidt had called on Diana and Alicia at nine in the morning, in great excitement.

"You must come and ice-skate with us!" they clamored.

Pauline prepared to come with them. All dressed for the cold, and were soon seated in the grand carriage Captain Mueller had provided. Diana noticed the heraldic crest on the carriage.

"What crest is this?" she asked, as they sat back in the carriage. The men faced them, their backs to the horses, and surveyed the two ladies with great satisfaction.

Diana wore her favorite dark blue with black braid, and a warm blue velvet hat perched on her golden coronet of hair. Alicia's outfit was a rather similar green velvet with black braid, and a bright green bonnet. Pauline sat between them, demure in black.

The young officers, dressed in their scarlet-and-gold uniforms, with black hussar hats, outshone them all.

"My brother-in-law's," said Captain Mueller with a charming smile at Diana. "I ran over there at seven this morning, woke them all up, and demanded the carriage! Of course my beautiful sister came down in her negligée, and scolded me. When I told where we were going, she said she would meet us there for chocolate. She longs to be introduced to you."

"Oh—how—lovely," said Diana faintly. The formidable and stunning Countess Elza Mueller von Hulsen! At last they would meet.

She had seen her about town, in concert audiences, in her box at von Korda's successful opera. But they had never been formally introduced. She had been aware of the woman's black eyes staring at her, when von Korda had taken her on his arm to escort her at intermission. Were they still lovers? Diana hated that thought.

At the Prater they soon had on ice skates, and each captain was eager to teach his lovely lady the art of ice-skating and dancing on skates. Both girls had skated in the past, and they soon remembered the art of balancing on the slim sharp blades. Before long they were sailing across the ice, clinging to the attentive arms of their escorts.

What a glorious day it was! Diana thought she would never forget it. The sky had been a deep sullen black-gray, and frost outlined the black limbs of the barren trees. But now the sun was daring to peep from between some clouds, the black was breaking up, and lighter gray prevailed. Where the clouds parted, some blue showed, and the sun dazzled their eyes as it glinted off the ice. The ice was firm under their feet, solidly frozen to a depth of several inches.

The winds blew Diana's cheeks a deep pink and caught at her breath. Captain Mueller set a pace for her, and she enjoyed the challenge; they fairly flew across the ice from one end of the pond to the other and back again.

Some sympathetic soul in a café nearby opened the doors and out floated the strains of a hired trio playing dance music. The melodies rang across the ice, turning the scene into an enchantment.

Captain Mueller looked dazzling and Diana felt so happy and light.

Everything was going so well in her world, but for one thing.

Von Korda's opera had been retained for the whole autumn season. It had been a great success, and he was very satisfied. Johanne had been engaged for a series of café dates in a very prestigious café, thanks to von Korda's efforts. Johanne had done so well, she had much more confidence now, and von Korda had been very pleased with her.

Diana had been improving rapidly under von Korda's guidance, and lately he had expressed generous praise for her work. Moreover, he had arranged several more concert appearances for her. In October she had had six dates with a small chamber group, and two appearances to perform duets for piano and violin. She and Alicia had done those. They had worked well together, and had enjoyed it. Von Korda had directed them both. He seemed to like Alicia, and undertook her instruction when her instructor was out of the city for a time.

There was only one problem. Von Korda seemed to have turned cool toward her. She puzzled over it. The change seemed to date back to the opera opening, but she could not imagine how she might have offended him. However, for the past month there had been little informality between them. Suddenly he was all business, as he had been in the very beginning.

In quiet dismay and disappointment she had turned to Captain Mueller. *He* liked her wholeheartedly. He flattered her, charmed her, made her laugh, enjoyed taking her out. They met often now in cafés, with Pauline always present, and sometimes Alicia or even Johanne Weiss. He was courting her, he told her, but with such a laugh she did not know if he was serious. He kissed her hand, looked to her lips longingly, but was never too bold.

Lukas had warned her against Captain Mueller. Why? Lukas was the lover of Mueller's sister, all the world knew it. Diana remembered that voluptuous woman ascending the staircase at the von Korda house, and flinched to think of them together, intimately.

If Lukas von Korda could have Elza von Hulsen as his mistress, then surely it could not be wrong for Diana to go out innocently with her brother!

Diana was feeling rebellious. She, too, wanted fun, before she had to settle down to a marriage she detested, to long hours of unappreciated hard work.

No matter how much she hoped to make a career of her music, some fatal fear inside her caused her to believe it could never happen. This would be her year of happiness, her year of music, but it was never to happen again. At the end of it she must return home to England, to her duties, to become once again the obedient daughter, and an obedient wife and—and mother of the children Montague would give her.

Now she laughed almost hysterically at a remark of Captain Mueller, pushing away the thought of the long dull years to come. She would have fun. She would not be cautious and refuse such innocent expeditions as this one. So Captain Mueller admired her, and made naughty remarks sometimes—she did not care! Lukas could warn her and frown disapprovingly—but *he* was reckless in his affair with a married woman, Gardell's sister!

It pained Diana to think of Lukas with the black-eyed beauty. To think of that generous mouth pressing on the seductive scarlet mouth of the married woman; the lips that had touched Diana's and made her dream headily of love. Elza was the kind that made men mad and reckless.

Elza obviously drove Lukas mad. Sometimes Diana could see sadness in his vivid blue eyes. Did he wish to marry Elza, but knew she would never be free of her cruel husband? Vienna whispered about Elza and the huge middle-aged Count Heinrich von Hulsen. Cruel, he was, a bully. Sometimes there were bruises on her white arms, and one could see when her sleeves were sheer that he beat her. One night at the opera she had a dark red slash across her face. Afterward she had gone to the country for a month, until the cut had healed.

Diana felt sick at the whispers. How did Lukas feel, to know his beloved was treated so? Diana turned again to Captain Mueller with a feverish laugh. She wanted to forget all that. Her companion was amusing, flattering, gallant. So he had a wicked reputation and people gossiped. She did not care! This was her year to have fun. Anyway, Lukas von Korda was deeply in love with Elza—he could certainly not be serious about Diana, though she did often lie awake nights remembering his kisses.

Enough of this. She would amuse herself with Gardell!

Though he called her "Diana," she still called him Captain Mueller. She rebuffed him if he tried to get intimate, but his attentions, his flowers, his boxes of chocolates, his evident appreciation of her charms, were all very pleasing. He even attended two of her concerts, when he could get away from his duties, and praised her to the skies.

"You are even more brilliant than I had thought," he had said gravely, after one performance. "You know, I am almost afraid of you, you are so talented!"

"Oh, pooh, nonsense, you are teasing me." She had laughed, but the praise had been sweet indeed.

Today he was at his most charming—laughing, making her giggle with his silly jokes, his exaggerated tales of some long-ago adventure in battle. She laughed until she had to cling to both his arms to keep her balance.

"How beautiful you are today, dear Diana."

"You mean, I am often ugly," she answered, laughing up at him.

"Never!" He pretended horror, and she giggled again. "Only today, your cheeks are more pink, your eyes are more blue, your beautiful body is more graceful, your feet are as fleet as Atalanta's—"

"Didn't she lose the race?" asked Diana demurely, her laughing blue eyes raised to his. "And Venus turned her into a lioness for not thanking her—"

"And her lover was turned into a lion—grrrr!" said Mueller, absurdly, growling into her shoulder, bending over her devotedly.

Diana's laughter trilled across the park in the cold crisp air, attracting the glances of many on the pond and in the café beyond.

The skating music changed to a waltz. Gardell Mueller immediately cried out, "Let us dance!" and drew her into his arms. She had no fear. He was so strong, she could feel the hard muscles of his shoulder and arm as she placed her arm lightly along his. His other hand clasped hers, and they were off! To the strains of the Strauss waltz they glided about the pond, and others made way for them, or joined them in the gay lilting melody. .

Diana's full skirts whirled about her long slim legs, and the cold air blowing against her heated body made her feel gay and giddy and happy. What could be more delightful than dancing here in the open air, their steps matching, their skates whirling on the frosty ice, as the sun shone above them?

The waltz finally ended, and they resumed a more sedate position, clasping hands and skating across the pond and back again.

Several times they paused by the side of the pond, walked up on the frosted grass, gingerly, and sat down on the nearby benches. There they would talk, sometimes with Alicia and Captain Schmidt who were also enjoying the skating and ice-dancing. Then back onto the pond they would go to enjoy it before the autumn sun melted some of the ice.

Finally about eleven, Captain Mueller called a halt. "I feel in dire need of hot chocolate and many pastries!" he cried boyishly, pulling her by the hand to the side of the pond. He unlaced her boots, took off the skates, and helped her put on again her own black smart high boots.

Then he changed his own skates, and they all four went into the café. She and Alicia went back to the pretty ladies' powder room, and washed their hands and smoothed their hair. They chatted a few minutes about how much they had enjoyed the ice.

When they came out, a lady was at the table with the captains and Pauline. A beautiful woman in a smart scarlet jacket and dress that showed off her hourglass figure, very slim waist, full breasts and thighs. The Countess Elza Mueller von Hulsen! In person, and up close, as Diana had never seen her.

The captains rose. "Permit me to introduce you to my sister," said Captain Mueller, with pride in his tone. "Elza, my dear, may I introduce to you— Fraulein Diana Ballantyne—Fraulein Alicia Huntingdon."

Diana looked full into the face and received a little shock. Elza was so stunningly beautiful! Creamy rose cheeks, large melting black eyes framed by long curling black lashes, a mouth that was red and large and imperious. Her hair was black, with long curls to her shoulders and the rest in a huge chignon, set off by a scarlet picture hat with black plumes. And her expression—she looked as fiery as a gypsy. Diana remembered that she and her brother were part Hungarian.

She smiled, shook hands, sat down. Countess Elza turned to her brother. "But how pretty she is!" she cried. "Like the picture on a chocolate box!"

Diana felt vaguely insulted. Had the remark been meant as an insult? The girls on the chocolate boxes looked so—doll-like! But perhaps she had meant to flatter.

Alicia eyed the woman with grave reserve, her laughter dashed for the moment. She said little, leaving the conversation to the men and Diana.

"How beautiful you looked on the ice, Gardell!" said Elza to her brother. "Remember how we used to dance on the ice at home? We would stay out for so many hours that we would go home frozen, and would have to drink much to get warm again!" She laughed, and her pearly teeth looked sharp and vixenish.

Diana was surprised at her thoughts. She felt this woman was dangerous. But how silly—perhaps she was prejudiced because she had been the object of the duel between von Hulsen and von Korda.

Diana drank her chocolate. She sampled a strawberry tart, but one taste told her it was too sweet. Had the day gone wrong? The feelings of excitement and pleasure were dying in her.

Elza finally rose and picked up her gloves. "There, I must join my other friends," she said prettily. "I was so entranced by your beautiful companions, Gardell, I forgot my own engagement. Good-bye, everyone, I will see you around Vienna!"

They smiled and said good-bye, and she reached up and kissed her brother's cheek lingeringly.

"Good-bye, my dearest sister," said Gardell, and kissed her on the mouth.

"Darling, darling Gardell," murmured Elza, and put her hand to his cheek before turning away.

Diana felt a sharp shock go through her as she witnessed this scene. Her family had been close, yes, but she could not imagine kissing her brothers like that, in public or in private! It must be true, what was said about the Hungarians being very emotional and demonstrative.

Elza left them, making her way to a table near the window. Then Diana felt another deeper shock—jealousy. For the blond-haired man who rose gravely to meet the countess was Baron Lukas von Korda.

He had been sitting there, observing them, and with him an older woman, the Countess Puffenbach, the one Alicia derided as the Countess Puff-Puff. She was a fluttery aging woman who sponsored charity events and had presented both Diana and Alicia in concerts for some of her causes.

Von Korda watched Elza coming toward him, and his face was hard and expressionless. From where she sat Diana could not read his blue eyes. He bowed, lifted the countess's hand almost to his lips, but did not kiss it. They spoke. He seated her and slowly sat down again. She leaned to him, spoke, and he laughed!

They were meeting in public! Diana felt deep shock. It was one thing to know they met privately in von Korda's home, and another to see them flaunt their affair openly. She felt ashamed of him.

Through her jealousy she felt disgust also. That he should so chase a married woman! She had honored and respected von Korda. And here he was meeting again the married woman over whom he had fought a duel—in public, unashamed!

Captain Mueller sat down beside her, in the chair his sister had just vacated. Pauline looked up from the stock of gaudy journals he always supplied her—he knew her taste for gossip and seemed to enjoy providing her with several of the latest titillating journals.

"I was afraid of this," he said in a low voice. Of course they were all curiosity. "She is meeting him again!"

"The baron?" asked Alicia, with a quick glance at Diana.

"Yes, the same. You know about the duel?"

Diana said, with reserve, "I have heard of it." The Austrians seemed fond of dueling, she thought. All of them seemed proud of the dueling scars on their faces. Duels had been outlawed in England almost a century ago, when too many of the prince regent's friends died in them. He forbade them to duel, and sometimes sent violators abroad for a year. Any dueling done now was done in secret, and it was against the law.

"Von Korda shamelessly pursued my sister," said Mueller, with a deep sigh. "Who could help loving her? She is adorable! She has always been stunningly beautiful! I can remember as a boy, I would come to her bedroom to watch her don her evening dress and jewels—I thought she was a goddess! When she married and left home, I did not want to remain—that was when I went into the army."

"And became your wild self," observed the smirking Captain Schmidt. Mueller jokingly threatened him with an upraised fist, and both men laughed.

The girls laughed also, Diana without mirth. She felt uneasy, disappointed in von Korda. The affair must have gone on for years. Did he have no shame?

Mueller continued, "I knew there was trouble with my sister and her husband—oh, I betray no confidences! All Austria knew they quarreled. She is very passionate, he is cool. She allowed von Korda's attentions, and at first her husband told her she was frivolous. He then accused her of more—wanton—behavior. Von Korda, to his credit, defended her, and they fought. It was a wild battle—I was there as my brother-in-law's second. They were pretty evenly matched. We stopped the fight when it looked as though it might go beyond the bounds of chivalry—but they tried to fight on!"

His nostrils dilated. He looked sullen and passionate, as though enjoying the memory.

"Both lunged at the same moment," he continued in a low tone, and all at the table were leaning forward to hear him clearly. Pauline's eyes were huge and fascinated. He seemed to be speaking to her. "Both were injured. We had to carry them off the field. My brother-in-law recovered, and reconciled with Elza, of course. Who could resist her? They were closer then, and are devoted to each other.

"But von Korda—his left arm was injured, and he retired to his castle and sulked for two years. When he returned, he played the piano no more, and we realized he had been vitally hurt in his left arm." Gardell did not sound at all sorry!

Diana was appalled at his story. She felt horrified at the tale of the love affair and the duel. How could he have forced his attentions on a married woman, no matter how beautiful? And the duel! Such wild and strange passions seemed foreign to her. She had been gently brought up, in such a cool manner. She could not imagine anybody dueling for her! She would not allow it, of course. These men were definitely not like the cool English.

Oddly enough, Mueller had said nothing of von Hulsen's cruelty. He evidently loved his sister deeply—didn't he care that her husband hurt her? It was a great puzzle to Diana. She had a strong suspicion that she did not know the whole truth yet. But of course it was not her business anyway.

"I warned my sister not to see him anymore. But I know von Korda has been pursuing her again. Look at them now!"

All instinctively turned to that other table near the window. Elza was speaking and laughing, while von Korda gazed at her intently, gravely, his blue eyes enigmatic.

"No," said Mueller. "He cannot stay away from her. And Elza—well, we are a passionate family! I fear for her. I begged Elza—but she is drawn to him—he is an attractive brute, I will say that!"

Diana would not have described von Korda like that. She would have said handsome, charming, serious, talented. The picture of him as an attractive brute irresistibly drawn to a forbidden woman was a strange one to her. She would have thought him more—more—

More what? she wondered as they ate pastries and

"No, no, you go on too fast," she protested, as mildly as possible, while her hands fidgeted in her lap under the café table. She remained cool, her smile unaltered. "I changed color merely because of your suggestions! He is very correct. He is an excellent instructor. I honor him."

He stared at her keenly, and she gazed back blandly. He shook his head. "Well, well, if he troubles you, you must tell me at once!" he said, still fierce. "It is bad enough that my own beloved sister is involved with him, but she is older, she is married. But you, a lovely unmarried girl, a stranger in Austria—no, it is too much—"

Alicia had been listening with a troubled expression, and now she intervened hotly. "Nonsense! Diana would not permit it, even if von Korda tried such a thing, which I don't believe he would. You go on too wildly, Captain Mueller. Diana is not the kind of girl to permit anything at all. She is a good fine girl, and I wish you would not say such things. Gossip starts all too readily this way. Honestly, even in New York they don't talk like this. And dueling—really!"

"Well, if I am wrong, I must say—I would be relieved. But von Korda is such a fellow—"

"Von Korda is a fine man, and I find it difficult to believe he behaved in this manner with your sister," said Alicia with such bluntness that Diana blushed. "However, that is neither here nor there with us. Diana is innocent of any wrong behavior, I assure you. I have known her for months, and she is utterly incapable of low behavior!"

"Thank you, Alicia," murmured Diana gratefully. She hoped that would end the distasteful conversation. Gossip did start quickly in Vienna, and grew to lurid proportions. She had no wish to be the object of any, and of course she and von Korda had a close working relationship at stake.

"I am happy to hear it," said Mueller, with a suddenly mischievous expression on his handsome charming face. His black eyes sparkled. "But Diana has a beautiful mouth, and I can well hope that one day she will be passionate as well! Only I hope she will show it to me, and not to any other man!"

Alicia shoved back her chair. "I find this conversation has become too loose," she said, with unusual forcefulness and coldness. "I think we must leave now. We are expected home for luncheon, and we both have practicing to do!"

"Yes, we must leave," said Diana, and stood also. Pauline, who had listened with silent shock, stood hastily also. "Thank you for the lovely day—we enjoyed the skating."

Alicia was moving toward the door. The captains followed, bearing forgotten gloves, with protestations that they had not meant to insult. Alicia insisted on hiring a carriage at the Prater gates, and they were off in a fiacre before Captain Mueller could persuade them into the borrowed carriage.

Diana was silent on the way home, while Alicia was muttering, "They go too far, they are too fresh! We must not allow gossip! I cannot believe all he said!"

Pauline looked with troubled glances at the two pretty girls, and shook her graying head. "They are handsome, but one knows what military men are! One hears rumors about them," she whispered.

"I cannot believe all he said about von Korda. I have found him charming, courteous, never fresh or insulting, not one gesture of insulting behavior!" said Alicia, shaking her red hair, in unconscious imitation of Pauline.

Diana said nothing. She should have stood up for von Korda, as Alicia did, but she was too emotionally involved. She did not want to believe ill of him, but he *had* dueled over Elza von Hulsen, he *had* fought for her honor. And he had met her again in the café! How often had they met since the duel? How often had he met her this summer and autumn? She felt jealous, she admitted it. She burned when she remembered that figure on the stairway. She had been strongly attracted to Lukas von Korda. He had been so very good to her, and she had even thought she might be starting to love him. But could there be love without trust? And he was not for her, a wealthy Austrian baron, a brilliant musician. No, she must forget about that. He was not for her—yet . . .

He had kissed her, and she could not forget those warm strong kisses.

But clearly he was still involved with the countess. He was her lover—everybody knew it but a few innocent women like Alicia. Diana felt weary at the thought. She was learning much about the world this year in Vienna, and it was not all pleasant. That her admired Maestro was involved in a sordid affair made her feel ill. Yet on meeting Elza, seeing her beauty, one could understand how a man could desire her. She was so vibrant and lovely, she made Diana feel pallid—like the girl on the cover of a chocolate box.

Well, if Lukas von Korda could continue to meet Elza openly, and keep her as his mistress, Diana could have fun also! So Captain Mueller was devilish, she knew that by the wicked lights in his eyes, by his daring speech. But he was fun, also, and she deserved some fun in her year of freedom.

At least she met him in cafés, and with a chaperon! Nothing could happen to her in the presence of the

sturdy watchful Pauline. She would be wary and enjoy
herself. And if Lukas von Korda scolded her again,
she—she just might confront him with a challenge!

But no—she would never hurt him so. She sighed
deeply and forced a bright smile as they climbed down
from the carriage.

Chapter 12

~~~~~~

The doors connecting the drawing room, the wide marble hall and the palm-filled conservatory were all open. Chairs filled the rooms and smart ladies and languid gentlemen filled the chairs.

The Countess Puff-Puff was giving a concert for charity.

Today there must have been more than two hundred persons present. Fortunately the late November day was cold and snowy, and a few opened windows were sufficient to cool off the overcrowded rooms.

Alicia opened her white ostrich-feather fan with a brisk snap and fanned herself vigorously for a moment. She was warm in her smart gray velvet gown and matching cloak. A small matching gray velvet hat sat on her fiery red hair.

Moritz Osterley leaned over to her. "A very large crowd, and all wealthy," he whispered in excitement. "Everyone comes to the concerts of von Korda!"

"Yes, you shall be very well heard today!" she replied. She patted his hand, knowing how excited he got when his musical compositions had a new audience. "They shall applaud you loudly!"

"Yes, and I shall give both hands in the applause!" said a smooth suave voice at her shoulder. She turned sharply, to meet the smile of Stanislav von Neumeister. Oh, heavens, could she go nowhere in Vienna without running into him!

"Hello, good day," she muttered, and turned back. Moritz Osterley beamed at Stanislav.

"How kind of you. How are you, Baron?" They shook hands, standing, clicking heels, bobbing heads at each other, she noted with intense irritation. "Yes, yes, I am very excited. Miss Ballantyne plays a composition of mine today, one of my latest piano sonatas!"

"Good, good, I shall be pleased to hear it. Are you going out to a café afterward?" Stanislav directed his look and voice to Alicia, but Moritz answered.

"I hope to persuade Miss Huntingdon—"

"No, no, I cannot today!" Alicia said hastily. She fumed inside. She dearly would have loved to go out, but she would refuse if Baron von Neumeister tagged along! She saw him too much. His blue eyes disturbed her, the way they were always watching her!

She turned her shoulders squarely to him, and nodded to various ladies in the hall. There was Johanne Weiss with her cellist, Arnold Lindau. Was that getting serious? They were often now in public, and Johanne wore a glow. . . .

Rosalie Stamitz was seated with Frau Lewisohn on one side and a young artist fellow on the other. The artist, Peter Hering, had invited all the ladies of the boardinghouse to his studio one morning. Alicia had gone and had been rather impressed with his serious work. She might have her father buy something of his. After all, he was a rising young artist, and her father liked landscapes like those he painted—of mountains and valleys and great trees, and flowers.

He had wanted to paint Alicia's portrait, and although she had refused for now, she suspected it might be rather fun to do before she went home. Sometime she must face the thought of going home to New York City, but not now.

Moritz sat down. "I see the Countess Elza von Hulsen coming in. What a beautiful woman!" he whispered.

Alicia turned her head to observe the glorious entrance of the countess on the arms of two beaux, dressed in her favorite scarlet. Her gown was of bright velvet, trimmed with black mink, her picture hat a masterpiece of crushed velvet with a wide brim which would surely block the view of three people behind her in the chairs. I don't like that female, thought Alicia. Is it envy? Or is she one of those women who bring out the worst in other women? Dresses too well, attracts too much attention, a bit of devil in her . . .

The Countess Puffenbach fluttered forward. People sank into their seats, and quiet descended.

The countess climbed the two steps to the platform where a magnificent grand piano stood. She was a fine hostess, thought Alicia. She genuinely loved music, and was devoted to charity, and the two were combined elegantly in her life.

"I am so happy to welcome you today," she said, and talked about her charity earnestly for about ten minutes. The audience was polite. The Baron von Korda in an elegant blue velvet suit with gold waistcoat stood listening at the side of the room. Beside him stood Diana, looking beautiful and composed.

"I should be going mad," whispered Alicia to Moritz, as the audience politely applauded the Countess Puff-Puff's speech. "How can she be so calm?"

"No nerves," whispered Moritz. "Magnificent performer!"

Diana was brought forward on the hand of von Korda. She and Alicia had chosen her gown—it was of white silk brocade embroidered in silvery spider-web tracery. The gown was an evening dress, with wide skirts bordered with white fox fur. The sleeves were brief: white fox on her shoulders that showed off her lovely strong white arms Her hair was dressed severely. Too severely, Pauline and Alicia had concluded, and had persuaded Diana to allow Pauline to bring forward a few little curls of hair on her broad white forehead and beside her ears. Now she looked demure and sweet as well as composed.

Von Korda spoke as Diana arranged herself on the piano bench and gently tested the pedals. She had brought no music with her, no sheets to distract her. Alicia had protested, "What if you forget?"

"I shall not forget, I have played the pieces many times," said Diana.

They had not even raised the music rack. The piano lid had been set back and propped up, and now Diana in white made a striking figure sitting before the dark shining piano.

"I am happy to present to you my pupil, Miss Diana Ballantyne. She will begin with three numbers of Frederic Chopin. First the Polonaise no. 3 in A major, the "Military Polonaise." Then two of his beautiful waltzes."

Happy applause greeted his words. Chopin was a favorite of audiences everywhere. Diana had quoted von Korda to Alicia, "We shall begin with the sweet wine of Chopin, go on to the meat and potatoes of Beethoven and Moritz Osterley, and von Korda's own sonata, then conclude with the pastries of Strauss! For the waltzes of Johann Strauss are as light, delicious, and sweet as the puff pastries of Vienna!"

Alicia glowed with pride as her friend began. In the first moments she appreciated the beauty of the lovely girl at the piano, her silvery-gold head outlined against the deep blue walls of the drawing room, her delicate profile as she bent over her hands at the piano.

Then she was caught up in the music, the drama of the playing. Diana was playing better and better all the time, she thought. There was more emotion in it now, yet she retained a lovely classic simplicity of style.

She finished, leaving the joyous sound of the Chopin waltz in their ears. The polite applause of gloved hands and beaming smiles acknowledged her performance. Alicia glanced over the audience, wanting them to like Diana. Most looked impressed and appreciative. But then she caught the cold critical look of the Countess von Hulsen, the scarlet-gloved hands in her lap, her wide black eyes staring right at Diana. Alicia felt a sudden shiver down her spine.

There was a slight pause, to allow a few latecomers to squeeze into the few remaining seats. Others in the audience stood against the wall of the conservatory, peering around palm leaves or over pots of forced roses. It was a very good crowd.

Von Korda came forward as Diana seated herself again at the piano after her bows.

"We have a fine new young composer in Vienna, and Miss Ballantyne will now present a piano sonata of his, which he composed especially for her. Mr. Moritz Osterley had his training at the Conservatory of Vienna." He went on to tell briefly of his training.

Then he motioned to the nervous composer beside Alicia. "Mr. Osterley is here today."

Moritz jumped up, clicked his heels together, beamed boyishly on them all, tossed back his long curly hair, clicked his heels again. Stanislav was loudly applauding behind Alicia. She could hear the sounding smacks of his big hands. Moritz bowed again and sat down, sighing with happiness.

Von Korda left the stage, and Diana began to play. Alicia had heard her practicing this sonata and knew the music was good, but even so she was amazed at its power and passion.

Moritz had so much music in his soul! Alicia listened critically, but found no fault with the music or the playing. Diana was intent on the music, her head bent to it, listening for the notes, bending back to allow her arms the full sweep of the keyboard. Her tone was rich, her playing sure, and the sonata itself magnificent.

The piece ended softly, and Diana let her hands rest on the keys for a moment. Then applause swept the room, and she stood, smiled, bowed, and held out her arm in the direction of Moritz.

He bobbed up, smiled shyly, nodded, and clicked his heels. Alicia and Stanislav applauded madly. When he sat down, Stanislav leaned forward at Alicia's shoulder and whispered, "Magnificent, dear fellow! I enjoyed it immensely!"

Alicia held herself stiff, as she felt his breath on her bare shoulder where the velvet gown revealed her white flesh. She felt his hand on her back as he braced himself against her chair—was he doing this on purpose? He was always touching her, seemingly innocently. But she was always intensely aware of him.

"Thank you, thank you! You are most kind, most kind. I cannot thank you enough. . . ." Moritz finally stopped thanking him, they straightened themselves in the chairs, and the music continued.

A Beethoven sonata was next, and Diana played it with power and feeling. How she could play! Alicia would close her eyes for a moment, feeling the deliciousness of the music flowing through her. Then she would open them, to see the form of her friend at the piano, playing with serious exalted face, her large hands crashing chords, or playing so lightly one had to strain to hear the soft notes.

At the intermission Diana disappeared through a door with the Countess Puff-Puff, and the guests stood up, talking among themselves and moving about. Alicia was forced to endure Stanislav, who deliberately kept the attention of both her and Moritz Osterley. People came up to them and congratulated Moritz. Alicia remained beside him silently, waving her fan slowly to hide her face.

While Moritz was talking earnestly to some small frail lady about sonorities, Stanislav turned to Alicia and took her fan from her. Deliberately he waved it at her and leaned toward her.

"This is not too much?" he murmured, his face close to hers.

"Give me back my fan!"

"You have such a temper." He sighed, his blue eyes mocking. "I do not mean to steal it from you!" And he fanned her again.

She would not please him by making a scene and snatching the fan from him. Instead she just stood, her eyes flashing at him furiously.

"The Countess Elza is not pleased by Diana's beauty," whispered Stanislav. "And I don't see her brother here."

Alicia forgot her own problems for a moment. "I thought she looked—angry," she muttered.

"Likes the limelight herself," he whispered, and she nodded, for once pleased with him. She knew he was staying with von Korda. She longed to ask him what von Korda thought of the Countess Elza, but of course she could not.

"Diana plays so very well," he went on, in a whisper, close to her ear. She hated to admit it to herself, but she suddenly felt a thrill that was purely sensual. He was a big handsome man, that was all—she was not moved by *him,* not himself personally. She detested him. "One could close one's eyes and think a man was playing!"

Alicia compressed her lips, but had to nod. "She plays strongly, and so clearly, and with such feeling," she said.

"Sometimes when she plays in the drawing room, in her lessons with von Korda, I have thought he had a man pupil there. But when I have gone down at the end of the hour and seen Diana emerging, looking so fragile and lovely, it always amazes me."

"She is not fragile. She is very strong, both physically and mentally," said Alicia firmly.

"I believe it," he said solemnly. "And so are you, my dear Alicia."

She was inwardly pleased, but frowned at him.

"You will go out today, after the concert?" he coaxed.

So he had been flattering her! What a fool she was, always to fall for his flattery!

"No, I cannot," she said, and sat down. He restored her fan to her as the audience returned to their seats, and the last whispers of conversation died away.

Diana played next a sonata of Brahms. Only the

musicians in the audience could appreciate its difficulty. Next she played a short flashy piece by Liszt, a "display" piece to show off her dexterity and virtuosity, which pleased the audience no end. The fact that it was fiendishly difficult to play escaped most of them, but not Osterley.

He was murmuring with admiration during the last measures of trills and complicated runs, then exploded with wildly clapping hands and cheers at the end. Stanislav imitated him, and their clapping almost drowned Alicia's applause. She beamed and beamed at the smiling girl on the platform, looking in her misty silver and silky white as though she would be capable of nothing more difficult than a waltz step.

Diana sat down again as von Korda stepped up on the platform.

"Next Miss Ballantyne will play a composition of mine. I had not completed it; but as she is a fine composer she has completed it for me, and is now going to play it. I do not normally name my compositions," he went on smoothly over their incredulous gasps. "However, Miss Ballantyne says it reminds her of the ocean waves and has named it the 'Seaside Sonata.'" He bowed and left the platform.

Near her Alicia heard a man mutter to another man beside him, "A woman composer? Nonsense, nonsense, he flatters her, he exaggerates! Von Korda is overcome with her beauty!"

Alicia glared at them, but they did not see her. She had watched in silence one day, as Diana had finished the last notes of a composition and had written them in the bass clef with her fine hand under the heavy black ink of von Korda's notes. One could see clearly on the music sheets what von Korda had written and what Diana had done, their handwriting and notes were so different. Alicia knew what her friend had done, even if the men in the audience would not acknowledge it. Nevertheless—Diana would be known someday, thought Alicia.

Diana played the music. The rolls of the left hand became the ocean waves, the sweet melodies of the right the sunlight, the birds, the joys of a beach in summer. One could almost hear the laughter of children, against the deep ominous rolling of the ocean waves. The sonata ended with a brilliant display of cross-hands playing, as the right drummed the deep chords and runs of the bass, and the left played a dreamy melody. With a final sparkle of sound it was over.

The audience applauded well. Von Korda seemed pleased as he took his bows, and Diana took hers, motioning with her white arm to the composer.

"To conclude," said Lukas von Korda with emphasis, in case the society audience was becoming restless: "As we all know, the jubilee of our beloved Viennese Waltz King is coming this next year. The fiftieth year of the conducting and composing of Johann Strauss will be celebrated throughout the land this coming year. Miss Ballantyne wishes to begin a celebration of her own in honor of him. She has brought together an arrangement of several of his most enticing waltzes. Miss Ballantyne."

He sat down. Diana fully enjoyed the following performances. She played the waltzes as though she were dancing them, swaying her slim body on the piano bench, smiling when a few overenthusiastic ladies in the audience began to hum along! The popular Waltz King was celebrated in satisfactory manner, and the applause was loud and happy at the end of the concert.

"Beautiful, lovely, how marvelous, how she can play, for a girl!" Alicia overheard the mutters, the comments. "Fine—for a woman—very nice, for a lady. She plays well. Very pretty!"

Alicia burned inside herself, but knew this type of comment was to be expected. Von Korda had warned her, and also Diana, though they did not want to believe him completely. She turned, smiled vaguely in Stanislav's direction, and piloted herself firmly through the seas of bodies toward Frau Lewisohn. Now she would go home! She would not go out with Moritz—he had plenty of friends here. And she would not run into Stanislav again today!

Johanne Weiss and her escort, Arnold Lindau, made their way through the crowd of well-dressed bodies to the entrance of the huge town house of the Countess Puffenbach. Johanne silently admired the huge marble statues in the hallway, the stained glass windows, and carved wooden chests, the elaborate pedestals holding baskets of fresh flowers.

So far had she come, to be in such a home as an invited guest of the artist! Diana Ballantyne had given her two tickets, and Herr Lindau had been delighted to come as her escort.

Carriages of all sizes, fiacres, and barouches, jammed into the streets outside. The squares were filled with horses and coachmen, footmen and carts and landaus, all crammed into every available foot of space.

Herr Lindau took Johanne's arm tenderly and pushed his way forward, keeping her slightly behind him. They finally found their way, squeezing through small spaces, and dashing across streets until they came to an open area beyond the boundaries of the crowd.

Johanne's smart blue crepe walking hat was shoved to one side, her skirts muddied along the way. But she was laughing and gay, and Arnold smiled into her bright eyes, as they strode away together.

"Whew, what a mob! There must have been a couple hundred there. What a smart group! That we have been in such society!" he marveled. "I cannot thank you enough for inviting me. It was most kind."

"I knew you would enjoy the music," she said. "Did you enjoy Diana's playing?"

"Oh, yes, above all things," he said, soberly. "What beauty she has. I walk now with the memory of the music under my feet, as if on a cloud. Her touch—how strong, how fine. Magnificent. And her choice of numbers, so smart. She appealed to the audience so cleverly."

"Yes, yes, it was Baron von Korda who chose," said Johanne. "He is her Maestro, her mentor. So very wise."

"Hum, yes. I enjoyed his own composition. He has much talent! Remember the chorale of the opera—" And he hummed the melody.

"How can I forget? My debut—and he is so kind. I have such offers of engagements. And if the opera is performed again next winter, he said he will engage me again!"

"He adores your magnificent voice. Who could help it?"

"Thank you," she murmured. He still held her arm, and though there was no crowd now, she did not feel like removing herself from its protection.

They turned into a smart corner café, where the owner recognized them both from previous visits. Johanne was making a name for herself in the music world and was starting to be recognized quite frequently. They were bowed to a table in the corner which they had chosen, and the waiter was beckoned imperiously.

They ordered black coffee and plain bread and butter, with jam. The coffee came promptly, and around them they were aware of people stealing looks at Johanne. "I am sure she is *someone*," insisted a high-pitched voice. "She looks like *someone*."

Johanne exchanged a little smile with Arnold Lindau.

"You see?" he whispered. "You are someone! But already I knew it! My children ask after you daily. You will come to dinner sometime soon again? Perhaps on next Wednesday?"

She did not sing Wednesdays, as he knew. "I think I may be able to come," she said, lashes lowered to hide her joy. He wished for her company, and the children asked for her too!

"Good. Good." He leaned back, smiling happily. "What a fine day it is! How happy I am! My children are well, my music goes well, and now today—what joy!"

She felt the same way, as though her cup was overflowing. Could it last? Could it be true, that he was coming to love her, as his eyes said?

She took refuge in a safe topic. "I thought the music of Herr Osterley showed much promise. He seems so young and foolish—I mean—"

"I know—do not apologize for saying your thoughts to me," said Arnold Lindau with a smile. "He has such a puppy-like air, he shakes his curls about, he bobs up and down. But he has a fine talent. One cannot judge by the outside, can one?"

"No, that is very true. His music shows much soul and emotion. Also I thought his structure was sound: the theme, then the variations, a fine fugue—"

"Yes, he carried one along. He composes as a happy child sings, and one is struck at first with the melodies. Then one listens again and hears maturity—it is surprising. Like my Cornelia when she makes a smart remark, and I realize it is wise. The other day she told me my face was smoother now, with fewer wrinkles. I must be happy, she said. She was right!"

They exchanged a tender laugh. He was telling her he was happier since he had met her, and she felt the same way!

Rosalie had slipped away from the concert with her artist friend, Peter Hering. Frau Lewisohn knew Rosalie posed for him, and though she did not approve, she knew the girl must make some money. So she let it pass.

Peter would keep his mouth shut. He was a diplomat, and a bit of a cynic. Rosalie said farewell to him at the opera corner, and sped on her way a few blocks farther, to her lover.

She was tempted to race up the three flights of stairs, but she waited demurely for the small lift to arrive, then entered, admiring as always the little velvet seat and the gold painted bars of the open cage as she pressed the button for the second level.

She arrived, opened the cage, closed it after her, and went to the opened door. Herr Franz Volger had heard her coming, and welcomed her. Dressed in a smart lounge robe of bright red, he was so handsome, with his large black eyes, his long eyelashes, his fine plump figure! Rosalie slipped inside and turned to him as he shut the door.

"My little tiny darling!" He welcomed her warmly, his arms enfolding her to his plump hard chest. His kisses smothered her mouth, her cheeks, her eyes.

Sometimes he hurt her a little, he would hug her so hard! But she welcomed it, she enjoyed it, a bit of rough play spiced their caresses.

"My darling Franz, my dearest snuggins," she whispered in his ear.

"Hum, hum, you smell so good! You taste so good!" He bit her smooth shoulder in a sharp bite.

"Ouch, you hurt your love," she reproached him, and drew back. She tapped his cheek sharply, daringly.

He grinned at her, showing his sharp pointed teeth. Pushing her before him into his overwarm living room, he indicated the tea tray.

"You will be hungry, so see what I have for you!"

Hot tea, hot cream, honey! And a tray of delicious pastries.

He adored such pastries. She could eat just one and be full, but she knew he expected her to go into raptures over this thoughtfulness. He loved his pastries, like a true Viennese.

"Sit down, sit down, my tiny darling, and tell me about today! Who was there?"

She sat down beside him on the plump overstuffed sofa, covered with a gaudy red, blue, and cream spread. She stuffed the pillows behind her back. Today she wore her favorite Alpine costume, of green with red roses splashed over it, and a crisp white lace blouse with huge sleeves.

She laid aside her gray cloak and her wide velvet hat, and attacked the tea tray with the proper amount of enthusiasm. He liked to "feed my darling, she eats like a bird!", he would say. When she began eating, it encouraged him, to eat and eat, and pretty soon he was too enthralled to notice that she was eating no more.

He helped himself to three pastries, and encouraged her in conversation. "The Countess Puffenbach—it was at her home?"

"Yes, yes, such a huge town house! Liveried footmen all over, and such a butler, a face like a horse—a refined horse," she hastily added, as he frowned. He worshiped royalty and all wealth's trappings. "The Baron von Korda was presenting his pupil, my friend Diana Ballantyne, and she gave me two tickets. . . ." She watched his reaction, slyly.

"You could have asked me," he reproached her.

She widened her big brown eyes. "Oh, no, we cannot be seen in public together, not on such an occasion! It is your own rule, Herr Vogler!"

He pinched her waist sharply enough to hurt. "You know I would have enjoyed it, my pretty bird!" He frowned. "Who did you take?" he asked sharply.

She knew he would have given up food for a week to have gone with that smart society crowd. Besides her attentions in their bed, she had discovered another way to win influence over him. Because she lived in Frau Lewisohn's house, and knew Diana and Alicia and through them the Baron von Korda, she was beginning to be invited to many society occasions. All she had to do was hint to Diana, and invitations were given to her. Diana was very generous that way.

But she would not give an invitation to Herr Vogler until he gave her what she wanted—a part in his coming operetta. She had had a bit part in the first one this autumn, but now she wanted more, much more. She wanted the lead!

"I took Peter Hering with me, the artist who paints me in my costumes," she said. "He is very safe. Frau Lewisohn approves of him, and he works hard and acts the gentleman."

"So—so—" He still did not like it. "And what countess was there, what baron, any prince?"

"The Countess Elza von Hulsen was there, very smart in crimson and black. I saw Prince Philip de Pinzon, very elderly, but listening attentively. He brought four friends, one I recognized as the Princess Alexandra. She wore blue and gold."

She made up some other prominent names for him as he pressed for more details. She knew he would not find out her lie. Even if a list appeared in the gazettes, it would never be complete. Generally, some royalty paid to have their names kept out.

When he was finally satisfied, he edged closer and put his arm about her.

"And another time, you will take your Franzel?" he cooed in her ear, nibbling the lobe gently.

"We cannot be seen in public, dear Franzel," she said very tenderly. "You are a married man. You will not leave your wife?" she added hopefully, watching him alertly through her lashes.

He cooled at once. "Nein, I cannot! She holds the strings of the purse, I told you one time! Her father still backs me! But one day I will have it all!" He contemplated the future with satisfaction. She wondered if he would ever leave his wife. It suited him to appear respectable, a family man with many children. Besides, he wearied quickly of his little operetta stars.

He bent and kissed her throat, lingeringly. She shivered in pleasure, and let him bend her back into the plump cushions. He was a skillful lover, and gave her much joy in their embraces. He licked at her throat as he kissed it, and she trembled and let him unfasten the laces of her crisp blouse, and the bodice.

"Let us go to the bedroom. I have such feelings for you, my little love," he whispered, and she moved obediently with him to the exotic bedroom of the suite he kept for himself near the opera house.

The bedroom was furnished with a huge bedstead with tall carved posts supporting a canopy that could be pulled down to shield them. He pulled it today, and it fell softly about the bed, a canopy of blue and gold, like one of his operetta curtains, and adorned with painted birds and flowers. They rolled over and over across the sheets of pink silk as he undressed her, flinging her garments gaily from the side of the bed. She giggled as her shoes landed on his dresser and crashed into one of his powder boxes.

"Oh, puff, puff," he said, and laughed as he pressed his kisses greedily all over her breasts and slim waist. "Tell me your names for me."

She pressed her fingers deliciously over his spine, up and down his plump back, as she murmured to him, "Oh, my Franzel, my love, my big bird, my plump dove. My cuddles, my squirming cuddles . . ."

She knew words both delicate and coarse, from her years of experience, and those words moved him madly. He pressed his body on hers, almost crushing her under him, as he pushed himself against her.

This was a safe week for her, and she could indulge all she wanted, and let him go the limit with her. She never told him what she would allow, but sometimes she would tease him to distraction, only to jump out of bed and run off and leave him. She would not risk a child, although she did not tell him that. Herr Vogler bragged of having several illegitimate children. She would have no such ties to him, no such sweet mementos!

"Oh, birdie, oh, pigeon," he muttered, and bit her breast sharply. She flinched, and smacked his buttocks with her hand.

"Don't hurt your pigeon!" she rebuked. "Not if you want your fun today!"

"I do—I do—give it to me." And they squirmed and fought on the silk sheets, until she lay back finally, and let him go into her, and pull in and out happily.

He was a big man, but when she was relaxed enough she could take him, she had found. So she made sure she made him wait long enough for her to be relaxed.

They both sighed with pleasure and satisfaction when it was over. She had come quickly to ecstasy, and that always increased his pleasure.

She petted him as he liked, and he groaned, and came again against her. She was a peasant and shrewd in her ways, but she knew how to please him and herself. She did not love him, but she enjoyed him as a lover. He was a passionate man, and it was not hard to pay for her success this way.

Presently they got up, and sat in their robes, to talk. He kept a fine blue silk robe for her in his closet now, and loved to pet her with little splashes of perfume after their lovemaking.

"I have some good news for my little darling," he told her, pulling her back with him on the couch in the bedroom.

She had a hunch it was about the next operetta, and she went still. "What is it? Chocolates?" she cooed.

"Better than that!"

"Flowers, my fine dove?" She patted his thigh, and bent and pressed a kiss on his hairy chest.

"Much better than that!"

"I cannot guess!"

"You know I am producing a new operetta, *Black Forest Maiden*?"

She caught her breath. He teased her a little further.

"Yes, yes, my new operetta. I need a new maiden for it with a fine sweet voice—and I have found her. She is Fraulein Speckel."

Her disappointment was keen, but she dared not show it in the slightest. He could be malicious and cruel, she knew that about him. "How splendid! With her lovely blond hair, she will look fine. Her voice is also good. A bit shrill in the high notes, but men will be busy gazing at her, eh?" And she allowed herself a malicious laugh.

He roared with laughter and spanked her bare hips. "You are a little devil, my hennie! And my maiden needs a pretty maid with brown hair. Guess who that will be? Eh?"

"Fraulein Hertz?"

"Nein, nein, it is my own baby!" He kissed her abruptly, roughly, rolling her over his lap. "It is you, my little Rosalie! Eh? Show me you are grateful!"

She made sure it was true, then showed him her gratitude. She was burning with anger that she did not have the lead, but he told her she would have a much bigger part than the maid's part she had had. The maid had one song of her own, and two duets, one with her mistress and one with the footman who was in love with her. Rosalie resolved to make the most of her songs, and steal the show from the doll-pretty Fraulein Speckel. She would get the notices from the critics, and forward her career.

When she left him at seven o'clock she was quite cheerful. She was lucky and found a fiacre at once, and it made good time through the streets. She was at the boardinghouse in time to quickly wash the perfume from her body, change for dinner, and be down at eight thirty, apologizing prettily for her lateness. "Peter is doing another portrait of me, and wished to finish it tonight," she said cheerfully.

Tomorrow she would go for her lessons to Herr Vogler in his studio. They would go over the music for the operetta, and she would sign her contracts and find out her pay. The money had better be good—to be sure, she would dangle before him the lure of the next Ballantyne concert. Yes, von Korda would have another concert for Diana, and Rosalie was sure she could get tickets from Diana.

So she smiled and planned, and kept her secret to herself. Tomorrow night she would announce the news that she had the second lead in the new Vogler operetta, and let them all celebrate with her. Alicia would call for wine and pay for it, with her usual generosity.

At dinner she turned to Diana, remembering the early events of the day.

"You played so very well, Diana. I was transported!"

Diana's face glowed, her blue eyes dreamy. "Thank you, Rosalie. I am glad you and Peter Hering were able to come."

"He wants to paint you, Diana, but I told him you did not have time. If you do have time, tell me, and I will arrange it. He works fast."

"Oh, I am sure he will find lovelier ladies to paint." Diana seemed truly unaware of her beauty. Rosalie eyed her curiously. Diana glowed when her music was praised, but when her beauty was mentioned, she seemed indifferent.

It was odd to Rosalie, who had lived by her wits and her beauty. It seemed only natural to her to take advantage of these things.

Chapter 13

Several critics had been present at Diana's concert. She waited eagerly for the reviews and had Hans, the odd-jobs man, gather up all the gazettes for her.

She read them with growing disappointment and hurt. Several of the critics were cool:

"Baron von Korda wastes his time with a female pianist, when surely there are more worthy young men who would reward his efforts with their fine future careers."

"Miss Ballantyne played well, and she shows von Korda's training. However, she also showed her weakness in the Liszt number. She has not the strength for such efforts. I found much to criticize in her playing, though I cannot devote much space going over it all. I choose to spend my time and efforts in more worthy causes."

And one anonymous critic was spiteful and nasty. "It makes one wonder. She is the only pupil of von Korda. It is rumored he spends much time with her. Of course she is very beautiful, and it is said her father is wealthy. . . ."

The boardinghouse females rallied around her, as if to protect her from the critics' spite. Alicia was fuming with indignation. "The Liszt was splendid! You have such power. . . ."

Diana smiled and shrugged. "Von Korda warned me to expect such reactions. His first reviews were ugly and cruel, he said, mocking his wealth and implying he had bought a teacher."

The furor died down, and she pretended to forget the reviews. But she was so disappointed. She could send no reviews to her father. These would only confirm what he had said all along, that she was foolish to think she could make a career of music.

Von Korda did not mention the notices at the next lesson. Perhaps he had not seen them; yet she felt that he had. The injustice burned deep inside her.

Christmas was approaching. She had sent gifts home in time for the occasion; some fine Meissen porcelain for her father, pipe jars and pipes and tobacco to her two brothers, leather pocketbooks and gloves to the housekeeper.

Her father sent her a gift from them all—half a dozen lengths of silk from his warehouse. Diana grimaced as she unwrapped the parcels that had arrived early. "For dresses for the holidays," said the note. The silks only served to remind her of his letter ordering her home, and she decided to give most of them away. The purple silk went to Frau Lewisohn, who was enraptured by its unusual beauty. The others went to her closest friends in the boardinghouse. To Alicia went the pale green silk, to Johanne one of the blue lengths. To Frau Hemmel she gave the dove gray, and to Rosalie Stamitz the rose silk with the golden threads.

Rosalie was especially thrilled with hers, and

thanked Diana repeatedly. "You are very good! Oh, I will make it up so beautifully!" And she offered to help make Johanne's dress as well. Johanne accepted, and both girls sewed and sewed for two weeks to make them.

Three weeks before Christmas Diana went to her lessons full of mixed feelings. The holidays were approaching, and she should be joyous. Vienna was filled with holiday decorations, the churches were practicing the special Christmas music. But the critics' words had dulled her usually high spirits. She began to doubt herself a little—not much, but enough to feel dispirited. She worked so hard. Was it all to be in vain? Must she go home and marry Addison Montague, and bear his children, and live out a life of sheer drudgery bereft of her music? Had she been fooling herself?

This December day she was greeted by von Korda with the news, "Ah, I am making plans to go to my chalet in the Alps."

"Oh—over Christmas?" she asked, setting down her music sheets on the piano, turning to hide her disappointed face.

"Yes. My mother is coming with me, and Theo. Margarethe and her family will be visiting for a couple of days, arriving on the holy day. I have been making many plans for January and February for you. What do you say? Will you come with us?"

She whirled around, her face surprised and eager. "Me?" She gasped.

"Yes. My mother will chaperon us. I have much work to do, some composing, some plans for concerts. And I wish to continue your lessons. I don't want to stop them for two weeks. Will you come?" He began to smile as she clasped her hands tightly at her breast.

"Oh, yes, yes, I should like it immensely! You are

most kind!" she said. "Oh, it would be such a pleasure—a chalet—in the Alps?"

"Yes. I hope you will like it. Bring your heavy boots and thick coats, some warm garments for the night. And your ice skates. If we are lucky we shall have some skating."

At her excited laughter he touched her cheek. A thrill ran through her at the touch of his fingers. He turned away abruptly. Did he feel it also, that invisible cord that seemed to run from her to him?

In a haze of delight, Diana packed three small trunks and four hatboxes with her garments and boots and a few small gifts. The von Korda party set out a week before Christmas with two traveling carriages, one barouche, two carts of luggage, and six footmen, in a stately procession southwest from Vienna to the mountains of the Alps over the Italian border. They traveled for two days, staying overnight with some friends in a castle in the woods.

Diana was made most comfortable, surrounded by luxury at every stage. At the castle she was asked to play for them all that evening, and her performance delighted everyone. Von Korda's mother was especially gracious. "We shall play duets when we arrive at the chalet," she said. "I have some music with me."

Frau Constantia von Korda was very sweet to Diana, asking about her progress, talking of her own children and grandchildren, inquiring if Diana was homesick over the holidays. She herself seemed even brighter and more sparkling, having given up her widow's black and gray garments some time ago, and appearing now in a gay crimson velvet traveling dress.

They arrived at the Alpine chalet toward evening, as the sky was reddening with the evening sun. The blue-purple shadows of dusk lengthened as the footmen carried in the luggage.

From the outside the chalet looked like any one of the sweet cottages Diana had seen from the road as they traveled. But it was four times their size. It was built of white native stones, and pine boards stained dark brown. A long balcony spread across the width of the front of the chalet. The roof from the first and second floors overhung the balcony so that snow might slide off safely free of the house.

With a courteous gesture von Korda bade Diana to enter. "Welcome to our home in the mountains, Diana," he said.

"Thank you, Maestro," she answered with a smile, and stepped inside. The spacious open hallway, set apart only by low decorative walls, gave way to a dining room and kitchen-pantry where huge copper pans hung from gray stone walls.

On the other side of the hall was an enormous drawing room in which rested a mahogany grand piano. It was flanked on either side by a golden harpsichord and a gold harp; and the low bookcases around the room were full of books and music quartos. But it was the wide windows that attracted Diana at once, big glass panes providing a wide view of the splendid valley below.

Frau Constantia von Korda showed Diana to her rooms. They walked up a lovely low-stepped winding stairway to the second floor. The first suite belonged to von Korda, the next room to his brother. Then came his mother's room, and then two guest rooms. And finally Diana's room. All these opened onto a huge hallway, with large windows facing the valley, and padded built-in windowseats, so one might sit there and watch the view and the small mountain animals that appeared from time to time. Tables of natural pine were set about, so one might read, or drink tea or chocolate, and lounge, von Korda's mother explained with a smile.

She opened the door to Diana's room, a charming pine-walled room with simple yet lovely country furniture—a wide comfortable cream pine bed, and matching dresser and mirror. A tall wardrobe for her gowns and coats. Her trunks were already there, opened, and a smart-uniformed maid was unpacking for her. The von Kordas employed several village girls to wait on table, cook, clean, do the laundry. Their pretty Alps costumes reminded Diana of Rosalie's dresses.

Beyond the room was a huge balcony, on the side of the house that faced the Alps. The sunset view of majestic snow-clad mountains, folds of blue snow, green pines, and vivid purple skies was irresistible.

Constantia von Korda joined Diana at the window. "When Lukas first built this chalet," she said softly, "he invited me to come and stay with him, just the two of us. I was troubled at the time. I would stay up nights, sitting at the window and gazing at the mountains. Finally I was able to accept what life asked of me. The mountains are good for the soul."

Diana turned, and impulsively kissed her soft pink cheek. Moved, the woman smiled at her, and kissed her in return.

"Now, you must feel free to come and go," she said gently. "You are quite free here. Lukas and Theo will beg you to come walking in the snow. Do so if you wish. Get up when you want, retire when you want, play the piano when you want. And we can talk together sometimes, if you wish."

With another quick kiss of Diana's cheek she left the room. Diana turned back to the window with a deep

sigh of contentment. Already she felt at peace, just
gazing at the immense and magnificent snow-clad
mountains.

In the night she wakened from a deep sleep to hear
a sound like rolling thunder. She got up in time to see
white snow cascading down the mountain just outside
her window, rushing down to the flat plain and sputter-
ing to a halt in white mist. Avalanche! But they were
not in danger; the house was built away from the
mountainside.

She sat up to watch awhile longer. The world was
dark, except for the white snow and the deep blue-
purple sky, its stars sparkling so brightly she could
scarce believe they were real.

The next morning she overslept. Nobody wakened
her. She wakened slowly and luxuriously in the bed,
and only when she looked at her lapel-watch, did she
discover it was noon.

The dark grayness of the day had made it easy to
keep sleeping. She washed in the huge bathroom in one
corner of her room, finding the water invigoratingly
hot. The plumbing must have been difficult to install in
this rugged landscape, but even so, one faucet ran ice-
cold water, the other steaming hot.

She dressed in a warm dark blue gown, then put on
a matching jacket, because the hallway outside felt
cold. Descending the stairs, she found the family
gathered in the drawing room.

"Ah, Diana, in time for lunch," said von Korda,
with a twinkle in his deep blue eyes.

"Do not let him tease you, Diana!" said his mother
quickly. "We all rose just a short time ago. So much
for schedules!"

"I had hoped to go walking in the snow," said Theo,

looking bright and happy in a gay red-and-white ski sweater. "But it is not good today. Too soft."

Luncheon was omelettes with good fresh country eggs, salted ham, onions, and mushrooms. Diana ate hot breads, little curved and folded crescents covered with poppy seeds and smothered with fresh butter and strawberry jam. These with hot coffee topped with whipped cream satisfied them all.

"I must go walking, soft snow or no," said Lukas, and he persuaded Diana and his brother to come also. They donned heavy boots, and Diana put on her warm mink coat.

They walked in silence, the only sounds the thundering of the snow in the mountains, and the occasional hopeful chirp of a winter bird. Lukas seemed to be deep in thought, and sometimes his right hand rose in a vague gesture, as though directing music. Theo was quiet, probably thinking about his studies.

Diana felt exhilarated. As they walked, the brisk wind turned her cheeks to deep rose, and made her eyes sting. In the last few days she had discovered something both ominous and beautiful: She was in love with Lukas von Korda. She wanted more than anything in the world to be with him always. It was an impossible wish, she knew, yet the thought made her feel more alive than she had ever felt before.

They returned to the house. Von Korda sat down at the piano and became absorbed in some melodies. His mother took out some frocks she was smocking, and Diana took up needle and thread to work with her. They chatted in low tones, at the other end of the huge drawing room from the piano. Theo was in his room reading.

"You embroider very well," said Constantia in a low voice. She studied Diana's design with satisfaction.

"Very neatly done. You have done it often?"

"I used to, with my mother. She was ill many years, and it was one thing she could do without strain."

"Are you much alike?"

"I think so. She loved music. She played the violin when she was young, but never seriously. She also painted, and embroidered, and made lace. She had a talent for making our home warm and pretty. She put flowers about, and always loved her gardens."

With Frau von Korda's encouragement Diana told a little more about her homelife, her mother, her father and brothers. She had learned to play tennis; she talked about that. She told about how her brothers had taught her to be a good sport, and not cry when she lost a game, or was hurt. Constantia smiled and nodded, and asked questions gently.

Presently Lukas turned about on the bench. "Diana, come here, I need you!"

She jumped up at once, then gave Frau von Korda a guilty look. The mother smiled and nodded to her to go. Diana went to the piano bench. Standing behind him, she gazed down at the handsome golden-blond head. Her hand reached out to touch his hair, but then she snatched it away again guiltily. When she was close to him, she sometimes had this desperate desire to touch him.

"Sit down beside me," he ordered absently. "I have an idea for the bass—chords in F minor—try it with me."

Under his direction she played the bass with the left hand, following the few notes he had inked on the music sheet. Concentrating, she listened to the treble part, then began to improvise chords in the bass.

"Yes, yes, that's it." He stopped her, and wrote in some notes rapidly. "Now—what then?"

Together they worked on the sonata, and finished it before tea. He gave a sigh of satisfaction. "I woke in the night and heard the music—then in the morning I had half-forgotten it. I must put some sheets of music and fresh ink in my rooms." He looked at Diana and added with a smile, "And in yours also, I think!"

"Yes, if you will! Thank you," she said with a laugh.

It was a very pleasant time. They both worked on their music. Lukas went over some compositions of hers and suggested a couple of additions, but professed himself happy with them. Diana helped him with his, and played the pieces for him when he had finished.

Theo was writing a paper about something, and rumbled to himself at times about his ideas. Constantia embroidered, directed the maids, and when she was alone, played the piano. Diana, coming in from outside, would hear her, and the music was sometimes sweet and soft, sometimes loud and forceful. Constantia rarely played for them, but twice in the evening she did so, at her son's urging.

"I do not play in public, my son!" she would protest.

"Since when is your son public?" he demanded, and pushed her gently down to the bench.

Diana enjoyed walking outdoors in the thick snow, unconcerned when she occasionally tumbled down in it and got wet. Outside the rumble and thunder of the snows in the mountains could be heard. The air was sometimes so sharp and cold it felt like a knife in her lungs.

Several times during their stay the skies cleared to a deep blue and the sun shone as in summer. The birds would sing, and small animals prowl and leave their tiny clear prints in the snow. When Diana went for walks with Lukas or Theo, they rarely talked. The air caught in their lungs, and they were satisfied to stride about, to walk on the crust of the frosted snow, to plow through new waves of blue-white. The pond froze deeply, and several times they were able to ice-skate, but they had to be careful. The country pond was not like the pond in the Prater, smooth and clear. It was rough, jagged, with sticks in it, and half-hidden logs, and crunchy snow along the edges.

Diana would sit on a log at the side of the pond, in the shelter of a massive green pine, and pull off her wet walking boots. Then she would pull on her ice skates and lace them slowly.

She got no special treatment here! Theo and Lukas did their own boots, and treated her as her brothers did. She must do hers herself! Somehow she enjoyed it, being treated as one of the family.

Then she would test herself cautiously on the ice, and strike out. No arms to lean on, though Lukas would glance over to make sure she was all right. Daringly she would thrust herself out on the rough ice, sailing to the other side of the small pond and back again. The air was so cold and crisp her own breath came in white clouds. She sang to herself happily, usually a waltz tune, and spun around and around dizzily.

How good she felt, and how she loved being with Lukas! She would look at him, cheeks red with wind, eyes blazing blue, sailing past her with arms outstretched for balance, yelling at Theo, laughing with carefree joy. How handsome he was, how fine! She loved him so much. Even if it could never come to anything, it was special just to love, and feel warm and good about someone so grand.

Theo sailed past her, hands clasped behind him, like a meditative parson, legs going like windmills as he moved faster and faster.

When Diana started to feel cold, she changed to her

boots, and left Theo and Lukas with a wave. She walked back to the house alone, went upstairs, and changed to a house gown.

She had been thinking music. A melody was in her head, disturbing her thoughts. She went to her small desk near the window. Picking up a pen and dipping it into the fresh black ink, she began to write on the music sheets, filling in little black notes rapidly on the staves.

The sound was all there in her head, and needed only be written down. She wrote and wrote until her wrist ached, then strode about the room, listening to the rest of the music in her head. When she sat down again, she wrote until dusk, when the maid came in softly to light her lamp.

"Fraulein would enjoy tea?"

Not wanting to stop, Diana shook her head and went on writing. The maid left quietly. Finally it was all down on paper, and Diana, sighing with pleasure, got up to change for dinner.

She dressed in a blue and silver gown, feeling brightened and exalted by the work. Lukas and Theo stood up as she came down the stairs. Lukas stared at her, then lifted her hand, the right one, still marked with some ink stains on it she had been unable to wash off.

"I should like you to play it after dinner," he said.

She laughed with some embarrassment. "Ja, mein Maestro!"

She played for them after dinner, from memory, for she did not need the music sheets. They listened in a silence of deep appreciation, and she was satisfied.

"Tomorrow, I will rip it apart for you," said Lukas lazily.

"My son!" his mother reproached. Lukas laughed,

and the next day he did not speak of it at all. When Diana asked, he laughed and shook his head.

"It is good, it needs nothing," he said. "You shall play it in a concert one day."

On Christmas Day they all exchanged small gifts. Christmas in Austria was mostly a holiday for children. Still, Diana gave Constantia a huge bottle of her favorite perfume, lilac. She gave Theo a book he had expressed a wish to have, and Lukas some blue silk ties she had made from her father's cloth.

They gave her gifts that showed their thoughtfulness: a book of Chopin's music from Constantia, a life of Beethoven from Theo, and from Lukas, a lovely gold and crystal inkwell and matching sanding box.

Chapter 14

Lukas was sitting at the piano as Diana came into the room before tea that day. Frau von Korda was still in her room, Theo was outdoors walking in the snow. For once she was alone with Lukas, and Diana felt a strange thrill of excitement.

Lukas had been playing with his right hand, but when he saw her approach, he let his hand drop to his knee. He looked at her and smiled, a curiously sweet smile.

At that moment she forgot all about his mistress, the Countess von Hulsen, and the fickleness and desires of men that led them to play fast and loose with women. She remembered only that she loved him, that he was the kindest man ever to her, that he seemed to understand her as no man ever had.

"I wanted to thank you again, Maestro," she said, and came to the piano bench.

He moved over slightly, motioned her to sit beside him, at his left side. "For such a trifling gift?" he asked, with a little mocking grin at her.

"That was kind, and I will enjoy using it," she told

him. "However, I meant—the fact that you have been so good to me. That when my father wrote, and said I must come home—you know. You were so understanding."

He moved slightly, impatiently, and his thigh brushed against hers. She felt the slide of silk against silk, and the warmth of his hard-muscled body against hers, and again that thrill of contact blazed through her. When she was so near to him, if they were not absorbed in music, she could scarcely think. She was all feeling, all emotion, alive to the closeness of his body, wanting to be closer still. She could understand then how women could lose their heads over men.

She could understand even how a woman like Elza von Hulsen could throw conventions out the window, and do anything to be near her lover! She was intensely jealous of the woman, but she knew how Elza felt. Diana felt the same way—if Lukas were her lover, Diana also would risk anything to be with him.

But of course he did not feel like that about her!

The silence between them had gone on too long. Diana cleared her throat and said huskily, "You do not know how grateful I am, that I have this year. Whatever happens in the future, I will cherish this time of music."

He frowned, seeming unusually tense. "It is not over, this year of yours," he said brusquely. "Anything could happen. . . ."

"If the reviews are ever good," she said, with a wry twist of her lovely mouth, "I would have some hope. Perhaps by spring they may be. I shall work hard."

"And if they are not good? What will your father do? He will not insist on your marrying that wretched fellow, will he?"

"I do not know. I fear so," she said in a low tone.

"The merger is going through. Father writes of how much they miss me."

"But it is madness to think of you giving up your music completely!" he cried impetuously. "You are very talented!"

"Thank you, Maestro. That is why I am so appreciative—you believe in my talent."

She looked up at him, her blue eyes full of gratitude. He gazed down at the earnest face so close to his. He moved, and she felt his stiff left arm slip about her waist. Diana did not even think of pulling away. She wanted this contact, she had been longing for him to touch her.

"Diana," he said softly. "Diana—how I wish—" He stopped and shook his head.

What did he wish? To help her further? Did he feel anything for her, as she did for him? Any fragment of desire, of love? She thought maybe he did feel desire for her, or he would not wish to kiss her and touch her. That was not love, yet—but, oh, she would have settled for that! But his mistress absorbed him. Diana felt again a keen stab of jealousy.

He drew her closer, slowly, as though waiting to see if she would protest.

She leaned against him, and he bent his head to her. His lips moved on her soft warm cheek. Oh, how she longed for a closer touch! She longed for them to be alone, completely alone, with no servants to interrupt, or Theo, or his mother.

Then she forgot the others, for Lukas put his right hand on her chin, and turned her face further to his. Slowly, his vivid blue eyes burning like the midday sky, he drew closer to her. Then his large generous mouth touched hers, tightened, twisting to force her to respond. Oh, how sweet his touch—how demanding . . .

She found herself responding wildly to him. Hardly realizing what she did, she lay against him, her hand clutching his arm, and her lips moved to kiss and kiss again. The large hand on her chin moved to touch her throat, and his teasing fingers caressed her skin. He kissed her again, and again, and his mouth grew hot, and he nibbled at her lower lip.

His hand slid from her throat, and his fingers moved to caress gently the rounded breast he had found. Even with layers of silk between his fingers and her flesh, Diana caught her breath in pleasure at his touch.

A thumb moved deliberately over her nipple, and he knew it rose taut to his caress. He lifted his head then, and gazed deeply into her eyes.

"If we had been alone in the chalet," he murmured, his mouth hard, "I would have come to your room that first night! It is as well my mother came with us! God, you are beautiful!"

Diana flushed wildly, her cheeks deep pink. His gaze went over her face, from forehead to eyes, to mouth.

Her lips trembled. She longed to invite him—but she could not. She wanted him—but she was a virgin, and he must know that. A girl like Diana did not have affairs—no, no, she must not think about that—She must not even consider such a thing.

"If I had come to your door, would you have let me in?" he whispered into her ear, and kissed the lobe.

She shook her head blindly. He laughed, seductively, and let her go. She sprang from the piano bench.

"Now you will be angry with me," he said, as calmly as though they had quarreled over a question of music.

She put her hands to her burning cheeks. "I do not understand you," she muttered. "You are protective—then you say things like that! What kind of man are you?"

"A man—like other men—who can desire," he said. "And you are a very beautiful woman. Have you given yourself to Captain Mueller?"

Diana gasped in shock. He raised his eyes swiftly, and his blue eyes were blazing.

"No, I have not, I would not!" she cried out.

He shrugged. "Sometimes I think women are all alike," he said idly. "You see him often, you seem to like him. Yet he is a demon, a rake, a womanizer. Do you find him attractive?"

"Yes, I find him attractive. Just as you find his sister attractive!"

Lukas stiffened. Diana held her breath. Had she gone too far? "Ah—his sister," said Lukas, without expression. "What do you know of her?"

"That you—dueled over her."

"So." He rose, and turned his back, gazing out the window to the blue-white snow, and the deep color of the evergreens. "No woman is worth it," he said. "I advise you to avoid Captain Mueller. But you will not listen to me. Women enjoy the taste of danger, don't they?"

All of a sudden he seemed to tire of that topic. He went out to the kitchen and teased the cook about something until the woman laughed and giggled with pleasure. Diana went to sit down, shaking over her scene with Lucas. What did he mean when he talked like that? Why did he kiss her? And to think of his coming to her bedroom made her nervous!

She was glad when Frau von Korda came downstairs. The more people about, the better.

The daughter, Frau Margarethe Greta Niemann, arrived for a three-day visit with her husband and children two days later.

The baby was only three months old. Margarethe

looked tired and ill, and her face was pale. Constantia took over the baby's care, and the maids hovered about her. Her husband huffed and bellowed and ordered the children about.

"You should have allowed me to send the carriages for you, it would have been more comfortable," Lukas reproached him.

"Nein, nein, too expensive!" he yelled. "I was comfortable enough!"

Lukas repressed his comments and turned away. The house seemed suddenly full of people, and especially filled with the noises of two small boys. The girls were very quiet. Young Karl was like his father, and demanded to go out to the stables and see the horses whenever he could. Other times he demanded to go ice-skating.

Roderick copied his brother, but had a sensitivity for music that Karl lacked. Julie was small and independent and inclined to be sullen. Kristel was adorable, with blond curls and wide blue eyes, and a thumb always in her pink rosebud mouth.

Presents were distributed the first evening. The children received dolls and wooden soldiers, sleds and ice skates, clothes and jewels, with happy screams. Julie dangled all her necklaces about herself, tried her bracelets on, along with her mother's, and strode about importantly.

They were all put to bed early, and then the parents exchanged news with their family. Diana wondered if she should leave, but Lukas shook his head at her when she mimed a gesture to the stairs.

Presently he took his brother-in-law with him to the stables to look at the horses, and the others talked more freely. Margarethe was weary, the harvest had been late, and her baby had been ill. Kristel had been sick, but was well again. Julie was learning her letters, and she was a good obedient girl. Diana remembered thinking Julie looked sullen, but perhaps she had been mistaken.

After they retired to bed, Diana lay awake for a time. Margarethe had looked wistfully at the piano, but shook her head on being asked to play. "I am out of practice," she said simply.

Was this marriage, then? Diana wondered. One child after another, the woman exhausted, the husband bullying. But surely someone like Lukas would not be like this! Yet—he was a man, he took service for granted. She tossed and turned, and it was midnight before the silence and the mountain air lulled her to sleep.

She awoke late and hurried downstairs guiltily. But the men had gone out in the snow, taking the boys with them. She drank coffee and ate hot rolls with Margarethe, who looked somewhat rested and more lively.

Constantia was at the piano, and Diana looked about for the girls. Kristel was busily undressing her dolls. Julie sat in a huddle under the piano where her grandmother played. When Diana bent down to look at the small girl, a sullen face looked back at her.

"Are you all right?" Diana whispered.

A nod. "I am listening!" she hissed.

"Oh. All right." Diana got right down on her hands and knees and crawled under the piano, too. Julie stared at her, wide-eyed. Diana sat as the girl did, with knees up, chin on her knees, arms wrapped about herself. She listened.

What a sensation! The music rolled and trembled about her, seeming to go right through her body, from her head to her heels. It was like being in the middle of an ocean of melody, with waves crashing overhead and underneath and through her. Chords thundered, runs tripped like waterfalls.

She sat there with Julie for a long time, in silence. They said not a word. Presently a small paw thrust itself into Diana's hand and squeezed. Diana squeezed in reply. Yes, this is wonderful, she answered the child's silent question.

Then the music was interrupted by the disturbing thud of men's boots and the sound of deeper voices.

Julie stiffened. Then someone bent and looked into their cave under the piano.

Diana opened her eyes and stared into Lukas's face, bronzed, red-cheeked from the wind, his eyes wide and blue.

"We are listening!" she whispered.

He muttered in German, "My God in heaven," and got up and moved away.

"Papa's coming," muttered Julie, and scrambled out of there in a great flurry of arms and long thin legs.

Diana slid out also, aided by a strong pull from Lukas. She moved to a sofa and sat down, and pulled Julie up beside her, just in time. Herr Heinrich Neimann strode in, bellowing.

"Where are my children. Come and greet me!"

Kristel ran to him, was caught up and hugged. Julie slid down and walked slowly to him, waiting until he had put Kristel down; then he lifted and hugged her. She left him and returned to the sofa, with an odd unusually adult look on her face.

So young, to be so wise about her father, thought Diana. She gave him what he demanded, but no more. She understood her place as her father's daughter.

His sons were his pride. He scolded them, he teased them constantly. He demanded that Roderick play piano for them that evening. "I have paid enough for his lessons! He would be better occupied learning his sums!"

Diana wondered that Roderick dared to play at all, but Lukas sat beside him on the piano bench and quietly encouraged him. The boy was unusually talented, Diana could sense that. But that night he played only two party pieces, and she did not really hear him play until the next day, when he thought himself alone but for his mother and Diana.

After they had left to go home, silence descended on the chalet once more. Theo returned to his writing, Lukas continued his composing, and Diana practiced her part of a piano concerto she and Lukas were working on.

He hoped to be able to obtain a concert for her with a symphony orchestra, and she must begin to prepare such numbers, he had said.

He was gentler with her after his sister had left. He seemed to have changed again, and showed another side of himself. When they were alone, sometimes he gently kissed her cheek, and he encouraged her kindly to speak her thoughts about the music.

Was he coming to like her more? Did she dare to hope that he might one day come to love her? And if so—what would happen? Would the Baron von Korda love her enough to want to marry her, and give up his stunning mistress?

Diana did not know what to think.

On one of the last nights before they returned to Vienna, she lay awake in the soft bed of her comfortable room. Thunder rolled in the hills, but it was not the approaching storm that kept her awake. She thought continuously of Lukas von Korda, and her mind would not slow down enough for her to relax into slumber.

Soon, back in Vienna, they would meet only for

lessons and concerts. She must have hoped when she came that they would grow closer, and they had, but it was not enough for her. Now that she knew she loved him, she kept watching for some sign that she meant as much to him.

He treated her almost like one of the family, but that was not enough for her hungry heart. His occasional kisses and embraces had roused her to desires she had never known before, to needs she had never imagined.

She turned restlessly in the bed, and finally got up, putting on her robe and walking slowly to the windows. Then she gasped, and her eyes widened.

Lightning was playing in the mountains, yellow against the white snow. Thunder rumbled, and she saw with apprehension that heavy snow was tumbling down from above, accumulating in great drifts in the meadows behind the house.

The masses seemed to come closer and closer! Could they reach the house? Perhaps the chalet was not so secure as she had supposed.

The house was quiet; not a single light shone out upon the snow from any of the rooms. Diana felt more and more apprehensive. Should she wake up the household, tell them to take refuge away from the bedrooms? Perhaps in the hallway they would be safe. At least it was on the other side of the chalet from the avalanches.

Another long rumble, and a huge mass of snow broke off from the rocks above and began to tumble down the steep slopes. Unable to wait any longer, Diana dashed out into the hallway. There she collided with a dark form.

She stifled a shriek. A hand reached out and grasped her arm firmly. "Diana. Were you afraid?"

It was Lukas, his deep voice calm and hushed. "Oh—Lukas—" She faltered. "The snow—avalanche—did you see it just now?"

"I have been watching," he said softly. "I enjoy the sight. I don't think we are in danger, however."

He put his arm about her, and she felt its hard muscular warmth like a warm bar about her waist.

"It—it seemed so close. I was concerned whether to waken the household." She gave a nervous little laugh.

She could see his white teeth gleam in a smile, even in the half-darkness. The snow outside shone and seemed to light the hall. Now that her eyes were accustomed to the grayness, she could make out his face and the dark shape of his head.

"They would not appreciate it, Diana!"

"I suppose not."

"But let's watch it together. The sight is spectacular, and the rumble of the snow is like music."

He drew her back into her bedroom with him. She was all too conscious of the bed with its mussed sheets and blankets. He drew her past it, however, to the large windows, and gazed out at the snow. Another rumble, long and deliberate, ended with a shower of snow and ice. She gasped, and he held her more closely to him.

"It looks close," he whispered, his lips against her ear. "However, I have just walked all about the house, and none of the windows are wet with the snow. So it is not coming any closer. Is it not beautiful?"

She nodded, and echoed, "Beautiful."

His arm moved more tightly about her, and he turned her deliberately. "Your heart is beating so fast," he teased. "I think you enjoy the thought of danger!"

What danger was he referring to? She wondered if

he meant a possible avalanche, or if he meant the danger of their closeness in the night!

She tried to draw away, though she longed to stay pressed to him. "Thank you, Maestro," she said. "I can sleep now."

"Can you? I think I cannot," he muttered, and bent his head. His lips found hers unerringly in the darkness, and she felt the warmth of his mouth twisting against hers to make her respond. She could not resist, and her lips opened under his. At once his tongue thrust into her mouth and touched hers, and it was as though a flame shot up between their pressed bodies.

Under his robe she could feel the heat and the pulsing of his body. It seemed to mold to hers, as though he could bend and move to follow her every curve, and match her form with his. Involuntarily she thought of them lying together on the bed, naked, her slim rounded body curving to imprint itself against his harder more muscular frame. At once she felt burning hot, raging with desires she had never known with any other man.

Her arms moved up to circle his neck, and one hand went to his hair. She had longed to caress his thick blond hair, and now she thrust her fingers boldly through the silken-soft waves. At her touch he went rigid for a moment, then began to kiss her more wildly.

He moved her toward the bed, his legs pressing against hers to move her backward. She had no thought of denying him; she wanted him, she longed for him. All maidenly modesty gone, she was caught in a gale of fervent longing, in a storm that raged in her as fiercely as the thunderstorm in the Alps outside. When he pushed her down on the bed, and followed her down, she was conscious of nothing so much as a fierce gladness that at last she would be fulfilled, that he would take her and end the sick longing for him that had plagued her. She would know—she would know his body on hers, she would adore his body with hers, she would understand what drove men and women together in a wild rage to consume each other with the flames of passion.

His hands moved over her robe, and opened the sash and the lapels, until she lay under him with only the white nightrobe on her silken limbs. He lay half on her, his legs sprawling over hers, his hands feverish on her arms and throat. His mouth pressed to her cheeks, her chin, her nose, in a series of little seeking kisses. His touch was hot. She felt his tongue licking delicately on her cheeks, as though he would eat her!

He made love in German, she discovered. The words spilled from him in little gasping whispers. "Lovely Diana, lovely girl, so silken, so delicious. How I have longed for this moment. I want you so much. So much. Ah. Your throat, the pulses beat under my lips. . . ."

His lips were moving over her feverishly, as though he would take her with his mouth. And his hands sought and found more silken softness. He had opened her robe, and pushed it down almost to her waist. When one big hand closed over her rounded breast, she gasped and arched her back in desire. She had never dreamed there was such passion in her. She wanted him, she burned wherever he touched. Now her nipple had come up in taut excitement, and he brushed it with his thumb, deliberately, to arouse her further.

"Lukas . . . Lukas . . ." she moaned. "I want you. . . ."

His mouth came over hers and stifled the sound. Deliberately, slowly, he raised the nightdress above her legs, until it lay in a crumpled roll under her back and thighs. One arm held her tightly to his body, and now his nightdress and robe were opened to her. She felt his naked limbs twining with hers, and knew the moment was near. She was about to know the delicious terror of a man's possession. How she loved him, and wanted him—

His hand on her thighs, he began to caress her rhythmically. She writhed in delight, her back arched, her arms clinging to him. She half-sobbed in pleasure at his skilled touch. Closer—closer—silently she begged with her arms, her legs, striving to come tightly to him—

Then the voice came, his mother's voice. "Lukas? Lukas? Where are you? The avalanches are coming closer!"

Diana scarcely heard her. Blood pounded in her head, and she was waiting, anticipating, longing for Lukas to enter her body. When he lifted up, she felt cold, disappointed. Her arms reached up for him.

But he was leaving her, snatching his nightrobe and outer robe about himself.

"Stay there!" he muttered, and yanked the blankets up over her.

She was sweating with heat, panting with need, and his leaving her made her feel as though she had been betrayed. She lay limp, unable to move, as Lukas padded to the door.

Angrily she marveled at the calm of his deep voice. "I am here, Mother, checking the windows. These are all right," and he closed her door softly, leaving her alone in the darkness.

She heard the murmur of their voices, as they moved along the hallway. Other doors were opened and closed as they gazed from each room to the snow outside, to see if the danger had come closer.

She waited for him to return, lying awake in the

darkness, fists clenched on the blankets, her body cooling. But he would not, she knew it. He would let his cool head prevail. Once he had left her and regained control of himself, he would not return.

Diana knew she should be glad they had been interrupted. Technically her virginity had remained intact. But spiritually, she knew she had given herself to him, and could never take herself back again.

She had wanted him so desperately, she had been willing to give him the most precious gift a girl could give to her lover, the one-time gift that could never be given again. But he had firmly refused it by leaving.

During the few days remaining of her stay, he did not approach her that way again. Oh, his gaze went thoughtfully to her, and she hoped that he still desired her. Perhaps back in Vienna he would begin to court her. Her heart leaped up at that thought. Perhaps he did not trust himself to be near her again here, as they had been alone in her bedroom.

Perhaps in Vienna . . . She hugged the thought to herself, and went about her packing more calmly.

Yet—she must expect nothing. He had made no promises, he had said nothing of love. And once in Vienna, he might return to the arms of his mistress once more.

Chapter 15

Returning from the peaceful Alps to gay Vienna was a shock. Diana had felt so marvelous there, alone with Lukas and his family. She had felt a part of them, playing duets with his mother, working closely with Lukas on compositions, laughing with Theo and teasing him like a sister.

Now she returned to hard work, discouragement, and the reviews that she had saved and put in a music folder. She read them over, and her shoulders drooped. Some of the remarks were so spiteful!

Alicia came over to chat about the holidays. "I went out several times with Captain Schmidt and Captain Mueller. I took a couple of girls from the house here, but how the men missed you! And when they learned that you had gone off with the von Kordas to their chalet—well, Captain Mueller's jealousy knew no bounds!" She laughed teasingly.

Alicia was curious about the chalet. Diana told her about how peaceful and beautiful it had been. "I would have liked it. I love to ice-skate and walk in snow," said Alicia, cheerfully, without envy. "When I go home, I'll try to talk Papa into buying a cabin in the mountains. Of course that won't be the same as the Alps!"

Diana fingered her music sheets restlessly. She did not want to go home. However when April came, she must go. She would have had her year, and she could not imagine her father would allow her another.

Alicia was gazing at her. "What troubles you, Diana? Do you want to confide in me? You always help us so with *your* sensible advice!"

Diana smiled and shook her head. "It is those reviews, Alicia," she said. "I could not send them to father, they were so bad. And when April comes, with no good reviews, no proof I have improved, he will order me home."

"Oh—and to marriage," added Alicia thoughtfully, her face reflecting Diana's own sadness. "Can't you fight it?"

"Not without money of my own," said Diana. "That is the key, isn't it? With no way to make a living, a woman is bound to her father, or her husband, or other relatives. Perhaps I could get music students—or teach in an academy for girls. But I have no training as a teacher."

"I know, I am in the same situation," Alicia sighed. "My father is very good and kind to me. But I have no money except my monthly allowance. He says women need none. I tried to persuade him to put some into a bank for me and let a banker manage it! But even that he would not do. No, when I want money beyond my allowance, I must go in and beg prettily!"

They sat contemplating their woes for a time and not finding any solutions. Neither was equipped to earn a living; few women were. Alicia jumped up. "Well, I should be practicing," she said, and left the room. Her face was sober.

We both have our one year of independence, Diana thought. Then I must go home and marry my father's choice, and so must Alicia, probably. Stanislav had gone home for a time. She wondered if Alicia's heart had softened toward him, but thought not. Alicia resented being married for her money, and Diana knew just how she felt. She did not care to be the instrument of a merger between two firms. It made her feel like a piece of property.

She got up and went to the piano, and vented her frustrations on the keyboard.

The next day en route to her Monday lesson, she felt tired from lack of sleep, and cross from contemplation of a future she could not control. She knew she was sensible and intelligent—yet she could not see a way out.

She entered the von Korda home at the side door as usual, but the butler hastened to meet her, his face rather red.

"Fraulein—beg pardon, if you will but step into the other parlor. . . ." He stammered over the words.

She was about to obey him, surprised, when she heard a soft laugh come from the music room on the other side, the large room where she had her lessons.

Then she heard Lukas von Korda's voice, stern, angry. Something impelled Diana, to move past the slow dignified butler, evading his hand, and stand at the door of the room.

And then she saw a sight that burned itself on her memory. The lovely black-haired Countess Elza von Hulsen lay against Lukas, her hands clasped on his arm, laughing alluringly up at him! Her lips were scarlet with paste, and on his cheek was an imprint of her lips, as though she had just kissed him, and left the mark there, a mark of ownership.

Diana stared, appalled, sick. The butler was stammering behind her. "Oh, Fraulein, if you would but come!"

He had been trying to spare her the sight of Lukas with his mistress! Protecting his master, thought Diana, furiously.

Elza turned away from von Korda, glancing toward the door. "Ah, your little English pupil." She smiled, her black eyes wicked. "I think I have shocked her! But she does not betray your secrets, does she, darling Lukas?"

"Miss Ballantyne—if you will wait for a few minutes—the butler will show you—"

For once Lukas von Korda seemed flushed, angry, flustered. Diana bowed with dignity, and then holding her head proudly erect, she turned away, and allowed the butler to show her into the room across the hall.

Evidently Lukas could not wait to return to Vienna to see his mistress again! And to think that Diana had been willing to give herself to him! As she sat on the edge of a hard chair and waited, she burned with fury and embarrassment.

A murmur of voices rose in the hallway, but she purposely did not look in that direction. Finally the murmur led to the back of the hall, to the side door, and died away. She heard a low seductive laugh and cringed at what Elza must be saying and thinking of the gauche English girl who had burst in on their rendezvous!

A door slammed. Diana jumped in her chair. The butler came and solemnly ushered her back to the music room. Diana took off her coat, and prepared to sit down at the piano.

Lukas came into the room. "I beg pardon for the delay," he said formally. His blue eyes glittered with anger, but she did not care. If he must conduct his affairs so openly, he must expect to be embarrassed!

How his handsome golden head had been bent to the glossy black curls! How he must adore her, to receive her in his home so openly. Had she spent the night with him? Was his mother here in Vienna with him? Did he carry on his affairs openly before *her*?

What Gardell Mueller had said was true. Lukas still loved the magnificent Hungarian woman, and could not stay away from her. But how could he? She was married! He had fought one duel over her—did he want another? Or did he love her so madly, he would risk his life to court her?

Worse—did he hope to persuade her to divorce, and marry her? He had never married. He was a very eligible man—handsome, wealthy, talented, respected! The man she loved was unworthy—but she could not help loving him!

They began the lesson. Today she wore a drab dark blue gown with no jewels, an outfit that matched her cheerless mood. The January day looked as gray as she felt. It was unusual for her to feel this way, and she could scarcely bear it. If this was love, she hoped to recover quickly!

She began to play the Brahms sonata she had been working on. During the first few minutes of the piece Lukas was striding restlessly from the window to the table, to the piano and back to the window. Finally he came to the piano and raised his right hand.

"Stop, stop, stop! This is dreadful! You have forgotten all I told you about this. It is not a funeral march! It is not a march at all! How dare you play it so! What is the matter with you?"

At the rebuke she felt like a cross child, like Julie with her little sullen troubled face.

She bit her lip inside until it hurt. "I am sorry, Maestro," she muttered, fingering the music sheet restlessly. "Shall I begin again?"

"Nein!" he said sharply. "I have told you before, Brahms was a man of great depths, and in this number—"

He strode about talking, but she could scarcely concentrate on his words. She watched his long legs in the blue silk stride up and down the thick Persian carpets, noted his characteristic gesture, the right hand clasping the stiff left arm.

"You are not listening! What is the matter!" he rebuked again in exasperation. "If I said that Brahms was an idiot, you would say, 'Yes, Maestro!' I tell you, you must listen to me!"

He thumped his right fist on the piano, and she jumped at the hard sound.

"I wonder why you teach me!" she hurled at him. If she made him cross, she did not care! "I wonder at you! Think of what the critics said of me. You probably agree with them! You don't really think I can make a career of music, do you!"

"Not if you play the way you are this morning!" he said roughly, scowling at her. "You must work hard, you cannot indulge your moods! Come good mood or poor, you must play well! You cannot afford to be weak and feminine and play well only when you feel like it!"

His rebuke stung her feelings. She caught her breath, her fists clenched as though she would like to hit him.

"You agree with the critics!" she flung again. "You do not think I can play well, because I am a woman!"

"You play well, when you forget you are a woman!"

he said logically. "You should play as a musician, not a woman or a man!"

"Why did you agree to teach me?" she blurted out. "I cannot understand why you agreed to that! You knew I was a woman, and they would not tolerate my trying to enter a man's world! And you think so also—you do not think I can—"

"I am teaching you!"

He turned away, as though to end the argument. She would not tolerate that. Something in her raged, the remembrance of his blond head bent to Elza's dark one. The knowledge that he loved an unworthy woman—and thought little of Diana! He probably did not even notice her, except as a pianist!

Her mixed emotions burned in her. She must carry on the quarrel; she would force him to see her!

"Why do you encourage me? Why do you waste your time with me?" she continued hotly.

He flung about, opened his lips to answer, then thought better of it, and scowled heavily at her. His face had flushed in anger.

Her fists were raised as though she would like to hit him. "Answer me!" she cried arrogantly, not like a pupil to her teacher. "Answer me! Why do you encourage me? Why did you not send me home, to be a poor obedient woman, doing what my father told me to do? Why encourage me, when you know our efforts are wasted?"

He muttered in German, "God help me!" and strode the few steps to her. He grabbed her fists in both his hands, the weak left one and the enormously strong one. He glared down at her.

She thought he would shake her hard, but instead he moved his left arm to her waist and pulled her to him. He had unexpected strength, and she gasped as she was pressed tightly to his warm body in the blue silk suit. His coat was open, and as he held her to his gold and blue waistcoat she could feel the hardness of his body.

He gazed down into her flushed face and bent his head. Before she knew what he was about, she felt the biting pressure of his lips on hers.

It was as though his rough touch set off an explosion inside her. Her anger blown away, she felt only the wildness and desire to respond. He kissed her again, and again, and her young lips replied. He pulled her hand to him with his, and slipped it up on his neck. Her fingers massaged his throat, and his right hand fell to her waist, to her hips, and pressed her to himself.

Sensations flooded her. She was aware of the roughness of his shaved skin, the curve of his throat and chin as they kissed, yet she did not know what she was doing. He bent her backward under his embrace, holding her with both arms, bending her back, as his lips touched hers again and again.

When he drew his mouth from hers, and began to kiss her cheek, her chin, and down to her throat, she felt bereft. Her hand coaxed him, trying to draw him back to her lips. She hungered for that warm intimate touch once more.

He was muttering something deeply as he kissed her white throat. "Adored, lovely—softness—my beauty . . ."

Oh, God, how she wanted his touch, his kisses. He went back to her mouth, held her roughly with his arms, so tightly he hurt her back and waist, as he drank deeply of her lips. Then abruptly she was shoved from him, at arms' length, while he gazed down at her with blue eyes blazing.

Suddenly he dropped his arms and moved away,

turning his back on her. The only sounds in the room were her harsh breathing and his. She could not move, only sway, in the receding moments of their passion. He was rejecting her again, as he had in her bedroom at the chalet.

He turned about, at the length of the room from her. "I must beg your pardon, Fraulein! I forgot myself. That was unforgivable!"

She stared back at him in silence, hurt by his words. He had not said what she wanted him to say. No. He had only used her to drain the emotion left over from his shortened meeting with his mistress.

She managed to say, faintly, "I made you angry." She meant, by interrupting him with Elza von Hulsen.

"Ja, ja!" he said, with emphasis, "very angry! Still, I should not have done that. Sit down again!"

He pointed to the piano bench, arrogantly sure of himself. She sank down weakly, not at all certain she could play. But he did not ask her to play.

"You must not listen to the critics. Cease to read them if you are so disturbed by them! I teach you because you have talent! You are willing to work hard! So! I am planning a concert in February. The Countess Puffenbach may sponsor this. If she does not, I have another plan."

He frowned in thought, whirled about again in his pacing.

"I wish you to play some piano and violin works with your friend Miss Huntingdon. I have selected some music for you to take home and discuss with her. See if she is willing. If so, I will talk to her instructor, and we shall make arrangements. Ja?"

"Ja, Maestro," she said meekly. She was relieved that he seemed to have forgotten his mistress for the time being.

"Hum. Now the Brahms again. Remember, it is dark, somber, melancholy. Try again. Play."

She felt dark, and somber, and melancholy, that he could forget so quickly that they had just been locked in a passionate embrace. She played it as he wished, and he was satisfied.

He had her play other numbers for him. He criticized her mercilessly, but she took it quietly. Nevertheless she was exhausted by the end of the two hours. He helped her gather up her music.

She managed to say bravely, "I must apologize to you, Maestro, for my—my display of temper today. It was wrong of me. You have been—very kind to teach me."

"Ja, ja. It takes time, but I do it because it seems to me worthwhile," he said, more kindly. "Now! My mother and sister are coming to Vienna tomorrow to stay for a week or so. No family but the baby! They expressed a wish to play some music with you, and become better acquainted also. Will you come as usual on Thursday, but plan to stay for the day and evening?" So, his mother was not in the house! She felt better about that earlier scene, though not much.

"I shall be happy to do so, Maestro. I shall enjoy it immensely!" Her spirits lightened. His family liked her; his mother wanted her to come, and so did he!

"Good, good. Now, be sure to speak to Miss Huntingdon and show her the violin and piano numbers I have given you. You may go over some of them together, but do not do much until I can tell you about them." Stern again, and serious.

He accompanied her to the door. She had worn her mink coat and heavy boots because of the thick snow and cold. "Do not come farther, Maestro," she said quickly. He was not wearing anything over his blue silk jacket.

He frowned at her. Then he said in a ridiculous high-pitched voice, like a small boy, "Yes, Mama! No, Mama!" They both burst out laughing, and it cleared the air.

He waited at the door and waved to her as she entered the barouche and sat down. She waved back, smiling, and went on her way.

Lukas watched her out of sight, then returned to the study. He had intended to work on a composition. Instead he paced back and forth, back and forth, until Theo returned from university, red-faced and breathless from racing the wind.

He could not rid his mind of the softness of Diana's form in his arms, the perfume of her body, the sweetness of her opened lips. How soft her white skin, how silky she was leaning against him. He remembered again what he had not been able to forget, that night at the chalet when he had almost taken her.

"God," he muttered, and shook his head. He had lost himself completely, lost all control. Had she been insulted? Did she hate him for his boldness? The critics must have hurt her deeply, for her to have burst out at him like that. But that did not excuse his behavior. He had treated her like a—a mistress! He muttered to himself. "I must not do this! She trusts me, as a guardian! I am her Maestro, not her lover!"

He was furious that Elza von Hulsen had come to the house this morning, and at such an awkward time. She had said she was worried about her brother, and wanted the advice of a man. They had scarcely begun to speak when Elza had clutched him and begun to weep.

What was the matter with the woman? Their affair

was long over, though he strongly suspected she wished to begin it once more. Well, he was done with it. She was a beautiful woman, and her passions were wild. She had pleased him for the short time they had been together.

But it was over! He wanted no more to do with her. He had to see her in the music circles; she had influence that could do his pupil good. But that was all!

When Diana had come in and seen Elza von Hulsen practically in his arms, Lukas had been furiously angry. The contempt in Diana's eyes—in her face! What she must think of the decadent Viennese!

He had almost taken her at the chalet. Thank God his mother had wakened and called him. He had wanted Diana madly—she was such an attractive woman. Yet he knew she was a virgin, not for his careless taking. She must save herself for her husband.

But how he longed to be her lover!

The word "lover" thrilled through him. He paused, smiling absently to himself. Lover. Her lover. How he would enjoy that. To unfasten those long thick strands of ash-silver hair and bury his face in them. To unbutton her demure gown, and put his face against those soft heavy breasts. God, how silky she was, how he had enjoyed the feel of her in his arms. He had put his left arm about her, his stiff arm, and she had not flinched. It had moved farther than he had thought— was he regaining strength in it? He moved it slowly, carefully. Yes, it moved well, but the fingers were stiff; he could not play skillfully with them.

His mother and sister and the little baby arrived in his carriage at five o'clock on Tuesday. He was happy to see them looking more relaxed. He had deliberately sent his own comfortable carriages for them, and five of his best men—he had not even asked his brother-in-law's permission this time. Best to go ahead and do what he wished.

He greeted them warmly, and fed them early, and sent them all to bed. They had a good visit on Wednesday, and on Thursday Diana came.

She was pink-cheeked and happy. "Alicia is most happy about the idea for the concert, Maestro!" she said at once. "We are so anxious to work on the violin and piano sonatas."

"Good, good! Ask her to come with you on Monday, and we shall work together all the day. Stay for lunch with us, and my family will meet Alicia also. I will speak to her instructor for her, and take care of all formalities of the lessons."

"You said you had an idea for the concert."

"Yes, something different. I have spoken to my mother. She agrees with me, and will help us. We shall go to Salzburg for the concert."

He watched her eager face with satisfaction. "Salzburg! Oh, Lukas!"

He beamed at her, realizing that she was using his intimate name more and more often. "Yes, Salzburg. We are going to my apartment there, with Mama as chaperon for you and Alicia. There we will present a recital in the very hall in the Residenz where Mozart conducted!"

Diana turned quite white and sat down on the piano bench. She put her hands to her heart. "Oh, Lukas," she breathed. "Where—Mozart—"

"Yes, yes, to the light of a hundred candles, with the white fresco setting off you and Alicia in elaborate gowns of Mozart's time."

She stared at his excitement, her own heart beating so fast he saw the tiny pulsebeat in her white throat. "Good—heavens," she said in English. He loved her soft clipped speech, the way she spoke English when she was terribly moved and the way she held her hands to her breast.

"But I will explain all this later. It is partly my mother's idea, and she will be there to help explain. For now, we must work!" he said gaily, and opened the music. "Now, Fraulein Musician, how did the Brahms go?"

"Much, much, much better!" She laughed. "Oh, you take my breath away, and then expect me to play a somber melody!"

They laughed, then worked away for quite two hours. When they had finished to their satisfaction, he took her upstairs to greet his mother and sister in the blue-and-rose drawing room. Luncheon was laid. They waited for Theo, who had promised not to let anything delay him.

Margarethe was looking brighter, he was happy to see. She did need to get away from the demands of her family at times. She and they talked music. Diana sat down at the small harpsichord in the dining room at one point to demonstrate something she had said. Margarethe went over to the instrument and leaned against it to ask a question. Lukas filled his eyes at the lovely sight—Diana in her favorite bright blue and silver, her hair in a coronet with demure wisps falling in front of her ears over her forehead; Margarethe in dark blue velvet, a long strand of pearls on her matronly breast, her plump figure still the shape of an hourglass. And his mother, in deep rose velvet on the light rose sofa, watching and listening, interjecting an intelligent comment from time to time.

Theo came in, cheeks rosy from the deep January cold. He went around, kissing the hand of each lady, and lingering mischievously when it was Diana's turn.

Lukas found himself watching intently, almost suspiciously as they laughed at each other. Was there some deeper feeling growing here?

No, no, they treated each other almost as brother and sister. He must not be silly. But who could help admiring her, coming to love her? She was so lovely, so smart and talented, so gentle and womanly!

Diana had helped him so much. As he watched her with his mother and sister and brother, he thought that she seemed almost part of the family now. They addressed each other by familiar names now, and with affection. She and Margarethe had liked each other at once, and so had she and his mother. And Theo had been devoted to her at once.

But she had helped Lukas most of all. She had pulled him out of a dismal depression. He had returned to Vienna almost defiantly, determined to make a career of music, though he could never perform on a piano in public again. But he had not been happy or eager. She had given him a joy in music again, an eagerness. He felt happy, alive, even joyous once more. And she had done it with her own enthusiasm for music, her eagerness for life and art.

On Monday she had demanded of him why he had accepted her as a pupil. He had been thinking about that. It had been fate, he decided, a kind wonderful fate that had brought her to his attention. He had admired her talent and her determined spirit, and had wanted to help her.

And in helping her he had helped himself so much more. He felt alive and vigorous, for the first time in several years. He had finished his opera and had gone through the effort and agony of getting it produced, and it had been a success! He was admired once more in Vienna. Moreover, he had regained his self-respect.

He had conducted again. He had introduced Diana in public and been proud of her, his student. And he was composing again! Music poured from his mind and heart; he wakened at night with music blazing in him, and he would rise and light a lamp and write it down for an hour.

Diana had done this to him. She, with her lovely face and demure manners, her cool British air, her vitality. In a few months she must go home. No, no, he thought, she must not go home! Her father must be persuaded to let her have another year, and then another.

After luncheon they all went over to his master suite. The curtains and draperies were drawn aside to allow the warm January sunshine to stream in.

Theo brought his violin, Margarethe sat at the harpsichord, and Diana and Constantia shared the piano bench. Lukas brought out his flute and piccolo—he could play them despite his crippled hand—and they had a merry, relaxing time of it.

The doors were left open. Lukas knew the butler tiptoed in the hallway, the maids sat in the hall on sofas to listen, the cook heard from the floor below and the coachmen could hear from the downstairs hall. All the afternoon from luncheon to late evening they played and played. It was sheer delight.

From time to time the musicians exchanged places. Lukas took the piano bench with Diana and played the upper part with his right hand, while she played the lower. His mother took a violin and Theo a cello, and they played those for a time. All had been musically inclined since childhood. And it had been far too long since they had made music like this.

Lukas brought out some of his recent compositions, and some of Diana's, and some they had worked on jointly, and together they all worked at those. Occasionally he stopped and rapidly scribbled some notes that would enable him to write out the rest later.

Lately the idea had come to him that he should publish some of his work. Why not also copublish some with Diana, some works of his and of hers, and put both names on the music?

After all, she had worked on finishing some of his compositions, and he had advised her on hers. Would she be insulted at the suggestion?

He knew the music world. If Diana published some of her compositions alone she would be insulted and derided. He had rightfully warned her that her performance would be reviewed critically because she was a woman; and as a composer she would be treated even more harshly. Some critics actually believed that no woman had the intelligence to compose good music.

But how would she take it if he suggested joint publication and joint authorship of their music? Would she be dismayed, upset? She was proud. Would she think he was trying to steal her compositions?

He was deep in thought about this, and as a result he was absentminded at tea and later at dinner. His mother smiled indulgently, and said, "My Lukas is thinking of more music!"

He was, and smiled, but shook his head. He would speak to Diana about this soon, and risk her pride and her doubts. If she had something published, even with him, it might convince her stubborn father that Diana did have talent, and he might allow her to continue her studies here in Vienna.

To Lukas, that had become very important.

He must be cautious with Diana. It was a wonder she still seemed to trust him, after the reckless way he had treated her at the chalet. His mind still mused over that night. He had been much stronger, had almost forced her—yet he had had the distinct impression that she had been willing.

He had no intention of marrying her, she must know that. He had been hurt badly, and shied away from marriage. Yet—yet she was so lovely, she had been so silken and yielding in his arms—Still, he must forget that. He must not be tempted to kiss her again.

Chapter 16

Sunday morning was cold and gloomy. Diana and Alicia had gone early to Catholic Mass with Cousin Helena. They enjoyed the colorful ceremony in the beautiful Cathedral of St. Stephen, and Frau Lewisohn had explained the Mass to them. Even when they could not understand the Latin words they loved the glorious music.

After luncheon Diana was practicing when Alicia tapped at the door. Diana opened it.

"The captains have arrived!" she announced joyfully. "The sun is trying to come out, and they say it is a perfect day for ice-skating. Afterward they want us to remain for dinner in a fine restaurant. What do you say?"

Diana hesitated, but only for a minute. "It sounds marvelous! What are you going to wear?"

"My warmest wool suit, and twenty layers under!" Alicia grimaced. "It is bitterly cold, you know. But we can always dash inside to the café!"

"Do ask Pauline—can she go?"

"She is eager to come! Captain Mueller has charmed

her, and you know he always has the latest gazettes to amuse her!"

Diana changed quickly to a thick blue wool and mink suit. She picked up her mink muff, and with the matching hat perched on her coronet of blond hair, she was ready.

Alicia met her in the hall, in her fine green and ermine suit. Together they made a smart and graceful appearance, and both captains beamed in appreciation.

Pauline soon joined them and they all went laughing out to the waiting carriage.

The January day was a bitter cold one. The wind was biting, the sun hidden behind sullen black and gray clouds. People scurried along the streets with heads bent, dashing indoors at the first opportunity. Only a few hardy souls were at the café in the Prater when the group arrived. The maître d' greeted them happily. Pauline was soon installed at a table near the window so she could watch the fun, and the table was piled high with her favorite lurid gazettes.

Diana shivered as Captain Mueller helped her change from her walking boots to her ice skates. "Whoo! What a day! Are we sure we want to skate?" she laughed.

He glanced up from his kneeling position, into her animated face. "I have waited for this too long," he said with unusual seriousness. "I have not seen you for a month!"

She glanced away from the burning black eyes, suddenly shy. She had no wish to encourage him. She thought of him only as she did her brothers, good sports, fun to be with.

He helped her up, then sat down to change his own boots. She went out on the ice, slipping a little. "Wait for me!" he called sharply.

She appreciated his protectiveness. In a couple minutes he joined her, taking both her hands in his and pushing off together smoothly across the ice.

The air burned their cheeks and noses; breathing drew icy wind into their lungs. But what fun! They laughed, and sang along with the music from the café. When the music became a waltz, they turned to each other. Gardell put his arm about Diana's waist, and they smoothly waltzed and turned and swung to the rhythm. Skating made them warmer, and the sun finally came out, turning the sky more blue. The bare tree limbs were outlined like a delicate ink drawing against the heavens.

Captain Ernst Schmidt was teasing Alicia or telling her jokes. Their laughter rang out again and again on the ice. How pleasant the men were, thought Diana with satisfaction. As long as they don't get amorous!

It was fun to have such handsome companions, such charming men to escort them about. Oh, occasionally they teased, and tried to get her and Alicia to come to their apartment on the Ring! But Pauline was always there to shake her head and keep them proper. The men accepted her decisions gracefully. Diana thought they could be devils if they had the chance, but if a lady was cautious they could do no harm.

The air was really too cold to stay out long. They went indoors after an hour, to remove their coats and warm up by the roaring fire in the cosy brick fireplace at the café. Then they sat down at the window to watch the few lone skaters out on the ice, to chat, and drink chocolate.

"I missed you very much," said Gardell Mueller seriously, turning to Diana.

Her cheeks burned with the cold and then the heat, and now with a little embarrassment. "It is very kind of you," she said formally, withdrawing a little as he bent closer to her. "I hope you had a merry holiday season."

Diana disliked it when he tried to kiss her or touch her. Now that Lukas had almost made love to her, she felt she understood men and their male natures better, and she realized she must be more cautious with Captain Mueller. They seemed easily aroused, these passionate men.

"Oh, it was very merry." Captain Ernst Schmidt winked and put his finger along his freckled nose. His red hair was mussed; he had not bothered to brush it back after removing his cap. Ernst always looked like a naughty boy. "I could tell you about one or two parties. . . ."

Gardell frowned at his friend. "And you talk too much!" he rebuked sharply, his black eyes somber. "I drank to forget, you know it!"

Schmidt looked at him and stopped. "Oh, very well . . ."

Diana wondered what he wanted to forget. Was it something about his sister? He evidently adored her. How different they were! Elza seemed so devilish and mischievous, so daring. Was Mueller like his sister? Was there a side to him that he did not show to Diana?

"Tell me about your holiday with von Korda!" Mueller had turned to Diana. "You went to his chalet in the Alps?"

She compressed her lips, to hear him phrase it so. Alicia looked up quickly from her cup of chocolate.

"With his family," she emphasized. "We made music much of the time. His mother and sister are very musically inclined, as is his brother."

"And you played the piano all the time?" he probed.

"You did not go out ice-skating, or walking in the snow—in the moonlight?"

He sounded downright nasty and jealous! Diana gazed at him thoughtfully. In moderate tones, she answered.

"The baron, his brother, and I went skating on a rather rough pond near the chalet. It was different skating there; the surface was more dangerous than here, but we enjoyed it. Sometimes we all walked in the snow, in the daytime. It is not safe at night, Captain. There are too many hazards, like tree trunks under the snow, and boulders."

There was a little silence after her sedate speech. Captain Mueller seemed distracted. Then he burst out, "I do not like it that you went with him! You know his reputation! I have told you about him and my sister! How could you go, knowing my feelings?"

Pauline gasped, Alicia stared from one to the other. Diana said quietly, "I hope you do not repeat this again! I respect Maestro von Korda and his family. They treated me with every courtesy. We were well chaperoned and my cousin approved of my going. Your insinuations are insulting."

Remembering the night when von Korda had made love to her, Diana blushed. True, he had not persisted, his mother's voice had saved Diana from a fate for which she had longed. But Mueller did not need to know all that!

Captain Mueller hit his fist on the table, making the drinking cups jump. Everyone in the café turned at the clamor.

He jumped up, then, shoving back his chair. He strode away to the fire and leaned there at the mantel, gazing into the blaze.

Captain Schmidt sighed and leaned forward. He

said, in confidential tones, "Gardell feels this very keenly. I tell you as a friend, he is very upset over von Korda and his sister. Von Korda continues to entice her to see him, even though it is only in the company of her close friend, the Countess Puffenbach. Gardell longs to have the affair over and done with, but von Korda does not listen to his pleas. And his sister is enchanted by him. It is too bad!"

Diana felt sickened. She knew all this, yet had not wanted to acknowledge it to herself. That von Korda should be so weak and so wicked! Yet she knew that there was deep passion in him. He had grabbed and kissed her—and he had fought the duel over the Countess von Hulsen with her husband!

"Perhaps we should go home," suggested Alicia.

"No, no!" Captain Schmidt jumped up, pushing back his chair. "This is too bad of Gardell to spoil our day like this! I will speak to him. Wait, he will be all right presently."

Captain Schmidt went over to his friend, and placing one hand on the crimson smart uniform shoulder, spoke to him earnestly.

They spoke about five minutes. Captain Mueller seemed to relax. He stood up straight and nodded, and Captain Schmidt clapped his shoulder comfortingly a couple times.

Then they returned to the table. Captain Mueller clicked his heels together and bowed to them. "My apologies. I should not have spoken as I did," he said quietly. His face showed remorse, his black eyes were wet with tears. Diana felt ashamed of herself, yet she wondered if he were acting the part.

"Do not think of it," said Alicia hastily. "Sit down. Shall we go out again? Is the ice safe?"

"I will find out," said Captain Schmidt with relief.

After speaking to the attendant outside, he returned. "It is very cold; the ice is safe!"

They went out again, and enjoyed the rest of the afternoon. Perhaps at Schmidt's suggestion, they changed partners, and he took Diana about, while Mueller escorted Alicia. They laughed and laughed, Schmidt was so very amusing, telling stories about his fellow guardsmen, about pranks they played on each other. It sounded like rough amusement, their military world! How like little boys they could be, thought Diana indulgently. She liked this side of them. If only they were always like this.

Mueller seemed to be exercising himself out of his gloom and despair over his sister. He was pleasant when they returned once more to the café.

"Tell me of your home, Diana," he urged.

She talked a little about that, of her town house in London, her father and two brothers, their social life.

"You entertain much?" he asked.

"Mostly father's friends," she said. "He has many friends and acquaintances in London and in the country. Many have been business friends of long standing."

"And you ride? And play tennis? That is marvelous for a woman," he remarked.

"Many women ride in the country," she explained. "Some even ride to the hounds. Fox hunting and deer hunting are very popular. However, I only ride for pleasure. And you—I expect you ride quite a bit?"

"Yes, on my brother-in-law's estate. He has a huge place, and they keep a dozen fine stallions and mares. Elza adores it above all. To see her in Vienna, one would think she was all society, balls, and cafés! But she loves the country best."

That was another side of the glamorous countess,

thought Diana. How Gardell's face glowed as he spoke of her! They must be very close.

They turned to Alicia next and politely urged her to tell of her life in America. Diana was very surprised at the way the American girl cleverly evaded their questions and talked only of life in New York, operas, balls.

After a splendid dinner the captains reluctantly returned them to the boardinghouse. Alicia changed to her robe and came to Diana's room to gossip and to talk about the next day with von Korda.

Diana asked her, "Why didn't you tell them some of your interesting stories about your early days, about your father and his work on the railroads, and living in a cabin? I thought that was so fascinating."

Alicia smiled and brushed her hair vigorously with her thick white brush. Diana watched the brilliant waves begin to form under her hand.

"Ah, Diana, you are not a snob!" she said. "Don't you know most Austrians are? Most Germans also!" And she scowled. "They think of us as middle class because our fathers work! Your father is a tradesman, they think! No matter how wealthy he is. And my father is looked down on, as a laborer! Sure, he worked with his hands, I can remember his swinging a pick! But I am proud of him for that! I love him, I admire him. He is the best father in the world. He works hard, he became successful by his own efforts!"

Diana stared. She could scarcely believe it. "But Gardell—and Ernst—you mean, they look down on us, because of our fathers?"

"Sure," said Alicia, practically. "We have no titles, my dear! And Gardell is related to a countess. Even von Korda has his title, his estate, his airs. Yes, dear, they are all above us! Maybe I feel it more because I live in America. We have no titles at all, you know—forbidden by the Founding Fathers! President Washington refused to be called a king!" she added proudly.

She chatted on about that while Diana pondered in silence. If Captain Mueller looked down on her—what did he expect of their association? She had imagined he hoped to marry her! She had meant to discourage him, although he showed no signs of proposing. Surely—surely he did not think of her lightly! He did not think to make her his mistress! No, of course not. Yet—he had never once mentioned asking her to dine with his sister. He had introduced her to his sister, but the countess had never once followed up on that, or invited her to visit with them and meet their society friends. And it must be because of the reason Alicia mentioned.

And what about von Korda? Did he look down on her because she had no title? She found that difficult to believe.

"Lukas's mother is a baroness, but she never uses the title," said Diana.

"Well, she is probably an exceptional woman," Alicia answered with a shrug. "It will be nice to see her again tomorrow. I have only met her once. Oh, well, let's talk about what we will play. Is Lukas a strict teacher?"

"Very!" said Diana, and they both laughed.

The next morning Alicia found out how strict. They began working on the numbers he had chosen for the Salzburg concert. There would be two works by Mozart, an early sonata for piano and violin, and a late, more sophisticated one. They would also play one of von Korda's sonatas for piano and violin and an arrangement of Schubert songs.

Alicia would play a Bach sonata for unaccompanied

violin as a showpiece for her talents. And Diana would play one of her own recent compositions.

"You shall choose which one," von Korda said that morning, studying her thoughtfully.

She was quite pale with excitement. "Really—in public—at this event—one of my own?"

"Yes. You realize—the reviews could be quite devastating, Diana. But I want you to find out for yourself what the critics say. This will be an ordeal for you. They will be harsh on both of you as women performers. For a woman to play her own compositions!—still, I think they deserve to be heard. Do you want to do this?"

"Yes, I do," she said. She was bewildered that von Korda was telling her so frankly what to expect as a performer and a composer. He knew she had been upset over the other reviews. Did he think she could not take it?

"Very well, what would you like to play?"

"The one I composed at Christmas," she said promptly. It was the most advanced of her own works. "I call it 'A Day in the Alps,' and it is—let me see— Opus Four, no. 3."

He smiled slightly at her precision and wrote it down in his heavy black handwriting. " 'A Day in the Alps,' very well. It should go well, if they are honest! It is a lovely piece of music, and your harmonies are well done. But you must brace yourself, Diana; there may be little applause. I only hope they will judge the work on its own merits, rather than on their own prejudices."

"I'll take that chance," she said quietly. She would prepare herself for this, she must. She had to play her own works in public one day, or nobody would!

Alicia had been listening in silence, her face serious.

Now she smiled and said, "If they say nasty things, I will break my violin over their heads!"

Instead of looking shocked, von Korda flung back his handsome blond head and laughed aloud. It was rare that he did this, and Diana was surprised.

"Please—do not waste a fine instrument so!"

They went back to their practicing and worked hard for three hours. Then von Korda took them upstairs to his drawing room, where his mother and sister greeted them eagerly.

"I heard you playing. You are splendid!" cried Margarethe, taking Diana's hand. "Mother has been telling me about your costumes, and I know you will both be beautiful!"

Theo came in soon, and over luncheon they discussed the concert. Lukas told them what music he had chosen. Everyone looked thoughtful when he said Diana would play one of his compositions and one of her own, but little was said about it.

The talk turned to their gowns. Lukas was planning the costumes, for which he took much ribbing from his sister, who teased him that he never used to pay so much attention to dress!

"I want them to fit into the setting," he said, unperturbed by her words. "Gowns of Mozart's time, in a setting he himself used, with candles. It will be elegant! The girls are both beautiful; they will look splendid. About the jewels—"

"As my gown is blue, I thought my sapphire and diamond set," said Diana. "But I would rather not wear bracelets or more than one ring. I am afraid they might clatter against the keys."

"And I want only a ring, and something in my hair," said Alicia. "A necklace would scratch my violin, and I won't have that!"

Lukas laughed again at her. Apparently he thought her very amusing and clever. Diana was surprised at her own jealousy, and tried to suppress it. Alicia was a dear friend, and damn it, thought Diana, with unusual vehemence, she *was* amusing and clever, yes, and very dear!

But she noted all that afternoon how Alicia could make Lukas laugh. Alicia was so lively and attractive, she kept them all laughing, until they returned to the work of planning for the concert.

She was to come with Diana to every lesson from now until the mid-February concert. Diana would not be alone with von Korda at all until after that concert. And if she did badly, or failed to make him proud, she might *never* see him again. She berated herself for being dismal and forced herself again to think only of the music.

Von Korda was arranging for a music publisher to print her sonata of the Alps at the time of her concert. He seemed hesitant about it, but she told him to go ahead, and resolved to pay him for it with some allowance money she had saved.

After tea Lukas sent them home in his barouche, and Diana found Alicia unusually silent.

At the boardinghouse Alicia said abruptly, "I want to show you something, Diana. I'll come right over." She then disappeared into her rooms.

Diana removed her thick coat and unpinned her hat. She sat down to take off her boots and put on her soft black house-slippers.

Alicia came back carrying a small sheaf of newspaper and magazine clippings.

"Diana, I debated whether to show you these," she said seriously. "I write often to mother, and of course I told her about you, and how beautifully you compose as well as play. Well, a woman—an American woman—as part of her concert played some of her own compositions. Mother sent me the notices, and, oh, Diana, they were so cruel to her! It is just as Lukas said." She shoved the clippings into Diana's hand.

Diana stared at her, and down at the clippings.

"Diana—if you decide not to play the sonata, Lukas will understand!" said Alicia passionately. "I would hate for them to treat you like this!" And she leaned forward and kissed Diana's cheek. "Read them, and burn them, if you like! I think it is hateful, but women must expect this, as he said!"

She went out and shut the door hard. Diana sank down on the sofa, lit the lamp beside her, and began to read.

She could scarcely believe the critics' venom.

"This woman—this female—daring to play such trite silly pieces on a reputable concert stage. . . . One hears she hired the hall and filled it with her friends; it did not keep the audience from booing."

"Harsh harmonies, trite themes—I recognized melodies of Schubert and Schumann and Chopin. How stupid of her to think she could get away with such brazen stealing!"

"Mrs. Smythe calls herself a composer. As a pianist and composer she would do well to go back home, mind her children, and sing them nursery songs."

"The performance recalled the old saying 'I would as soon think a woman can perform well in public as that a dog can stand on his hind legs and give a speech.'"

One more serious longer account concluded, "Women have smaller brains, they must reconcile themselves to that. They are not suited for difficult work such as composing. And they have not the stamina for concert performance. Let Mrs. Smythe perform for friends in her parlor, I am sure she will do very prettily. But it is not for her and other women to attain such high exalted positions as men do."

About an hour later Alicia stuck her head in the door.

"Are you all right?" she asked anxiously. "I have been scolding myself for showing them to you!"

Diana smiled at her. "I am all right," she said calmly. "Come—look at this."

She pointed out several places in the reviews. "Look," said Diana, "they say she has copied the melodies of Schubert and Schumann and Chopin. Another said—here—she has copied the style of Liszt! And then they say her melodies are silly. How can both be true?"

Alicia stared at the lines. "You are right! Of course! How can both be true? If her melodies sound like Chopin—how can they be trite? And the style of Liszt is immensely difficult—he was a master pianist!" She began to laugh. "Oh, Diana, aren't they hypocrites?"

"I think so," said Diana, and put down the clippings. "I feel better. I hope Mrs. Smythe notices that also, and goes right on playing and composing. She must not be discouraged—I know *I* don't mean to be discouraged!"

"And you will play your own sonata at Salzburg?" asked Alicia.

"Nothing but a snowstorm will stop me!"

Chapter 17

Johanne Weiss and Arnold Lindau had been spending more and more time together. Often he came to the café at night as she was finishing, and had a midnight supper with her before taking her home.

They spent every Wednesday together now. He had a job with a symphony orchestra, that took up much time, and of course he was devoted to his children, but he managed to be with Johanne as often as she would permit.

She grew to like him so very much. The more they were together, the more she liked him. He had a gentle nature, yet he was masculine, firm, strong. His sense of music was deep and he was very talented, capable of playing several instruments in addition to the cello.

On one Wednesday in February they had gone home together after his rehearsal and spent the rest of the day and evening at his apartment with the children. Johanne had prepared dinner that evening, noodles and meatballs, while the children clustered about her, always under her feet.

She could not rebuke or scold them. On the contrary, she loved it!

"You said you would play the piccolo tonight, Papa," reminded young Hugo. "I want to learn to play it better. Show me how to make trills."

The child had his own little instrument, and Arnold took out his larger one, and they began to work together. The older girl Cornelia listened quietly, but Maria became restless. She climbed up into Johanne's lap, asking, "Do you know any stories?"

Johanne did not like to disturb Arnold and Hugo, so she whispered, "Later!"

Maria was not very patient, though. She pouted a bit, and twisted about on Johanne's lap. Arnold looked at them, his eyes crinkled up in love and amusement.

"We can talk with our piccolos, Maria," he said, and played a merry little questioning tune on his.

She stared. Johanne said, "Yes, and I can answer him," and she sang a high trill that matched his trill.

Hugo laughed aloud, and said, "Go on, go on!"

Arnold smiled, and put the piccolo again to his lips. He made it sing a merry little phrase, and Johanne answered it. Another, and she answered again, then added a little trill, like a question. Arnold answered, and she trilled, and he whiffled another, creating a musical dialogue.

They played at this for about ten minutes, piccolo asking and soprano answering. They made the game into a song, a duet for two lovers.

Cornelia listened with a sober glow on her small face. Hugo fingered his piccolo eagerly, as though longing to join in. But Maria sat with her mouth open, her face upturned first to Johanne and then to her father, like a small bird hoping to be fed. Such big brown eyes, so melting and trusting, so wistful and hopeful.

They were all adorable. Johanne had come to love them as she loved their kind good father. When they had finished, Arnold put the instruments in their cases and said, "And now to bed, my darlings!"

There were the usual weak protests, but Maria was yawning. Arnold put Hugo to bed, and Johanne tucked Cornelia and Maria into their little beds in the next room. How sweet and small their little bodies were, she marveled as she lovingly drew a blanket over each. Maria reached up to kiss her, and when Johanne planted a tender kiss on her forehead, then Cornelia wanted a kiss also.

Softly the doors were closed, the last good-nights whispered. Then Johanne returned to the living room, and stood waiting. Should she go home? It was just eight thirty.

"Could you stay for a bit?" Arnold asked hopefully. She nodded, and sank down shyly onto the sofa.

He sat down beside her and gazed at her lovingly. "The children need you as much as I do," he said presently.

She looked down at her large hands. They felt empty, now that the children were in their rooms. "You know—you know—that I cannot have babies," she said awkwardly, feeling embarrassment.

"Perhaps not. But I have my three, and how they need you! They adore you. They need a mother, and my house needs a woman in it. You make my rooms glow, and when you leave the light goes out."

"Oh, Arnold . . ."

"It is true," he said, nodding. "You know that I love you, I have loved you from the first moment I saw you. There is a true woman, I said to myself. But I did not dare to dream you would even look at me—until you sat down with my children, as though they drew you to them."

"I noticed you early," she confessed shyly. "You were so tall, so fine, and you played so—so divinely. When you play, your face takes on such a wonderful glow."

He took her hand in his. "Johanne, will you marry me? You know my feelings."

"I would—like to. But I have said—my husband said—I am—frigid—cold—You deserve better. . . ."

He shook his head slowly. "You are not cold, I do not believe it. You hold my little ones like a mother already, with sweetness and gentle warmth. How Maria loves to cuddle up to your body. I long to do so myself!"

"Oh, Arnold . . ."

He did not touch more than her hand, but his warm brown eyes went over her quickly. "Yes, I long to," he whispered.

He did not take advantage of the fact that they were the only adults in the flat. He would never take advantage of her, she thought. He was so kind, so good, so thoughtful.

He would love her, with warmth and sensitivity, as he did his children. Oh, how she longed to take what he offered!

"But what if I have no children?" she whispered. It troubled her so much.

"If you did, I would love our babies. If you do not, we have our three already. You know—I think maybe your husband was very wrong about you. You said he married again, and he still has no children. I think it might be he who cannot have children," he said seriously.

"But we cannot marry just on the hope . . ." She faltered.

"Hope? I hope to have a warm loving woman in my bed, a gentle mother for my children, a wonderful lady who loves music as I do—we like so many of the same things, *Liebchen*," he murmured, and then he moved over and kissed her cheek softly.

He called a neighbor presently, and the woman sat with her husband in the flat while he took Johanne home. Johanne was happier than she'd ever been. She had to share this with someone.

As she came up the steps of the boardinghouse, she saw that Diana's lamps were lit, and once inside, she tapped shyly at her door.

Diana opened it at once, her warm blue eyes bidding Johanne welcome.

"Come in, come!"

"I am disturbing you?"

"Not a bit of it! I cannot make this come right." She gave a comical grimace at the sheets of music paper before her on the large table. "It will be better for being left for a time." She closed the door and drew forward the overstuffed chair for her guest.

"I have news that makes me happy," said Johanne, putting her large hands together nervously. "Herr Lindau—has asked me to be—his wife!"

"Oh, Johanne! How wonderful! You are so much alike!"

Diana could not have said anything that pleased and relieved Johanne more. She smiled at Diana. "Yes, we are alike, we love the children, music—homelife . . ."

"And you have agreed to marry him?"

"Ja. Soon, I think. My contract for singing in the café is over at the end of March. He asks that I not renew it, but marry him soon after. He earns a good living as a cellist, enough to support us."

"You will stop singing?"

"Nein," Johanne shook her head. "He does not ask that. He says I have a wonderful voice! But I shall take what contracts I wish. If Baron von Korda should ask me to sing, I will sing whenever he wishes. He is such a wonderful man, it is to him I owe my present happiness! For he hired me for the opera, where I met Arnold."

"I think you would have met Arnold one day anyway," said Diana positively. "It was meant to be! God meant it."

Johanne put her hands at her breasts. How wonderful to think so! "Ja, ja, ja," she repeated, sighing with pure joy. "What a marvelous man is Arnold. What beautiful children. God is good to me!"

"You deserve it, Johanne. You are a good woman."

"Never good enough," said Johanne seriously. "But I will go to Mass early tomorrow and thank the saints, and the Blessed Virgin, that such joy comes to me." She stood to leave.

Diana kissed her impulsively on the cheek and sent her on her way with many good wishes.

Rosalie Stamitz heard the news at luncheon the next day. Everyone in the boardinghouse was delighted for Johanne, and all kissed her and wished her well. Rosalie felt the little pang every unmarried girl feels at an engagement. Could this have been me? one thinks. But no, thought Rosalie, not me!

So she was able to kiss Johanne and congratulate Herr Lindau when next he came, and be happy for them. But marriage was not for her! Such a life she saw as another form of slavery. When women became truly clever, as Rosalie was, she believed they would realize what true freedom was, and how to get it!

On Friday evening Rosalie dressed for her part in the operetta *Black Forest Maiden* with special care and pride. The Baron von Korda had purchased two boxes for the night. He was bringing a large party, and Herr Vogler was ecstatic. Lately the attendance had begun to go down, and there was worry that they might have to close soon.

If Herr Baron von Korda praised them, though, and reported to his friends how fine the operetta was, it might stay on another month.

Vogler came to Rosalie's dressing room before the show. "You must sing well tonight, darling! And everyone must do well! Dance your little heart out!"

She meant to. She had fine plans for tonight. She smiled at him with her best demure smile and murmured, "As you say, Franzel!"

"Not in public!" he scowled, glancing at the maid, his voice low and harsh.

Rosalie changed her expression and nodded primly. "Ja, ja, Herr Vogler!"

At her first entrance she glanced about warily and saw the two boxes on the right. The Baron von Korda sat in the first one alongside his mother, in blue silk, and Diana Ballantyne in silver. There were others with them, and in the second box sat his brother Theo with Alicia and Johanne and Herr Lindau. A fine crowd, and all applauding with every number. The house was but half full, but she would sing and dance to them like an inspired goddess.

In her first major song, she sang a duet with her stage mistress. Fraulein Speckel always faced the audience, and Rosalie had to scramble about to sing outward. Tonight she turned her back on her mistress, in defiance of orders, and sang right to the Baron von Korda! Normally Rosalie's voice blended well with Fraulein Speckel's second soprano, but tonight Rosalie let her own voice soar up and up, to show up her rival!

Fraulein Speckel would have loved to kick her, Rosalie knew! But the audience applauded loudly at the duet, and Rosalie stood beside the lead singer as her equal and accepted her applause with merry little flirtatious curtseys that drew all eyes from the star.

At the intermission, Herr Vogler snarled at Rosalie. "You forgot your place, Rosalie! Do as I told you!"

"Ja, ja, Herr Vogler," she agreed mechanically, but without any intention of doing so. She wanted von Korda to hear her voice.

In the second act she had a solo, and she sang it as well as she had ever done. The house was absolutely silent as her pure soprano soared. She let the notes linger, closing her eyes so she would not see Vogler anxiously motioning her to go on! No, she would hold the notes, to let all hear how magnificently she sang, even if her dramatics did show up the lead.

Rosalie's interpretation was in great defiance of Vogler's orders. It threw the operetta out of balance for the second lead to sing so flashily, to extend her little part. But Rosalie wanted von Korda to hear her, and hear her he did. He leaned forward in the box listening to her. And at the end he applauded and applauded.

The others applauded also, and for several minutes the action stopped as the house made the floor shake with stomping and yelling. Rosalie took bow after bow, until Vogler, with a false smile, nodded to her, and began to play the chorus again.

He permitted her one more chorus, then began the next music very loudly, so she must turn and welcome her mistress. Oh, how Fraulein Speckel was angry! Her china-blue eyes flashed, and when she had a chance she pinched Rosalie sharply on her arm. "Vixen!" she whispered. "I'll get you for this!"

But Rosalie did not care. She had been heard by someone important!

The duet with the footman was in the middle of the last act. The footman was too scared of Vogler to cooperate with Rosalie, and when it was over he turned and marched away. She had to finish, curtsey, and run off the stage.

In her dressing room her friends crowded in and congratulated her. "You sang marvelously!" Diana said.

The Baroness von Korda congratulated her on her beautiful voice and her costume. Vogler stood in the corner and beamed with pleasure. From his expression Rosalie thought she had gotten away with her little scheme.

And the Baron von Korda shook her hand, raised it to his lips, kissed it, and said seriously, "You have a very fine voice, Fraulein Stamitz! Your tones are so pure. We must speak again about this, when your engagement is over. Who is your instructor?"

"Herr Franz Vogler, the conductor," said Rosalie, introducing them proudly. Vogler bowed and scraped and clicked his heels.

After they left the room, she changed with the help of the weary backstage maid and prepared to leave. Vogler returned.

"Your friends are waiting with the carriage," he said. "Leave us," he added, nodding to the maid, and she left, shutting the door, with a curious look at Rosalie.

Rosalie was in her costume again, the Alps dress she

wore to the theater. "What is it?" she asked pertly, as she reached for her cloak. "You are pleased with me tonight, Herr Vogler?"

With a grim angry face he reached out for her. But instead of kissing her, he began to shake her, his fingers pinching as he took hold of her slight body like a bulldog worrying a small French poodle.

"You dared to defy me! You dared to defy me!" he said, his voice gritting between his teeth. He shook her like a rag doll, so hard she thought her hair was coming loose.

"You're hurting me, Franzel!" she whimpered. Now his fingers dug cruelly into her shoulders.

"Hurt you, is it? Hurt you? I should strangle you! You threw my operetta all out of proportion tonight, and you did it against my direct orders! Who do you think is the lead, eh? Do you think because I make you the understudy, that you may take over on stage? God, I could kill you! And the Herr Baron was laughing at me, because my conducting was thrown off!"

"Nein, nein, he did not laugh! He respects you."

He did not hear or pay attention, so gripped was he by fury. "You will never do it again, you hear me? Never! Or I will have you thrown out! You will never sing on stage again, not in Vienna! You will return to your farm and your cows and your stinking beer halls!"

He gave her a final shake, and shoved her so hard she fell against the dressing table. She felt the corner dig into her back. She would have a bruise there tomorrow, she knew.

He straightened his coat, adjusted his hat, picked up his cane in trembling hands. He longed to strike her with it, she could tell. She cowered, truly frightened, against the table.

"Never again," he said, and left the room.

After a moment Rosalie straightened up. Her friends were waiting for her, she must put on her cloak and go.

Diana tapped and opened the door. "Dear Rosalie, are you ready—what is it?" she added sharply.

"Nothing, nothing, I am ready."

Rosalie turned her back to put her cloak on, but Diana saw her face in the mirror.

"What is it? What did he do?"

"Nothing! Let us go!" She brushed past Diana rudely. Diana said no more, but followed her out to the carriage in silence.

Von Korda helped her in as though she were a grand lady, but even his attentions could not take away the sting of her aches. Her shoulders hurt where Vogler's fingers had stung and pinched. And how her back ached!

Back at the house, she could scarcely enjoy the dinner and the champagne and the compliments.

She did not go to Vogler the next morning, as she usually did. She was too afraid. His temper could last for days. She would test his mood at the evening's operetta performance.

Instead she took herself to a café where she knew she would find Peter Hering. She sat down with him and offered to pose for him again. After all, if Vogler did throw her out, she would need more posing jobs.

"Sure, fine, how about this morning?" asked Peter in his casual way. He clicked his fingers for the waiter and ordered fruit juice for her. He knew she did not like hot chocolate and pastries; they put weight on her so quickly, and she was proud of her petite figure.

She drank the juice, and followed him to his studio. In the large cold attic room she removed her cloak and went to take her pose.

"Push your sleeves back, darling, let's see your white shoulders," said Peter, putting a fresh canvas on his easel.

She bit her lips. She had forgotten about that. "What about leaving them like this?" she asked quickly.

"Nonsense, why such modesty before your friends?" he joked. He came over, and carelessly pushed the white puffy sleeves down from her shoulders. Then he stared. "My God in heaven! Rosalie, what happened?"

She shoved the sleeves up again. "I fell."

"Onto both shoulders? Was it Vogler?"

Reluctantly she nodded.

"God, you're asking for trouble! He is a beast! What happened—was it last night? I thought von Korda's party was coming—didn't they show up?"

"Yes, they came. I—I made trouble," she said, avoiding his gaze. "I wanted them to hear my voice, the way it really is, not smothered the way Vogler—well, I went too far. He was furious that I sang so, they applauded—he had to do another chorus of my solo."

"Is that so bad? That might cause the operetta to run longer! People are tired of that fat cow's voice!"

She smiled reluctantly. Peter was a darling, so supportive and kind.

"He said I threw the show out of balance. But I wanted so much for von Korda to hear me! And he did, and said we must talk after the operetta closed."

"Well, it might be worth it then, darling!" Unperturbed, Peter took out his paints and began sketching her quickly. "Toward me, your skirts up a bit more to show your ankles. That's it. . . . So what now?"

She shrugged, turning her head the way he wanted. "I'll go on. Maybe von Korda will help me, maybe not. Vogler is still helping me now."

"Do not become too dependent on Vogler. He

changes his fancies with the wind—all Vienna knows it."

She was silent, and Peter became absorbed in his painting. He had the gift of complete concentration. She watched his slim form moving about the canvas, his quick fingers with the long brushes making the strokes. How good he was, how kind, asking nothing from her but to pose. And he always paid her at once, knowing she needed the money.

Lately Vogler had been rough with her in bed. She had almost come to dread their meetings. He must be a little mad, she thought at times. He liked to bite her breasts, and when she showed it hurt, he would do it again.

And he might discard her now; she was no longer a challenge to him. He changed mistresses with the wind, as Peter said. But for now, he still wanted her—she must take advantage of that, and get all the musical exposure she could. If she could star in his next operetta, she would be made!

She still needed the security of Vogler's favor and money to pave her way in the cutthroat music world. Girls with talent equal to or less than hers would get the coveted jobs instead of her, if their patrons had enough money to back the new shows. He could advance her career. She must keep him sweet, loving her enough to continue his favors to her. He had been furiously angry with her, however, and it would cost her dear to soothe him and make him show her his love once more.

Love! She made an ugly sound in her throat. Love. It was not love that they shared, it was sex. It was as impersonal as the mating of hogs in the pen, or sheep in the meadows.

Now, with Johanne and her Arnold, that might be

love. There was a radiance in their faces, a gentleness in the clasp of his hand, in his protectiveness as he helped her from the carriage.

But Herr Vogler knew not love, and neither had she ever known it. Maybe love was for just the Johannes of this world.

"Darling mine," said Peter plaintively, "what is that terrible expression? Are you going to kill? That is not my lovely meadow maiden! Come, now."

She gave him a radiant smile, and adjusted her gown to show more of her ankles.

"That is better! Why don't you sing me a song? One of your little melodies to soothe the cows!"

So she sang for him, one of her pretty little songs, and they laughed and he painted her well. He was finished by four, and she hurried back to her room to change for the theater.

Vogler was still furious with her that evening, but said no more, showing his wrath by glaring at her from the podium. She was careful to sing and dance just as he had directed, and gradually he relaxed, and gave her a nod of approval at the end.

She would be a good girl, she resolved, until the operetta closed. Then she would sweet-talk him into giving her the lead in the next one.

With good luck, and her skillful way of extracting favors from men, by next autumn she should be on her way to her goal.

It would take all her patience and her charm, but she would do it. Herr Vogler's vanity was his weak point. She could flatter him, seduce him, let him think he was the love of her life. Yes, she must be a brilliant actress offstage as well as on.

Chapter 18

Lukas von Korda stood back and surveyed his two protégées critically. But perfectionist though he was, he could find no fault at all.

They stood in the anteroom to the large concert hall, shortly before the Salzburg concert. His mother was carefully adjusting the silvery blue ribbon at Diana's white throat, fastened with an oval brooch of silver set with diamonds and sapphires.

Diana wore the gown he had had made for her, of the classic eighteenth-century style. The bodice was demure, an oval at her soft white breasts, only showing the tops. The color was pure deep blue, and the side skirts in a pannier arrangement with hoops at her sides were of blue and silver stripes. The bodice was fastened with frogs of silver down to the waist. For jewelry she wore only the brooch, and a matching hair clasp of the same jewels.

Lukas's gaze moved to Alicia. Baron Stanislav von Neumeister was with them again, and seemed unable to remove his gaze from her. He stared like a small boy in a bake shop! thought von Korda in amusement.

Alicia's flaming red hair was dressed like Diana's, unpowdered, and she wore a court-dress of green, fashioned after a gown Mozart's sister wore in a portrait that was once painted of her and her famous brother. A high bouffant, with long curls at the throat, set off her white skin. In her red hair sat a large butterfly brooch hairpin, made of silver set with diamonds and emeralds. An emerald-green ribbon set with the same jewels circled her throat.

Between them they were wearing a fortune in jewelry, von Korda thought ironically.

Well, everyone would stare. He had warned them of that, separately and together.

"I have deliberately dressed you so they will stare and take notice of you. Many comments will be made, I hope! I want everyone to sit up and remember you. Only know this, nine out of ten in the audience will admire your costumes and stare at you. The other one tenth will also listen to your music. And one out of one hundred will listen intelligently!"

Alicia had laughed, but Diana had heard him out, her face rather pale. "Just so they review us," said Diana.

"They will—but how, I do not know."

The concert was near, and he had done all he could. He knew they would play competently, perhaps brilliantly. The rest was in the hands—and pens—of the critics.

"It is time," said his mother, anxiously.

Alicia gave a nervous laugh and flirted her lashes at Stanislav. Von Korda wondered if she was beginning to like him a bit more. He hoped so; he was a likable fellow, and Alicia was not as serious and dedicated about her music as Diana was.

Diana gave a small decisive nod, her thoughts already on the music. She was ready, Lukas knew by the look in her blue eyes.

He opened the door and stood back. Alicia went out, holding her violin by the throat, her bow in her other hand. Diana followed her. They carried no music, for they disliked such distractions, and both girls memorized easily.

A loud murmur of surprise greeted the two ladies as they entered the large concert hall. Lukas von Korda waited a moment, then followed them quietly into the hall and took his place in the seat that Theo had held for him.

He was disappointed that Margarethe had not been able to attend. Her husband had refused permission, saying she had been away from home too much this winter.

He sat down and waited. His gaze went briefly about the familiar hall. His own suite of rooms in a nearby building enabled him to come to Salzburg often, for concerts or simply for vacations in the charming city.

The concert hall was large, with a small platform in the center on which rested the grand piano. Its ceiling was of white stucco, with a design of baby angels and cupids peeping from the corners and linked by a motif of stucco wreaths and vines. The *Rittersaal* was a very beautiful and elegant room. The middle of the ceiling was adorned by an oil painting, *The Breaking-in of the Horse Bucephalus by Alexander the Great,* painted in 1714.

Mozart had been here, more than one hundred years ago. When Lukas closed his eyes in this room, he could feel the presence of the youthful genius, conducting his own compositions, the serenades, divertimenti, the charming early symphonies.

When the girls began to play, the illusion of Mozart's presence was even more startling. They played first the Mozart early sonata for violin and piano.

The notes were clear, and they played well. Neither showed any sign of nervousness. Von Korda glanced about furtively at the audience, and was faintly amused. So many were staring at the girls through lorgnettes! He wondered if the fine ladies even heard the music, they were so busy studying the design of the gowns, the placement of the throat ribbons, the jewels.

But he had planned for this—a feast for the eye and ear.

The first piece concluded to enthusiastic applause. The critics, however, did not applaud; that was beneath some of them, and the others were staring critically. Lukas found himself grinding his teeth. His mother touched his arm gently, smiling a warning.

"Be calm, they're doing so well," she murmured, under cover of the applause. Stanislav, next to him, heard not a word. He was clapping so hard he could be heard all over the room, and a grin split his handsome face!

Von Korda listened more critically to the next composition, but found no fault at all. They were playing one of his own sonatas, Opus 12, no. 1, for piano and violin. Diana had finished the arrangement, but had insisted on not having her name on the program with his. "You did it all, really. I only wrote down what you wished," she had said to him.

Much applause followed. The audience always loved it when the composer was in the room. Diana and Alicia each held out a white hand to him to take a bow. He rose, bowed to the audience, and sat down again.

A slight pause, then the third piece, the last before the intermission, this one planned as a crowd pleaser. Diana had arranged some of Franz Schubert's familiar and popular songs for piano and violin, and the girls played them well. Some of the listeners hummed softly and swayed to the music.

The intermission seemed endless to von Korda, who stood it out in the corner of the room. Alicia tuned her violin, and frowned as Stanislav complimented her. "Thank you, thank you very much, but please do not bother me now!" she said curtly.

Diana diverted his attention, with a twinkle in her blue eyes. "She must tune her violin, but I don't have to tune the piano, Stanislav. How do you like our outfits?"

"Beautiful, stunning, you are both delectable!"

Finally the intermission was over. Von Korda stayed behind with Diana, as Alicia went out alone. From the little anteroom they listened to Alicia play her solo— an exquisite complicated Bach sonata for unaccompanied violin. She played it beautifully, and the room was completely silent for her. But it exploded into applause as she finished.

Alicia came back. "Whew, it is getting warm in there," she commented.

Stanislav had followed her out, like a big eager puppy. Now he promptly offered his large white handkerchief, and she accepted it and dabbed at her forehead.

"It was marvelous," he said to her soberly. "You are so talented. I wish my mother and family could have come to hear you."

"Thank you." She wiped her upper lip and sighed. "Maestro?"

"Very well done," said Lukas, and she smiled in relief.

Von Korda went over then to open the door for Diana. "Do well," he said. She nodded and gave him a quick smile.

This was the difficult piece; this was the reason for the concert. Diana would appear alone, and she was going to play one of her own sonatas, "A Day in the Alps." If they did not applaud, he would kill them, he thought soberly.

When Diana was halfway to the piano, he escorted his mother back to their seats. Stanislav and Alicia remained in the anteroom, with the door ajar so they could hear.

There was a little murmur from the audience, a critical one, as they stared from their programs back to Diana. The young English girl was going to play one of her own compositions! In the same program with two pieces by Mozart! Well, they would see what they would see!

He felt keenly the biases of the people in the audience, especially those of the gazette critics present. He knew them all. One had written an anonymous searing criticism of von Korda himself, on his first appearance. "He plays because he is wealthy, and can afford to buy an audience," the man had said. Theo had seethed. Von Korda had quietly gone about identifying this anonymous critic by watching for the same writing style in other reviews. He had felt contempt for the man, to mask such criticism in anonymity, while he signed his name to praises.

However, the man had a powerful patron, and what he said was read with respect. He did have some musical judgment, when he did not let his emotions cloud it.

Von Korda was proud of Diana. She seemed oblivious to the murmurs when she began.

The first movement was soft, as though she remembered the daybreak in the Alps, the glorious rising of the sun as it flamed out over the snowy meadows and above the tall blue mountain peaks.

Then the middle movement, as a storm rumbled over the Alps, echoing in the valley, the thunder and the avalanche like twin sounds of doom. The movement became very rapid, the sound *fortissimo;* von Korda was startled himself at how much power Diana released into the room. Her large hands crashed into the chords, thundered over the long runs. Her head was bowed over the piano, but he could see her profile was grave and intent.

The final movement began strongly, then moved into a questioning passage that had puzzled him since he had first heard it. What had been in Diana's mind? He had never asked her, feeling a composer had the right to keep his inspirations private. But what could she have been thinking about?

A brief repeat of the middle theme ensued, and then a variation of the first theme reappeared, in a tender minor key. Rather like a remembrance of the morning, as the evening sun descended on a tranquil scene.

The sonata ended in a minor chord, which Diana had insisted on. He had originally questioned her judgment, but now he saw it was right, that minor sound, fading in the room.

He led the applause. She had been magnificent. His brother Theo was clapping and beaming, and his mother applauded with all her strength. Others clapped also, and one critic joined in, his face smiling reluctantly. So he did like it! Lukas had hope.

The applause died, replaced by murmurs throughout the room as Diana bowed once more with calm dignity, and Alicia came forward for the last number.

The late Mozart sonata pleased the audience. It was something they were familiar with. They settled back to enjoy it, and the applause at the end was good, resounding and full. Diana and Alicia took bows three times, then glanced at von Korda. He nodded.

Alicia tuned her violin while Diana stood at the piano. In her clear clipped German, she said, "Thank you very much. We would like to play for you another piece by our Maestro, the Baron Lukas von Korda. This is his Rondo in E minor."

She sat down, disregarding their murmurs of surprise. Von Korda smiled grimly. They had expected an encore by Chopin or Mozart or Bach. So had he! Diana had surprised him again.

He settled back to listen critically. They had only gone over this twice with him in practice. It was a work he had composed when he had been tired and ill, about five years ago. It showed some despair, a sort of romantic agony, he thought. But it went well, Diana's judgment was vindicated, and the applause was hearty. He stood reluctantly to accept their applause for him, and then the applause died, and the concert was over. Two months and three lifetimes of preparation, and the concert was finally finished.

In the anteroom both girls turned anxious faces to him. "I was very proud of you both," he said briefly, and that seemed to be enough. They smiled and glowed, and turned to accept the congratulations of the friends who crowded in.

Three of the critics came and bowed over their hands. Von Korda stood close to Alicia to fend off vicious questions, and his mother did the same for Diana. They were both wise about the concert world of Austria.

It had gone well. He was satisfied.

They all adjourned to a reception at his nearby apartment, on the second floor of a magnificent building overlooking the Salzach River. What a fine view there was from some of the windows—of old bridges, and of the castle fortress on the hill. Old Hohensalzburg Fortress was Lukas's favorite, and he often looked up toward it before beginning a day of practice.

The apartment was huge. Guests clustered about the long buffet dining table, elegantly laid with huge platters of cold ham and beef, bowls of exotic fruits brought by carriage from Italy, and plates of pretty pastries made by the best bakery in Salzburg.

They moved then to the huge drawing room, done in rose and silver. As they ate they chattered and gossiped. All admired Diana and Alicia in their magnificent old-fashioned gowns and jewels and took note of each other in their fashionable evening attire. Everyone seemed to enjoy himself.

Lukas saw two nasty-tongued critics hovering near Diana, and moved quickly in that direction. She had her usual clear calm expression, her eyes smiling, her lips red and soft. They probably thought she was easy prey, but he knew better. Still, he would not see her distressed.

He was in time to hear one man say, "You know, it is because of your beautiful gowns that you were applauded, Fraulein Ballantyne!"

"So Maestro gave me to understand, sir," she said, without turning a hair. "One hopes that people did hear us, however. We came to play music."

The other man stiffened and snapped, "If your patron were not so wealthy as to buy out the hall, you would not have given a concert at all! It is a pity that a more deserving pupil did not have the occasion to perform!"

Lukas flared up protectively from behind them. "It would be difficult to find a more deserving pupil than I have, sir! Miss Ballantyne has a magnificent talent. You will all know it one day."

They turned to face the more formidable enemy. "But she will not last long, Herr Baron!" said the first man. "She is too pretty to be unmarried, nein?"

When they had all left, the words haunted him. Yes, Diana was too pretty to remain unmarried for long. And her father was too wealthy for her to be unnoticed by fortune hunters.

He had reluctantly come to admit, that he himself was in love with Diana. Yes, he loved her! She was so fine, so good, so lovely and talented. She was warm of nature, under that British cool that he had scoffed at. He had been coming to love her, admire her, respect her since they had first met.

Then—in the Alps, in the chalet, he had come upon her, calmly sitting under the grand piano with small Julie, hands clutched in hands, with closed eyes, ecstasy on her face, loving every minute of the music that poured over her.

Such a silly thing to do—to sit under the piano! But so natural, so sweet, and Julie had adored her for it. And he had turned away from the sight, feeling stunned with the knowledge he had tried to deny—that he loved her! Later, in her bedroom, he had come close to taking her. He knew then how deeply he was in love.

He had fought it off. He could not marry her. He wanted to help her with her career, he had vowed to do so. Yet, he loved her, wanted her, with his mind and his body.

However, if he married her, he would be betraying her as much as her father—betraying her talent. She would have to stop playing as his mother had stopped. She would become a wife and a mother, tired and worn with her duties, with little time to play even for her own amusement.

How could he, respecting her, do that to her?

He rose early the next morning, unable to sleep. Early as he was, he heard someone already playing the piano very softly. He dressed and went to the drawing room, to find Diana playing with foot firmly on the soft pedal.

"Did I waken you?" she asked, concerned, ceasing to play at once.

"No, but come to breakfast! Then we will go out and walk. I want to show you Salzburg."

They had arrived three days before, but the girls had been practicing so much they had scarcely gone out. Diana smiled and agreed. "I should like that very much."

"Is Alicia awake?"

"She wakened, then went back to sleep."

Lukas was pleased to have Diana to himself. She made no objection to going out without a maid, and they put on their thick wool cloaks and started out.

Salzburg was a gem, and with a light covering of snow it was a golden jewel set in silver. They walked down some of the narrow cobblestoned streets, pausing to admire windows of alpenstocks, or dirndls, or concertinas, or a lovely display of gems. Then they would stroll on, looking from café windows where people could be seen sitting with newspapers over their morning coffee, to breathtaking views of the Hohensalzburg Fortress, and the blue Alps beyond.

Diana's eyes sparkled, her cheeks rosy from the wind. How lovely she was, he thought. He curved his hand protectively under her elbow to assist her, but she was light on her feet, and skillful at maneuvering along the cobblestoned walks.

The window of a music shop attracted them. Diana looked over the displays, and with a single purpose they both turned into the door of the shop.

The owner came forward, bowing, recognizing Lukas. "Is there anything I can obtain for the Herr Baron?"

"I am looking for fresh piano music. Who are the composers now in Salzburg?"

While they talked, the owner brought out sheets of new music. Lukas looked them over, and Diana strolled about to observe everything. The owner kept looking toward her.

"The Herr Baron's protégée played so well last night!" he murmured, a light in his old eyes.

Lukas beckoned to Diana, brought her over, and introduced her. They shook hands. "Thank you, you are most kind," she said, smiling at his praise.

"Nein, nein, I love music. There is talent in those fingers," he said reverently, and raised a hand to his lips.

"Old Frazer liked your work," Lukas said, after they had departed, having ordered some music delivered to the apartment. "He has good taste, I always knew it."

"It was kind of him to say it," reflected Diana. "It takes courage to admire the work of a woman, doesn't it? He must be very sure of his judgment. I am glad there are such."

She looked up at him with a glance both demure and mischievous. He laughed and took her hand in his, giving it a gentle squeeze. He was so proud of her! She would become famous, he vowed it! She had such courage in that slim young body.

They went home after their brisk three-hour walk.

Theo had been out with his friends and had returned with some of the journals. Theo started through them after luncheon.

"Bad?" asked Lukas, quietly, seeing his face after glancing at one.

Theo grimaced at him. He was seated at Lukas's desk in the study. "Bad enough. Don't show the girls."

Diana said from the door, "Yes, I want to see them all." She came in without an invitation. "May I?" And she held out her hand.

Lukas nodded. Theo handed the review to her, finished cutting up the journals, and put the neat sheaf of reviews on the desk. Then he departed, tactfully. Alicia was talking with Frau Constantia von Korda in the drawing room, and from the study Lukas could hear their laughter.

He held a chair for Diana and she sat down at the edge of the desk. Taking half the reviews, he began to go through them.

When he had finished, he waited, then took the stack from her. She was reading more slowly, critically. Lukas was frankly looking for some good words, some gleam of hope, that would recognize the girls had talent.

Two of the items were from gossip columns. There was much gush about the gowns, the jewels, the reception in the beautiful apartment of the Herr Baron, what the Baroness von Korda had worn—Lukas had scarcely looked at his mother in her amethyst gown with the jewels in her gray hair.

Another critic was cool and very stern. The girls had much to learn. The early Mozart was not bad, the late Mozart needed more work. It was vanity for von Korda to have his pupil play his work. He showed promise, but his work was not to appear in the same

concert with Bach and Mozart! And for Miss Ballantyne to play her own work—well, the less said the better. Women were not composers; he had never met a
decent one, and never hoped to.

Another critic was nasty, and Lukas, reading his
words, shook his head. Anonymous, but he thought he
knew who it was. He laid aside the last one.

"Overall, not too bad," he said objectively. "They
did recognize that both of you have talent, and of
course you need more work. Nobody is perfect at
twenty-one or -two! But you both have unusual ability—oh, my dear, what is it?"

He felt thoroughly shaken. It was unusual for Diana
to cry, and when he saw the tears rolling down her
cheeks, he would have done anything to comfort her.

"Oh, child, do not mind it. . . ." He sprang up and
took her hand. She shook her head helplessly.

"I am sorry, I had not meant to—it is so nasty!" She
gave a little cry, part sob, part laugh, and took out her
handkerchief. It was woefully inadequate.

He found his big handkerchief and tenderly mopped
her face and her closed eyes. Her skin was as silky as
he had remembered from the times he had kissed her.

"You have to get used to this. I warned you!" he
said, angrily.

"I know—forgive me—I'll go to my room until I
can c-control . . ." She stood up, bumping into him as
he stood beside her.

He could not help himself. She was so soft, so weak
for once, so dependent. . . . He caught her in his arms
and drew her close. Her head went back, the teary eyes
were startled. Furiously he pressed his lips to hers. He
was angry that he had so little self-discipline, but he
could not help it!

She did not fight him. Her hands found their way to

his hard shoulders. Through the cloth he could feel her strong hands, the fingers pressing him, and he went a little mad.

Oh, God, he thought. She was not fighting him.

His kisses fell on her chin, her silken cheeks, roamed desperately to the ears, to the soft spot beneath the ear, to her throat, to her shoulder, pushing aside the white wool. What skin she had, so perfumed, so velvety. She was like a peach, with pink skin, like a peach—

He kissed her passionately, holding her to himself with his hand sliding on her slim rounded hips. She moved against him, and involuntarily his masculine body responded. Desire rose in him so hotly that he was afraid of his own passions. Yet he could not let her go. Lips clung to lips, her fingers pressing his shoulders so tightly he could feel the strength of those hands—

She responded, her sweet half-opened lips moved under his, shyly, gently. He drank from them, with hunger he had never felt before. He had known women, but those were experienced women, and he had been too aware of their experience, too cynical about their feelings.

This was different. Diana was young, graceful, and inexperienced with men. Cool, until awakened. God, how he longed to be the one to waken her!

He drew back before it was too late. His skin felt flushed and hot. Her cheeks were deep pink, her eyes shut. Slowly they opened before his intent gaze, blue eyes that were dazed and sleepy. To see her in bed, just wakening! Like a sunrise, the blue sky in the silvery gilt of her lashes like the feathery sweep of a thin morning cloud—

He was all too aroused, and too aware of his desire. He had to let her go!

He stepped back. Her arms fell from him, and she looked stunned and shaken at his abrupt change of attitude. He felt stunned also, but he must recover even if she did not!

"You must go to your room," he said curtly. "I will send a maid with tea."

Tea for a crushed and hurt spirit! He dared not offer the comfort and passion he longed to.

She nodded, and with bent head left the room. He stalked up and down the room, over and over again, cursing softly under his breath.

He could ask her to marry him! For a moment, he considered it. But no, no, damn it, he could not!

She was so young, twenty-one, not quite twenty-two, and he was thirty-three and very experienced. He was injured, crippled and scarred. She was vital, on the threshold of a great career. He was older, cynical, willing, perhaps, to settle down; but only if he found the right woman to please him, coddle him, obey him.

No, no, it would not do. It would ruin her career if she married him. He pictured his mother, repressed, her fingers too tired at night to play even in the nursery. How could he do that to Diana?

He pressed his hand to his temples. Was he insane? He was unsure whether he wanted to marry anyone. Margarethe and her husband managed the estate. It would go to their sons, if Theo had none. He could play the bachelor game all his life, and it would harm nobody. Did he want the ties of marriage? No, not with just any pretty girl—

But Diana. God. He paced and paced. He wanted her with his body. He longed to be closer to her, to know her thoughts, to enjoy the inquisitive mind behind that clear broad forehead and those beautiful sapphire eyes.

How she had changed his life in a few months! Instead of wakening late in the morning, hating to face a new day, he roused himself early, eager to find out what would happen, what Diana would bring to the lesson, what she would say about his new composition, how she would complete the unfinished work he had given her. Or what she would say about an item in the gazettes, how she would laugh with his brother, or listen tenderly as his mother spoke of her grandchildren.

Diana had brought him back to life. How could he reward her by marrying her—crushing her—finishing her hoped-for career?

Was there no way out?

No. Married women became wives and mothers, and their talents must be channeled into no other direction. That was the way life worked. He knew it.

If Diana wanted to become a great musician, she must not marry. She must work hard, strive. And he could help her by teaching her and guiding her and sponsoring her—not by marrying her.

He brought his fist down on the desk so hard it made his fingers sting.

Chapter 19

Rosalie Stamitz changed out of her operetta costume wearily. The dresser took it from her with a sympathetic glance. The dresser was old and tired. She had seen such girls come and go over the years. None remained long. They wore out, married, or went back home.

"So—we close in a week, eh? I'd best wash and iron this costume tomorrow, though. We will need it for the week."

It was mid-March. They had scarcely hoped to last so long, but the show had lasted, and the closing would be a jolt. Vogler had not spoken much about his next venture. Would he do one this summer, and star her? He had not told her, but kept her waiting and wondering.

The dresser helped Rosalie into her own dress, an unexpected courtesy. She usually did only what her duties required, but something about Rosalie was so sad tonight.

"Thank you, Frau, you are most kind." Rosalie picked up a brush and pulled at her errant curls. She longed to go straight home and fall into bed. She was so tired, and so fearful. What would happen next in her life? She had a little money left; she'd saved enough to get by for two months if there were no work—but beyond that she needed to have work.

She had no illusions left about Vogler. He could be a magnificent lover or he could be a pig, according to his mood. She had allowed herself to be his latest victim. She had asked for it, accepting this price for her success.

He came to the door, partly open now as the dresser went out with her costume.

"Ah, Herr Vogler, I'm taking the gown to wash and iron it."

"Ja, ja, go ahead. It is but for a week now!" he growled.

"Thank you and good night. It went well tonight, much applause!"

The house had been a quarter full, and the applause had soon died. There were only two curtain calls tonight. The last week was often a sad one.

Rosalie watched him nervously in the mirror as she put on her broad-brimmed flowered bonnet and tied the ribbons. She managed a pert smile.

"Ah, Herr Vogler, you look so smart tonight!"

He preened, smoothing his silvery-beaded waistcoat and pulling in his fat stomach. "Ja, ja, it is new," he said proudly. "Come, now, you are ready?"

He ran his pudgy hand down her back, before reaching for her cloak. She recognized the signs, and, oh, God, she wanted to go home and sleep!

And it was not a safe time for her. Why tonight, why tonight? she moaned to herself. He had not wanted her all the week, why tonight?

But perhaps he would tell her about his next project! She had heard rumors about a new operetta, a summer project to be put on in the Prater. Could he be directing it?

She made herself smile and talk lightly as they walked the few blocks back to his apartments. On the way up in the lift he would not keep his hands off her, though the hall porter was smirking at them both as they rode up in the open-grilled car.

In his apartment he pulled at her cloak even before she removed her hat. The table was set with rich pastries that made her sick to see. She felt such rebellion welling in her. She hated both him and herself.

But what else could she do? She had to be nice to him, she had to. She needed that job. And the next job, and the next. The endless prospect of having to please him and others like him made her feel dirty.

She must be tired. Usually she could laugh inside and play her part.

She stirred herself. She must not be defeated!

With a toss of her head she let her glowing curls spill about her white shoulders. "Do let us chat tonight, Franzel!" she chirped brightly. "We have not gossiped for such a long time! Did you see Madame Chin-Chin in the audience?"

The audience was usually a safe topic. He counted the number of guests personally, and studied their faces from behind a corner of the curtain as the show went on. He could remember who had been there on any given night. More and more he left the conducting to an assistant, so he could study the audience. Several members of the cast snickered about it, but the management did not find it so amusing.

"Yes, yes, so funny! She weeps over the sentimental parts."

He laughed and sat down at the table, and drew a plate toward himself. She sat down opposite him with a sigh of satisfaction. Perhaps tonight she would evade his advances.

She let him talk, encouraged him. She managed to eat one pastry slowly as he devoured five and drank cup after cup of hot chocolate smothered with whipped cream.

"Any word about the summer, Franzel?" she asked gaily, as though it did not matter.

"I might go to the mountains with my family," he said gruffly, and scowled at his last pastry on the plate.

She felt a thrill of fear. "You, to the mountains? Is an operetta being produced there? I cannot imagine you not directing in your magnificent way—"

"Another man got my job!"

He stood and began to pace through the large room. He was scowling, and swearing, his face turning red. He had put on his lounge robe. Rosalie twisted around to see him, her eyes wide.

"What did you say?"

"I said—another man got my job! I was promised an operetta in the Prater—for all Vienna to see! Now suddenly someone else is doing it. I will kill the man! Upstart! He pushed his way in. He must have influence. If I find the man behind him, I will kill him also! I have worked hard, I have the reputation. I know how to find the right singers for each part. I have discovered many fine singers—I know how to direct just right—I know how to pace it—by the heavens, they cannot do this to me! I had their promise. . . ."

He rambled on so rapidly she could scarcely make out his words. But a thrill of pure fright went through her again and again. The summer—wasted—he did not have the job. Who did? What would happen to her? She could not live on the modeling jobs, Peter did not have much money himself. She twisted her lace hand-kerchief nervously in her small hands.

Could she find another job? What other operetta conductor was there like Vogler, who would trade favors with her? Oh, God, could she start in with another man? Vogler was getting worse all the time. Sex was a more brutal game with him.

"Well, what are you thinking about, little fool?" He stopped snarling long enough to glare down at her. "Are you sorry for your Franzel, eh? Silly fool! Laughing at me, are you?"—as she tried a timid smile.

"Oh, no, Franzel, I'm not laughing. I am so sorry—"

"Sorry for me? Eh? Well, don't be! I'll be back on top—only it may be the winter before I am! March, eh, and then April, and the summer to come. I will get them for this. I do not forget such slights!"

"But you are the best conductor of operettas in Vienna!" she said swiftly. He liked to hear that. Usually he softened when she said that. Tonight it did not work.

"Then why did they hire another man to conduct *Golden Girl* this summer in the Prater?"

She could scarcely take it in. *Golden Girl,* a new operetta, rumored to have glorious music, beautiful parts and costumes—by an as yet anonymous author—it would be magnificent.

"Oh, Franzel!" she said with a gasp. "*Golden Girl*—if only I could have a part in it. Do you think you could help me—"

Before she could fully realize the indiscretion of her words, the rash folly of them, he had struck her.

His big pudgy hand flashed out with incredible speed and accuracy, and he had smacked her across her face, on her left cheek, and his big diamond had scraped her. She felt the sting of it and put up her handkerchief. It came away bloody. She stared blankly at the blood spot.

"You little bitch! You cowherd! I'll send you back to your pigpen!" He cursed her in a slow, steady stream of filthy words and threats. "You little mercenary bitch! You think only of yourself! God, I could kill you!"

By the red light in his small black eyes, she thought he might, but she could not move from the chair. She pressed the lace handkerchief to her cheek and thought, "I cannot play tomorrow. This will show. . . ."

She sat still, and he paced and raved until he was exhausted. Finally he turned to her, calmer, his voice hoarse.

"Well, bitch? Well, bitch? What do you say?"

She stared at him blankly, shock still in her eyes. He frowned, reached out, and pulled her hand from her cheek. He stared, and the professional side of him emerged. "God, what about your cheek? The operetta tomorrow!"

She could not answer.

He blew out his breath in a big puff, as if letting his anger escape. "Well, well, we'll put something on this. We must fix this up. Tomorrow night if you wear a lot of makeup, it won't show."

He went to the bathroom, returned with some salve, and smeared it clumsily on the cheek. Then dropping the ointment box on the table, he said, "Come to bed. We'll talk."

She did not move. She said, "I must go home. I must rest. I must sleep."

"Come on to bed, I said!"

"I must go home," she insisted, in a strange level

voice. She could not endure it if he touched her, much less tried to have her tonight.

"Damn it to hell! Girls are all alike, little bitches!" He cursed her heavily, but went to change his lounge robe for his coat, and she got up and put on her bonnet. She was ready in her cloak and bonnet when he returned. His face was red and angry again, and he glared at her, as though her bloody swollen cheek were her fault.

"You should not make me angry," he warned her heavily.

"Ja, Herr Vogler," she said automatically.

He took her out to the carriage which waited in the cold street. The coachman stared at her, though she was partly shielded by the bonnet. She had the sensation that everyone was staring at her, all the night people strolling the streets.

Vogler muttered to himself from time to time, but she remained silent, staring out the open carriage window at the lighted streets, her fists clenched in her lap. The cold rainy March night suited her mood.

At the boardinghouse he helped her out. Another carriage drew up briskly behind them. Rosalie turned in curiosity, and saw Lukas von Korda step from the carriage and turn to assist Diana.

"Thank you, it was a lovely evening, Maestro!" said her gay voice. Rosalie shrank back inside her cloak.

Diana turned and saw her. So did von Korda. There was a moment's pause before the men saluted each other and spoke briefly. Rosalie scurried up to the door as Gretchen opened it.

She went into the hallway and hoped to make it up the stairs to her room without being observed. Gretchen was staring at her keenly, wide-eyed with shock.

Diana followed her in after a brief good-night to von

Korda. Then she followed Rosalie up the stairs, moving swiftly.

In the upper hallway she stopped Rosalie with a hand on her arm. "Come into my rooms for a moment," she said with gentle firmness.

Rosalie mumbled, "I cannot—I'm tired—must get rest."

But Diana insisted. She opened her door and pushed Rosalie inside. Her face was serious as she lit a lamp and removed her thick cloak and bonnet. Rosalie remained defiantly near the door.

Diana began, "Rosalie, it is near two in the morning. What were you doing out at night alone with that man? You must not—" Then she saw Rosalie's face in the lamplight.

Diana felt sick. She had been suspicious of what was happening, since she'd started to hear the footsteps creeping up the stairs late at night. Alicia had spoken to her about it. "I'm afraid our little Rosalie is having an affair. It can't be that disgusting Vogler, can it? He is twice her age, and married!"

"Oh, Rosalie," she whispered. She came up to the smaller girl, who flinched from her. With gentle hands she untied the bonnet strings and took off the wide bonnet. She stared at the bloody bruise. "Vogler?" she asked.

The big brown eyes closed briefly, then opened. She nodded, and said dully, "I made him angry. It was my fault. I'll wear heavy makeup tomorrow."

"You are running a terrible risk. He has a bad temper."

The pretty mouth twisted. "I know it!"

"Come and sit down. I have a good ointment."

Rosalie sat down in the big chair. Diana went to the bathroom, wet a cloth, and returned with a towel and box of ointment. Deftly she bathed the red cheek, working around the cut, then gently bathed the cut itself. She rubbed some ointment on it and asked, "Is that better?"

"Yes—thank you."

"Tell me what happened."

Rosalie eyed her warily. "I told you."

"You are having an affair with him?"

Rosalie frowned. Finally she nodded. "It is the only way to get a part in an operetta with such as he."

Diana felt a stab of fear for her, at her hopeless tone. "But, Rosalie, that is not the only way to get a singing job! You have a magnificent voice. Von Korda admires it very much."

"He is not directing operettas. Vogler has his own say about casting. Could I have gotten a job on my own abilities? Not in Vienna, not in Austria. You have to pay their price!"

Diana listened gravely. She could scarcely believe it, but in the bitter voice there was a strong ring of truth. Rosalie started to rise, until Diana stopped her.

"All the time—you have had to pay—this price?"

Rosalie nodded, both cheeks matched now in redness. "Yes, it is the usual," she said dully. "All the cast—they have their patrons, usually an instructor, highly placed, or with money to pay for favors. I have no money, so I pay what I can—" She indicated her body with an ugly gesture.

Diana drew her breath sharply. She must not be condemnatory or preachy to the girl. After all, she had never been in Rosalie's situation.

"But it's very dangerous. Vogler has a bad temper. Has he hurt you before?"

Rosalie nodded. "Usually not in a place that's noticeable," she said calmly. "One expects it. One protec-

tor I had threatened to mar my face if I did not—"
She stopped, frowning. "You do not want to hear this.
You have been raised differently from me."

"What will you do now? Does Vogler—will he need
you for another operetta?"

"That's what is wrong. No. He did not get the job
he wanted. They will do a new operetta called *Golden
Girl* this summer in the Prater. I guess he counted on
conducting, but someone else got the job. He is in a
fury about it." Rosalie brightened a little. "If there are
open auditions, I might get a bit part. I can sing!"

Diana thought about it. "When does *Black Forest
Maiden* close?"

"At the end of this week. I have enough saved for
two months' worth of rent and food," said Rosalie
quickly. "Don't worry about me! I can always pose—
Peter Hering uses me all the time." She tried to sound
brave.

"I will see what I can do. But oh, Rosalie, do not—
do not go with him again, will you?"

"I don't know," muttered Rosalie, shaking her head.
She stood up wearily. "I thank you for your concern,
Diana. But I must do whatever is necessary to further
my career. I have no other way to make a living. I will
die before I go back to the farm."

She went out and shut the door gently. Diana had a
feeling she meant it, that she would literally die before
she returned to the ugly place from which she had
come. And Diana could not blame her.

She undressed and went to bed, but sleep was slow
in coming.

On Thursday morning she had a lesson. Lukas was
working her very hard for a concert in April (My last
one, thought Diana, for her father would surely demand that she return home after her year was up). She

was determined to do well. She refused to think beyond April; the rest was a blank in her mind. Perhaps she would have good reviews, and her father would relent. Perhaps a miracle would occur, and she would get a magnificent job as a pianist.

Lukas planned to direct a small chamber concert group, designed to show off his growing group of protégés. Diana would perform a solo and also play with the group, as would Alicia, and Johanne would sing. Herr Arnold Lindau would be in the chamber group, and one or more of the numbers would be works of Moritz Osterley.

Lukas greeted her pleasantly as she came in, flushed from the March wind. "Good day to you! I hope you are staying for the afternoon, for mother will be very upset if you do not. She asked me to invite you, and I am not sure if I mentioned it."

His blue eyes twinkled with fun. She laughed and replied demurely, "You did mention it, Maestro, your memory is not at fault. I shall be happy to remain."

"Good, good."

She played for him, a difficult Bach piece, which he corrected over and over. Although she listened to him carefully, she could not seem to get it right.

Finally he got impatient. "What am I saying wrong? God in heaven, you are not dense!"

She put her head in her hands. "Let me think, Maestro. I think I am confused. You say this is sorrowful, full of grief?"

"Yes, but not somber. There is a difference." He went on to explain, striding up and down. "One can have grief, without being pulled down, and one must find the shades of difference. . . ."

They came to a meeting of minds, and she managed to play it as he wished, to their shared relief.

At the end of the lesson they went upstairs. Diana was thinking again of Rosalie and her problems. She had seen the girl go off Wednesday to the evening theater, one cheek flaming, the other rouged awkwardly to match.

Frau von Korda was quick to notice that Diana's mind was absent, and murmured in sympathy, "The lesson was difficult?"

Von Korda was listening, frowning. Diana smiled, and teased, "As always, Frau von Korda. But most stimulating and inspiring!"

They all laughed.

"But you are worried about something?" the baron's mother gently insisted, patting her hand.

"Yes, I am. It is about a girl at the boardinghouse. You remember, Baroness, and Theo and Lukas, how Rosalie Stamitz sang so well in the operetta we attended?"

"Yes, yes, in *Black Forest Maiden,*" said the baroness. "Such a sweet pretty little girl, also."

"Well, yes. Yes, so pretty. And she has worked her way up in the ranks of singing, and out of the chorus. However, I find she is paying a dear price."

Her gaze was caught by von Korda's intent stare. She knew he was recalling that they had returned home very late and seen Rosalie with Herr Vogler.

"So many girls do," murmured Constantia von Korda, with a sigh. "She is not eating enough?"

"No, that is not it at all!" said Diana. "No, her— conductor is also her instructor. And he is rather a rough man. Last night I found that she had been struck hard by him. Her cheek is cut and swollen. I am upset by this, and I think she should not continue with him."

Lukas intervened. "He has a bad reputation, Diana.

I was not pleased to see he was her instructor, as well as conductor of *Black Forest Maiden.* Can she obtain—is she having difficulty obtaining another instructor?"

Diana turned to him with relief. She had hoped he would take an interest in Rosalie. "I do not think she has tried. She feels tied to him, because he casts as well as conducts the orchestra for the operetta."

"Hum. I think I can help there. The operetta ends this week. I will see her, I believe, and direct her to another teacher. What about work?"

"She hopes to find something this summer. She said there is rumor of a new operetta to be given in the Prater, by name *Golden Girl,* and if there are open auditions—"

She stopped, puzzled, noticing a smile that spread over Theo's face. Lukas was groaning audibly.

"Nothing is secret in Vienna! You cannot even whisper in hearing of a tree!"

"Even the name is out," joked Theo.

"You know about it?"

"I am the patron of it," Lukas said, with resignation. "You may as well know. Moritz Osterley is just finishing the score. It is a very charming and pretty work, and I predict all Vienna will be singing it this summer."

"You are going to conduct?" cried Diana, clasping her hands with delight. "Oh, if Rosalie could just get a job in the chorus—"

"She deserves better than that," said Lukas, smiling. "When I see her about changing instructors, I will tell her about the operetta. There are parts for three young girls. I am fairly sure she can be the first soprano. The others will be second soprano and contralto. Three sisters of course, with the Golden Girl the first soprano!"

He laughed aloud, as she cried out and clapped. He raised a hand in warning. "Not a word now! It is still a secret! However, I think I will take over young Rosalie, and use her in our April concert as well. That should tide her over until summer."

"Oh, you are the best, the kindest man in the world!" cried Diana, in rapture, smiling radiantly at him.

There was a little silence in the dining room. Constantia was smiling to herself. Theo was looking from Diana to Lukas, and Lukas was looking down at the table.

Lukas cleared his throat. "Thank you, Diana. In view of my behavior to you this morning, that is most gracious!"

"Oh, you are very kind," she said, in a most restrained way. "However, did you say you will conduct? You have time?"

"No, no," he said, more naturally. "I am looking for another conductor. We are going to decide on that before long. Now, what about sending Rosalie to me tomorrow morning, or better yet, come with her to me. She will feel more at ease. I will have young Osterley come and hear her, and we might settle the matter tomorrow. She can come in the morning, can't she?"

"Oh, yes, perhaps about eleven? She does go to bed so late."

"Yes, yes, at eleven. I will notify Osterley. Let me see, I have the music here. You can take home two of the songs for her to see briefly. And no word to Vogler, if you will! He has been sniffing around, trying to get a job on this, and I won't have him!"

"Not a word," Diana assured him. "And Rosalie will not say anything, except she may on the last night tell him she will no longer be his pupil. That is all right, isn't it?"

"Quite right. We'll get her out from under his influence, that's for sure. Her voice is very lovely. With a little good training, and practice—ah, I just thought of a man. Professor Rodino—the Italian. You recall him, Theo?"

"Yes, yes, that little gnome of a man, brilliant!"

"He is accustomed to the Italian singers, but caught on quickly with the Austrian, and speaks many languages. He is so patient and good—yes, yes, he will be fine with our little Alps maiden!" He smiled at Diana.

Diana gave a great sigh of relief, and relaxed. Lukas would take care of Rosalie. She need no longer worry about her little friend. Rosalie was so courageous and brave; for all her youth and defiance, though, she needed help. It made Diana shudder to think what Rosalie had gone through with Vogler, and in her previous years, to get where she was.

The experience might have destroyed a weaker girl. And perhaps it had destroyed something in Rosalie, her gentleness, her womanliness, her faith in people. Something inside her seemed tough and wary, as though she had been hurt too much.

Well, this would help her, anyway. Diana trusted Lukas. He would make a great effort for Rosalie, that could be depended on. He liked her voice, and surely he would help her career, without ever demanding the price that the Voglers of the world demanded. Pig, she thought, swine! Rosalie must get out from his world!

Chapter 20

Alicia felt both excited and irritated. Baron Stanislav von Neumeister had returned to Vienna and was staying at the home of Baron von Korda. Why could he not stay away, in Germany, in his leaky castle.

With Moritz Osterley at her side, she laughed and chatted feverishly with Lukas von Korda's guests. He was giving an elegant dinner in his huge home. The lower drawing rooms and hallway were filled with stylishly dressed guests. There must have been three dozen people there, many of them titled.

Stanislav's tall bulky frame stood out in the crowd. Alicia watched him from the corner of her eye as he bent attentively to a stunning young countess in purple. *She* had money and title. Why didn't he ask her to marry him? she thought nastily.

She had to admit he made her heart flutter, but that just irritated her all over again. She knew why he wanted to marry her; he wanted her father's money, that was all. Why did he pretend to be so fond of her? She remembered the times he had kissed her, and a warm blush had come over her. She hated his pretending! It was just the money he wanted—she knew it—any wealthy woman would do!

Moritz nudged her like a big unhappy puppy. "Did you know, the baron has decided not to use my music at the April concert?" he asked, his face dismal.

"Yes, Moritz, but it is not any fault of your music!" she reassured him earnestly, forgetting her own problems for the moment.

"But why, then?"

She could not answer him. It was still a secret. Lukas had determined to use entirely music composed by him and by Diana, as a showcase for their talents. He had written some fresh songs for Johanne and Rosalie to sing, and Diana was busily composing some beautiful music for a small chamber orchestra to include Alicia. But they would not use Moritz's music.

"He wanted you to concentrate on—you know what," she said mysteriously.

"I know, I know. But it is almost done, and I could write anything he wants!"

"Of course you can, but this time is different."

"He is weary of my music, I know it!" Moritz was unusually pessimistic.

"Now, Moritz, that is not true! He admires your talents very much!"

Someone paused to speak to them, to shake Moritz's hand and bend over Alicia's. They spoke, smiled, and he went on.

"I think he is weary of me," mourned Moritz.

"No, he is not!"

"What will I do if he drops me?"

"He will not drop you! You know his plans for the summer! But we cannot speak of them aloud. The very walls have ears!"

He did not even smile. She felt sorry for him. He

was dear to her, rather like having a younger brother in Austria. She searched for some way to reassure him. He was so very talented, but he had lived from hand to mouth for so long. Now he dreaded going back to that desperate existence.

And he knew as well as she did, how some patrons were temperamental, backing one's work, then dropping one as the "fashions" of culture changed. She did not think Lukas von Korda was like that, but Moritz was high-strung and nervous.

"Do not worry, darling Moritz! If he did drop you, which he will not, I would sponsor you!"

He looked skeptical. "You tease me," he said. "You are a musician, as I am. How can you help me? One must have much money to sponsor concerts and operettas and all that!"

She lowered her voice. "But I have much money, darling Moritzel! Don't worry. You shall not lack for a patron. If I ask, my papa will sponsor you," she added confidently.

He looked puzzled. "Ah, you tease me!" he said gloomily. "I am serious. If the baron becomes tired of me and of my work, I shall be back at the bottom again. I will have to find another patron. Oh, the misery of being without money!"

He would have been comical but for the real misery in his face and his expressive hands. Stanislav had been watching them. Now he caught Alicia's eye and started for them.

"Ah, how are you this evening? How do you do?" said Stanislav eagerly, raising her hand to his lips. His dark blue eyes looked deeply into hers before she could glance away. "How beautiful you look! How stunning!"

"Thank you, I am sure. You remember the composer Moritz Osterley, my dearest friend?" said Alicia

brightly, clinging to Moritz with her free hand, and trying not to feel the thrill slipping up and down her spine
at Stanislav's touch.

Stanislav frowned down at Moritz. "Yes, how do
you do? You are well? Fine." And he scowled at Alicia's hand on the dark gray sleeve of the young composer. "I believe I am taking you in to dinner," he told
Alicia.

"No, no, I am going in with Moritz," she said defiantly, raising her round chin at him.

"But Lukas promised me—" He broke off at Alicia's
bright flashing look.

So—Lukas was plotting against her with that young
German!

She had begun to suspect it at Christmas, when
Lukas had told her he had invited Stanislav to stay
with him this spring. And now here was Stanislav, just
as Lukas had said. They were close friends, she
thought. But oh, how could he do this?

Lukas had come to them. "Here you are, Alicia," he
said, with his calm authority. "Stanislav will take you
in to dinner. Osterley, there is a lady who wishes very
much to meet you, she admires your music so very
much!" And he took Osterley off with him with a neat
twitch of the hand.

Alicia refused to see Stanislav's hand held out to
her. She played with her white ostrich feather fan. "I
would think your duties called you in Germany, Herr
Baron," she said in dulcet tones.

"They do, delicious Alicia," he said in a low amused
tone. "But something else calls me so from Vienna,
that I cannot resist!"

"Ah, some little charmer, no doubt."

"You are right!" And his bright blue eyes flashed

down at her significantly. "How—very—lovely you look. You would grace my castle!"

She compressed her lips angrily, and looked around rather desperately for Diana. But her friend was at the other side of the room, her hand on Theo von Korda's arm. Diana looked so elegant and self-assured, in her China silk gown of palest peach and cream lace. A tall peach colored ostrich feather was set in her hair, and amethyst jewels decorated her hair and her wrist.

Stanislav took Alicia in to dinner, and she amused herself by looking about the long tables in the dining room and drawing room. Countesses sat next to barons, and musicians next to dukes. She had never seen so many tiaras together except at the New York Metropolitan Opera House.

"What are you thinking about, dearest?" said a voice in her ear, and his lips swiftly touched her ear as she turned.

"Don't *do* that!"

"Don't speak to you? But that would be rude!" The mischief in his eyes told her he was teasing.

"Don't—you know!"

"Tell me!"

She turned a white shoulder to him and spoke at length to the man on her other side. But the man was deaf and elderly, with a broad ribbon across his chest—probably some military man—and conversation was difficult. With a sigh she returned to Stanislav, who now was speaking to the lady on his other side.

She was deserted. Moodily she sipped the chilled soup, munched on soft croissants, studied the ladies' gowns, and pondered when she might go home. Diana had hinted lately she would be returning to England in April.

"But, darling, why go home?"

Diana had shrugged. "You know why. I have not had good reviews. I must earn my living at music or go home. I'm trying to think what to do."

Diana had been in an unusual mood lately. She had been composing until late at night. Alicia often heard the soft music coming from inside her suite. But she was not her usual bright happy self. Instead it seemed an effort for her to smile; she was moody, brooding.

Was she in love? Alicia wondered. She had seen her friend gaze tenderly at von Korda when she did not think herself noticed.

Oh, Diana was in for trouble, if she had set her heart on that man! Certainly he was eligible, handsome, wealthy, titled, and even more, so very talented in music! But he showed no signs of wishing to marry. And Captain Mueller kept hinting that Lukas was still seeing his married sister, the devilish Elza.

What a tangle people did get themselves into! Alicia gave a big sigh at the thought, her eyes soft as Stanislav turned at last, abruptly deserting the garrulous lady on his other side.

"What is wrong?" he whispered.

"Oh—I was just thinking—how mixed up people can get, to be sure! If I had the way of it, I would soon sort them all out!"

He smiled down into her eyes at her fierce determined nod. "And how would you do that? Do you know how things ought to be, dearest Alicia?"

She flushed. She despised herself for the way she reacted to his whispered caresses, the touch of his thigh against hers at the closely set table.

Even as she tried to move herself away from him, he drew closer. "Do have some of these little pastries; they have bits of snails and shrimp in them," he whispered.

She nodded, tried them, thanked him primly. But she was all too aware of the brush of his hand, the movement of his leg against hers.

"You look like a young girl in that gown," he murmured. "So adorable, so pretty, like a girl at her first party."

"I am not a young girl!" she shot back, offended. She had thought she looked particularly sophisticated tonight, in the beaded dress. "I am twenty-one now!"

"So old," he said gravely. "Is it not time you were married, then?"

"Ohhh," she said between clenched teeth. Lukas von Korda was gazing at her, and she glared back at him. "Why, why must you bother me?" she whispered. Von Korda bowed, and raised his wine glass to her from the head of the main table. She had to smile and bend her head.

"Do I bother you?" murmured Stanislav tenderly. "You trouble my sleep. I have you in my dreams!"

His words were the most romantic sentiment any man had ever expressed to her. She hated herself that she was so secretly thrilled by them, and could think of nothing to say in the way of a smart reply.

He placed a filled wineglass at her hand, and nodded to a footman to serve her the next course. He paid such delicate attentions to a girl, he would turn one on her head, thought Alicia fiercely. If only she did not know his real motive for all this!

Oh, the cursed money, to come in their way. But if she did not have the money, she reminded herself, she would never have met him at all!

Not met him. Oh, she would not have liked that, she decided absently, as von Korda rose, proposing a toast to his guests. Stanislav could be irritating, and maddening, and too attentive—but he filled her dreams too.

She could not help what she dreamed about—his kisses, his embraces. One morning she had wakened to find she had dreamed that she was in his huge bed at the castle, and he was kissing her passionately!

"What are you thinking about, my delicious?" he said in her ear.

She went very warm and knew she was blushing. She had just remembered that dream.

Dessert was spectacular: ice cream bombes were set aflame to choruses of admiration from the guests. After this treat they adjourned for black coffee and brandy in the drawing rooms. Alicia deliberately left Stanislav and sought out Moritz Osterley.

He eyed her gravely. "That man is very fond of you," he said. "Someone says you are engaged. Is that true?"

"No!" she said passionately. "My father wants it, yes, but all the Herr Baron wants is my dowry!"

Moritz went a little pale. "Dowry? He is very wealthy, then, as you said?"

"Very," she said, for once heedless of her words. "All the Herr Baron wants is the five million dollars for his castle and his lands and his—" She stopped herself abruptly, for Moritz was gasping, his mouth open.

"Five—million—dollars!" he said, and Alicia could have died. "Do you mean it? I never heard such a sum in my life!"

"Forget it—I am indiscreet!" she muttered, and tried to change the subject. Moritz listened to her chatter about gowns and music, about the season and the fat duchess in her black dress that made her look like a pincushion. But he scarcely spoke. She could not be sure she had managed to erase her words from his mind, and she went home angry.

"What a stupid thing to say," she kept muttering to herself.

The next day, Sunday, she found it difficult to concentrate on her music. In the morning she could hear Diana working, composing probably, for the sounds of the piano came irregularly. At noon Alicia went down to the big Sunday dinner, but she was restless and ate little. Diana seemed absentminded, staring into space humming.

"Are you going to work this afternoon?" she finally asked Diana hopefully.

"I don't know—do you want to do something?"

"Oh, I want to go out. It has been raining and raining, and I'm going mad!"

"Why don't we? Pauline would go with us, we have worked hard lately. And my one piece is almost finished. I don't want to complete it until Lukas has approved what I have done so far. The last movement depends . . ." Diana paused, tilted her head to one side, and frowned into space.

"I think you *need* to go out! Do let us go!" And they asked Pauline, and had the odd-jobs man get a fiacre for them.

It was pleasant to ride about Vienna. The late March rain fell like a gray curtain to make the city like a stage setting for their amusement. The girls pointed out sights to each other and to Pauline; the scurrying figures of men with their huge black umbrellas, the wisps of green leaves on the winter-bare trees, the carts of the chestnut sellers, and tattered posters advertising last winter's opera productions.

"Soon it will be spring and all will be fresh and new," said Pauline. "You will enjoy the May concerts, and then the summer! Ah, the puppet shows in the parks, and the singing and the waltzing at nights, and the lights in the Prater . . ."

Alicia could not meet Diana's look. Both were thinking they would be gone by then. Their year was up. Both would go to their homes, Alicia to America, Diana to England. Would they ever meet again?

"Do let us go to a café in the Prater, the one near the ice-skating pond," suggested Alicia. "Nobody will be there, but we can enjoy the chocolate, and the trees, and the pond."

She would remember it all, when she was back in New York City, venturing out from her family mansion on Fifth Avenue, her maid beside her. She would remember how it had been here in Vienna with Diana, and the others. With Stanislav, and his daring blue eyes, and his leaky roof, and what might have been—if only he had loved her and not her money.

The café was almost empty. The waiters scurried about, serving hot chocolate, bringing piles of gazettes to read, and trays of rich pastries. "I shall be fat by the time I get home," said Alicia gloomily.

Diana smiled. "And I also. But it will be pleasant to remember—"

"You are not going home, young ladies?" Pauline asked curiously.

"Soon," said Diana, and set down her cup carefully on the saucer. Her clever long fingers traced an idle pattern on the red-checked tablecloth.

"Is there no hope?" asked Alicia quietly.

"Only if I have very very good reviews in April. Father might listen then."

They were both silent. There was little chance of that. The critics had not been kind this winter, why should they be in the spring?

"Ah, here you are, here you are!" Gay voices made

their heads turn, to see Captains Mueller and Schmidt swinging in, their uniforms of scarlet like bright plumage in the dark room.

Behind them came Moritz Osterley, smiling, small, like a little pageboy with them. He glanced at Alicia and then away, like a guilty child. She felt a funny pang. He had not said anything, had he? Curse her indiscreet tongue!

The waiters joined another table to theirs, and they all sat down. The laughter and teasing words at their table filled the room, and made the few old-timers smile.

Captain Schmidt was beside Alicia, Captain Mueller beside Diana, smiling, happy, flattering.

"You look like the Goddess Flora!" Captain Schmidt admired Alicia's gown of bright flowered chintz. "Now I can believe in the sunshine!" He grimaced at the streaming gray windows.

"And you, Miss Diana, you are like the sun itself," complimented Captain Mueller.

"Thank you, thank you, gentlemen! You are so kind, you make our spirits rise!" said the smiling Alicia. And she did feel happier.

The young men drank their hot drinks quickly, and drew deep satisfied sighs. Then their inquisitive looks went from one girl to the other.

"You are not engaged to the stuffy Baron von Neumeister, are you?" asked Captain Schmidt, putting his hand on his heart, and gazing soulfully at Alicia. "You have broken my heart!"

"Oh, I didn't know it was there to be broken!" She laughed. "I thought you had given it away, piece by piece, to all your beautiful charmers!"

"Naughty, naughty!" He shook his head at her. "But come, tell me, rumor has it that he marries you for millions of dollars! I did not know your father was so wealthy!"

"Is it true?" asked Captain Mueller. "Little Osterley here swears he heard it from your own bright lips! It cannot be! I know Americans are very rich, but surely nobody has five million dollars!"

Alicia squirmed as Diana's startled gaze went from one to the other. Pauline looked stunned. Moritz had turned away, afraid to look at her.

"I was drunk," he mumbled. "I did not mean to say it."

"But is it true?" persisted Captain Schmidt. "If it is, I am amazed. I must say—Mueller and I were saying—"

"Yes, yes, what a waste, on that German baron! You are too pretty to be thrown away on such a brute!"

Alicia could smell their breath now, and knew they had been drinking. But that was no excuse for their rude indiscretion. And Osterley—she had never thought he would repeat it—though it was her own fault that she had said it.

"What about you, Diana?" Captain Mueller turned to her, his black eyes bright and searching. "Is your papa also a rich tradesman?"

Diana could not seem to speak. She looked helplessly at Alicia, for once at a loss for words.

"I must say, my young ladies, this is not a proper topic," began Pauline bravely. "We must leave, if you do not change the topic."

They ignored her, as they would have a buzzing little bee.

"Tell me, tell me, Alicia," said Captain Schmidt boldly. "Is your father wealthy? A simple yes or no!"

She did not reply. Her mind sought frantically for a

way to get out of this. She hated their persistence, and hated more the knowing looks of their faces. They reminded her so bitterly of the young men who had flocked about her at the school dances, the brothers and sisters and friends of her classmates, and how they had said to each other in her hearing, "Alicia Huntingdon—yes, that Huntingdon! Railroads and steel! Buckets of money!"

Diana said quietly, "I think that is not your business. We really must go now—it is growing late."

She moved to pick up her cloak. Mueller reached for it first and stroked his hand over the fur. "Mink—and diamonds," he said slowly. "I think we have missed a bet, young Schmidt!" He began to laugh.

"Yes, and emeralds and sapphires, and ermine, and ostrich feathers!" Schmidt began to laugh also, his face turning red under his carrot top. "We cannot let that big German have her, eh?"

"No, no!" Mueller still held the cloak, away from Diana's grasp. "I'll tell you what! Schmidt shall marry you, Alicia! He is always in debt! He needs the money more than Neumeister does! What about it? Marry Schmidt, he is crazy about you anyway!"

"You can marry her English friend, our cold Diana!" Schmidt said, smirking, as Alicia sat frozen with fury. Osterley was looking more and more alarmed, his head swiveling from one to the other. "Yes, yes, and we will both be set for life, eh? Rich wives, rich wives! That is marvelous, and both so very pretty!"

"That is enough!" Diana rose, and with calm dignity held out her hand for her cloak. Mueller reluctantly let her take it. "I think we shall leave at once. Come, Pauline."

"Oh, I say!" Mueller sprang up, seeing her face. "I am so very sorry!" he said charmingly, catching her arm. "I did not mean it! I have had a bit too much to drink! Don't be offended! It was a joke."

"A very poor joke," said Diana frigidly. "We are not likely to be amused by it."

"Oh, I know, I know. Come on, Schmidt, apologize, you clod!" Mueller kicked his friend brutally on his ankle. "I'm frightfully sorry, Diana! I meant nothing—I didn't know how wealthy you were, I should have guessed, and you are sensitive about it, probably! Has your father picked out your fiancé for you? No doubt, you poor girl!" he said, his black eyes wild, in what was intended to be a soothing voice.

Alicia had pulled on her cloak, and Pauline was struggling into her gloves. They were on their feet, ready to depart. Moritz Osterley stammered, "All my fault—my big mouth—terribly sorry—I never should have said—forgive me—oh, God, what a terrible thing—"

Several waiters had rushed over, seeing the ladies about to leave. The maître d' hurried to them, muttering about the bill.

Diana took some money from her purse, and tossed it on the table. Alicia had never seen her friend make a rude gesture before. In her clipped tones, she said, "To pay for all of this—" And she turned and walked away.

"Oh, I say!" cried Mueller. "Don't be angry. Don't leave—I'm so sorry—we didn't mean—"

He and Schmidt followed them, apologizing and getting in their way, and trying to get them to come back. Diana turned her cold profile to them and did not speak to either of them. Alicia said, "I'm sure you will be very sorry for your remarks, but you had best get sober!"

And they swept out with Pauline running after them.

In the sheltered overhang Diana motioned for a fiacre. It swept up to them and Captain Mueller reluctantly helped them in, still begging their pardon charmingly.

As the carriage started out, the young officers fell back.

Alicia said, "Diana, I am so terribly sorry—it was my fault! How could I have said—"

"Impertinent young men!" said Pauline, gasping, and still outraged; though half the conversation had been in English, she had caught it all. "To speak so to my ladies!"

"It is probably for the best," said Diana, with strong distaste in her voice. "They were always so gallant— but I think they showed their true colors today. They really would marry us for a joke—and for our money! Lukas warned me about Mueller and Schmidt, but I would not listen."

"Young military men!" scolded Pauline. "Impertinent and rude and brash! I should never have permitted this," she admitted with regret.

"I expect I was very rash," said Alicia, sighing. "But they were so flattering, and always sending flowers—"

"It is too bad," said Diana. "It ruins the memories, for me. The skating, and the music—the dancing . . ." She sighed and pushed back her bonnet with a restless gesture. "I meant no harm—but, oh, I wish they had not said that. It is so unpleasant to find out what is really underneath the handsome faces of those men."

"I know," said Alicia. "Papa warned me, always. And I tried to listen—but somehow—in Vienna—"

"Music, dancing, song, wine." Diana smiled sadly. "It is all intoxicating. Perhaps it will be best to go back home."

Alicia caught the wistful look in Diana's eyes, and knew it was intended not for the gay young officers who had disillusioned them today with their crude remarks. It was for someone else entirely, a handsome Austrian who could break one's heart. Poor Diana, she thought. She is caught also.

Yes, perhaps the sooner they went, the better. But no matter how long the years grew, they would never forget what had taken place this year in Vienna. When an orchestra played a gay Vienna waltz, each girl would remember the year she had loved, and lost.

Chapter 21

"It is still not right." Lukas von Korda was bending over Diana's shoulder as she played the refrain again. "I want it in a minor theme, but that is not right."

"How about—" She tried another chord, then another. He kept shaking his head, then began to stride about the room. She knew he longed to take her place at his large grand piano and play it out himself. But he could not.

She concentrated, playing it softly again, experimenting slowly with one chord, then another. Then she paused, thinking, her eyes closed. "Yes," she muttered, and played a chord strongly, and went on with that melody.

Lukas turned about, listening intently. "That's it! That's it! Do it again, let me write it down!"

She played it again as he sat beside her at the small table drawn up beside the piano. He scribbled rapidly on the music page as she played. They worked at it, together, almost as one mind, and finished it. "Now play it all," he said, and jumped up to move restlessly about, listening carefully.

This would finish the little song cycle he had composed for Johanne to sing. It would be dark and serious, gentle, the story of a girl maturing to wifehood and motherhood. It was even more beautiful than the little song group he had composed for Rosalie to sing, a bright lilting series suited to her gay soprano voice.

As Lukas muttered over the music, and beat the time again, Diana thought over their ambitious repertoire. It had been Lukas's idea, a tribute to Johann Strauss II.

He had decided that he and Diana would write some compositions commemorating Strauss's fifty-year conducting career. All Austria and Germany were excited by the coming event, to climax in October of this year, 1894. On April twentieth a small chamber group would play in a hall Lukas had hired, before twelve hundred people.

"It will showcase your talents and mine," he had told Diana. "This will demonstrate to all Austria that your talent is no fluke. And if the critics don't write good reviews, it will be clearly out of prejudice. All Vienna will know better, for they will have heard what you can do."

She was caught up in his joyous excitement. He was so positive that she would do well. She had worked hard on her compositions, and he on his. The pieces were designed to demonstrate how well they worked individually and together.

Lukas had assembled a fine little chamber music group. Diana would play the piano in all the numbers. Alicia was the first violinist, Arnold Lindau would play the cello and the piccolo. He had found also a second violinist, a violist, a bass cellist, and a flutist.

Johanne would sing, as would Rosalie. Diana had been delighted at the smooth way he had taken over

Rosalie's career, introduced her to a new instructor, and removed her from the clutches of Herr Vogler. The conductor had been absolutely furious, but he could say nothing. It was Rosalie's right to change instructors, and she did not need him anymore.

Rosalie was already privately practicing the music for the summer's new operetta, *Golden Girl*. It was obvious she was happy. In her free time she was busily sewing her own costumes, all of precious golden silk.

"Well, that finishes it, Diana!" announced Lukas. "That is the last series of pieces. Let's go over all of them now. If it all fits, I'll have the copyists in, and get copies made for everyone. We must go right into rehearsals."

They brought out the music and got it in order.

The overall program was called "Vienna Dreams," and it was dedicated to Strauss. The conductor himself had condescended to agree to attend, in the front box. That alone would assure a fine audience, for all Austria adored him.

The overture was called "Austrian Scenes." Diana and Lukas had composed it together, and it was written for the entire chamber orchestra, with Diana as piano soloist. It would be fifteen minutes long, and would set the mood, with scenes of the Alps and of Vienna indicated by the melodies for the various instruments.

Next would come "Countryside," a song cycle for Rosalie's clear soprano voice. Both humorous and romantic, its lyrics told of a young country girl's dreams of the Vienna she imagines. She would be so gay in Vienna, she sings, with no cows to milk, no cheese to make, no farmers to fight off. Instead she would be popular, dancing every night. This composition had brought out a rarely seen side of Lukas, thought Diana; he had never before composed such funny songs with merry feminine rhymes that tickled the fancy.

Third would come "The Prater," written by Diana. It was a gay longer number, an instrumental piece whose themes evoked the images of Vienna: an organ grinder and his monkey, a puppet show, the clatter of the fiacres, a scrap of waltz tunes as skaters danced on the ice. And through it all was a wistful theme for the Viennese people, as they contemplated the end of the era of their beloved emperor, and their beloved Waltz King.

A brief intermission would follow.

Beginning the second part would be "Nostalgia—an English Spring." Diana had written this, a sonata for piano and violin, combining the sounds of England and Austria. It was a more serious number, in classical sonata style.

"Romance" would be sung by Johanne. This was a longer song cycle of about twenty minutes, the story of a girl who becomes a bride, then a wife, and finally a mother. Lukas had composed this with Johanne's rich talents in mind. If it went well, he thought he might use it as the basis for a new opera.

To conclude would be "Vienna Dreams," a series of different chamber music pieces. There would be waltzes, songs, duets, a piece of nostalgia, gaiety, all kinds of music that signified Vienna to Lukas and Diana. The entire chamber group would be involved, and this would be the climax of the afternoon concert.

Diana looked at the final pile of music proudly. Lukas was looking down at her with an odd smile.

"Well, there it is, Diana. The climax of our first year together. What do you think?"

"I think we have done the best that we can for now," she said thoughtfully. "If I had more time . . ."

She fingered the top sheets with a sober look on her face.

"What do you mean, 'if?' " he said heartily. "When the critics witness what we can do together, they must give in and admit you are a fine musician. You will play every number. You have composed more than half of these. And your name should be on all of them, for you helped me complete all the songs also!"

"Thank you, Maestro. I only hope if father sees good reviews he will allow me another year."

"He has to, in all fairness," said Lukas brusquely. "Once he knows what you can do, he will know that you must have your career! Your talent cannot be allowed to be smothered. It is not for you to be a wife and mother alone. With time you will be acknowledged as a great pianist, and a fine composer."

She hoped he was right. The words had a sting in them, however. She had come to love Lukas von Korda. She wished he loved her, that he would want to marry her. But there was always his mistress, Elza. And besides, if he did want to marry Diana, she would have to give up her life as a musician, just as surely as if she married Addison Montague! Only if she remained unmarried and independent could she carry on a career. What an irony, she thought.

Within a few days the rehearsals were under way. Lukas usually held them in his huge drawing room. Only the final rehearsals would be in the hall he had hired. For now, they all gathered three times a week, carving time out from their other commitments to practice.

Rosalie and Johanne came faithfully, whether needed or not. They simply could not stay away. They listened to the others rehearse, were always ready for their parts, and handed about cups of hot coffee, platters of pastries, sheets of music, and whatever else was required.

By April tenth they sounded almost ready, Diana thought. Who would have thought they would sound so grand? She listened, bursting with pride, as the orchestra played the melodies she had had in her head, and had put down in small black notes on music sheets in the privacy of her room. What a thing it was, to hear in full glory the music she had once heard only in her imagination.

Lukas must feel like this also, she thought, as she glanced at him, intent on his directing. He rapped on the conductor's stand.

"Now, this next part," he began, "is to be played with a light joyousness that characterizes the composer's feeling for Vienna. But underneath, there in the cello and the bass cello, there is the little melancholy, the sadness—"

How well he understood her. She had scarcely needed to explain what her music meant. Their minds met so often, so readily. When Lukas could not complete a number, she could help him. When she stumbled, and frowned over an accompaniment to a song, he would know it, and explain in a few words what she needed to do.

Did he not feel it also? She wondered, as he worked with the cellist over a part.

Alicia came over to her and whispered, "Did you receive more flowers from Mueller?"

Diana nodded, scowling. "I gave them away! I want nothing from him."

"Schmidt sent more, with a funny note. They want us to go out again, but I for one am indifferent. That last time spoiled it so. I wish I had said nothing—"

"It is just as well to find out what kind of men they

really are." Lukas had tried to warn her, yet it had still been a shock to find how hard and thoughtless they could be, how callous and crude. To speak of marrying them for their money—as though they meant it! What a miserable life each of those captains would make for any fine girl who might marry him. There was no goodness or thoughtfulness in either of them. They were all selfishness, searching for a pleasurable time, wanting only to pass the days and nights irresponsibly in a continuous search for a gay life.

She suspected Elza von Hulsen was like that also, from what she had seen of the woman. How could Lukas possibly love her and keep her as a mistress?

"Now," said Lukas, tapping on the stand. "Our little Alps maiden, little Rosalie—come over here!" He smiled kindly at the glowing girl as she ran forward in her little black slippers. "Stand here, Rosalie, where you can have room to move—off the carpet, so you can do the little dance in the middle."

She nodded happily, smoothed her skirts, then fluffed them up again. All white gauze this morning, but that afternoon she would wear golden gauze. The public would not know she had the part of the first lead in *Golden Girl,* but later they would remember!

She watched alertly. Diana began the accompaniment. The chiming of the bells indicated by the piccolo came in, then the bird song of the piccolo and violin. Rosalie began to sing, in her light bright voice, of the joys of the countryside. But, oh, how she longed for the lights of Vienna, the dancing and singing. Here she had a little duet with the piccolo. It was humorous, the rhymes were clever, and Lukas was smiling as she sang.

"Good, good, Rosalie! Just right! Now, in the next part, remember to sound wistful, a little sad. Your smile goes away, you are tired from the day's work, you sit on a bench and sing of what might be."

Theo sprang forward to set the bench for her. She smiled and thanked him. She listened gravely and intently to every direction from von Korda, and obeyed orders well, thought Diana. At the same time she had the true creative instinct of a good artist. As she sang the words that had been dictated to her, her face and tone reflected her mood clearly.

Yes, Rosalie would do well. Already her new instructor, the elderly Italian Professor Rodino, had helped her. He was bringing out new facets of her personality. Her style was no longer flamboyant, but more restrained. Yet she was gay and bright, her every note clear as a bell.

At the end Lukas met Diana's eyes, and he gave a brief nod of satisfaction. He had helped Rosalie for her sake but by doing so he was helping to develop the talent of a good young artist.

"Very good, very good. We will work no more on that today. Rosalie, ask Professor Rodino to help you with the clarity of the words in the second number. They are more difficult. I want every syllable understood by the back row."

"Oh, yes, Maestro! I will do it! Thank you, Maestro!" And she would, thought Diana. She would work hard, and her performance would be as perfect as she could make it with determination and hard work.

That afternoon they worked also on the third piece, "The Prater," and Lukas was as patient with the orchestra group as Diana could have wished. He seemed to bring out all the sounds she wanted in her composition. It was with a great sense of satisfaction that she gathered up her music at the end of the rehearsal.

"On Wednesday at the same time this week," said Lukas briskly. "Then on Friday. Everyone can make it at ten in the morning, yes? No? Who cannot come? Very well, what about two in the afternoon, yes, that is well? Very well, it shall be two o'clock on Wednesday."

They trickled out, putting on coats and carrying instruments, streaming to their carriages or walking down the tree-lined street outside the elegant town house.

"I'll take you ladies home," said Lukas. "The barouche will be ready instantly."

The butler helped them into the barouche; she and Alicia, Johanne and Rosalie, and Lukas with his back to the horses. He seemed happy today. Rehearsal had gone very well.

Johanne was humming one of her songs, absently. She caught Lukas's eye and smiled a little guiltily. He smiled back at her.

"Only a few days now, eh?" he said.

"Yes, Maestro. It will be beautiful."

"I hope so, I hope so." he said cheerily, as though he had no doubts. "And the reviews will be excellent."

The girls laughed a little, as he meant for them to do. The cheery clip-clop of the horses' hooves seemed to echo their laughter. Oh, it must go well, it must! Diana thought. And then she could write to her father, and beg for another year. "One more year, oh, please, Father, everything is going so well, I cannot stop now." She had been mentally composing a letter to him for a month.

They arrived at the boardinghouse. Outside the green leaves had begun to open on the plane trees, and flowers bloomed in the little plots beside the road. The door of the house opened, and Diana expected little

Gretchen would come out, smiling and happy for them.

But instead a tall man came out, with blond hair, and a stiff walk, his cane swinging. "Father," she said faintly. She thought the blood went to her feet, entirely leaving her head. "It is—Father."

"He's come for the concert?" asked Lukas sharply. "He knows about the concert?"

"No," whispered Diana. "I had not—written about it. I wanted to wait for the reviews."

It was April the tenth. Her father had come—her year was up! She could not think straight.

"I must meet him," said Lukas. He got out, helped all the ladies out, and moved with them up the walk to the house.

Diana went to her father and moved into his arms. He bent and put a kiss on her cheek. His mouth felt cold. "Well, well, Diana. You were not here to greet me!" he said, and it sounded like an accusation.

"We were rehearsing, Father," she said. "Did you have a good journey?"

"Yes, yes. We did, splendid. We are putting up at a rather decent hotel in town. Your cousin has invited us for dinner this evening, before we start back in a few days."

They moved into the hallway. Lukas was right behind Diana, his good hand supporting her arm. His very presence gave her strength.

"We will go into the drawing room," said Mr. Ballantyne briskly. He marched in and she followed, Lukas at her heels. Then she saw the other man in the room.

He moved forward, his face pallid and weary from the long journey. His hair, the color of weak tea, flopped over his forehead. When he put out his hand

and pressed hers, it was damp as usual. His thin long mustache moved with the motion of his thin lips as he spoke.

"Ah. Diana. Ah. Splendid to see you. Ah."

She had forgotten what a thin high voice he had.

"How do you do, Mr. Montague," she said quietly. She turned back to Lukas with relief. His blue eyes were very alert and sharp. "Maestro, permit me to introduce you. Herr Baron Lukas von Korda—my father, Mr. Homer Ballantyne. Mr. Addison Montague."

"Her fiancé," her father chipped in, smiling in his quick formal manner. "So anxious to see you again, my dear! He willingly agreed to undertake the long difficult journey to Vienna!"

"So kind," said Diana, swallowing.

"Well, well. So good of you to teach my little girl! A bit of a waste of time, in my opinion, but she wanted it. And I find it difficult to refuse my girl what she wants. Herr Baron, you have children?"

"Not yet, I am not married," said Lukas von Korda gravely. "My time was not wasted, I assure you. Miss Ballantyne has a fine talent, and a great future, in my opinion."

There was a brief awkward silence. Mr. Ballantyne was frowning heavily, making Diana fearful of what he might say. A cold despair came over her.

"Well, well, we must thank you anyway," said her father. "Of course, all this must be set aside for her marriage. She is to marry my good young friend, Mr. Montague, in the near future, you know! We are merging our companies."

"Indeed," said von Korda. "Well, well, you have come at a good time." Diana was not sure if he was imitating her father deliberately, or absently.

"Indeed? The spring is fine here, but it is fine in England also."

"Of course, of course. However, I meant that our concert will be on Friday of next week, the twentieth. Diana is playing, of course, also several of her friends. I have composed some pieces and so has Diana, in honor of the great popular composer Johann Strauss II. You must remain for it, of course!"

Mr. Ballantyne hesitated. "Diana is in it? But we had planned to return home on Monday next."

"Impossible," said Lukas cheerfully. "She is to perform in the concert. She has no time for vacations until afterward."

"Vacations?" said Mr. Montague, in his high voice. "But she is returning home with us, for our marriage!"

Lukas turned to Diana. The others could not see his near eye, and he deliberately gave her a broad wink. There was mischief in his dear strong face.

"The concert will be a true test of Diana's abilities," said Lukas calmly. "You must remain for it. She plays in every number! I will see that good tickets are sent for you. Herr Strauss himself will be in the first box. You shall have the box across from him, seated with my mother, the Baroness von Korda. I hope you brought formal attire? If not, I can recommend—"

"No, no, not necessary, we have suits. But my dear chap, we had not meant—"

"It is absolutely necessary! You will be enchanted with your daughter's progress," said Lukas heartily. "Now, you should know that much of Diana's time will be taken up in rehearsals during the next few days. I shall have my young brother to show you around, and of course you will come to dinner on Sunday. My mother the baroness will want to entertain you."

"The baroness?" repeated Mr. Montague, his china-blue eyes brightening. "We shall be with—the baroness?"

Diana could hear him now, telling everyone in London about his dinner with the Baroness von Korda, how he had sat in a box at a concert with the baroness. She had never heard von Korda use his titles so often in a few short minutes!

When von Korda departed later, he had their promise to remain for the concert, and to come to dine on Sunday. And he would send the carriage for Diana as usual in the morning, for their practice. Diana, of course, had not planned to come on Wednesday until afternoon, but she said nothing of that. She would be all too happy to be out of her father's path, and that of her would-be fiancé, Mr. Montague.

She could not marry that man! She could not! Just to stand there in her cousin's drawing room and contrast his stooped back, his weak face, his straw-colored hair, his hanging arms, with the perfection of Lukas von Korda—!

Lukas was all that was fine and strong. He stood tall, his chin high, his face so strong and handsome. There was courage in him, and toughness. Nobody could defeat him!

She accompanied him to the door. He squeezed her hand, saying, "The carriage will come at nine thirty, and you will remain for luncheon, of course. We have much to discuss on the program. And your lesson is on Thursday, as usual. On Friday we rehearse once more."

"Thank you—oh, thank you," she said softly. He smiled down at her tenderly, his face softening.

"Make no promises to them," he whispered, and

gave her hand a final squeeze, before going out the door.

She turned back to face her father and Mr. Montague with excitement and renewed strength.

Chapter 22

It was Friday April 20, 1894—the morning of the concert. Diana had thought the day would never come, but it was here.

She had put on a dark blue morning dress, and she and Alicia were going over some of the numbers easily, just to warm up.

If the critics were kind for once, if the reviews were good—oh, maybe father would be kind also! Diana turned over the page, gazing absently at the music she knew by heart. Oh, could it be that she would have another year? Could it possibly happen? She must have faith and hope for the best.

Her father and Mr. Montague had been kept busy. Theo had kindly shown them all over Vienna and eastern Austria. He had not given them time to pester Diana, nor interrupt rehearsals, nor nag her to pack or make plans for the journey. No, they had gone for rides in the von Korda carriage, been guests at luncheons and dinners, been taken to museums and art galleries and shops.

"Nervous?" asked Alicia, setting down her violin. "I am, I have butterflies in my stomach!"

"I am nervous in a way, but not about the music. I'm sure we will all do our best," answered Diana.

Alicia's green eyes flashed. "He cannot take you home, just like that!"

"Oh, yes, he can," said Diana. "He holds the purse strings, and you know what that means. I might be able to get some jobs teaching music, or playing the piano, but it would take time to build up a living." She attempted a smile. "But I shall not borrow trouble. Today the concert is our only concern."

Someone tapped on the door. Alicia went to it. They both expected to see Johanne or Rosalie, but instead the Countess Elza von Hulsen stood there, dressed in black with a huge bonnet half-shielding her face. Both girls stared at her blankly.

She swept in, pushing open the door from Alicia's hand. "You must come at once." She said it to Diana, imperiously, her black eyes flashing.

Diana rose automatically. "I beg pardon—what—"

"You must come! Lukas sent me. He is badly injured. I don't know if he will survive. I promised to come for you."

Diana's heart was beating wildly. "Oh, God," she whispered.

"What happened?" Alicia was asking sharply. "A duel—an accident?"

"I'll tell you on the way. There is no time to waste. I did not want to come for you"—the tall woman's eyes flashed with disdain—"but he begged me and I could not refuse him. My carriage is waiting—hurry!"

Diana reached automatically for her cloak hanging on the peg near the door.

"Wait—I'll come also." Alicia put down her violin and dashed across the hall to her room for her cloak. Her face had gone chalk white and her scarlet hair set off the whiteness in which her eyes blazed.

They hurried down the stairs, the countess in the lead. Diana felt numb, dizzy, only gripping the railing helped her keep her balance.

Cousin Helena had come from the back room. "What is it?" she asked sharply. "Where are you going?"

"Lukas is hurt," Diana told her in a gasping voice. "The countess is taking us to him . . . oh, God—"

"What has happened?" demanded Helena Lewisohn. "Let me come with you."

"No, we must rush!" cried Elza von Hulsen, waving her off imperiously. "It was a carriage accident, early this morning. He's bleeding. The doctor has little hope."

She dashed out, with the two girls after her. The coachman was waiting to help them inside the large closed carriage. Diana was startled when a hard hand caught her elbow and pulled her inside and to the seat.

She glanced up, panting from her haste, and met the black gaze of Captain Mueller. "You're here," she said.

"Yes, I had to come. Hurry—come up here, Alicia." He yanked at Alicia's hand. Captain Schmidt reached out and pulled her up beside him on the seat and held her with an arm about her.

The countess came up last. "Hurry," she said to the coachman. "There is no time to waste!" She settled back into the seat beside Diana, who was crammed between her and Captain Mueller.

"Now, tell me what happened," said Diana, in a

choking voice. "You said there was an accident—a carriage . . ."

The countess von Hulsen put her hands over her face. "Wait," she said in a choked voice. There was silence in the carriage. One curtain was pushed back as a result of their hasty entrance. People along the streets gazed curiously at the smart-looking people in the carriage. It was about twelve, Diana thought.

The concert was scheduled for four in the afternoon. It would have to be canceled, of course. They could not go on without Lukas von Korda.

And how could she go on without him? Diana gazed blankly into space. She scarcely noticed Captain Schmidt with his arm comfortingly about Alicia. She scarcely felt Captain Mueller's strong arm about her own waist.

Lukas—dying—bloody—from a carriage accident early that morning! Where had he been so early in the morning, the morning of their terribly important concert? But of course, she realized in a daze, he must have been with Elza von Hulsen!

Oh, God, he must still be carrying on his affair with her. Her brother was right; Lukas could not stay away from his mistress.

She pushed her hair back from her face. Lukas dying. Never again to see him standing tall and straight, with the conductor's wand in his clever hand, his half-smile as he began the music. The eager light in his blue eyes, the enchanted expression as the music gripped him.

Oh, if only he could have stayed away from that woman. She had brought him nothing but trouble. Diana felt she hated her, yet the woman had been good enough to come for her.

Why had she come? Why come for Diana? Did Lukas think so much of his pupil?

As she asked herself these questions, the carriage raced through the streets of Vienna. She glanced out the half-opened curtain and saw a familiar face. Moritz Osterley was staring at them. Quickly Diana leaned forward. "Moritz!" she called. "Go to the house of Frau Lewisohn—tell her—"

Captain Mueller yanked her back, and Countess von Hulsen hastily yanked the curtain closed.

Diana gasped from being slammed against the back of the seat. "What are you doing? I only want to tell him—"

"Little fool, do you want all Vienna to know about Lukas?" snapped Elza.

"But they will all soon know," began Diana, in bewilderment. "And that was Moritz, a friend."

Alicia looked puzzled and suspicious. Suddenly she sat up straight and tried to push Captain Schmidt's arm from her waist. "I am all right," she said to him. "Let me go. I want to ask—"

"No questions now," said Elza. "Ah, we are turning in." She was peering beyond the curtain, holding it back slightly from the window.

The carriage had slowed. The sounds of the horses' hooves changed as they went from smooth pavement to cobblestones, and the windows darkened. They must have turned into the mews between some apartment buildings, thought Diana.

The carriage pulled up with a jerk. "We are arrived, Captain Mueller!" said the coachman.

The door opened. Elza got out with the coachman's help. She strode up the steps of the back entrance, and a door opened for her. Diana saw a smart footman standing there, his face calm and indifferent.

Would he be so calm if Lukas were dying inside?

She had no time to think. Captain Mueller helped her out and hustled her up the steps into the building. They went up through a back entrance and into a smartly furnished room, of luxurious red velvet and golden trim.

"Where is Lukas?" she asked, gazing about anxiously. She started for the next room.

Alicia had come in on the arm of Captain Schmidt. The door slammed shut after them.

"Alone at last!" said Captain Schmidt dramatically, and began to laugh. He pulled Alicia into his arms and pressed a kiss on her face. She tried to draw back, but he was holding her tightly. "How I have longed for this moment! Elza, you are so clever! You got both of them for us!"

"And you shall marry her, Schmidt!" said Mueller carelessly, flinging off his gloves and throwing them onto a table. "She has so much money, your troubles are ended!"

"Where is—Lukas?" said Diana numbly. She was beginning to realize it had all been a trick. But what a ghastly trick, not amusing at all. She began to get angry. "Was this all a foolish joke? Take us back at once!" she demanded imperiously.

Elza began to laugh. She flung herself onto the deep red velvet sofa, luxurious with cushions, and laughed and laughed. "Oh, what an actress I am!" she crowed. "They believed me completely! Look, she still gazes about for her poor bloody wounded Lukas! Oh, I am sick with laughing! It is the best joke I have ever played!"

In Diana's mind relief vied with fury. She had been so anxious over Lukas, she had been so terrified—and now to find it was a cruel stupid joke!

"We must leave. Come, Alicia!" she said coldly, and started for the door.

Alicia tried to wrench herself from Captain Schmidt, fighting his grasp. Diana's arm was caught by Captain Mueller.

"Not so fast, my icicle!" he murmured, his black eyes amused. "We did not bring you up here to let you go so swiftly! No, no. I have longed to have you here, and you must remain a day, a week, a month!" He laughed, mockingly, at her shocked face.

"You are insane," she said coldly, drawing herself up. "Of course I shall not remain. My reputation——" She stopped abruptly at the look on his face, the knowing jeering look.

"Of course—your reputation!" mocked his sister. Elza lay sprawled across the velvet sofa, with cushions tucked under her hourglass figure. Her skirts had ridden up, showing her slim ankles and half her legs in the black stockings. She looked seductive, wild, coarse. "What a bright girl you are, Diana Ballantyne! Your reputation!"

And she flung back her black curly head and laughed in a shrill screech.

"She means, my dear, that you shall not go to the concert today! All of smart Vienna will be there, with Johann Strauss himself, and Lukas von Korda directing! But the pianist will not appear! And thanks to my clever sister, Alicia Huntingdon will not come either! No, no, she will be safe in the arms of her lover, Captain Ernst Schmidt." Mueller bowed mockingly at his colleague.

Alicia struggled furiously, her face white and her green eyes blazing. But she could not free herself from the arms of the powerful captain. He bent over and pressed a kiss on her white straining throat. She tried to slap at him, but he evaded her hand, laughing.

"And when it is over, you will be glad to marry me, dear Alicia!" he mocked her, his carrot hair standing on end. "All Vienna will be laughing at you!"

She stopped struggling and stared at him proudly, scornfully. "I'll never marry you, no matter what happens," she said coldly. "My father will kill you instead!"

Captain Schmidt went a little pale. Alicia took advantage of his uncertainty to wrench herself from his arm. She sat down quickly on a chair nearby, and gazed at him haughtily.

"Yes," she said, "Father would kill you. And he would certainly never consider letting me marry you. He is too smart for that. You would try to bleed him dry. No, I am convinced, what he would do is kill you." She nodded decidedly.

Captain Schmidt flung himself sulkily down on the couch beside Elza. The woman sat up straight and adjusted her hat.

"Nonsense," said Elza. "Just go ahead with our plans, Gardell. We have planned it long enough. You want Diana, and are convinced you can melt the coldness in her. If your taste runs in that direction, you can have her! I have done what I can for you."

Gardell kept control of Diana with one hand cruelly on her wrist. When she tried to pull away, he merely tightened his fingers. She stopped struggling, fearing he would break her wrist.

"You know where my tastes are." He smiled complacently at his sister. His gaze ran over her rounded form. "You are the one who taught me how to love, my dearest! She was my first lover," he said to Diana, not caring who was listening.

Instead of being ashamed, his sister was smiling, and gazing up fondly at her brother.

"And you learned so very quickly, my darling," she said languidly, letting her eyes rove slowly up and down his handsome figure. "You were always a delight to me."

Diana could scarcely believe the scene. She felt soiled and disgusted, that they could talk this way—and mean it! She had thought for a moment that they were lying, making a scene to shock her. But she soon realized it was true, they were decadent and proud of it. Such sordid relationships horrified her, and from the look on Alicia's face, she felt the same way.

The footman stepped in, glancing uncertainly about. "Tea, sir, or coffee?" he murmured respectfully.

Diana noticed Gardell Mueller's hand had loosened, and she promptly slipped her hand from his and sat down in a chair near Alicia.

"I would like tea, if you please," she said in a clear composed voice.

"Coffee for me," said Alicia, quickly.

"Nein! Bring some brandy," said Gardell, frowning.

"No, I thank you, just hot tea, and lemon," said Diana, to the footman.

Elza made a snort of disgust. But the footman bowed and left the room. There was an odd silence. Diana studied her hands. There would surely be a bruise on her left wrist. What time was it? She could just see her lapel watch. It was twelve thirty, and the concert was at four.

Elza's quick look had caught her glance at the watch. "Yes, my dear, in a few hours all Vienna will know where you are!" She said sneering. "I shall go home and change for the concert. I would not wish to miss the sight—as dearest Lukas von Korda, the Herr Baron Highness himself, has to go on without you, or cancel the concert! Then he will be humiliated!"

"You wish to humiliate him?" asked Diana, as though only idly interested. "Your brother tried to convince me that you two were madly in love! But I expect he was lying as he often does." She kept her tone quite calm.

"Oh, he was in love with me," laughed Elza. "I enchanted him. He could not stay away from his adored mistress. I fear the duel disillusioned him, however. He told me he despised me. But I think he still adores me, he cannot help it."

"I doubt that he does," said Diana gently. "You see, I have come to know the Baron von Korda quite well. And he has such excellent taste, Countess von Hulsen. He could no longer love you, once he had learned what a liar and a cheat you are."

Mueller swung on her ferociously. "Are you insulting my sister like this? Do you dare—"

Diana faced him fearlessly. She would rather have his blows than his kisses. "Exactly. And you also, Captain. Once one has seen beyond your charming handsome exterior, one cannot but shudder at the devil behind it. You are despicable."

His face twitched, his glare was murderous, and indeed there did seem a devil visible beyond his handsome face. He was speechless with fury.

Elza stood up. "I quite envy you the task of taming her, Gardell," she said, smoothing down her black lace gown. "But I must be on my way, much as I would like to witness the session that follows. I must change my dress—I think I shall wear my new scarlet silk with the fox hems. I cannot wait to see my dear baron's face when you do not come!"

She laughed at Diana as she swept past her. Before leaving the room, she threw her arm about her brother's neck, and kissed him lingeringly.

"When you are finished with her, darling, come to me, and tell me all about it!" she said, and kissed his mouth again, her free hand trailing over his scarred cheek.

"Every detail, dearest!" he promised.

The footman came in and set a tray with china and a teapot before Diana. She straightened, pulled the tray neatly before her, and began to pour, as though in her own drawing room.

Elza laughed, but her eyes flashed fury at Diana's calm. Her brother escorted her to the door. There was no chance for Diana and Alicia to escape, both captains were on guard. Diana exchanged a quick look with Alicia, as if to tell her to stay calm and ward off the men's advances as best they could.

Gardell Mueller shut the door after his sister and came back into the drawing room. "Get out," he said to the hovering footman.

The man gave him a startled look, and retreated backward, bowing himself out.

"Now, Schmidt. You can tame yours, and I'll have mine," said Mueller, his black eyes gleaming.

Diana continued to drink her tea, taking little sips of the hot liquid. "Do try the pastries, Captain," she said quietly.

He gave a short laugh, hesitated, then finally sat down on a chair beside her, and reached for a pastry. His white teeth shone as he snapped it in two and began to chew on it. Alicia stirred her hot coffee with the tiny spoon and gazed thoughtfully at the swirl of liquid.

Diana was thinking, that if necessary, she would pour the whole teapot over one of the captains.

Somehow she and Alicia must think of some way to get out of here. Perhaps the footman would help—there had to be some way.

Chapter 23

Lukas von Korda was on edge. This concert was so very important to him, because it was important to Diana. It must go well! Her father must be convinced of her very real talent, and permit her to continue with her career.

At two o'clock he called for the carriage. "I'm going over to get the young ladies and take them to the concert hall," he told Stanislav abruptly. "We can rehearse for a time before we are to begin."

"I'll come with you," said Stanislav eagerly. "I can turn the music—or something," he said with a laugh at Theo's merry look.

"Shall I come?" asked Theo, rising. "I'm ready also."

"No, you take Mama and claim the box with her. And be ready if I need anything. Thank you."

Lukas was dressed for the concert. He had been ready for an hour, looking dashing in his blue silk suit, his sapphire studs, his white ruffled shirt. Stanislav followed him out of the carriage. The German baron looked handsome in his gray silk suit with diamonds.

Lukas wondered how his courtship of Alicia was progressing. He liked the man; he wished he could give Alicia a shove in his direction.

And yet—what if Alicia wished a career as Diana did? Lukas frowned slightly at the scenes of Vienna outside the carriage. Alicia did not seem as dedicated as Diana, yet she also was talented.

They pulled up at the house of Frau Lewisohn, and both men went in. Gretchen opened the door to them, and her eyes went wide.

"Herr Baron," she stammered. "But you are hurt—Frau Lewisohn said—"

Frau Lewisohn came hurrying from the back room. Her face had gone pale. "Herr Baron—you are all right?"

"Hurt? What do you mean?" asked Lucas sharply.

Frau Lewisohn pulled herself together with an effort. "The Countess von Hulsen came two hours ago, in great agitation. She came for our Diana. She said you were injured, very hurt—calling for her! Our Alicia went also. It was—oh, God—"

"A trick!" cried Lukas, furiously, going pallid. Damn that woman, she made mischief constantly. "Did the captains come also?"

"I did not see them. It was the countess in black—very upset she looked." Frau Lewisohn was wringing her plump hands. "Oh, God, what has been done?"

The doorbell rang again. Gretchen hastened to open the door. Moritz Osterley dashed in, his curly hair on end.

"I saw your carriage, Maestro!" he cried. "Are the ladies returned? It is time to go—oh, God, is there mischief?"

His wise brown eyes were troubled. Lukas turned on him. "What do you know of this?" he asked sharply.

"I saw the von Hulsen carriage—the countess in it, and Captains Mueller and Schmidt with Alicia and Diana—almost two hours ago—going a great pace along the street."

"Carried off!" roared Stanislav, having kept silent as long as he could. His face was flushed and angry. "Carried off. Damn them both. Where could they go?"

"Captain Mueller's apartment, perhaps," suggested Moritz. "They have such parties there. . . . I play for them," he added in a mutter. "But they would not do anything to the ladies, would they?"

Lukas strode out without a word. He was shaking with angry fear. Diana, in the grip of Mueller—he had warned her, but she would not listen. She had trusted that charming wastrel. Stanislav and Moritz ran after him, and climbed into the carriage.

"Direct the coachman, Osterley," Lukas said abruptly. "You know the way."

The horses leaped forward. Osterley stuck his head out the curtains to direct the coachman quickly along the boulevards. Lukas clutched his left arm with his right. He had not even his sword! But he would kill them.

Stanislav was muttering ominously, "If he has touched my darling girl . . . God, I will kill him. I will beat him to a pulp."

Osterley directed the carriage into a narrow mews, and to the back door. "We can get in more easily this way," he whispered, as though he might be heard by the captains. "This is the way their women come in."

He flushed at Lukas's look. "I play for them," he said, with a shrug. "It makes me a living sometimes."

A footman stood near the back door. He let them in without question, merely giving them a curious stare.

Osterley led the way, with a nod at the man. "We are expected," he said cheerily.

Lukas flung open the door to a gaudy living room of crimson and gold, and he drew in his breath. Alicia was fighting off the carrot-haired Schmidt. He had torn her dress, but she continued to fight him, and had drawn her fingernails in a red scratch down his cheek. Diana stood beside a chair, her head back, as though daring Mueller to touch her.

At the intrusion they all turned at once. Lukas would never forget the look on Diana's face, the wonder, the intense relief at the sight of him. A strong smell of brandy hung in the air, and broken glasses lay on the floor near the wall.

Lukas and Stanislav had the advantage of surprise over the captains, who had been absorbed in the effort to subdue the women. Stanislav caught up the smaller Schmidt and was shaking him like a rat, banging his red head against the brocaded wall.

"You devil, you fiend in hell! To touch my lady! How dare you! I'll kill you, you bastard! Damn you— damn you—damn you—" And with every curse came a hearty thump of the head against the wall.

Lukas said to Diana, "Get back!" And she stumbled back against the sofa, clutching its arm as she did so. He turned on Mueller, and gave him a hard cuff with his fist. Mueller was not long taken aback, however. He came after Lukas, and began to hit him.

Lukas was enraged. He disregarded his stiff left arm, and struck Mueller again and again with his right fist. Blood began to sting his knuckles as he jabbed the hard chin, the cheek and ear and nose. He hit again and again, so furious he overpowered the other and did not count the blows Mueller managed to get to him.

The footman stared from the doorway, and Moritz Osterley cried out encouragement.

"Again! again! Oh, good blow! Get him again, Maestro! There you are. Bang, bang, you have him now."

One more hard blow, and Mueller went down in a tangle of boots and rug. Stumbling backward to evade Lukas's fist, he had caught his heel.

Lukas gave him a final hard kick with his boot. The captain gave a groan. "No more, no more!" he moaned, clutching his side.

Lukas desisted and gasped for breath. "Diana—over to Osterley—by the door," he gasped.

Diana nodded, and slid along the wall over to the door, where Osterley waited. The footman made no move to stop her.

Stanislav gave Schmidt one last hard blow to the teeth, and the man slumped to the floor. Then he grabbed Alicia in his arm, and half slung her with him to the door.

Lukas paused, gazing down with contempt at the two uniformed men on the rug. "Now," he said. "You will leave Vienna."

"No," groaned Mueller. "Cannot go."

"You will go! I shall speak to your colonel. Your behavior has been a disgrace to your regiment for the past year! He shall post you to some far frontier, where you might finally make yourself useful to Austria! I shall inform him that if you do not go, then civilian charges shall be pressed against you."

Mueller gave him a sullen look, his hand pressed to his bleeding cheek. "He will not make us go. He is fond of us."

"I warrant he is fonder of his own skin!" said Lukas in a chilled tone. "No, you shall go, or you shall

be charged with carrying off and assaulting two innocent females of good reputation. In case you have any
thought of trying to get away with this behavior, I will
tell the gazettes of your misdeeds. All Austria shall
view you with the utmost contempt!"

"We will continue to be received, however," cried
Mueller. "My sister shall see to that!"

"Your sister shall not be here," said Lukas positively. "Some words in the right quarter—and she shall
be off to her country estates, and not return to Vienna
for a year. I will see to that. No woman, no matter
what her title, can manage such a trick as she did today, without paying for it."

He left the apartment with the others, and Stanislav
assisted the ladies into the carriage. Diana was trembling, Alicia was in tears. God, how could they play in
a concert now? He would have to call it off.

But Diana said, as she drew together her torn gown,
"We shall have to change quickly. It is past two-
thirty."

"Yes, yes." Alicia drew herself up and brushed back
her tumbled red curls. "I'll change my gown, and we
can do our hair in the carriage. My jewels are laid out.
My violin and music—"

Lukas was proud of them both. They had courage.
Diana turned to him as she sat beside him.

"Oh, Maestro," she said, and took his right hand in
hers. "You are bleeding."

"It's not bad," he said. "I'll wash it with some ointment at Frau Lewisohn's. Did he—hurt you?" he bit
off the words savagely.

"My wrist," she said simply, and held it up. There
was a dark bruise all about the wrist. "It hurts a bit,
but I'll soak it for a minute in cold water, and put a
bracelet over it."

"You can play?"

He wanted to take the injured wrist and put it to his lips. It was an effort to pretend calm.

She nodded her mussed gold head. "Yes. I'll play. We shall do well, Maestro."

She glanced about at the other men. "Thank you all," she said, with a misty smile. "I prayed you would come to our rescue. You were magnificent."

Osterley's chest swelled out like a rooster's. "I knew you would be there at the apartment," he said proudly. "I directed the carriage."

"I hoped you would understand when I called to you. I did not realize then what villains they were," she said quietly.

Stanislav turned to Alicia, safely encircled by his arm. "Nothing like this shall ever happen to you again," he growled, almost threateningly. "I shall marry you and keep you safe! Do you hear me?"

She stared up at him, her green eyes wide. "Oh, Stanislav," she said meltingly.

He bent, and before them all, he pressed his lips to hers. Lukas felt a little embarrassed, but even more, envious. How frank was Stanislav in his adoration of Alicia, and his feelings toward her.

"There, we are engaged, and shall be married soon!" said Stanislav proudly, squeezing her so hard she squealed.

"If you do not break my bones first, Stanislav!"

"Oh, am I hurting you, my dearest beloved?" he asked anxiously.

"No, no, I am all right." She gave him an adoring melting look that Lukas envied. What he would not give, if Diana would look at him like that! But what was he thinking? Such relations were not for them—

though he longed for the right to take care of her, and to promise to protect her from such trouble again!

Alicia rested her head against Stanislav's shoulder for the remainder of the ride. Diana gave a slow long shudder, and had finally relaxed by the time they reached Frau Lewisohn's house.

Frau Lewisohn's door was flung open by the good Frau herself, and the maids were clustered in the hallway. Rosalie in her bright gold dress and Johanne in her deep blue came from the drawing room, faces distressed and anxious.

"How are you? What happened?"

"We must change quickly and get to the concert hall," said Diana quickly. "Explanations later. What time is it?"

"Three o'clock. Pauline and Gretchen, go up with the ladies and help them change."

"We will do our hair in the carriage," called Alicia, racing up the stairs. "My violin—my music—"

Diana ran after her. The maids raced up at their heels, and Lukas turned to Frau Lewisohn.

"I require some cold water and some salve, good Frau Lewisohn."

She opened her mouth to gasp questions, then shook her graying head and led them back to the bathroom on the first floor. She soaked his hand, and brushed up his clothes, and put salve on his and Stanislav's wounds.

By the time they had returned, the girls were racing down the stairs again. Diana wore her blue-and-silver striped gown, and her hands held her jewels, her hair brush and music. Alicia carried her jewels and brush, and Pauline handed her violin case to Stanislav.

"I'll do your hair for you in the carriage," announced Rosalie, holding up her cloth bag. "I have mirrors and combs, and all. Johanne, you will come with us and hold the mirrors. Where is your music? Do you have mine?"

Lukas found time to be amused at the little Alps maiden, and how she bossed them about. She was a little jewel! He got them into the carriage, Stanislav and Alicia, Diana and Rosalie, Johanne and himself. Frau Lewisohn had sent her odd-jobs man out for another fiacre, and she and Frau Hemmel and Moritz Osterley were setting out in that.

In the carriage Rosalie set about combing and brushing Alicia's glorious red-gold curls, until they were in perfect order, with a long sausage curl beside her neck. Then she carefully set in place the emerald and diamond clip, and fastened it snugly. She placed the green ribbon on the white throat, fastening it with the emerald and diamond brooch. They were halfway to the concert hall when she finished. Johanne held up the mirror for Alicia to examine herself.

Then Rosalie turned to Diana, and began to brush and comb her thick blond curls. Lukas longed to take the brush from the girl and do it himself. How silky her hair, how fine spun the tresses! But Rosalie knew just what to do, and he restrained himself.

What a clever and useful girl was Rosalie! She saw just what needed to be done, and hurried to do it. One could tell she was accustomed to show business, probably from her years of work in beer halls and dance halls and operettas. Lukas would see to it that she had the best work possible that he could manage.

Golden Girl would be just the start for her!

The golden locks were brushed, and coiled in a style similar to Alicia's. Diana fastened a bracelet over her wrist, to hide the bruise. Lukas swallowed his rage, as the bruise disappeared from view. The ribbon was set about her throat, the diamond and sapphire brooch fastened, and the matching hairpin set upon her golden hair. Then Diana, too, was ready, just in time as the carriage rolled up.

"How do we look, Maestro?" asked Alicia with a smile, but her voice trembled.

"You all look marvelous. You shall do very well," he said, forcing himself to sound calm. But in truth he wondered if his own hand would shake.

"Later on I want to hear the whole story!" said Rosalie, decisively. "But the concert comes first!"

Chapter 24

~~~~~~

Lukas helped Diana from the carriage, and felt her tremble slightly against him as her body brushed his.

"You will do well," he said firmly. "You are well prepared. You have only to relax and you will play like the angel you always are!"

She gave him a radiant smile, and her blue eyes sparkled. "Thank you, Maestro. I will do my best for you."

He wondered if she realized what she was saying. "My best—for you!"

They waited in the wings. It was already five minutes until four. Arnold Lindau came over to Johanne, and they whispered for a moment, his face drawn and concerned. It would be all over Vienna by tomorrow, thought Lukas. And the Countess von Hulsen's part in this vicious plot would be known. She would be ostracized. Perhaps she would take herself to the country of her own will. But if she did not, Lukas would see to it that she was informed by the authorities that she was no longer welcome in Vienna. He burned with rage inside that she should have dared to reach out and try to hurt Diana! What malice was in her, what devilish mischief and will to harm?

Well, she should not be any longer a threat to Diana, he would see to that. And the captains also. Captain Mueller would be sent a thousand miles away, for years.

Lukas moved the curtain slightly. He could see Johann Strauss II, the magnificent Waltz King, in the front box, with his handsome head high. In spite of his age his hair was dark. Probably a wig, thought Lukas. At this distance he looked fine, well made up, his elderly frame in a handsome golden brocade coat. The ladies and another gentleman in his box were equally handsome, well-dressed in bright clothes.

Johann Strauss would do them proud. He had been kind to agree to come, but then he was known as a kind, generous man. Many in the audience kept gazing up at him, nodding and smiling, and applauding reverently for him.

It was now four o'clock. Lukas peeped about at the box where his mother and Theo and their guests sat, Diana's father and the other man whom he despised. Diana would never marry Addison Montague, he would see to that! He was not worthy of her, not by far. He would crush her strong spirit and ruin her career. No, that could not be allowed to happen. The concert today would prove to her father that Diana should be allowed to continue with her music.

The curtains parted. The players strode out, Diana went to her piano, and Lukas followed them, smiling, to take the podium. Applause swelled, both for them and for Johann Strauss, as the players bowed and curtseyed to him.

Strauss rose, splendid in his gold suit, and bowed

grandly to the stage. Then he turned and bowed to the audience, which went mad with applause.

In the tumult the activity in the third box back on the other side went unnoticed. But the Countess Elza von Hulsen rose, magnificent in her red silk and fox, and with a stormy look ran from the theater. Lukas saw her, and rejoiced that she would not remain to sour the concert. She was too furious to remain. Her plot had been smashed, and she should soon know she was no longer welcome in Vienna, he thought.

The applause rose and fell. Johann Strauss bowed and sat down again. Lukas turned to his small group and gestured for them to be seated at their instruments. Rosalie and Johanne seated themselves in chairs to one side. Rosalie brushed back her golden skirts with a dramatic gesture as she sat down. Johanne was more demure, tall and goddesslike in her deep blue.

Diana sat down at the piano, her shoulders straight, her face serious and intent. She looked at Lukas, waiting.

Lukas lifted his baton, and they began to play.

Diana had been shaking. Indeed she had wondered if she could play at all. But discipline and practice took over, and she began firmly at the downbeat of the Maestro's baton. Once the music started, she was at once caught up in the spell of the notes she and Lukas had created between them.

The overture, "Austrian Scenes," went well. She could feel the listening silence of the audience. From the piano bench she could glimpse the face of Johann Strauss in his box, nodding and smiling.

At the end came the applause, loud and hearty. Lukas gestured for them all to rise and take their bows. There was a slight pause as they turned their music to the next piece. Diana sat in silence, her right hand on her left wrist. It ached, but she must ignore it.

Next Lukas gestured to Rosalie. The pretty girl came forward smiling, in her golden gauze with the roses embroidered on it. How pretty she was, how professional, with her dancing step.

Rosalie sang so clearly one could hear every word of her gay songs. They had not counted on the laughter that greeted some of the rhymes but Lukas conducted skillfully, and Rosalie watched him alertly, and went on with the singing whenever the laughter died enough for her to be heard.

In the third song she went into her dance. The waltz steps made her golden skirts swirl about her legs, showing her trim pretty ankles. When her song cycle was finished, she curtseyed again and again, smiling. How the audience loved her! They called to her, "Rosalie, Rosalie!" Many remembered her from the operettas.

She took a final bow and went back demurely to her chair beside Johanne. Then the chamber group began to play Diana's composition "The Prater," which blended the gay sounds of the park against the sad undercurrent of the minor theme. She played with all her heart, watching Lukas's direction, and enjoying the way he was absorbed in the music with them.

What a storm of applause followed! It startled her; she had not expected this. Lukas led her forward to take more applause as the composer. As the audience clapped, the musicians did also, some tapping their bows on the music stands, others stamping their feet on the wooden floor of the platform. She bowed, smiled, Lukas's hand holding hers high. She glanced up to see Herr Strauss beaming and applauding her. She looked also toward her father, but he was frowning down at

her. She felt a chill. Was he only surprised at her? Did
he not approve of the music?

Then came the intermission. She went back into the
hallway, and Theo was there.

"Everyone is raving," he said jubilantly.

"Go back and listen in the lobby," his brother ordered him. Theo grinned and obeyed.

All too quickly the intermission ended and she and
Alicia went back on stage, for their violin and piano
sonata. "Nostalgia—an English Spring" was listened to
intently. Alicia was poised, but her face was chalk
white, Diana noticed. She wondered if she was as pale
as Alicia. What a frightening day they had had! She
dared not think yet what Captain Mueller had intended
doing to her. When Lukas had strode in, his face so
stern and condemning, so coldly furious, she could
have bent down and kissed his feet.

The music was a serious piece, and Diana was surprised it was applauded as heartily as the other numbers had been. She and Alicia bowed again and again,
and then Lukas sent the other members of the orchestra out once more. As he passed Diana at the piano, he
gave her a quick pat on the shoulder. "Good, good,"
he muttered. That buoyed her up for the rest of the
concert.

Johanne sang next, and the audience listened intently to her songs of a woman, "Romance." Diana
glanced quickly up at Johann Strauss. A movement
had caught her attention, and she was not surprised to
see he had lifted a big handkerchief to his eyes! He was
a man of sentiment and sensitivity, as one could tell by
his own music.

Before the last number, Lukas made a graceful
speech to Johann Strauss. He stood with his head
turned to the Waltz King.

"Our beloved Waltz King, we have dedicated our music to you this day, in respect and love. It is you who represent Vienna, and all Austria, for we have danced to your waltzes, hummed your melodies, sung your songs, even made love to your music!"

There was a strong titter of laughter in the audience.

Lukas went on.

"In the compositions of Miss Ballantyne and myself, we have striven to show what you mean to us, how you have influenced our own music, as well as how we love Vienna. May we have the honor of playing this last number especially for you, Herr Strauss, with our congratulations on your Golden Jubilee!"

The audience went wild. They rose, clapped, screamed, yelled, for quite ten minutes. Herr Strauss stood time and again, bowed, thanked them, bowed to Lukas who bowed in return. Finally everyone calmed down again, and Lukas turned back to the musicians.

He lifted his baton, and the music began. The finale, "Vienna Dreams," was a musical suite of waltzes and songs, alternately nostalgic and gay, dreamy and sad, gentle and joyous. Diana and Lukas had written it in only a few days together. The notes seemed to spill from them effortlessly.

At the end there was more applause. Johann Strauss stood to applaud them, and they bowed to him and to the audience. Diana caught sight of her father's face, frowning and uncomprehending. He was not Viennese; he could not understand all this.

A little cold chill ran down Diana's back, despite the overwhelming warmth of the audience.

Afterward they went on to a large restaurant where a buffet dinner awaited them. The whole audience was invited, and the well-dressed society crowd swarmed about the players and singers.

Diana's hand ached, her mouth hurt from smiling, but she was so happy! It had gone well. Several critics came up to her individually. One eyed her sharply and said, "I can scarcely believe you have composed such music!"

"Thank you, Herr Tauber, you are most kind," she had said demurely, as though he were complimenting her.

"You wrote all that the program said?"

"Ja, Herr Tauber. All of it. Maestro von Korda and I composed much together. I hope you enjoyed it?"

He said so, grumpily, as though cross with himself. Diana shared a smile with Theo, who hovered nearby.

Another critic came up with his wife, and before he could begin to say anything sharp, she was gushing about how much she had loved every note!

A large circle of admirers gathered about Johann Strauss, but still he found time to compliment Diana on her talent as a pianist and as a composer.

He leaned to her and whispered, "And you are so young and pretty! You really wrote all those pieces?"

"Yes, sir, I did. Thank you. The music is in my head, and it must come out. I can hear it singing in me."

He stopped smiling and eyed her keenly. "Then you do have a great talent, my darling lady. Nourish it and cherish it, eh? It is a rare quality, especially in a lady. But rare in anyone, eh?"

"Thank you, Herr Strauss. You are most kind."

"Nein. I am not kind about music. One has talent, or one does not. Von Korda, she is your pupil?" He turned abruptly to the baron, who had appeared at Diana's side.

"I have that honor, sir."

"I have told her to nourish her talent, to cherish it.

It is rare, one does not find that every day. Work, work, work, eh?"

"That is correct. One knows that you know the world of music, and have experienced all the difficulties and triumphs that it has to offer."

The compliments that they exchanged were not empty ones, despite their flattering tones. Diana listened, holding her breath, so she would not miss a word they said to each other.

"You have recently known the depths, eh, Baron? Now you are climbing once again the heights. I went to your opera *Juditha,* and wept over it. It was magnificent!"

"I thank you from my heart."

"You will create more? Of course you will. You have talent in the light songs and the serious, in the classical methods and the popular Viennese style, eh? I envy you, your talents are endless!"

"From you, that is a compliment I shall never forget."

All around were listening. Diana saw Lukas's mother smiling and proud, a tear in her eye. How proud she was of her son! If only my mother were here to listen to me, Diana thought, and to smile at me at the end of a concert! Her father stayed in the background, uncomfortable in the rush of German language which he did not understand. Addison Montague slouched near the buffet, eying hungrily some elaborate salads.

A critic pushed himself closer to the Waltz King. "Herr Strauss, what do you think of the talent of the Baron von Korda?"

"Magnificent!" said the Waltz King promptly, and patted Lukas's lame arm. "He can no longer play the piano, but now he plays on our heartstrings!" It was a graceful knowing compliment, and Lukas appreciated it.

"And what of his pupil, the lady Miss Ballantyne? What do you think of women playing the piano and trying to compose?"

Johann Strauss took the question seriously, not frivolously. "You applauded as I did, sir. We both know she is young and has much to learn. But such melodies come from the heart and mind, and show she has music in her. She is talented. She will work hard, and one day she will play for many. We are fortunate to be here and listen to her first compositions. One day we shall say we knew Diana Ballantyne when she first played in Vienna!"

Lukas smiled down at Diana, and she smiled back glowingly. Oh, how her heart raced! To be complimented in public, and by someone like the gracious Waltz King! She would never forget this moment.

Johann Strauss moved away, claimed by others of his admirers. The dinner went on, but Diana scarcely knew what she was eating. Theo brought her fresh plates of food to nibble at. Little curls of Austrian ham, German potato salad, slices of roast beef, cucumber in vinegar, varied delicacies of pâté, caviar, and jellied veal. Then there were the pastries—cherry and strawberry, chocolate and custard.

Rosalie scarcely ate. She danced from one group to another, listening, laughing, as though on air. Johanne and her fiancé Arnold Lindau stood near the wall eating in silence, exchanging smiles, their faces quietly happy.

Alicia clung to Stanislav's arm. He was dazzled by her, gazing at her as though unable to believe his good fortune. What a handsome couple they were, so suited to each other, thought Diana. If they could manage to forget it was her money and his need that had brought them together, they might make a fine match of it.

But what about her music, Diana wondered. Would Alicia be able to go on concert tours, as she had talked of doing? Could she remain in Vienna and study, while her husband returned to Germany and worked on his estates? She could not imagine that happening.

Her father managed to come closer to talk to her. "We will come over tomorrow morning," he said. "We must talk about our plans."

"Yes, Father. About ten—or eleven?"

"Ten o'clock," he said. "We shall come to Frau Lewisohn's at that time, but not remain for luncheon. You will tell her? She most graciously invited us, but I cannot endure the Austrian meals," he added in a mutter. "We will dine out at a British restaurant, at twelve."

"Yes, Father."

"We are going now. This has gone on and on. Shall we take you home? We can get a carriage—"

"I must remain until most of the guests have departed," she said hastily. She did not want to go. She wanted this magical evening to last forever!

"Very well, very well. Someone will take you home?"

"I will go home with Cousin Helena."

His face cleared. His responsibility for her was over for the day. "Fine, fine. We shall see you tomorrow at ten, then. Be ready."

He spoke to her as though she were ten or twelve years old. She smiled after him sadly. After a year of deciding matters on her own, of consulting no one but herself, it was hard to submit to his authority.

She felt a little cold chill again. Her father had not enjoyed the evening. Did he not realize it had been a success? Diana had performed in every number; she had helped in the composition of practically the entire program. Did he not realize what she had created with Lukas? Couldn't he appreciate that Diana was proving herself as a musician?

It was true, she had not earned much money this winter. But she had progressed rapidly from a school-girl pupil to an accomplished and recognized performer, a pianist and a composer. Lukas von Korda recognized this; why couldn't her father? Or did she misunderstand her father's indifference? Perhaps he understood, and would tell her tomorrow, that she could continue with her training and study.

She slept uneasily that night, haunted by fears. She had nightmares of Captain Mueller grabbing at her, hurting her wrist, tearing her dress. She wakened, sweating, and flung off a blanket. Sitting up for a time, she tried to soothe herself by recalling the success of the previous day, the praise from Lukas and Theo and their mother.

But then she began to worry about what her father would say in the morning. What if he did wish her to go home? How could she present her case?

She rose early the next day, unable to lie abed. Coffee and rolls were brought to her room. After breakfast she dressed in a demure gray housedress, her hair in a simple coronet. She must convince her father she was businesslike and seriously decided on a career.

At ten Pauline came to inform her that her father and Mr. Montague had arrived. She felt uneasy. She hadn't expected the younger man. Still—what else would he do? He was not a seasoned traveler, for all that his family was in the Near East trade. She supposed he worked mostly with the accounts in an office.

How dull he was. What little he had to say, was never of much interest.

Diana went downstairs and into the drawing room. Her father said, "Good morning, Diana," and looked her over critically.

"Good morning, Father, Mr. Montague."

She did not offer her hand to either man, but sat down in a straight-backed chair and looked at her father as he seated himself.

"Well, there is nothing now to prevent us from returning home this next week," said her father briskly. "I shall obtain our railroad tickets on Monday."

She felt a little jolt and sat up stiffly. "Father, I do not wish to return home to England," she began calmly, her hands still in her lap. "As you saw yesterday, I am beginning to make a name for myself in music."

"A name for yourself, miss?" snapped her father. "I was very embarrassed! You performed in public, on a platform! That is not what I would expect from a daughter of mine!"

Diana stared at him. "What did you suppose that I did, Father?" she asked, genuinely puzzled. "A pianist must perform in public, and for pay if possible. That is how—"

He shook his graying head. His narrow face seemed thinner and more chill than it used to be. He looked a typical businessman, crisp and colorless.

"Not a lady," he said positively. "Your mother would have been horrified, as I was! No, a lady performs on the piano only in the presence of her own family and friends. Preferably in one's home. One does not appear in public, showing one's legs."

"Showing one's legs!" gasped Diana, gazing down at her cloth-covered knees. "Father—"

"That other girl did. That little girl with all the curls, in the yellow dress."

With some difficulty Diana recognized Rosalie in the description.

"But she was dancing to the waltz, Father. She has appeared in operettas. If you had seen any of them you would realize it is done—"

"She did not only show her ankles, that would have been indecent enough. But she showed her legs up almost to the knees! I was horrified."

"Quite horrified," echoed Mr. Addison Montague, nodding from his chair at the side. "I do not know what my father would have thought. One does not act like this in England."

"But Father, I did not show my legs," said Diana reasonably. "I am a pianist, and a composer. Herr Johann Strauss praised me. I have reason to hope for good reviews this next week in the gazettes—"

"For what purpose?" snapped Mr. Ballantyne, growing a little flushed at her unreasonableness. "It will do you no good! You shall come home, and marry this fine young man."

Mr. Montague gave a pallid satisfied smile, and shook back his limp weak-tea hair.

"You must take your rightful position in our household, Diana. You have had your year, you must admit that. Now, this foolishness must end. Only fast women perform in public, and you have never been fast! I wish you to give it all up. You shall play for your family, and we shall enjoy it. That is enough for any decent female."

"Yes, yes, Miss Diana, and we have missed you," said Montague, with a little smirk. "My father was so disappointed when you did not hasten home to us at

Christmas. He longs for you to return and get settled with us."

With growing dismay Diana realized they were taking her assent for granted. It never entered their minds that she did not want to return to them, that she did not want to marry him, that she did not want to be their slave from now on!

She must make her position plain.

"Father, and Mr. Montague, you must listen to me," she said firmly, straightening her back, and planting her feet solidly on Cousin Helena's faded carpet. "I do not wish to marry Mr. Montague. We are not at all suited. I am a musician, I wish to carry on with my career. In time I can earn a living at this, by teaching and performing. It will take a little time, but I am willing to work hard."

Mr. Ballantyne was frowning with intense disapproval. Mr. Montague gazed at her incredulously, his mouth hanging open. She had to look away from him to conceal her disgust. In that pose he looked like a limp codfish.

"I am proving myself," she went on before they could speak. "I am becoming successful. My instructor has faith in me, as I have in myself. You must have faith in me also, that I can do what I have set out to do."

"Diana!" said her father very sharply. "Has nothing I have said made an impression on your mind? It does not matter that you have musical talent. Many women do, and they amuse their families with it. What matters is that your father tells you to return home and obey his wishes. What matters is that I have promised your hand to Mr. Montague, and that he is eagerly awaiting your marriage. You have your duties and your responsibilities to us, and you must perform them. I will hear no more. You must be my good obedient daughter, not this naughty young lady!"

"I do not wish to be disobedient, Father—"

"Good! You will then obey me!"

"But I will not marry Mr. Montague," she said slowly and firmly. "I do not have the—the regard for him that I should have to marry. It would be wrong to marry."

There was a brief silence. Mr. Montague stared at her, fuming.

"The regard will come," said Mr. Ballantyne shortly. "I will promise you that, Diana! You are innocent of men, I thank God for that. You do not know what you are talking about. But when you have been married— and have children—and have fulfilled your marital duties to your husband, you will have this regard for him. Time will bring it."

"No, Father, I shall not marry him. And I shall continue my musical work, I am determined on that point."

"Rude disobedient daughter!" said Mr. Ballantyne. His hands shook as he lifted his fists in futile rage. "I cannot imagine what I have done that heaven has visited this grief on me. How embarrassed I am, Mr. Montague, that you should witness this display of shocking filial behavior! Diana, we shall take our leave of you now. Go to your room, and think over your words and your threats. I shall return on Monday, and have your apology. I am grieved and wronged by you!"

He stood and glared at her, then stalked to the door.

"I am sorry, Father. I mean it, however." She stood for them to go out the door. She felt weak and ill. Never before had she defied him in this manner.

"I hope you will soon be sorry," said her father. "I hope God will soon bring you to the right. Your family awaits you at home, the poor invalid father of your fiancé, your brothers, and the servants who depend on you. We have endured this year without your services, and we have missed you. But I would never have consented to your coming here should I have realized it would encourage you to such disobedience and defiance. I am ashamed to call you my daughter."

She could not answer this. She thought she had a right to live a life of her own choosing. The thought of marrying Mr. Montague and being slave to them all was unendurable. Somehow she must find some way to escape them. When they had departed, she went up to her room.

Pauline brought her luncheon on a tray, with a pot of hot tea. Cousin Helena had overheard enough to sympathize with Diana, and had sent it up.

Diana changed to a thin blue robe, and brushed out her hair, hoping the brushstrokes might soothe her troubled spirits.

Over and over she went through the prospects. She might find some work teaching music to young pupils. Older and more experienced ones wanted male professors with social contacts. But she might take young ones, and teach them here in Cousin Helena's house.

And she might supplement that by work in a café, accompanying singers such as Johanne Weiss and Rosalie Stamitz. And that was another possibility—she might play in the orchestras for operettas.

She considered these ideas, and how much money she would need to make if her father cut her off completely. It would take courage, but that she had. She smiled wryly as she thought how much more courage it would take to go home and marry Mr. Montague! Now, that would take nerve! She could not face the possibility.

Perhaps Lukas would help her get pupils, or steer

her toward positions that would pay money. But she could accept no money from him; she had too much pride for that. She bit her lip. If only he loved her as she loved him . . . but that was not to be.

Diana admitted to herself that going home to England seemed especially intolerable because it meant she would have to leave von Korda. She might go to London, live there, take pupils—it might be easier than in Vienna. But it would mean never seeing Lukas again.

Never see him standing on a podium, wearing a half-smile of encouragement as he glanced over his orchestra. Never see him pace the floor of his drawing room as he considered the music she played. Never hear him explaining a difficult point in composing. Never work with him again. Never—never—

No, she could not go. She must resolve to defy her father, no matter what the cost. She could not endure to go home to the life she had lived before, housekeeper for her father and brothers. And even worse, she could not take on a husband, a father-in-law, more and more duties—and the hateful necessity of sleeping in the same bed as a despised husband and bearing his children.

No, she must find some other way to make a living and remain in Vienna.

Alicia tapped on the door about midafternoon, glowing with excitement. "Stanislav has left." Saying this, she sighed. "To think how I hated him at first."

"Sit down on the sofa, talk to me," urged Diana. It would help her get her mind off her own troubles.

"Oh, he is such a man," murmured Alicia, curling up in her green silk robe. "We are to be married in a few months—he has written to my father already! I think Papa and Mama will come to Vienna this summer."

Diana smiled and encouraged her to talk about wedding plans, the castle in Germany, how marvelous Stanislav was, and how he was furious at Captain Schmidt and wanted to tear him apart.

"Were they not terrible, Diana? I never dreamed that Ernst would be so—so hateful!" Alicia frowned, and her emerald eyes shadowed. "How men can be so charming on the surface, and all the time want only one's body!"

"We were warned, I must say," said Diana. "I could not believe it—but now we must believe, and stay away from such men."

"Oh, Stanislav will see to that," said Alicia. "He will never permit me to be alone with another man again!"

"And your music, Alicia?" asked Diana, with seeming casualness. "What about your violin lessons? Is there someone he knows who can teach you?"

Alicia grimaced, and fingered her hairbrush. "I fear not," she said slowly. "I must give up my lessons. I cannot appear in public again, either. Stanislav told me it would not do. It is my position, you see. I shall be a baroness."

"I see," said Diana. She did, all too well. "No more performing, then?"

"Well, I can perform for our family," she said brightening. "He has a piano, a fine one, and the pastor's assistant plays. Also, his sister is not bad. We can play duets, I am sure. Of course, I will have much to do. He is going to have the castle renovated, and the rooms that are so shabby—my dowry will help a great deal. Then we shall entertain, Stanislav promises. We shall not be shut off from the world!"

Diana let her ramble on, talking of how wonderful

Stanislav was. He had promised she might perform for their guests at the castle; he often had guests there much of the summer, and at Christmas also. They might travel to the United States, he'd said.

Diana thought, I could not settle for that. Even if Mr. Montague agreed to those terms she could not endure such a life. If she married him, she would be so busy, she would have little time for playing the piano, and no time for composing.

Alicia finally stopped raving about Stanislav. "But what about you, Diana? Did your father come this morning? What did he say? Must you go home soon?"

"I don't know yet, Alicia. I don't know."

Alicia looked at her with a troubled gaze. "Won't he allow you to remain in Vienna? You did so well at the concert, everyone raved. Von Korda was so pleased with you!"

Even to hear his name was sweet agony. If she went home, she would probably never hear his name again. Diana shook her head, and the silver ash-blond hair spun about her face.

"I don't know. I have to think. Alicia, I don't know."

Chapter 25

Lukas was pacing up and down the carpet in the upstairs drawing room. The luncheon plates had been carried away. His mother sat embroidering a petticoat for one of her grandchildren, while Theo read intently.

Lukas felt uneasy. The euphoria of the concert was dying away. It had gone well. The applause had been so much more than he had dared hope.

His mother glanced up at him. "Lukas, you are not happy? We have heard nothing from Diana."

"No, nothing. Did her father say nothing to you during the concert?"

"Very little." She sighed. "He did not seem pleased, however. Once he said something about ladies who perform in public. I think he said it would not do in England."

Theo laid aside his book. "I think he is not pleased with his daughter's success. He would rather she became a housekeeper again."

"A housekeeper!" Lukas snorted. "What a waste! She is brilliant. Her musical talent is rare. She is a strong pianist, a fine interpreter, and also a marvelous composer."

He caught the little sad smile on his mother's face. "Once I also had compliments and dreamed of a career, my son," she said softly. "But I became a wife, a mother, and a housekeeper. That is the lot of females, no matter how talented."

She was unusually bitter. Theo gazed at her thoughtfully. "Do you regret us, Maman?" he asked plaintively.

"My darling, no! But I wish I could have been able to indulge my love of music also. I can feel for Diana. She must be truly torn. Well, she may not have a choice. I understand she has no money of her own." She picked up the smock once more.

Lukas turned about abruptly. "I shall go and see her," he announced, and left the room.

He called for his carriage, and paced the hall, too restless to sit down and wait. He set out then, into the late-April Sunday afternoon.

In the carriage he frowned to himself. If Diana had to leave, what could he do? But surely her father now recognized her talent! All Vienna had recognized it, surely her father did also.

In the next year, he thought, he could proceed to teach her more about counterpoint. He would encourage her to compose some chamber music—that would be good experience for her. He would assemble a more permanent group to perform regularly in Vienna, and go also to Salzburg—yes, that would be good!

At the boardinghouse the usual Sunday afternoon calm pervaded the building. Pauline let him in, beamed at him, and said, "I will inform Fraulein Ballantyne that you have come to see her, Herr Baron."

"Thank you, Pauline."

Soon he heard Diana's light footsteps in the hallway, and heard her voice murmuring to Pauline. She opened the door and came into the darkened room.

"Good afternoon, Mæstro." She held out her hand to him, and he closed his own over it. In the half-light he eyed her keenly.

Her face seemed colorless, and dark shadows circled her blue eyes. In a dress of pale blue her figure was as slim and pretty as ever, she moved as gracefully, yet something seemed different. It was as though she were drooping.

"Please be seated, Maestro."

She seated herself on the sofa, and he sat opposite her on one of the straight chairs. She had shut the door after herself as though she cared nothing for the proprieties.

"Diana, were you satisfied with the concert?"

Her mouth moved as though she would smile, but could not. "It went well, Maestro. Also, I have to thank you for rescuing Alicia and me from—those awful men." Her shoulders moved in a little shudder. "If you had not come, it would have been so very terrible. . . ."

Lukas felt chilled inside himself. "If I had come too late," he blurted out, "I would have killed them both."

She raised her gaze to his, her blue eyes wide. "I believe you *would* have done that. Thank you," she said gravely.

"Let's forget that. They are leaving Vienna. Just be very careful, and always take Pauline with you."

Diana's white hand rose to her face to brush back her silvery hair. "My father wishes me to leave Vienna with him this week," she said dully. "He insists I am to marry Mr. Montague."

"What?" burst out Lukas, sitting up more rigidly. "That cannot be. That is nonsense!"

His worst fears were being realized.

"My father does not believe a nice female performs in public," her tired voice continued. He had never seen her so discouraged and dispirited. "He is very angry with me, that I have begged to remain here in Vienna, and continue my music. Oh, Lukas, I do not know what to do. Am I so foolish, to think I could teach, or perform, and earn some money?"

His mind was in a turmoil. She was so beautiful, so talented, she had worked so hard to prove herself. And her father with one word could force her to give it all up. It was not fair, it was a crime that he could do this to her.

She stood, as though too upset to remain calmly seated. He stood also, automatically, and watched her as she moved about the room, to the window and back, her hands clenched together. Those talented hands, that played so very well. He could see them on the keyboard, playing those magnificent runs, pounding out a blazing series of chords.

"I was very disobedient to him," she confessed. "Always before, I tried to do what I was told. When I wanted to rebel, I repressed my spirits, and did what he told me to do. But this time, oh, Lukas, I cannot force myself to give in. To return to London, to marry a man I cannot even respect, much less like, to bear his children, to work for them all—oh, God, what am I going to do?"

She brought her hands to her face, and she was shaking. He strode to her and put his hands on her shoulders, shaken himself by her plight.

"Diana, Diana, you must not do this," he said forcefully. "That fate is not for you, I swear it! As I listen to you, I can only realize that your father is wrong about this. Yes, he is a good man, an intelligent man, but he does not realize that your talents are far beyond those of an ordinary female. This is no light frivolous decision you must make. This is serious."

She lifted her face from her hands to study his face, so close to hers. He gazed into her wide blue eyes, saw the trembling pink mouth.

"You—you do believe—that I have a right to rebel?" She quivered. "I do not want to be a disobedient daughter, but, oh, Lukas, I cannot face what he plans for my future! Is there some way I can remain here—"

"Yes, as my wife!" he said firmly.

A gasp came from her opened mouth. He bent and pressed his lips to hers. The taste of her mouth was like honey. He put one arm about her and drew her closer. He kissed her again. She was shaking, his strong Diana!

He felt the warmth of her slim body against his hard body, and felt exultant. Yes, this was what he wanted and needed. This beautiful fine woman to be his wife, the mother of his children. But more than that. From the moment they had met, they had begun to be as one person in music. She meant so much to him.

He tried to explain that to her. He drew her to the sofa and sat her beside him.

"Diana, from the moment we met—the time we began to work together, do you remember? It was as though the fates had ordained it. You made me come back to life. I had felt dead, my music meant little to me, because I could not play the piano as I had. But you were my inspiration. I began to compose again, I began to dream music again. Yes, from the time we first began to work together, I dreamed music once more."

"Oh, Lukas, do you mean it?" she whispered. She drew back from the close tender hold of his arms and studied his face. "You are not just sorry for me?"

"Sorry for you!" He began to laugh. "No, no, my darling! I am sorry for me—that it took me so long to realize what you meant to me. What time we have wasted. I could have claimed you long ago. But you, my darling—wait, I'm going too fast! I love you madly—but what do you feel for me?"

He studied her face anxiously. A light was dawning in the large blue eyes. "Oh, Lukas," she whispered.

"Do you love me?" he demanded.

She nodded shyly, and pressed her face to his shoulder. "Oh, for so long," she mumbled. "I tried not to. I thought you did not want a wife and children. You were so supremely alone, you did not seem like us mortals. . . ."

"Oh, Diana, I am human. Feel how human I am!" And he turned her face to his and pressed his lips to her cheeks, her nose, her chin, then to her mouth again hungrily. "It was that I waited so long for the right woman, the perfect woman, to be my wife, my mate, my companion. . . ."

They kissed, and hot blood raced through his veins. He longed to claim her at once, not to wait for marriage. She was so full of passion under that British cool. Her lips clung to his, her hands linked about his neck, and she pressed herself to his body, yielding so that he wanted more and more of her touch.

"God, darling," he whispered. "And we are alone in this room! I should send for your cousin at once."

She laughed, drawing back a little. Her cheeks were

no longer white, they were blush-rose. Her blue eyes sparkled with joy.

"Oh, Lukas. How I have longed for this, and thought it was impossible. That you should want me for your wife," she murmured, and her hand stroked his neck gently. "To have the right to touch you like this." Her other hand ruffled his thick golden hair.

"My darling, my love. We will tell your father at once. There will be no nonsense about leaving me."

"And I shall not mind now giving up my music career," she said bravely. "To be your wife, the mother of your children, that will be more than sufficient! I shall listen to your music, and encourage you—"

"Oh, no!" he said sharply. She blinked, jolted. "No, Diana! Is that what you thought I meant? Oh, my love, that you would have sacrificed yourself for me!" He was touched deeply that she would have done this, just as his mother had done. His mother had been crushed, but Diana should not be!

"Is that not what you meant, Lukas?" she asked, puzzled. "You did want me—to marry you?" And she blushed beautifully.

"Yes, I wish that, and we shall marry, my love. But you are more to me than a wife, the mother of my children-to-be. From the first we were like born companions in music. You encouraged me to compose. You could finish something that I began. Our minds were in tune always. Your bright spirits lifted me up from the despair where I had sunk after my injury. You made me wish to live again, write again, create music. Ours will be more than a marriage of bodies, we will have a true marriage of minds and spirits."

"Oh, Lukas!" She glowed, flinging her arms about his neck, and pressing her lips to his cheek. "You mean it! You really mean this!"

"With all my heart, my darling," he assured her tenderly. "I have seen what happened to my mother and my sister. Do you think I would allow my own wife to endure that? No, no, you shall have it all, all that you wish. I shall encourage you to play, and be so proud when you are applauded. And your compositions I shall conduct myself!"

"Lukas, I am the happiest woman in the world." She rested her face against his shoulder. "And you are the best, kindest, most thoughtful man in the universe."

The door opened. Cousin Helena Lewisohn walked in, then abruptly stopped and stared. "Diana—Herr Baron! I am shocked!" she cried. "What is going on? You are alone here, and like this?"

Diana sprang up, her hands to her cheeks. "Oh, cousin! I am sorry—but I am so happy."

Lukas stood also, and held out his hand to Frau Lewisohn, smiling. He was so handsome, so fine, and how he glowed, thought Diana. "You may congratulate me, cousin. I am to marry my beautiful Diana!"

She gasped. "But Diana is to marry—I mean—"

"Nein, she marries me!" said Lukas firmly. "But I must send for Mr. Ballantyne and ask his permission." He made a comical face. He reached out his good arm, and Diana went to him like a bird to her nest. "My darling? May I send for your father?"

"Oh, yes, Lukas! Or he will be buying my railroad ticket tomorrow morning." She laughed, as though that fear had not haunted her for weeks.

"We cannot have that. Let me write a note to him—asking him to come. Frau Lewisohn, some notepaper, and a pen?"

She supplied them, and Diana wrote a quick note to her father, as Lukas was too excited to write good English. She had rarely seen Lukas lose his composure. It was delightful!

The excitement spread throughout the boarding-house. Frau Hemmel came from the back parlor, and learned of it, and told Pauline and the other maids. The maids conveyed it to Rosalie and to Johanne, and they came down to the drawing room to share in the thrilling news. Alicia was out with her Stanislav.

"I knew you would not leave Vienna," declared Rosalie. "I have second sight! I could see you staying here forever! And you will write music, and play with us, and we shall all be famous, I know it!"

She gave a decided nod of her curly head, and they all laughed. Johanne offered her shy best wishes to them both.

"When do you marry?" Lukas asked her. "Three months? Then we shall beat you to the altar, for I shall not wait that long. Ours shall be in one month!"

"Nein, nein, we cannot have her ready so soon!" cried Cousin Helena. "Her dress to make, the dinner to plan—"

Lukas was laughing, sweet and teasing. Diana had never seen him so happy. She hoped he was truly happy; for she was incredulous at her good fortune. She had been in such despair, and now to know that Lukas loved her! He wanted her, he wished to marry her. And even more, he wanted her to continue with her music. He believed in her, he would encourage her, he would want her to go on playing and composing.

Homer Ballantyne arrived in Lukas's carriage prepared to receive his daughter's submission to his plans for her. What a shock for him that the ground floor of Cousin Helena's house was filled with laughter and shouting, plans and teasing about the forthcoming wedding.

Cousin Helena tactfully shooed everyone away from the front parlor, except Mr. Ballantyne, Lukas, and Diana. She pushed the others to the back parlor and sent for a fabulous tea, so they could celebrate. She had seen this coming. She knew the Herr Baron von Korda cast a longing eye on her beautiful cousin, and would not allow her to slip from his grasp.

In the front parlor Lukas explained more soberly. "I have long loved your daughter, Mr. Ballantyne. She is a fine woman, and you should be very proud of her. You cannot blame me for wishing to make her my wife."

"Well, well, this is a great shock to me, and to her fiancé," said Homer Ballantyne, disapprovingly. "You know she is engaged to a fine young man, and we plan to merge our companies. I do not see—"

Lukas listened with his usual calm patience. Diana was fidgeting as she sat on the sofa, her ankles crossed, her hands twisting together over each other. Lukas gave her a tender understanding look, and she relaxed.

"Diana has done me the honor to confess her love for me," said Lukas finally, as Mr. Ballantyne temporarily ran out of words. "We have much respect for each other. We have many interests in common. It will be a marriage of minds which have true compatibility."

"Well, well, but Diana will not be with me in London," said Mr. Ballantyne, rubbing his face. "I confess I miss her very much. Nothing is comfortable without her."

"I can understand that, but you must expect that when she marries, she will leave you for her new home and family anyway. My mother loves her already, and has longed for me to marry and have children. I can assure you, I have plenty of money. Your daughter will not want for comforts. I have a castle in the country that has been in the family for many centuries, as well as the Vienna town house and a chalet in the Alps. . . ."

Diana was embarrassed as Lukas enumerated his possessions. It was not for these that she loved and wished to marry him! But as he went on, and her father relaxed and looked less troubled, she realized this was important to them both.

"My family jewels will be hers," went on Lukas. "I will not ask for a dowry, as I understand you are absorbed in a merger, and it may not be convenient for you to take the money from the firm."

"Well, well, that is most kind of you to suggest. But of course, Diana must have her dowry. That is only right. She has money from her grandparents' side, but it is now in the firm. We shall discuss this next week, before lawyers," said Mr. Ballantyne, more comfortable with the businesslike tone the discussion had taken on. "Perhaps we may arrange to leave the money in the firm, and we shall send quarterly funds to you for her shares. Of course, the merger will not go through now. I cannot carry a man who is not a relative. Perhaps I shall arrange a marriage for my elder son; it will be more advantageous."

Diana was glad when they finally stopped discussing that. She felt a little sad that her father should readily decide to send money to Lukas, who had so much, but had not thought to give her any part of it for herself, to keep on with her music. Well, that was to be expected.

Mr. Ballantyne conveyed his satisfaction that his daughter was going to marry a wealthy man. He agreed to stay a week, to talk over matters with Lukas's lawyers and make the marriage settlement.

"And you must return in two months for our

wedding, Father," said Diana gently. "Do you think Lewis and Andrew will be able to come?"

He smiled and kissed her forehead. "I shall arrange that they do, of course," he said. "We shall miss our girl very sorely, I tell you!"

"Your loss is my gain," said Lukas, with a twinkle in his eyes.

"Yes, yes, a fine housekeeper," said Mr. Ballantyne, sighing. "And she cooks very well also."

Diana could have hit her father, but restrained herself. Lukas showed amusement in his eyes, and that satisfied her.

"And I must say, I am pleased that she will be married and settled," added Mr. Ballantyne. "She will no longer make a fool of herself playing the piano in public."

Lukas laughed. Diana finally joined in, thinking of their plans. What would her father say, if he one day saw her playing on the stage, with Lukas conducting?

But it would be, Lukas had said so. Lukas would not force her to give up her beloved music.

Diana thought she would have the best of both worlds: music to satisfy her soul, and a husband who was tender and understanding. And the music that rang in her mind would be set down on paper, and she would play it for the world to hear, just as she had dreamed of doing.

Later Lukas took her back to his home to tell the news to his mother and brother. They had dinner together, and laughed and talked, and rejoiced.

Frau von Korda expressed her deep satisfaction. "Since I first met you, Diana, I hoped that Lukas would see what a lovely wife you would make for him."

"And a sister for me," said Theo, with his sweet kindness.

She thanked them for their goodness to her, and their welcome into their family. Later when she and Lukas had some time alone in the music room, she told him, "I feel I am already a part of your family. How good they are. Your mother is as dear to me as my own mother was."

"I can tell you, she feels most relieved," said Lukas, jokingly. He seemed much lighter of mood than she had ever seen him. She felt this must be the way he had been ten years ago. "She had despaired of my marrying. And now I have given in, and will make a reformed husband."

His words reminded her of the stunning Countess Elza von Hulsen, and a shadow passed over her face. Lukas touched her chin gently.

"You think I was a merry rake?" he asked gently. "I was rather loose in my behavior for a time, but I soon found that life was not for me. After the duel I never had an affair again, nor do I wish to. And now that I have my dearest love, so much finer than I deserve, I shall not look at any woman in desire again, except the one who makes me the happiest husband in the world."

Diana blurted out, "But I thought Elza—I thought she—I saw you with her. And she was at the house—"

Lukas frowned. "I think she arranged matters to make it appear we were still close. But we were not. I was sorry for her; that husband of hers is a brute. But no more. She can go to her country estates and remain there with him, and I care not what happens to her. She is so full of malice and evil—yes, evil—that I believe she deserves whatever she gets."

After his stern words she said no more about that.

She was happy to forget the countess and her wicked brother.

Diana leaned against Lukas's chest and sighed with happiness. To think that only last night she had been full of doubt and uncertainty, unable to think where to turn. And this evening all doubts were resolved, the future certain and bright.

"Oh, Lukas, I am so very happy!"

He held her close, and his lips touched hers tenderly. His mouth was warm and eager, and her lips parted to allow his tongue to caress her mouth. His touch was so thrilling, she forgot where she was. Her arms twined about his neck, her slim body pressed to his muscular frame.

He pulled her yet closer to him, his left arm almost as strong as the right. His mouth kissed the lobe of her ear, her cheek, her chin, then returned eagerly to her expectant lips. Their kisses deepened, and against her thighs she felt how he desired her, for he was stirred and demanding.

When he drew back he was breathing heavily. "Two months," he muttered. "How could I have agreed to wait so long? I must have been mad!"

She laughed, her cheeks poppy-red, her eyes starry. "Oh, Lukas . . ."

"I almost took you that night at the chalet."

"Yes, and I would have let you! I had never felt so with any man."

"I should hope not!" He gave her a mock-stern look, then his eyes softened, those intense blue eyes she loved. "You love me?"

"So much, so very much!"

Irresistibly drawn together, their bodies swayed, and his arms caught her tightly once more. He bent her back, letting his lips touch her white throat, and slid them down to her breast, where he had opened the buttons. Diana thought of the time that would come soon, when she could yield to her deepest impulses and give in to his demands. She would come to this house as his bride, and in the bedroom upstairs, she would become his wife, yielding everything to him. But it would be in love, in joy, in passion that she would surrender. There would be no fear, no distaste, no cold reluctance.

"My darling, my dearest love," Lukas murmured against the curve of her breast. He was holding her tightly again, and his one leg had slid between hers, forcing her dress to ride up, almost to her knees. She felt the driving passion in him, the bold way he held her.

His hand slid down her back, over the sweet curves of her hips, again and again, urgently pulling her to him. If he had taken her then, she would not have resisted. She felt such a storm in her that nothing would calm it but his sweet possession.

It was Lukas who finally drew back and gazed down into her flushed face and dreamy eyes. "I must stop," he said with a groan. "I must take you to your cousin's. Did she truly say two months?"

Diana managed to laugh at his tone, and turned to press her face against his slightly rough cheek. How masculine he felt, how strong, how possessive—and she loved him so!

"It will go fast," she whispered, and that was a promise.

The second volume in the spectacular Heiress series

The Cornish Heiress

by Roberta Gellis
bestselling author of
The English Heiress

Meg Devoran—by night the flame-haired smuggler, Red Meg. Hunted and lusted after by many, she was loved by one man alone...

Philip St. Eyre—his hunger for adventure led him on a desperate mission into the heart of Napoleon's France.

From midnight trysts in secret smugglers' caves to wild abandon in enemy lands, they pursued their entwined destinies to the end—seizing ecstasy, unforgettable adventure—and love.

A Dell Book   **$3.50**   **(11515-9)**

The unforgettable saga of a magnificent family

IN JOY AND IN SORROW

by JOAN JOSEPH

They were the wealthiest Jewish family in Portugal, masters of Europe's largest shipping empire. Forced to flee the scourge of the Inquisition that reduced their proud heritage to ashes, they crossed the ocean in a perilous voyage. Led by a courageous, beautiful woman, they would defy fate to seize a forbidden dream of love.

A Dell Book   **$3.50**   **(14367-5)**

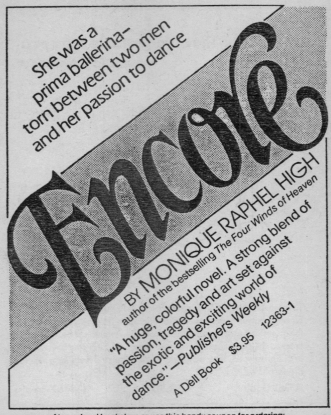